a hope
for emily

BOOKS BY KATE HEWITT

A Mother's Goodbye
The Secrets We Keep
Not My Daughter
No Time to Say Goodbye

a hope for emily

KATE HEWITT

bookouture

Published by Bookouture in 2020

An imprint of Storyfire Ltd.
Carmelite House
50 Victoria Embankment
London EC4Y 0DZ

www.bookouture.com

ISBN: 978-1-83888-243-3
eBook ISBN: 978-1-83888-242-6

Dedicated to Mindy
I know we haven't been in touch in a long time,
but I think about you often. Love, K.

PROLOGUE

I found out about you today. I held the stick between my fingers and stared at those blazing pink lines and felt amazed, joyful, and terrified all at once. I couldn't believe it, so I took another test. Actually, I took three. And then I wondered how I should tell your father—hide the test in his bag? Write a card? Text? No, of course not text, but I really don't know. What's the best way to say a surprise? Right now you're my secret, and I'm holding you close. I'm hugging you tight, because you're mine.

I'm calling you 'Bean' because apparently you're as big as that—or almost. A lima bean, the internet told me. A small one. I'm eight weeks pregnant now—I didn't take a test before, even though my period was late, even though I sort of suspected, because the truth is, I was scared to know, to feel disappointed or overwhelmed or... something.

But I finally took the test—well, all three in the package—and I sat and stared at those lines and I knew, I knew it was the best thing that had ever happened to me. Even if it was scary. Even if I wasn't sure I could handle it—pregnancy, birth, being a mother, the whole nine thousand yards. You're my bean, and I already love you with everything I have, with a love that feels so huge and overwhelming and wonderful and scary, because it's bigger than me. How can something I feel inside be bigger than me? I don't know, but it is. It absolutely is. And I know that whatever happens, wherever this journey takes us, you're my little bean, and you always will be.

Love, Mama

"Emily's care team has come to the conclusion that further treatment or testing would not be advisable at this stage." The words sound rehearsed, but the tone is heartfelt. I know it's been a long journey to this decision; I know Greg and his team have tried everything—every scan, every experimental drug, every possible therapy. Nothing has worked. Nothing has shifted the horrible non-diagnosis that Emily has always had. And yet still I resist, because not to is inconceivable.

"How could it not be advisable?" My voice rises, strident, worse than crying. I am turning into the angry parent, and in the three years since we began this terrible journey, I have tried so hard not to be that.

I've been the good mom, the one who always says thank you, who brings cookies and boxes of chocolates to the nurses, who remains upbeat even when I've felt like staggering or just lying down on the floor of Dr. Brown's—Greg's—office and curling up into a ball.

I've treated Greg like the leader of an expeditionary force, a fearless explorer, braving this new and uncertain terrain. *What can I do to help? How can I support you in this endeavor?* I've been so *good*, and now this? He's just walking away, along with all the other specialists and surgeons, nurses and neurologists, everyone who has been trying to figure out what is wrong with my daughter? They just don't *care* anymore?

Suddenly I am furious; the rage courses through me, a cleansing river. *No.* I will not allow this to happen. Emily is five years old. She has her whole life in front of her. She must.

I clench my fists, open my mouth, but Greg gets there before me.

"Rachel, I really am sorry to have to tell you this." He smiles at me, sorrowfully, and I believe he is sorry, of course he is, but it isn't enough. He places his hands palm down, flat on his desk, next to Emily's file. "I know it is particularly difficult in cases like these, where there are so few answers."

"There are *no* answers." I sound fierce, bitter, and I try to rein myself in. There's no point antagonizing the one person who has the power over my daughter's care. Her life.

"I know that's been very frustrating for you."

Frustrating? He makes it sound like a paper jam in a printer, a bit of morning traffic. I know he doesn't mean it that way, Dr. Brown has been great—with *has* being the operative word, it seems. Past tense. Looking at his slumped shoulders and tired eyes, he is a far cry from the neurology expert with the firm handshake and purposeful stride who assured James and me that he was going to get to the bottom of this, two and a half years ago.

He was going to figure out why Emily was slurring her speech. Getting migraines, at only three years old. And later, when she started to stumble, and had seizures, and began to lose her vision—yes, he was going to get to the bottom of all of that, too.

But he didn't. He failed, and I don't blame him for that. How can I? There were so many tests, so many attempts at diagnosis. Brain scans and blood work, MRIs and mental and physical assessments, on and on and on, the cycle of fear and hope, followed by more uncertainty, tempered by a treacherous relief—at least it's not *that*. Neuroblastoma. Moyamoya disease. Metachromatic leukodystrophy. There are so many terrible and rare conditions out there, and Emily doesn't have any of them. But no one knows what she *does* have.

Dr. Brown has done his best for Emily, I know that, and I don't blame him for not being able to diagnose her condition, whatever it is. But I can blame him for being ready to stop trying. For giving my daughter up as a lost cause, when she has so much to fight for. To live for.

"Sometimes this happens," Greg says. He's said it before, but not in quite so final a tone. "Boston Children's Hospital is one of the leading treatment and research centers for neurological conditions in the entire world. We have more resources and research at our disposal than just about anywhere else." He spreads his hands out, a gesture of sorrowful defeat. "But we haven't been able to diagnose Emily past SWAN, as you know."

Of course I know. SWAN, Syndrome Without A Name. The non-answer, the endless question that constantly torments me even as it offers that treacherous sliver of hope. It's impossible to explain the bizarre mixture of hope and fear you have, when there is no diagnosis. When there is no diagnosis, it could still be some weird virus, an infection no one caught that can be quickly cured. When there is no diagnosis, it could be the newly discovered fatal disease that only one in five million children get, and your child is the one that has it. And so I veer wildly from one to the other, one moment sure that Emily will wake up one day and smile at me—she *has* to—and the next half expecting this to be her last. It's overwhelming and exhausting, like living with an intense adrenaline rush and a body shot of Novocain all at the same time.

I take a deep breath. "But why stop trying to find out, since you don't know?"

"Rachel, Emily has been in a state of unresponsive wakefulness for four months, with no visible improvement." He shakes his head sadly. "As you know, from her recent MRI, her brain activity has been seen to be minimal for some time."

"Forty percent is not minimal," I flash back before I can stop myself. He sighs—a sound I hate. "So what are you saying?" My voice trembles. "It's not worth trying to find out what she does have?"

"I'm saying I no longer believe Emily is a viable candidate for continued testing," he says steadily. "I'm not giving up on her, Rachel, although I can understand why you think I am. If a new drug that I think would help Emily became available, I would put her forward for a clinical trial."

"But you don't think that's likely." I sound bitter.

"No," he agrees heavily. "I'm sorry, but I don't."

I can't believe it's going to end like this, after years of searching for answers, desperate for a diagnosis. I held onto hope, for all that time. "Dr. Brown, please don't do this." My voice catches; I am begging. "Emily is only five."

"I know." He looks emotional, swallowing hard, but I am not moved. Not now. He might feel badly; he might go home tonight, raking a hand through his hair as he reaches for a beer. *I had to let a patient go. It was tough.* But he can't feel it the way I do, with every fiber of my being, every last wrung-out corner of my heart. Of course he can't. I wouldn't expect him to, and yet I want—I *need*—more than this.

"I and the rest of the team have done our absolute best by Emily," he insists, a throb of feeling audible in his voice. "I promise you that. But her condition has only worsened since she first came here, and her consistent lack of progress suggests an irreversible decline in her mental and physical capabilities. The team agrees that the best thing for her now is to be referred to the pediatric palliative care unit."

He takes a glossy brochure and pushes it across the desk towards me, but I jerk away, as if it is covered in spikes, hissing like a snake, "I don't want a *brochure*."

"I know you don't," he says quietly.

We wait, the silence heavy and oppressive. Dr. Brown's hands are back flat on the table. I can't think of him as Greg anymore now. I won't.

I take a deep breath, and it shudders through me. He registers the sound, the grief in it, and simply waits.

He must have had a thousand moments like this one. Pediatric neurology is not a happy field. Not a lot of positive outcomes on this ward. But *this*? Palliative care? That's for old people, surely. People with terminal cancer, people who have already lived their lives. Not Emily, who has hair like blond cotton candy, who is only three and a half feet tall, who is five. *Five*. This is not right. I can't let this happen.

But I don't think I am being given a choice.

After another few seconds of silence, I finally take the brochure. I flick through it, my mouth twisting cynically. Massage rooms and music therapy. Caring doctors with white coats and sympathetic smiles. Lots of couched language—*family-centered, offering relief, based on need not prognosis.* I hate it all. I put the brochure back down on the table.

"Surely there's something more you can do." There has to be. Because I know as soon as Emily leaves this ward, this place where things happens and tests are done and results are still a possibility, no matter how slight, her life might as well be over. Instead of medicine, I'll need a miracle. But maybe I needed that all along. Maybe Emily did. I can't bear the thought.

"I'm truly sorry," Dr. Brown says. "Really. I wish…" He stops, shaking his head. This is not the time for wishes.

"Is there really nothing else you can do?" I am caught between despondency and rage. "No tests… no scans…" I am grasping at flimsy straws, I know that. I see it in his face.

"The entire team is in agreement about this decision, Rachel, and it is not one we've made lightly, I assure you."

I know it can't have been, but does that make it any easier? I glance down at the brochure again. It looks like a nice place, but also an awful one. A place where people go to die.

"Dr. Brown…" I look up at him, seeing his compassionate gaze, his hands folded in front of him. I swallow. I don't want to ask this. I don't want to *know*. And yet I have to. "What, in your opinion, is Emily's prognosis?" I force myself to ask. "I mean… how long will she be in this…" *State of unresponsive wakefulness.* That's the current, politically correct term; the old one is a *persistent vegetative state*, which I hate. It makes my daughter sound like a thing, a zucchini stuck in a bed, and some of the medical team still use it. Dr. Brown makes sure not to, but I don't really like any of the words they use, the clinical way they say them, even though I know they have to be that way. "I mean, I know you don't think she'll get better." The words are jagged splinters sticking in my throat.

Ever since Emily slipped into a coma first, and then deeper still into the state she's now in, I've been trying to be realistic. I've known she's not going to open her eyes one day, smile sleepily, and say "hi, Mommy." I know that, and yet right now I realize I can tell myself I'm being realistic and still fool myself.

I have told myself all along that I was prepared for setbacks, for permanent damage, for Emily to never speak or even move again. I was, and yet right now I know I wasn't. Because, all along, I've been hoping for the sudden diagnosis, the miracle cure, or at least some *treatment*. Something to make things just a little bit better, instead of this downward spiral towards... I can't bear to think it. I won't. Not yet.

"Emily could be in her current state for years," Dr. Brown says quietly. "Although the average life expectancy of someone in her condition is usually under five years." He pauses. "Unless you decided her quality of life did not merit continuing with life-sustaining measures."

It takes me a moment to realize what he's saying. "You mean... kill her?" I can barely get the words out. *Did a doctor really say that?*

"No, not that," he answers swiftly. I wonder if he's thinking about lawsuits; it's so important to use the right words. "When parents or relatives decide the quality of life is not worth continuing with life-sustaining measures, they can agree to withdraw the gastric feeding tube, for example, from the patient in question."

"Starve her." I am disbelieving, icy.

"She would be made entirely comfortable." Comfortable? Is that even a word he can use here? "Obviously," he says after a very *uncomfortable* pause, "that's not something you need to consider right now."

But I will have to one day, seems to be the implication. One day he'll encourage me to make that decision.

My stomach churns and I rise from my seat. "I'll need to discuss all this with James." He should have been here, but he had a work meeting and didn't realize how important it was. Neither did I. "When we've had a conversation, we'll be in touch." I don't know what that conversation will sound or feel like, because even though we are determined to be amicable, James and I don't always agree about Emily, about her care. He trusts the doctors more than I do; he's willing to simply go along. It hasn't mattered so much until now, but I have to hope—I have to believe—he will agree with me on this.

"I am sorry, Rachel," Dr. Brown says yet again. How many times has he uttered those useless words? "Do talk to Emily's dad, and then get back to me. We're hoping to move Emily to the palliative unit next week, as long as her condition remains stable."

I nod tersely, unwilling to verbalize my acceptance of that plan. I could still fight it. There has to be some way I could fight, some legal avenue James and I could go down.

I walk stiffly from the room, along the corridor to the ward where Emily has been for the last eight months, since a chest infection meant another hospitalization. She was only supposed to be in for a few weeks, until her condition stabilized, but even after she recovered from the infection, her condition continued to spiral downwards, until she slipped so deeply into a sleep, she has never seemed to wake up.

Sometimes I torment myself with my lack of memory of the last time Emily spoke. The last time she smiled or reached for my hand. If I'd known it was the last time, would I have remembered? Would I have held onto it? I'm sure I would have, but, as it is, I can't remember any of it at all.

It all happened so gradually, an erosion of ability, of possibility, that I was desperate not to acknowledge. When she first started slurring words at only three years old—well, she was young, and children developed at different stages. Then she started stumbling, and having terrible joint pain, as well as migraines. For that whole year, Emily was in and out of preschool, going for tests, scans, therapies. For that whole year, I held on to the hope that this could be solved.

Then, just after her fourth birthday, when we took her to Cape Cod for a week of sun-soaked days on the beach, she had her first grand mal seizure. I think I knew then that we'd entered new territory, an unknown shore, and there was no going back.

A nurse looks up from her station and smiles at me, the curve of her lips fleeting and sympathetic. An aide is pushing a trolley slowly down the hallway; I hear its wheel squeak, and from another room I hear a mother's murmured voice, the ensuing silence. This is a ward of children who are in similar states to Emily, children with neurological conditions, diagnosed or not, that are serious, untreatable, and in many cases terminal.

Children in comas, temporary or not; children with brain damage of varying degrees; children, like Emily, who have moved from a coma into a state of unresponsive wakefulness, the more hopeless scenario, as I have come to discover, because it signifies, as Dr. Brown pointed out, minimal brain activity. The scenario where you wonder if they're awake, because they're breathing, chest rising, eyes opening and closing, and when you squeeze their hands, sometimes they squeeze back. It's not very much to pin your hopes on, but you do. Of course you do. You pin them all.

Although, the truth is, I don't know the conditions of the other children on this ward anymore. I stopped chatting to the other parents a while back, because I just couldn't. I don't think they could either. We all have enough sorrow in our lives already; we don't need the burden of bearing someone else's, not even for a five-minute conversation.

Now I breathe in deeply the smell I've become so used to—antiseptic and stale at the same time. I know this place—the bright lights, the murmured voices, the heavy doors, the sunlight that streams through the window and yet feels so far away, the view of the parking lot, the people moving below, some with balloons, others with wheelchairs, everyone living out their hopes and griefs on a silent, sober stage.

Now, as I come into the room, she lies in bed, her eyes closed, her breathing regular. Sometimes her eyes are open, and it almost feels as if she can see me. Her gaze will track to the door and back, almost as if she's trying to tell me something. *What if she is?*

She has been able to breathe on her own since she recovered from the chest infection, and besides the monitor registering her heartbeat and the feeding tube, she looks normal, a word I've started to hate. What *is* normal? Who gets to decide that?

"Hello, my darling girl." I keep my voice cheerful even though sometimes it feels like the hardest thing I've ever done.

I move around the room, touching her shoulder, adjusting the blinds, twitching a bedsheet. Anything to feel busy and useful, to lend a bizarre sort of normalcy to this situation.

Looking at her now, if you didn't know any better, you'd think she was just sleeping. You'd think she'd wake up any minute, blinking sleepily like I try so hard not to imagine, smile at me and mumble something. *Hello, Mommy.* Or even *I'm thirsty.* Or maybe *where am I?* I'm not picky about what she might say. I'm not picky at all.

But that hasn't happened, and it's hard to hold onto the hope that it might, even as I guard against wanting something impossible. Sometimes I think I'm not being fair to Emily, to keep my expectations low. Shouldn't we want the absolute best for our children? Shouldn't we do everything we can to give it to them? Isn't that what being a parent, a mother, is all about?

Or is it about this, sitting quietly next to a girl who might never truly wake up, and talking about all the things she might miss, but just can't tell us so? The most recent studies have shown that patients in this state might actually be more conscious than we realize, something that is both wonderful and terrifying.

Might, James said, with such awful emphasis. *You can't trust these studies, Rachel. You can't pin all your hopes on them, on one research experiment that tells you what you want to hear, when there are so many others with different results.*

But then what can you trust? Where do you find hope?

I take Emily's limp hand in my own; it is small and warm and so terribly lifeless. I can't let them do this. I can't let them give up on her. If they stop looking for a diagnosis, they'll never find a cure. If they write her off as someone who is only going to get worse, there's no way she'll ever get better. I'm not willing to consign my only child to being dismissed and then dying. I'm not ready, and surely, *surely*, neither is she.

Gently, I squeeze Emily's fingers. It doesn't always happen, but sometimes I feel something back, a light pressure, a barely-there squeeze. I thought I was imagining it at first, wishful thinking, but then Dr. Brown told me that patients like Emily can exhibit natural reflexes. He was quick to tell me it was nothing more than that, gently warning me that it didn't mean anything.

But if it was just a reflex, why doesn't it happen every time? Despite his well-intentioned warnings, I chose not to believe him. It's more than a reflex to me.

And so, I squeeze her fingers again, gently, like a question. *Are you there, baby girl? Is some part of you still with me, still holding on?*

I hold my breath and wait, pray, *hope*, and like the tiny miracle I know it is, after a few endless seconds, she squeezes back.

CHAPTER TWO

EVA

One line. One damn, *damning* line. I push my high-heeled foot down on the pedal to lift the lid of the bin, wrap the test in toilet paper and throw it away. Then I leave the toilet stall at work and wash my hands, gazing firmly at my reflection—highlighted hair, blue eyes, determined smile that drops as soon as I look away. Yes, this is me.

A woman I know vaguely from another department comes into the bathroom, giving me a friendly smile, and I force my lips upwards again, an act of sheer will. I am fine.

Briskly I dry my hands and turn away from the sink. My heels click on the tile floor, a pleasing sound. I straighten my shoulders, lift my chin. *I am fine.*

This is the fifth pregnancy test I've taken. The fifth time I've let myself hope just a little, because my period is a day late and that twinge in my midsection *might* be a symptom. Or it could just be a menstrual cramp, which invariably it is.

Every cycle, I tell myself I won't take the test early this time. Why waste the money? Even when you buy the cheap strips on Amazon instead of the top-drawer digital tests from CVS, month after month it still adds up. Pregnancy tests are expensive, and negative ones suck. So why put yourself through the pain? Hope followed by disappointment. Much better, much easier, not to hope at all. Except hope, I've found, doesn't work that way, no matter how hard I try.

Back at my desk, I pull my laptop towards me and do my best to immerse myself in work. Try not to think about how maybe I did take the test too early. If I swing by CVS on my way home from work, I could get one of those more expensive tests, the ones that promise they are accurate just ten days after ovulation. Then I'd really know.

See how it goes? Hope. Disappointment. Hope.

I focus on my computer screen and the latest results of the digital ad campaign we ran for our new line of vegan, ethically sourced lipsticks. I work for Maemae, a boutique company that specialises in organic, cruelty-free, high-end beauty products, the current "crème de la crème" of the natural beauty world. For this campaign, I decided to focus on how the lipsticks' ingredients were ethically sourced in challenged areas of the world. People are meant to care about that sort of thing nowadays, but judging from the results of the ad, they don't. Mara, my boss, isn't going to be pleased with the lacklustre results.

I've been with Maemae almost since they started seven years ago, founded by Rio Adachi, a Hawaiian-Japanese business-woman with an amazing drive and focus. She's moved onto an organic sports clothing line in LA, but she comes to our office once a year to check how things are going and give us all a boost, filling the open-plan office with her crackling energy. From the way she talks, you'd think we were all working on the cure for cancer rather than overpriced, if decently made, cosmetics, and for a long time I felt as if we were. I felt like an intrepid explorer, fearlessly on the forefront of a brave new world. Now, six and a half years later, I can't help but think I flog makeup online.

I feel a twinge in my belly. Was that a symptom? Or is my period coming? *Why* am I still hoping? Not that I'd admit that I was, to anyone, not even to my husband, who has taken each month's disappointment in his stride.

He doesn't share my urgency for a baby, and why should he? He already has a child, has already experienced the love, the joy, and, sadly, the terrible grief of parenthood. I understand why he's wary. Anyone in his situation would be. But I tell myself it will be different this time round… for both of us.

Now with my fingers still resting on the keyboard as I gaze unseeingly into the distance, the noise fading away around me, I focus on the present—my work, my marriage, my pregnancy, because one day it's going to happen. I will see those two pink lines. I will get to be a mother, after all these years, and press a petal-soft kiss against that perfect, round cheek.

A phone rings on the desk next to mine, startling me out of my thoughts. Maemae—meaning pure in Hawaiian—has an egalitarian, open-plan office, with all of us working and think-ing together. All Rio Adachi's offices are open plan to "maximise synergy"—whatever that means—and while I can appreciate the all-white aesthetic, the big windows and streamlined desks, the clean purity of it all, sometimes I crave a little space. A little privacy.

Like right now, when my belly twinges again and I am bat-tling both hope and disappointment, unsure which one would feel better.

"Eva?" Mara sticks her coiffed head out the door of her glass-walled office. As open plan as this place is, she still gets her own space. "A moment?"

I snap my laptop shut and carry it into Mara's office, knowing she's going to take me to task over the low figures. Except she won't actually get angry, which I think I'd prefer; she'll sigh and shake her head and seem disappointed. Kind of like my mother, who has been bewildered by my life choices since I was seventeen.

Inevitably, that's exactly what happens. Mara acts as if she's disappointed in our customer base who didn't respond to the *National Geographic*-type images of refugees and war sites that we paired with the single, slim-line lipstick. I acknowledged it was a rather jarring fit, but I thought that it would make an impact.

"I think," Mara pronounces, as if she is making a deep statement about the meaning of life, "people don't want to combine their politics with their cosmetics."

I nod sagely, even though inwardly I am rolling my eyes. These days, it seems as if people want to combine their politics with everything, and yet they don't want to be made *uncomfortable*. God forbid I bring a little reality into their lives. Heaven help us if I try to make this about anything more than makeup.

"We'll adjust the images and try again," I say briskly. "I still believe our customers care about our products being ethically sourced. The Beeautiful eyeshadow is one of our more popular products." Made with sustainable beeswax, it has a creamy finish and a subtle palette of neutral shades.

"Perhaps that's because it's a good eyeshadow?" Mara returns, and I shrug my agreement. I'm not the one who decided on ethically sourced cosmetics. I'm just trying to sell them.

I used to love working for Maemae. Seven, five, even two years ago, I was an ambassador for the company, an evangelist for organic, cruelty-free makeup, for making a difference in the beauty world, for doing something that mattered. But sometime in the last year or so, the gloss has begun to wear off. Perhaps because it feels just that—glossy, superficial, and pathetically unimportant compared to what a lot of people are doing.

Or perhaps it's just because I'm tired of being the corporate career woman. *I want a baby.* Not that I've told anyone at work about that. I was reluctant even to tell them I'd got married, knowing how Mara would mentally take me down a few rungs on the career ladder. I remember overhearing a dismissive comment of hers about a woman in the accounting department, when she went on maternity leave with her first child. *Even when she comes back, it won't be the same. She won't work the way she used to.*

Sometimes, though, I fantasize about not coming back. About having a baby and moving to the country, somewhere upstate, a rickety farmhouse with a vegetable patch and a couple of chickens. It's all ridiculous, I know. I've never lived anywhere but in a city, whether it was Boston or New York or Claremont, and my husband's job is here, as well. Yet I still dream; I picture myself in something loose and linen, my hair down my back and my feet bare, my baby in a sling. It's not me at all, but then what is?

Fifteen minutes later, I've left Mara with the promise to redesign the campaign; the genius of digital marketing is that I can do that with a few clicks of my mouse and little expense.

Another cramp twinges in my belly and I make a detour back to the bathroom, swearing out loud when I see that my period has come. Another month wasted. Disappointment is a twisting in my gut, a sour taste in my mouth, even though I've been expecting this, or at least telling myself to.

I wash my hands, and when I look at myself in the mirror, my eyes are hard, my expression fixed and grim. I can't quite fake it this time. I will be fine, I always am, but I'm not right now.

The disappointment still clings to me like a mist as that evening I leave Maemae's offices in downtown Boston and head towards our apartment in Beacon Hill. It's a twenty-minute walk and I usually use the time to clear my head, breathe deep, unwind after eight hours of mental focus and determined energy. Tonight, though, I can't shake the sadness.

Five months of trying. And I'm thirty-six. What if it doesn't happen? What then? I'm not ready to think of contingency plans, but I'm already afraid I'm going to have to.

It's a beautiful evening, the trees lining Boston Common bursting with pink puffballs of cherry blossom. It's the first really warm day, the kind where people can shed their jackets and coats and stroll easily through the city's parks instead of walking quickly, head down against the icy cold and biting wind. The kind of evening where I might arrange to meet up with friends somewhere trendy and fun—a wine bar in the Back Bay, or a new tapas place on Tremont Street. As it is, my phone stays in my pocket.

My steps slow as I come to the street of gracious brownstones where I live, in the kind of apartment you'd expect to see on some Boston drama or sitcom, with a big bay window and a bike chained to the iron railing, flower boxes under every window and bookcases flanking the fireplace that we're not allowed to use.

It's a beautiful apartment, but it's overpriced and it's not a particularly good neighborhood for families, far too expensive, but I suppose we should enjoy it while we can. At least, that's what I keep telling myself, trying to stay upbeat.

Even now, I am wondering if I should mention this latest disappointment. I always tell myself I won't, just like I tell myself I won't test early, and then I do. I can't help it; I want my husband to share my sorrow, and I know he won't, not entirely, even if he tries to act as if he does. I'm afraid I can see something like relief in his eyes when it's another negative test, another month of no, and it hurts me every time. I know he doesn't want this as much as I do, even if he never says it outright.

But tonight, as I step into the marble-tiled hallway, sunlight slanting through the big windows of the front room and catching the dust motes in the air, I realize something else is already going on.

James is standing by the kitchen island in the back of the apartment, his cell phone clamped to his ear, a shuttered look on his face that he always has when he's talking to his ex-wife. Before I hear a word he says, I know it's Rachel on the line.

I slip off my heels and pour myself a glass of wine from the bottle James has already opened, although he hasn't yet poured himself any. I give him a fleeting smile, which he doesn't return, acknowledging me with just a nod.

I can hear the unfamiliar, strident sound of Rachel's voice through the phone. I've spoken to her exactly once, on the phone, about four months ago, when she called the landline instead of James' cell.

We were both startled, I think, by the reality of the other person; she was soft-spoken then, almost apologetic for bothering me. I stammered something about passing on the message that she'd called, and then we both hung up, feeling, I suspect, relieved.

I heft the bottle and gesture to James, but he shakes his head, angling his body away from me. It must be a serious call, then, like it was the last time Rachel called, when Emily slipped into a coma. James had gone out to meet Rachel, see Emily, and was gone for hours. When he'd finally got back, he'd looked both shocked and exhausted, his eyes unfocused. I'd asked him what had happened, and he'd shaken his head, struggling to get the words out.

"She's in a coma," he'd said finally. "She just... lost consciousness. They're not sure if she'll wake up." His voice had been ragged, but when I'd tried to comfort him, he'd flinched away. "I can't talk about it," he said then, which was what he always said, and I let him go, because what else could I do? I have never known how to be, when it comes to Rachel and Emily.

James told me straight away about them both, something I appreciated. He was upfront about his emotional baggage; he didn't try to hide it the way some people do, even when you can see it trailing behind them, a battered train of wrecked relationships or fears of commitment, hidden complications or abuses or pain. They think they're hiding it, but no one really can.

If anything, James told me more than I might have wanted to know, at least all at once. I think he wanted to get it all out, and afterwards he cringed a little, as if waiting for me to back off. To say this was not what I had signed up for. Because, of course, it wasn't, and yet at the same time it was. I knew I wanted to be with a man who is there for his wife and child. And although Rachel might not agree with me, James was, and is, there for Emily. And that counts for a lot.

But it doesn't make it easier, in moments like this one.

I take my glass of wine and curl up on the big, squashy sofa in the living room, glancing out the bay window that faces the street, waiting for James to finish his call. I wonder what Rachel has phoned him about. Has something happened to Emily? My mind shies away from any potential scenarios; they're all grim, and I don't know how I feel about any of them. I've never met Emily, or, for that matter, Rachel. From the one photo I've seen of James' little girl, I can imagine what she looks like, but it's something vague and hazy, a pale, blond girl lying in a bed, someone who is not quite real to me.

In the year that I've known James, it has never really felt like my business, to ask about Emily, and yet it seems ungenerous not to. I've tried to stay interested yet on the periphery; it's hard to strike the right balance. I bought Emily a present once, a soft toy in the shape of a dolphin, because James had told me, in one of his rare moments of actually talking about Emily, that she'd loved the New England Aquarium. He took it to the hospital, and that was the last I heard of it. I didn't know whether to ask about it, and when I do ask about anything Emily-related, James' answers tend to be terse, so it's easier not to ask at all, even if that feels wrong.

I sip my wine, my mind slipping over what I do know about my husband's former life. Rachel and James were married for six years; they had Emily when they were both thirty-five, and when she was just over three years old, she started exhibiting symptoms—slurring words, migraines, joint pain.

It sounded awful, and according to James it became progressively worse. I don't know the exact details, but I know that for a year they took her for tests and searched for a diagnosis, and then just after her fourth birthday, she started having seizures and spending more time in the hospital than not. Six months ago, when she was a little over five years old, she went in for a chest infection, ended up slipping into a coma and then a persistent vegetative state.

I met James when Emily was almost five; he'd been separated from Rachel for three months, which didn't feel quite long enough to me, but he insisted they'd been drifting apart for a while before that. How long "a while" is, I've never asked.

In all the time I've known him, James has visited Emily three times a week—Tuesday and Thursday evenings, all of Saturday—without fail. I admire that. It's a lot more than some men would do.

I take another sip of wine as I both try to listen to and ignore James' replies to Rachel.

"Rachel, Dr. Brown is the professional here. He wouldn't make this decision without thinking through it very carefully. And if the whole team agrees…" He stops, and I think I can hear the rising tones of Rachel's reply, even from the living room.

James lets out a short, sharp sigh, a sound of weariness edged with impatience.

"I don't want to fight you on this." Another pause, and then his voice softens. "I know it's hard. Of course I know it. I feel the same, Rachel, even if you don't believe me. I do." His voice catches. "Don't you think I miss her?" Another sigh. "I *know* that, I didn't mean she was… Yes. I know."

I get up from the sofa, not wanting to eavesdrop. This conversation, like so many others they've had, feels too intimate for me, and it's usually made worse by the fact James won't want to talk about it afterwards. I'm not threatened, not exactly. It's just, when James and Rachel talk, I feel… extraneous.

I go into the bedroom to change, taking my time, drinking my wine, and when I come back into the living room, James is slumped on the sofa, his wine half-drunk in front of him.

"Sorry about that," he says, his voice flat.

"You know you don't have to be sorry."

I sit in the chair opposite him and sip the last of my wine. We've been married for eight months, together for a year, and yet moments like this still unnerve me. I don't know how to handle them; I don't know what James wants from me. I don't even know what I want from him.

"Want to talk about it?" I ask, although I know he won't and, in any case, I'm not sure I want to know. While part of me is avidly, obsessively curious about Rachel and Emily, the front I give to James and everyone else, even myself, is that I'm good with it all, that I've accepted the situation, that I am doing my best to be supportive without prying or feeling threatened. And for the most part that is true. It is just so often I don't know what the right thing to say or even to feel is.

I sip my wine, even though there isn't even a mouthful left, and wait.

James sighs heavily as he rakes a hand through his hair. "I don't even know." He lapses into a morose silence, and I wait another beat. A cramp bands my stomach, reminding me of what I've missed out on again. "The medical team has advised that Emily go into palliative care," he says, his voice toneless, almost indifferent, but I know that's a front too, because I see how he blinks rapidly as he throws back the last of his wine in one reckless gulp, his throat working, his mouth tightening to hold it all back.

"Oh, James." I think of Emily, the little girl I've never met, now moving from a search for a diagnosis to a wait for death. That's what palliative care is, isn't it? "I'm so sorry."

"Yeah." He rotates his glass between his palms, his head lowered, his hair flopping forward. I wish I could go sit next to him, put my arms around him, give him the comfort he surely needs, but I can't. I love him, and I know he loves me, but Emily and Rachel and everything about them has been our no-fly zone since he laid it all out on our second date. We just don't go there. Ever.

"How is Rachel feeling about it?" I ask cautiously. It's not my business, but I can't help but recall Rachel's raised voice on the phone, and I wonder about the woman I've never met. Is she coping? Does she handle it all the way James does, with stoic silence? Or is this the moment that will break her, and if it is, what can—or should—I do about it?

"She wants to fight it. Insist Dr. Brown and the others keep trying to find a diagnosis."

I digest this information for a moment, wondering what it means. What more can they do? James has told me only a little about all the tests and scans and therapies, endless ways to try to get Emily better, and clearly none of them have worked. "Can she do that?"

"It would mean a lawsuit. It could get ugly." He sighs, lifting his head. He looks so tired, his dark blue eyes filled with weary misery. "Especially if I don't agree, which I won't."

For some reason that jolts me, his firmness, even though I know it shouldn't. James has already told me that he has been grieving Emily for months, years. When she went into a coma, he thought it was the beginning of the end. This is just the next step, natural, and yet so not. So very much not.

I've seen one photo of Emily; it's in our bedroom, on top of James' dresser. She's a toddler, hoisted in James' arms, giving the camera a joyous, gap-toothed grin, her flyaway strawberry-blond hair caught up in a high, wispy ponytail. It was taken, he told me, just a month before the symptoms started in earnest.

Every time I look at that photograph, I feel a wave of sorrow for the little girl I'll never know, and an uncharitable envy for the life James has already had that has nothing to do with me. I asked him if I should meet Emily, knowing it had to be up to him, and he said no. He told me he didn't want me to see Emily the way she was now, and I accepted that. How could I not? But I wonder; I wonder about the photo albums that surely exist somewhere, that James never shows me. I wonder about the photos that still must be on his phone, that I've never seen, and I wonder why he won't show me, even as I know I am not brave enough to ask. Is it because it hurts too much? Or because it's too private? Maybe both.

"So what are you going to do?" I ask when James doesn't offer any response.

Another shrug, so defeated. "I don't know. I'm hoping Rachel will see sense. It's been three *years*, Eva, and Emily has never improved. She's been in this—*state*—for four months. She isn't going to get better. The doctors have told us that, and Rachel needs to accept it."

"But you don't really know that." The words slip out of me before I can stop them. I don't know why I said them; I don't know the first thing, really, about Emily's condition, except that it's undiagnosed, despite all the testing they've done.

James looks at me in surprise, a flash of woundedness in his eyes. I feel as if I've betrayed him.

"I only meant," I clarify quickly, "that since Emily's never been diagnosed, you can't know what will happen."

His mouth twists. "You sound like Rachel."

Which doesn't seem like a compliment. "I'm just saying, I understand why Rachel might want to fight the doctors, even now." Suddenly my throat feels tight and I lurch upright from my seat, emotion coursing through me that I thought I'd buried a long time ago. "I'm going to get a refill. You want one?" I hold out my hand, and James gives me his glass. I smile, or try to, and he gives me something like a smile back. We're okay. We won't talk about this anymore, and we'll be okay, like we always are, because we love each other. Because James is wry and self-deprecating, and I'm focused and a little smart-mouthed, and together we work. When we're not talking or thinking about Emily, we laugh. We joke. We play off each other, and it's fun and easy and light, and yet in moments like these it's as if it all vanishes, as if we're nothing but this tension and silence and sorrow.

I want to get us back to where we work, and so the last thing I want to do now is argue with my husband about how his ex-wife behaves, or seem to be on her side. Not that there are even sides in this situation. Everybody is just trying to do what's right, aren't they?

Except sometimes it's so hard to know what the right thing to do is. And sometimes, I reflect bleakly as I slosh more wine into my glass, sometimes you know what the right thing to do is, and you still don't do it.

CHAPTER THREE

RACHEL

I blink in the dim gloom of the ubiquitous Starbucks where James asked if we could meet. It isn't the kind of place I'd choose for our conversation, but it is near his work, a boxy office building on the outskirts of Brookline. It's the busiest time of the month for him and he said he could only do his lunch hour, which stung. This is our daughter we're talking about.

I take a deep breath and scan the tables, full of moms with toddlers or women decked out in exercise gear, as well as twenty-somethings setting up their mobile workstations, with their laptops and latest iPhones and large lattes. The air is full of the rise and fall of murmured voices, the hiss of the espresso machine, the clatter of cups.

Finally I see James at a table in the back corner, and I start towards him, managing a nod, if not a smile. I feel brittle.

He half rises from the table as I come forward. "Let me get you a coffee."

"I'll get it." I force a smile to belie the sharpness of my tone. "I'm already up."

I turn back to the line at the counter that is snaking towards the door, business people checking their watches, bored college students scrolling through their phones, their thumbs moving so fast, I doubt they're even registering what's on those essential screens.

I join the line, needing a moment to gather my composure, assemble the front I always put on when I'm with James. Just as with Dr. Brown, I try to be the good guy in this scenario. I'm the friendly ex, the one who understands, who is trying to make things work, who accepts James' choices, even though, in truth, a hard knot of bitterness and hurt has taken up residence in my gut and hasn't shifted or lessened in the sixteen months since James told me, quite simply, that he "couldn't do this anymore".

I'd just come in from another endless day at the hospital, where Emily was being monitored after her fifth grand mal, or tonic-clonic, seizure—a terrifying experience that had left my hands clenched at my sides and my mouth open in a silent scream. Still no answers, just more blessed dead ends. She didn't have a neuroblastoma, thank God. It wasn't epilepsy. But as relieved as I was to know those things, I still wanted answers.

She'd been exhibiting symptoms for a little over a year at that point, and had been seriously ill for nearly six months. She couldn't talk or walk very well, and had sudden, violent mood swings and bouts of anti-social behavior. I felt as if I didn't know who my little girl was anymore, but I was still trying to get her back.

I dropped onto the sofa, my whole body wilting, as I nodded my weary agreement. "I know, James. I don't feel like I can do it anymore, either."

After the first seizure, when Emily was about to go into her second year of preschool, we'd both agreed that I would be the one to take a leave of absence. As an actuary for a life insurance company, James earned three times as much as I did as a high school English teacher. Besides, I wanted to stay by Emily's side; I needed to be there, and it soon became clear that James struggled to handle it.

Looking back, it's hard to remember exactly how we felt, how worried we were, when Emily first started slurring words and stumbling. I remember thinking she was just clumsy, something that now shames me, although I tell myself it shouldn't. James was dismissive; it was so much easier, so much more comforting, to think it was nothing, or something she'd grow out of.

But as the weeks passed and she stumbled more, not less; when the headaches started, along with the joint pain and the inexplicable mood swings… it became harder to think it was just a phase or a virus, a three-year-old having an off day.

And then that first appointment with a neurologist—Dr. Stanger, I think, although we only saw her the one time, before we were referred up the chain. I remember how grave she seemed, how seriously she was taking it all, and that scared me more than any of Emily's symptoms. It scared James as well, and then the doctors' ignorance made him angry, and everything felt as if it were spiraling out of control—Emily's condition, our emotions.

Going to doctors' appointments and physical therapy sessions—back in the beginning, when these things seemed as if they could hold answers—started to feel like an escape. Perhaps that should have been my first clue that our marriage wasn't as strong as I'd assumed it to be. That this was coming.

"I don't mean it like that, Rachel," James said after a heavy-laden pause. I was easing my sensible shoes off my aching feet, my head lowered, but I looked up when I registered his serious, final-sounding tone. "I mean us."

I stared at him dumbly, barely able to process what he was saying. *Us?* I couldn't remember when I'd last thought of *us* as a concept. How could I worry about making sure we had a date night when our daughter had been sick for over a year and was only getting sicker? When every last iota of our emotional energy surely had to be focused on Emily and helping her to get well?

"Is this really the time for this sort of conversation?" I asked, striving to sound reasonable, even though I felt like flying at him, fists raised, temper finally unleashed. *Are you serious? Our daughter is ill. Seriously ill. And you're going to complain that you're not getting enough quality time or sex or something like that?*

"I'm sorry, Rach. I really am. I know there's no good time for this. I thought about not saying anything, just stumbling through, but... I don't think that's the right choice for either of us."

I straightened, his words, and worse, his tone, filtering through me. He sounded so *resigned*, as if it was already over. *We* were. "What... what are you actually saying, James?" I asked, each word wooden as it came from my mouth. I felt stilted, everything in me off-kilter, knocked off balance by this entirely unexpected—and unwanted—conversation.

All we'd done for over a year was think and talk about Emily. Evenings spent online, searching for the miracle needle in the endless haystack, the bit of research that would tell us what was wrong with her, when even a team of the world's best neurologists didn't know. Days spent sitting by her bedside or helping her to walk, talk, *be*—keeping her in preschool, trying to salvage some normality from the total disruption of our lives.

"I think... I think we need some time apart."

Even though part of me had known he was heading there, that he had to be, it still came as a shock. It felt ridiculous, that he could say this now. That he could even think it.

"You're *leaving* me?" My voice was faint with disbelief; I realized I couldn't even summon the energy to feel angry. Emily was in hospital for the third time in three months; in the last six weeks, she'd lost her ability to speak, her hearing and vision were becoming compromised, and her mobility was continually getting worse, and he wanted his own space? He thought that would *help*?

James scrubbed at his eyes with his fists; I saw how tired he looked, and more than that, how distraught, his lips trembling before he pressed them into a line. And yet, despite all that, he nodded. Resolute. "I suppose... I suppose I am. If you want to look at it that way. But I think it's better for both of us."

"How else am I supposed to look at it?" I was almost curious, the professor investigating a problem, too dazed to look at this from anything but a distance. How did he think he could spin this? What other explanation could there possibly be?

James dropped his fists and looked at me directly. "Tell me the truth, Rachel. Are you happy?"

I had a sudden, wild urge to laugh, but I didn't. Of course I didn't. "No, I'm not happy. Our daughter is in the hospital, having had *another* huge seizure, and the doctors still can't find any answers as to why she is losing all her abilities and functions." One by one, like dominoes falling, always falling. Nothing ever getting better. There were some days I thought I couldn't stand it anymore, not without screaming or even exploding. My voice rose to a fraying thread, ready to snap, as I glared at him. "How do you *think* I feel?"

"I mean with us," James said on a sigh. "Are you happy with us?"

I shook my head. "James, I can't even think about us, with Emily the way she is. I'm amazed you can." I sounded accusing; I couldn't help it. This felt so *absurd.* Quality time could come later, surely. Our sex life could take a hit.

He took a deep breath. "Emily has been sick for over a year, Rachel—"

"I *know*—"

"And the way things are going… I don't think she's going to get better."

His words felt like an assault, worse than a slap. Physical violence, as if he'd taken my body between his hands and broken it. In all the time since we'd first gone to the pediatrician with our fledgling, hesitant concerns, he'd never said that.

Neither of us had ever voiced it, not to each other, not to anyone, because to do so was to give in, to give up. We'd held fast to the latest research, Greg Brown's list of credentials, the cases where children were cured, healed, or at least the symptoms helped, the degeneration arrested. And yet here James was, saying the opposite. Admitting defeat. I couldn't stand it.

"You don't know that." I forced the words out through stiff lips.

James shook his head, a slow, determined back and forth. "Her condition has only deteriorated since this whole thing started—"

"Because they don't *know* what her condition is, and so they can't treat it." My voice was spiraling higher and higher, a screeching yelp of fury and fear. How dare he give up already? How dare he think I would?

"They've tried, Rachel. They've tried over and over again. Antibiotics, anti-seizure medications, more MRIs than anyone should have in their lifetime, never mind in a year—"

"What is your *point*?"

James deflated, shoulders slumping, head lowered. I had no sympathy for him. *He* found this hard? I'd been at the hospital all day, every day. I'd been the one to hold Emily's hand as she went into the MRI, to wait on endless hard plastic chairs for results that never came. I'd brushed her wispy hair from her forehead as her eyes pooled with tears and she looked at me in helpless confusion; she was losing the ability to speak, but I knew what she wanted to say: *Why is this happening to me?*

James had been there for some of it—a lot of it, even—I could grant him that. He'd come to every big appointment, visited after work almost every evening, spent most weekends by her bedside. He'd been good that way, but he didn't understand the relentless, day-in and day-out existence I'd been living. He couldn't. And yet he still wanted out of it all.

"I know you've been taking the brunt of it," he said slowly, his head still lowered. "Of Emily's care. I know I come out looking like the big jerk in this scenario, Rachel. Of course I know that."

"Yet you're still going to do it anyway." *Leave me.* The words echoed through me like an empty wind.

He looked up, his eyes bloodshot, tear-filled. Pity stirred, even though I didn't want it to. This hurt him, too. I couldn't pretend it didn't, that it hadn't been hurting him all along. "I'm sorry," he said. "I just... can't."

"Can't what?"

"Can't live like this anymore. And I don't think you can, either."

Desperation made me scrabble for something. "James, do we really have a choice? I mean, I understand that you're unhappy, and I'm sorry. I'm unhappy, too. I want better for our family, for our marriage. But with Emily—"

"I'm not talking about Emily. I know you don't think we can even think about us, Rachel, but we're still married, we still have lives." I opened my mouth, but he overrode me. "I'm not trying to be cruel or selfish, but not everything is about Emily."

I shut my mouth with a snap. I didn't know how to answer that, because to me everything *was* about Emily.

"We're not happy together," James stated more quietly. "We've barely spoken in months."

"On Cape Cod—" That golden week, now over six months ago.

"Even then it was all about Emily, and that was fine. I enjoyed spending time with her. I'll cherish that week forever. But..." His voice wavered and broke. "I can't keep going on like this, Rachel. We're living like strangers, semi-hostile strangers, even. I feel like you resent me for taking up even a second of your time."

I rolled my eyes. I couldn't help it. "Are you seriously going to tell me that you're not getting enough attention?"

"No, because I'm not a dog you have to pet or a goldfish you have to feed." He spoke with cold dignity, his emotion hardening into something scarier and far more final. "I don't want your attention, Rachel. I don't need my ego stroked."

I was silent for a moment, absorbing everything he'd said, despite my instinct to reject it. "I don't resent you," I said, but the words sounded hollow. The truth was, I did, and I didn't even know why. For being healthy? For not seeming to care as intensely as I did? I wasn't even sure, but I knew it wasn't fair.

"I think we'd both be happier if we took some time apart," James said quietly.

"You really think that would help Emily?" I burst out. "Because if you *cared*—"

"It's not a *competition*." The words burst out of him, as if he had wanted to hold them in but couldn't anymore. "Of course I care, Rachel. Why do you always act as if you doubt that? We're not competing for who loves or knows our daughter best, or who cares the most about what's happening to her, or who feels the saddest or most hurt."

I stared at him, stunned into silence by the force of his feeling, the impact of his words hitting me like hammer blows.

"I know it's not a competition," I said after an endless moment. "Why would you even think that I thought it was…"

"Because you act like it is. All. The. Time." He spoke flatly, the fight gone out of him, while my mind spun. This was new. This I hadn't heard before, even though, now that I looked back at it, I'd recognised James was feeling restless, growing distant. Or perhaps I was. Either way, I knew things between us hadn't been great, or even good, for a while. For months, we'd been moving around each other, first politely, then with simmering resentment. I hadn't wanted to acknowledge it because of Emily. Always because of Emily.

I shook my head slowly. "I don't even know what to say."

"I'm not sure there is anything to say." James smiled sadly, the corners of his mouth barely lifting up. "I know you can't see it from where you are. I know, to you, I must sound unreasonable and selfish, especially at a time like this."

Yes, he did, and it irritated me that he could admit that and yet still not want to change his position. But even as those thoughts ricocheted through me, realisation crept in, cold and unwelcome. Even now I was seeing things as a competition, just as James had said—I'd come in feeling more tired, more put upon, more in need of sympathy and support, and I was the one rolling my eyes at his excuses, feeling more aggrieved and more certain that I was right.

Except I wasn't anymore.

And sitting there, with everything in me aching, I didn't think I had the strength to fight for both my daughter and my marriage. Besides that, I wasn't even sure I wanted to. James certainly didn't, and who was to say he wasn't right? Maybe the tension between us was taking its toll without me even realizing. Maybe it would be easier, being on my own. I wouldn't have to worry about anyone but my daughter.

"What do you want to do?" I asked dully. "Emily might be coming home in a few weeks." The doctors hadn't made any promises, but I was still hopeful. "Don't you want to be here?"

"If she comes home, then yes, of course I'll be here. Every day."

"You mean you'll visit?" I couldn't keep a sneer from entering my voice at the implication. A part-time dad to a seriously disabled child. How low did he have to go?

"Tell me you want me to stay." James looked at me levelly, challenging me to admit what I realized was true. I didn't. "Tell me you want to, and I will. Tell me you love me, and we'll handle this together, hand in hand, whatever it takes."

I looked away, ashamed by how he'd seen a lack in me that I hadn't. "That's not exactly fair," I said in a low voice. "Considering you've already told me you want to leave."

"I don't want to leave. I just… think it's best. For both of us. Tell me the truth, Rachel. Aren't you a little bit relieved by this?"

I bit my lip, not wanting to go there. It was so much easier to feel aggrieved. And it was going to be unbearably hard, to do this on my own. Even if James came over every day; even if he took over on the weekends. Whatever arrangement we managed to make, I would still bear the brunt even more than I already was. And yet… he was right. Some small, treacherous part of me felt relieved.

"I didn't ask for this," I said finally, my voice clogged. "I don't want it."

James cradled his head in his hands. "I didn't either, Rach, but this isn't working. If anything, I feel like it's making it worse. Harder for both of us. We need all our strength to deal with Emily, not gripe at each other."

"I haven't been *griping*…"

He gave me a weary, level look. "Can you seriously say you haven't been annoyed with me? Even angry at times?"

I looked away, half-forgotten memories of sharp words, pointed looks, coming back to mock and accuse me. *But I've been under such a strain…*

James let out a weary breath. "Maybe we…" he began, but then he let that thought trail away, and I didn't dare to ask him to finish it. Maybe we should never have got together? Maybe we just weren't strong enough to endure this kind of trial? I couldn't bear to hear him say anything like that, to make our marriage a mistake or a regret.

We'd been good together, James and I, in a quiet way. I still believe that, even now. We'd been set up by mutual friends, assured by both that we were perfect for each other, and we'd admitted this over that first dinner, laughing and rolling our eyes at well-meaning marrieds determined to get their single friends blissfully together.

At the end of the second date, as he held my hand, James murmured shyly that maybe we were. *Perfect.* It was a big word, a lot to aim for, and yet we *fit.* I laughed at his jokes; he listened intently when I spoke. We made each other smile.

It wasn't fireworks with us, maybe not even a slow burn, but we were both in our mid-thirties and we'd already had the adolescent obsessive relationships that inevitably flamed out. We'd gotten over that. We wanted something different, something deeper and stronger, except right now it seemed as if it wasn't.

Was this how marriages were supposed to end, with a sigh and a shrug? Weren't they not supposed to end at all? What about our vows? The whole "for better or for worse" we'd signed up for? The questions pinged through my brain with no answers but James' sad, guilty look.

"Where will you go?" I asked finally.

"There's a Residence Inn in Needham. I'll go there until I find something more permanent."

Permanent. *Forever.* I felt, quite suddenly, seasick, as if I were on a ship that had begun to list and the deck was shifting underneath my feet, everything around me bobbing in an unknown sea. How on earth could this be happening? I was losing my husband? I might be losing my daughter?

But no, I couldn't think like that, I couldn't let myself, because if I did, I knew I'd fall apart, a mess of bones and broken pieces—and I can't think like that now, either.

I reach the counter and the chirpy barista greets me with a bright smile.

"And your name?" she asks when I give my order, her Sharpie poised to write on my paper cup. I wonder how on earth she manages to maintain her perky expression, customer after indifferent customer.

"Rachel." My name comes out like a whisper. I'm so tired; I barely slept last night, staying up for hours trawling the internet for the success stories that will be my evidence today, and then staring gritty-eyed at the ceiling of my bedroom as I went over my opening argument with James, as sharp as any lawyer, determined to make my case and win it.

He can't give up on Emily. He may have given up on me, but I won't let him do to the same to our daughter.

Grabbing my latte, I head back to where James is waiting, hands folded on the tabletop, looking unnervingly composed.

"Thanks for meeting with me." I'm determined to stay purposeful, firm, like this is a board meeting I've called. I put my bag on the floor as I slide into the chair opposite him. "I know you're busy."

"I'm always happy to meet you, Rachel." There's a thread of quiet compassion in his voice that I don't like. I know James has moved on, of course. He kindly kept me apprised every step of the way. Meeting Eva at some bar downtown. Dating her, for all of four months. Getting engaged, seemingly on a whim, as soon as our divorce was final, and then the surprise destination wedding in St Lucia. At every point, he informed me, quietly, bracing himself, as if he expected me to rail and storm, and I never did.

I stayed calm, no-nonsense, supportive, even. I acted as if I accepted the end of our marriage—and part of me had. Another part of me, the part that's knotted in my gut, definitely hasn't. But at least I recognize that, and I do my best to deal with it—quietly, on my own.

But now is not the time to think of our marriage, or its allegedly irretrievable breakdown. I need to focus on Emily.

"I know you believe the doctors have considered Emily's case carefully," I launch in before I've so much as sipped my coffee. "And I think they have, to a point. But the reality is they don't know what Emily has, and so they can't make any definitive statements about her prognosis. Whatsoever." I pause to take a breath, ready to talk about the latest research, the case studies, but James gets in there before me.

"Rachel, Dr. Brown told us at the last appointment we attended together that, from the latest scan, Emily's brain function is at forty percent."

"Yes, but—"

"And patients with that kind of limited brain function don't recover." He speaks quietly, sadly, and that is so much worse than if he was strident.

I swallow hard. "Sometimes they do. Not completely, perhaps, but they can still gain some awareness and even some speech and mobility back. It's happened, James."

I've read so many studies, so many would-be miracles, and so many sad stories. I know them all. I know about Karen Quinlan, who surprised everyone by being able to breathe after they removed her ventilator, expecting her to die; I know about Martin Pistorious, the "Ghost Boy" who spent eight years locked in what appeared to be a coma, while in fact he was conscious. He's married with a child now. How can I not hold onto a story like that? *Hope* like that?

"I know it's happened, Rachel, and it could still happen with Emily. Removing her from the ward isn't consigning her to nothingness. She'll be in a fully staffed facility, with all the life-sustaining measures she needs. This isn't the end." But the tone of his voice suggests that it will be one day soon, and I can't stand that.

I look away as I take a sip of my coffee, trying to marshal my thoughts. "Is this what you want?"

"For Emily? Considering her circumstances? Yes. She'll be comfortable, Rachel. I looked up the brochure online—they have massage therapy and music rooms. Won't those be better for her than endless MRIs and blood tests, poking and prodding her to no avail?" He sounds beseeching, almost tender. He makes it seem simple, the obvious choice, but I know it can't be.

"They're giving up, James." I can barely get the words out. I take a paper napkin between my fingers and start to shred it, tearing off careful, even strips and rubbing them between my fingers. "They'll forget about her. They won't try any new treatments, or enter her into any clinical trials, or prescribe any new medication that's just been FDA approved. She'll just be a name on a list. A statistic. An *expense*."

James is silent. He's heard it all before, of course. I said it yesterday on the phone. I meant to try a different tack today, because I need him on board. I need him to agree with me to fight Dr. Brown and his team. To keep Emily on their ward, so they can continue to look for a diagnosis.

I was going to be upbeat today. I was going to pelt him with all the amazing statistics, the incredible new research into brain function, the studies that show there *can* be recovery, if doctors will just give people time and space and the right therapy. So little is known, the field is wide open, even if Dr. Brown is reluctant to say so. Basically, no one can say anything definitive about the human brain. How it functions. How it heals.

But my positivity has been derailed by James' pitying tone. I know he means well, but I can see how his mind is made up, just like it was when he told me he was leaving. He's sorry, he's sad, oh yes, but this is happening.

I take a deep breath and feel it shudder through me. Why am I the only one who wants to fight? To *try*?

For a second, I let myself remember how it used to be—the day Emily was born, when it went on and on and I was crying and swearing and grunting like an animal, and James stood next to me the whole time, telling me I was amazing, and then shutting up when I told him to, because I was so tired and overwhelmed, I couldn't take anything, not even encouragement. And then, suddenly, a surprise even after everything, nine months of pregnancy and thirteen hours of incredibly hard labor, Emily slid into the world and James let out a cry of wonder and joy.

I remember that sound; it was as pure as a bell, ringing through the room. It made me laugh, despite the pain still banding my middle, even before I'd seen my precious daughter, because it was so happy. *I* was so happy.

"It will be better for her, Rachel," James says gently. "She'll be more comfortable. More at peace." He makes her sound like a dying granny. He touches my hand and I have a sudden, itching urge to smack his face, or maybe just cry.

"Better for you, maybe," I choke out before I can think better of it. "Then you can forget about her. Move on with your new wife, your new *life*."

James blinks in surprise, looking hurt. I've never said anything like that before. I've never even intimated it. But right now I'm too hurt, too raw with this fresh grief, this *betrayal*, to monitor my words or take care with my tone.

"You know it's not like that, Rachel," he says quietly, a hint of censure creeping into his tone, and I know I can't talk to him like this. When I'm the one who seems unreasonable.

I lurch up from the table, spilling my barely touched drink.

James rights the cup and then reaches out to me with one hand, his fingers brushing my coat. "Rachel—"

"Forget it," I spit. My fury feels limitless now, coursing through me in a red, red river. I've been so good, I've been so understanding, and now this? "I should have known," I practically hiss. "I should have known I couldn't count on you."

I whirl away from him, heading blindly out of the café. Near the entrance, I bump into one of those high-end, primary-colored strollers, a big behemoth used for jogging, with a cupholder and basket underneath big enough to stow a TV. The baby inside starts to cry, and the mother draws herself up like a cobra, ready to hiss and strike.

"Fuck off," I snap before she says a word, shocking myself and everyone in the vicinity, and then I storm out of the café.

Dear Bean,

Today we found out how perfect you are—a perfect little girl! Can you believe that, Beanie? I can't. I looked at the screen and laughed in amazement and joy, because I could see you. I really could. A girl. My little girl. My daughter.

I keep saying the words to myself, like trying on a new outfit, making sure it fits. Maybe if I keep saying them, they will start to feel real, because right now they don't. I keep shaking my head at myself, amazed that we've gotten this far. My belly is round, I feel your flutters, we're having a girl!!

Your father looked so proud when he saw you on the screen, little legs kicking away like you had to get somewhere, fast. You have places to be, Bean!

"Here's one who doesn't like to sit still," the technician said, and laughed. And your daddy… he grew six inches taller just looking at you. His chest swelled and his face couldn't hold his smile.

"Well, hello there," he said to you, which made me smile. I could see it already—how he would sing you to sleep, your head nestled under his chin, your tiny hand starfished on his chest.

I could see it all, Bean. It was all there in front of us, shining, perfect, waiting to happen. I didn't have any doubt about that. No doubts at all.

Love, Mama

CHAPTER FOUR

EVA

"Beer or soda, Eva Diva?"

My dad smiles at me hopefully, using my old nickname, as he proffers the cooler with its many cans jostling for space amidst the melting ice cubes. It's Saturday, a properly warm day, with blue skies and birdsong, and my parents have invited James and me over, along with my brothers and their families, for a barbecue. Something I try not to dread, but invariably do.

"I'll have a beer, Dad," I say with a smile, not because I actually want a beer, but because I know it will forestall any when-are-you-going-to-get-pregnant conversations that my father hints at and my mother asks outright. *You know your eggs start to wither and shrivel at thirty-five, Eva? You don't have all the time in the world, even if you think you do.*

No, I always want to say, *I don't think that, Mom.* But I never do, for a whole lot of complicated reasons.

My father's face falls just a little as he hands me a can of Budweiser, the family drink. I grew up in a solidly working-class family in the south Boston suburb of Roslindale, back when it was a generational, immigrant community of Irish Catholics and a few others besides. Now it is in the process of becoming expensive and gentrified, peopled with a mix of college students, singles, and young upwardly mobile families. Most of my parents' friends and neighbors have sold up since the prices have skyrocketed, but they've held on, stubborn to the last.

We are standing on the back deck, overlooking a postage stamp of carefully tended yard, the Boston skyline visible over the trees in the distance. I can smell the smoky, charcoal aroma from the old-school barbecue my dad has already started, mixed with the cloying pine scent of the air freshener my mother overuses. Home. A place that makes me feel a dozen different things.

"James!" My dad's voice becomes jocular, the man's man tone he seems to reserve for my husband in particular. "Beer?"

"No thanks, Brian." James never drinks beer; he doesn't like the taste, something my father refuses to understand or accept. I'm sure he thinks if he keeps asking, one of these days James will take a Bud from him.

"Are you sure?" Dad asks, and James smiles and shakes his head.

"Sorry. I'll have a Coke, though." His gaze is a little distant, his manner a bit reserved, as it always is when we visit my family.

James is the only child of wealthy parents; his father was in finance, his mother lunched and played tennis. He grew up in Connecticut, went to boarding school when he was eleven and then on to Tufts here in Boston, and everything about my family—from the beers to the nosy neighbors to my back-slapping brothers—is foreign to him. It doesn't help that my two brothers are the kind of guys with hearty laughs and booming voices; Patrick is a firefighter and Steve a paramedic. They married young, have three children each, and stayed in Roslindale. I'm the anomaly in the family, and I suspect I always will be. I feel it most when I'm at home, like I'm wearing clothes that don't fit.

"So how's the insurance world, James?" my dad asks, which is something else he always does on these occasions that never works. My dad is a plumber and doesn't really understand the corporate world. Doesn't really want to. He basically thinks life insurance is a big scam.

"It's good." James' smile seems a bit forced. I know things have been tense since Rachel called with the news about Emily. I don't like to ask, because James makes it feel so private, but I know he met her during his lunch break and they argued.

Emily is moving to the palliative care unit on Monday, and James is taking off work to be there for the day, with Rachel. I haven't asked him how he feels about it, because I know he won't tell me, but it feels like I should—like I should at least try to *seem* supportive.

I take a sip of my beer even though I don't like the taste. All my childhood, I've been trying to fit in with my family, keep up with my brothers, even though I knew I never could. They outpaced me at everything, no more so than with our choices of career—saving lives versus marketing for makeup? No contest. And it's not even real marketing, according to my mother, who wrinkled her nose and said, "But it's not in a magazine?" when I told her about one of the ad campaigns I'd organised.

Another sip, and the beer doesn't taste any better. I'm still feeling crampy, wishing my period would finish so I can start on the next cycle of hope. I haven't even told James I'm not pregnant; with the situation with Emily, it hasn't felt appropriate, and it's not like it's news, anyway. Yet part of me still wishes he would notice, ask, *care*.

When I told James I wanted to start trying for a baby five months ago, he looked shocked and not altogether sure, which I'd kind of suspected would be the case, even though I pretended to myself that it wouldn't be.

"A baby? Already? I mean…" He tugged at his collar.

"I'm thirty-six, James, and I want a family."

"You never said you wanted children." He sounded faintly accusing.

No, I hadn't said it, because I'd thought it was obvious. Didn't most people want children? Weren't you supposed to say if you *didn't*? And yet, even then I knew that wasn't true. I hadn't always wanted children; in fact, for a decade I definitely didn't. And perhaps it was this ambivalence, or just my fear of this exact response of James because of his situation with Emily, that kept me from bringing up the topic earlier.

"Do *you* want children?" I asked after a moment. "I mean, more children." I felt guilty for forgetting about Emily, even for a second.

"I don't know," James said after a pause. "Someday, I suppose. I haven't really thought about it too much yet."

We'd been together for just seven months then, married for three. By some standards ours was a whirlwind romance, but as we'd said to each other, when you know, you know. Why wait around, waiting for things to get stale, making sure you agree on silly things like music choices or what toothpaste you use?

Yet looking at James' uncertain expression then, I knew we should have had this conversation before we decided, on a whim, to fly to St Lucia for a destination wedding, no guests, just us. My mother had been devastated.

We should have had the conversation, but we hadn't, and the truth was that part of the reason we hadn't was because I'd been afraid. I'd rather hear nothing than no, and I'd told myself I could talk James around eventually. Of course he'd want another child, in time. He'd be a great dad. He *was* a great dad.

"Well, surely it's something to think about now," I said. "I know we've only been married for a few months, but I'm not getting any younger, and neither are you." I smiled to take any sting from the words. "And just think how cute our babies would be."

He tried to smile. "Definitely cute, as long as they looked like you."

I smiled back, willing this to be easy, even though it felt forced. "It might take some time, you know. It often doesn't happen right away. And then, of course, you've got nine months to wait."

"Right." He still looked discomfited.

I leaned forward, put my hand on his knee, wanting to remind him of what we had shared... all the memories, all the laughter.

At the start of our first date, I spilled a full glass of red wine all over his suit. I was mortified, and James looked stunned, and then, to my horror, I started laughing. Really laughing, the kind that makes your stomach muscles hurt. Maybe it was nerves; maybe it was just because it all seemed so ridiculous.

"You are never going to want to see me again," I'd gasped out, half-joking, even as my heart had lurched at the thought.

"That's definitely not the case," James had said. "But I think I need to change."

He went to a Gap down the street to buy a pair of jeans, and came back while our starters were served, joking about how hipster he was, in a suit jacket and tie and jeans. And I think I fell in love with him right then, for taking it all in his stride, for being so easygoing, for making me laugh even more.

With my hand on his knee, I looked into his eyes, willing him to remember. "I want to be a mother, James. I want to be a family with you."

He met my gaze, looking torn. Upset, even. "Eva... it's just that I didn't realize..."

Something in me prickled. "You didn't realize? What did you think I wanted?"

"I don't know." He shifted away from me, so my hand slipped from his knee. "I mean, yes, I suppose, *eventually*. But it's just, you're very career-focused, Eva, that's all. And I didn't think... you don't seem..." He stopped there, but the damage was done.

"I don't *seem*? What? Maternal?" I meant to sound scoffing, but I only sounded hurt.

James ducked his head, apologetic. "No, of course I don't mean that," he said, reaching over to touch my hand, giving me one of his lopsided smiles that I loved so much.

The trouble was, even as he laced his fingers through mine, I knew he sort of did mean it, just as I knew I couldn't really blame him. I *didn't* seem maternal, and I was afraid that I wasn't.

I'd focused on my career for the last fourteen years, with an almost grim determination to succeed. I made sure I had the right image—the expertly done hair, the perfectly threaded eyebrows, the gym-toned body. On the outside, I looked like the stereotypical career woman who had no time for baby bumps or dirty diapers. But that wasn't the real me, not anymore, and maybe not ever.

But is that blossoming, bump-bellied earth mama me, either? I don't know. I haven't had the chance to find out. I just know that I've wanted a baby, with a desperation that has grown with every passing month and negative test. I want to feel that solid, pleasing weight in my arms, breathe in that sweet, milky scent. I want to kiss a soft, downy head and close my eyes and think *at last, at last, mine.*

I want it with a ferocity borne of a fear that it's never going to happen, that it can't, because maybe it shouldn't. Yet another layer of complexity to my relationship with my husband, because I couldn't even begin to explain any of that to James, and I certainly haven't tried.

At the end of that painful conversation, James agreed to think about trying for a baby, and a few weeks later he brought home a bottle of wine and, with a glint in his eye, he carried me to bed. Afterwards, we lay with our legs twined, our fingers laced together and resting on my belly, which he gave a little, meaningful pat.

"Maybe it's already happened," he said, smiling at me, and my lips trembled with incredulous joy as I smiled back. In that moment, I thought it was all about to happen, it was *promised.*

But as month by month has gone by, each one with a single line on a stick and a flash of relief in James' eyes that I do my best to ignore, I wonder if it ever will happen, if anything is promised.

As my brother Patrick comes in with his family, the kids running from the deck to the yard with boisterous, banshee screams, and Tiffany, Patrick's wife, hugging my mom as she puts the Jell-O salad she brought on the kitchen table—we brought some Brie—I edge closer to James.

"You okay?" I ask quietly, feeling like I should at least *enquire*, and he glances at me, startled and a little wary, as he always seems to be when I work up the energy and courage to ask about Emily.

"Yes, I'm okay."

"I know this development with Emily…" I venture cautiously, tiptoeing on the thin ice of the unspoken, but wanting to—*needing* to—test its weight, even though part of me is so afraid of the hairline fractures that I suspect will result. "It's hard."

"It's the right thing to do." He speaks in a final tone, and I let it go, as I always do, with something like relief. At least I tried.

James first told me about Emily and Rachel on our second date. Thankfully I didn't spill any wine. We'd first met in a noisy sports bar in downtown Boston, where I'd gone with friends for an afterwork drink and James had been dragged along by one of his colleagues. Neither of us had really wanted to be there, and as we sat on the edge of our respective groups, neither of us involved in the raucous give and take of the chatter, we caught each other's eye and gave commiserating smiles.

When I went to get a refill of my white wine, James did too, and we ended up chatting as we waited for our drinks. I thought that would be the end of it, and felt a little sad—with his floppy brown hair, kind eyes, and quiet manner, James seemed like the kind of self-deprecating, decent guy I hadn't yet been able to find.

But then, as I was leaving, he came up to me and asked me for my number. Shyly, seeming a little uncertain, which made me like him all the more. He called me a few days later, and we had dinner that weekend, with the wine fiasco keeping things light.

But when the second date came around, as our appetizers were cleared, James put his palms flat on the table and said in a serious-sounding voice, "Look, I need to tell you something."

My heart lurched—wouldn't anyone's—but I kept my voice light as I raised my eyebrows and smiled. "Okay," I said.

"I'm divorced," James told me. "At least, I'm in the process of getting a divorce. I separated from my wife four months ago. It will be finalized soon."

"Okay," I said again. In my mind I was trying to decide whether four months was a decent enough length of time or not.

"But there's more," James said, his manner one of someone laying down a burden that had become too heavy to bear. "I have a daughter, Emily. She's four."

"Okay." I couldn't think of another response; it was something more to absorb. My mind felt like an oversoaked sponge. I took a sip of my drink, stalling for time as I tried to sort out my thoughts. Married, with a child. You expect that when dating in your thirties; there are always complications, the inevitable baggage that someone who is not fresh-faced out of college has collected along the way. But I wasn't sure yet how I felt about it then, coming from James. "What happened?" I asked eventually. "With your marriage?"

James shook his head slowly. He looked so genuinely sad that I felt afraid. There was history here, more than the tired, old usual. I could see it in his face—the shadows in his eyes, the graven lines from nose to mouth. "We grew apart," he told me. "But not... not in the usual way. Emily got sick..." He spoke haltingly, every word coming at a cost, and I remained silent as I listened to him explain.

How, a year and a half earlier, Emily had started having symptoms. Small things at first—stumbling a bit, but she was only three, so who was to say it wasn't normal? Slurring words, when she'd only just started speaking clearly. Sudden high fevers that seemed to have no cause. Headaches, although they hadn't realized at first, because she hadn't had the verbal skills to explain; she'd just cried and sometimes clutched her head. Joint pain that made her writhe and sob.

It all sounded heart-wrenching in the worst way, and my eyes welled up listening to him explain how they'd gone to the doctors, who had first dismissed their concerns, but then they'd gone again, and then there had been tests, so many tests, but never any answers.

"And she just kept getting worse," he said quietly, his head lowered, his palms still flat on the table, fingers spread out. "Ten months ago, she had her first seizure, a big one. Tonic-clonic, it's called. She's been in and out of hospital since then, mostly in, for the seizures and also some infections and other problems. She has trouble walking, can barely speak, and still no one can say what's wrong with her."

"That… that sounds so tough," I said after a moment. Such a ridiculous, offensive understatement, but I was grasping for words, still absorbing it all, trying to figure out how I felt. I barely knew this man, and yet he'd bared his already flayed soul.

"It was," James said. "And is. I'm sorry I'm laying this all on you now, so early, and I know it might make things awkward, but I feel like I have to tell you. Because it's a big thing. Maybe too big."

I heard the note of vulnerability in his voice and it made me ache. What was too big—too big to warrant the commitment of time, energy, emotion that our relationship would be? Was this? With a tremor of fear, I wondered what would qualify as *too big* for James. What could I tell him that would make him walk away?

"So did you and your ex-wife split up because of Emily's illness?" I finally asked.

"Yes," James said, "and no. But mostly yes." He sighed, lifting one of his hands from the table to rake through his rumpled hair. "We grew apart, and started to resent each other. We weren't communicating at all. But we also approached the whole thing differently, I suppose. We both wanted the best for Emily, of course, and we still do, absolutely. But a while ago what that might mean started to look different for both of us."

"What do you mean?" I asked, a bit warily.

James hesitated, wanting to choose his words with care. "Rachel's been obsessed with finding a diagnosis. Emily keeps deteriorating, but she seems to think if we can just find out what's wrong with her, it will all go away. A magic pill or some course of therapy… she doesn't use those words, and she'd probably deny what I'm saying, but that's essentially what she's hoping for. A quick fix, relatively speaking."

I could understand why she would wish for such a thing, do everything in her power to try and obtain it. Wouldn't any mother? Any parent? "And you…" I paused, feeling my way through the words. "You don't think Emily can be… cured?"

"No, I don't." The statement was so terribly bleak. "I know that sounds heartless, but I think it's better for everyone to realize what's going on. And from everything the doctors have said, all the stuff I've read about degenerative neurological conditions… they don't just go away. They don't even get better." He blinked rapidly, and I almost reached over and placed my hand on top of his. I lifted my hand, let it flutter near his, and then put it back in my lap. Touching him at that moment felt like an invasion, too much of an intimacy. This was only our second date, after all.

"I'm so sorry, James."

"It's been a long process of grief," he said quietly. "Watching Emily decline, day by agonising day. Losing all her abilities… talking, walking, maybe even thinking. It's hard to know how much she's taking in, how much she's aware of us now. She communicates, but…" He shrugged. "It's just so hard to know. But Rachel doesn't see it that way. She refuses to grieve, to let go. She feels like doing that would be a failure, some sort of betrayal of Emily. And then it started to be a competition for her—who cared the most, who did the most. One I was never allowed to win." He looked up at me then, a vulnerability in the cast of his features that moved me. "I know that doesn't make me sound…" He blew out a breath. "Whatever. I don't even know. I don't come out looking great in this, but I honestly felt—I still feel—that leaving was the best thing for both of us. We were bringing each other down. We couldn't help each other."

I nodded, signaling my acceptance of his narrative, even though my thoughts were tangled, a knotted mess of compassion, wariness, suspicion, and affection for this man who had been so honest with me, who was trying so hard to do the right thing, in so many ways.

"So do you have partial custody of Emily?" I asked.

"Yes, in terms of medical decision-making. We both need to agree on any treatment she has. But no, in terms of her living with me. When she's not in the hospital, she's with Rachel, because she's set up for it… Emily has a lot of physical needs." He swallowed, his gaze downcast again. "I see Emily three times a week… Tuesday and Thursday evenings, and all day Saturday, either in the hospital or at Rachel's, if she's there, although more and more it's been at the hospital, because of her seizures, infections…" He drew a quick breath. "One day it will always be at the hospital, I think."

"Okay," I said, because I didn't know what else to say. It was too much to take in; I couldn't even begin to absorb all the implications.

James grimaced. "I know it's not a lot of time."

The guilt in his voice, in the hunch of his shoulders, made me want to comfort him. It was actually a lot more than most divorced dads spent with their kids, as far as I could tell. There was a guy at my old job, back in finance, who saw his son once a month, if that. When I'd overheard someone asking him about it, he'd just shrugged and said, "What can you do?" as if it was entirely out of his control. Perhaps it had been.

James took his hands off the table, put them in his lap. He looked up at me, resolute now. "I'd understand if you wanted to walk, or even run, away now. This is complicated, I know. Emily is a big part of my life. And as for her prognosis… we just don't know. How long, or how much, or…" He stopped, not wanting to say the words, and then stayed silent, waiting for what felt like a verdict.

He'd made me a judge, with the power to condemn or forgive. It was a terrifying feeling, and yet I already knew what I'd say. How much I was willing to accept, for a man like James—a man I was already falling in love with, who made me laugh, but also was one who cared about his family, who had shown what he was made of when it mattered. How many people could say they'd done the same?

"Everything is complicated," I told him, which was as close as I ever got to telling him about my own emotional baggage, those battered bags trailing behind me that, just like everyone else, I pretended didn't exist. And James smiled, and nodded, and the relief that flashed in his eyes was like waves breaking on the shore. He'd told me the truth, and I'd accepted it. We could move on, together. We could start building something new, just for us.

And we did move on, but it was in such a way that it felt impossible to revisit that conversation, to take it down avenues I hadn't dared to consider when I'd barely known him.

Once James had explained about Rachel and Emily, it was as if a door had closed, a door to a room whose dimensions I could not conceive of. And while all too often I was happy to have that door shut, and not to think about that room at all, at other times I felt its presence in our lives, as well as my ignorance, like a physical thing.

I'm not sure exactly when I realized just how much of a no-go area Rachel and Emily were. Early on, before we were married, I asked James something about them, I don't recall what, and he gave me a look, a cross between hurt and annoyance and said, "I've already told you about that."

I remember the *that*—not them. It sounded strangely, disconcertingly impersonal, even though I knew he couldn't have meant it like that. I knew he would have been appalled if I'd thought that he did. And yet that was when I began to realize, dimly at first, and then later with painful clarity, that James neither expected nor wanted to talk about Rachel or Emily with me, because he'd already told me, and it had nothing more to do with me; it was finished, and we never needed to discuss it—*them*—again.

And so, without me agreeing, or even realizing, Emily and Rachel had become a blocked-off area for my marriage, despite the three days a week James spent with his daughter. And, for the most part, I've told myself that that's okay. I don't want to talk endlessly about Rachel and Emily; I don't even want to think about that much. I might feel I have to ask, yet it's a relief not to press. Not, even, to know.

And yet, at times like this, when something big is happening, when I feel like James is closing himself off to me, and the tectonic plates of our relationship are subtly shifting, the ground beneath my feet run through with fault lines, the lack of communication, of openness and honesty, scares me and I realize how alone I feel, even when James is right next to me.

Yet maybe all that will be in the past now. In just two days' time, Emily will go into palliative care. Will that be the beginning of the end, as both James and Rachel seem to think, in their different ways? No more treatment, no more possibility of that wished-for miracle diagnosis and cure? My heart aches for Rachel, and yet…

Is it wrong, I wonder as I sip the beer I don't want and James stays silent beside me, to feel the tiniest bit relieved by it all? Is it terrible?

"Oh, Tiffany!" my mother squeals from the kitchen, and, jolted out of my thoughts, I turn to see her throwing her arms around my sister-in-law, who smiles and gives her soft tummy—three kids will do that to you—a self-conscious pat.

I freeze, my inquiring smile turning into a rictus grin. Cody, her youngest, is only eight months old. Surely not…

"Can you believe it?" my mother calls out as she links arms with Tiffany and parades her out to the deck as if she is her personal trophy. Patrick is smiling in a self-satisfied way, clearly the cock of the walk, and James' expression is blandly curious, his gaze still distant. I feel sick.

Steve bounds up from the yard, where he's been playing tee-ball with the kids.

"I'm going to be a grandma again," my mother trills, beaming, and then, as I knew she would, she looks pointedly at me.

I can't even smile. I can't believe Tiffany is pregnant again. Four kids under five? All I want is one.

Patrick nudges me. "Better get a move on, Diva," he says, the nickname from my childhood that I actually kind of hate. It wasn't even true, anyway, at least not much. "What do you think, James? Time to start trying?"

My family are nosy, to the point of utter obnoxiousness, although they don't realize it. The one aspect of my life they don't ask about is Emily. Everyone skirts around that one. But in terms of trying for a baby? Fair game.

James ignores Patrick's question and kisses Tiffany's cheek. "Congratulations, Tiffany. That's great news."

Tiffany gives me an apologetic look. "I was putting my maternity clothes aside for you, Eva, but I guess I'll need them now."

"I guess you will," I say, trying to sound jokey, but I can't. I glug my beer. What am I supposed to say to any of this?

Later, in the kitchen, while we're dishing out the salads, my mother says in a low voice, "There's nothing… wrong, is there, Eva?"

"Wrong?" I am thinking of how quiet James has been about Emily, how it is making me feel so uncertain, on top of my own disappointment.

"You know, with your… female parts." She gestures towards my pelvis just in case I didn't understand. "It's just, you're not getting any younger, and I know you've said you want children one day…"

Had I let that slip once, when I was feeling hopeful, my period three days late? She sounds so wistful, yearning, just as I am, and yet I can't make myself commiserate with her. "James and I haven't even been married a year, Mom. Give us a little time, okay?"

"But you're thirty-six…"

"I know." I dump some potato salad into a glass bowl; it comes out in a congealed, rectangular lump. "Trust me, I know."

My mother gives me a look that is half sympathy, half exasperation, and touches my hand. It's as far as either of us will go towards admitting that this isn't simple. But, of course, my mother has no idea how complicated it really is.

CHAPTER FIVE

RACHEL

On Monday morning, James and I meet at the doors to the children's palliative care unit. It's a much quieter place than the neurology ward—no doctors striding purposefully down the corridors, no squeak of wheels as monitors or ultrasound machines are moved importantly from place to place, no persistent beep of some essential machine or other.

The atmosphere is hushed, expectant… or am I just imagining that, because of what I know happens here? The parents going in and out look quiet and tired, but accepting too, in a way that makes me both prickle and ache. I don't want to be like them. I won't, not yet. I still want to fight, even though I've had to agree—and in some part to accept—this move to palliative care.

James touches my shoulder as he greets me, a look of concern on his face that annoys me. We haven't spoken since our meeting at Starbucks; we arranged today by text. He's probably wondering if I am going to be able to hold it together. I'm determined that I will, at least until I get home where I can cry in private.

"How are you doing, Rachel?" he asks, all sympathy, and I shrug a reply. I want to tell him we should be feeling the same in this situation, that we're *both* deserving of his thoughtful compassion, but I don't, because I know it would be petty. Besides, I've already decided I'm going to fight for Emily, not against James. I just don't know what that will look like yet, but I will.

Dr. Brown meets us in the waiting room a few minutes later, his expression serious but friendly. "Emily seems comfortable in her room," he tells us. "She was moved about half an hour ago, and it went very smoothly, I'm happy to say."

We both nod our acceptances, and James murmurs some sort of thanks. I can't quite manage that yet; there is a burning in my chest that is threatening to work its way up my throat and I am trying not to let it.

I know how difficult it can be to move someone in Emily's state just from one bed to another, with all the potential complications, risks of infection, and laborious transferring of equipment; moving buildings would be a challenge, indeed, and one we were requested not to be present for, in case it didn't go well. What that would have looked like, I can't bear to imagine.

Dr. Brown touches my shoulder lightly, just as James did. "Would you like to see her new room?"

I nod jerkily and follow him down the corridor; the lighting has been dimmed and everyone talks in murmured voices. It should feel soothing, but it doesn't. Dr. Brown had offered a tour before they moved Emily, but I'd declined, a matter of principle that now feels a bit petty.

There are colored, cut-out handprints on the walls, with different names written on them. I peek in a room where the door is ajar and see a wall with a colorful Noah's Ark mural and an empty crib. I look away quickly.

"Here we are." Dr. Brown pushes open the door to Emily's room.

My heart squeezes with impossible amounts of both love and fear as I see her lying in her bed, her small body barely making a bump under the sheet. Dr. Brown has told me before how her growth has been affected by her condition; although she's now two months shy of her sixth birthday, she's only a little bit bigger than she was when she was three, when all of this started. It feels like a lifetime ago. Perhaps it was.

"Hey, sweetie." I pitch my voice cheerful and firm, as I always try to do, normalizing what is entirely and horrifically abnormal—a tiny girl lying in a bed, eyes open, body still, and nobody knows why. She seems lifeless, yet with her eyes blinking, heart beating away, her lungs taking in breath after breath after breath. Four months like this, and it never feels less strange.

I touch her curls lying limply against her forehead; her hair feels brittle now, and it used to be so soft, curling about her apple cheeks, her rosebud mouth. James used to joke how he could eat her up.

When I'm at the hospital, I try to do as much for Emily as I can—giving sponge baths, brushing her hair, trimming her nails. Once I cut the tip of her finger, and I let out a stifled cry as blood welled up, a bright crimson drop, but she didn't flinch or react at all. That hurt worse than the fact that I'd cut her.

Today I've brought some nail polish and hair clips, a way to make this time special, although I know it will feel like a gross parody of the real thing, a mother and daughter girly time with giggles and hugs. I try not to think of it that way, try, with desperate intensity, to focus on what I can—the sparkly bow I'll put in Emily's hair, the way her fingers sometimes seem to squeeze mine. It's so little, and yet it has to be enough. But even as I brush and polish and chat, I know part of me will resist everything I am doing, and another part of me will revel in it, because at least she is here, breathing, beside me.

I leave the bag of clips and polish on the table next to her, for later, and instead flit about the room, adjusting the blinds, smoothing her coverlet, patting her hand. Dr. Brown is talking to James in a low voice; I hear assurances about regular consultants coming in, a tour of the unit, good communication, keeping her on lists for experimental drugs and clinical trials. He's told me all of it already, all the promises that nothing is going to change, while we all know that everything is. Emily will be out of his sight, an afterthought, perhaps, at the end of a long working day. *I wonder what happened to...* or, if we're lucky, *maybe I should check on...*

And yet, even though I am corroded inside with bitterness, I know I can't fault him. I can't fault anyone, from the nurses who have always been so gentle and kind, to the medical team who are purposeful and efficient, to the support staff—the aides and cleaners and caterers—who give me sympathetic smiles as they quietly move about, doing their jobs with the minimum invasion or fuss.

The standard of care has been amazing, and if I had to fill out a survey, I'd give everyone five stars. But that doesn't change the fact that my little girl is lying in bed, staring at the ceiling, and I haven't heard her speak in nearly a year. It doesn't change the fact that I will do anything—*anything*—to help her.

A round-faced, smiling nurse with a warm, rich Caribbean accent, comes in and introduces herself as Alma, and assures me she'll answer any of my questions, get me anything I need. Dr. Brown invites us to take a tour of the ward with the nurse, even though I am reluctant to leave Emily.

Dr. Brown says goodbye, promising to "check in" soon, and so dutifully James and I follow Alma around the unit, listening to her chat about life on the unit. She is cheerful without being annoying, laying a hand on my arm on occasion, giving me a smile that tells me she knows what I am feeling, the prickliness that comes out on me like a rash. I can't let myself like anything, not even Alma, even though she is the kind of person you want to hug, because to do that would be admitting defeat, even in some small way.

The unit is formed as a square with four corridors, and a nurses' station in the middle. I see the massage and music rooms that were bigged up in the brochure, and a little kitchenette at the end of one corridor where I can make coffee or tea if needed.

There's a lovely playroom for the children who are well enough to play, although it's empty when we poke our heads in, some blocks forgotten on the floor.

I take in the sofas, the toy kitchen, the colorful bins of plastic figures and puzzles, and swallow down the howl of resentment that wells up inside me, because Emily won't ever use this room, unless they find a diagnosis. And a cure.

James asks practical questions about the facilities, the music therapy and massage room he seems so keen on, while I listen numbly. I already play Emily music. I already massage her limbs, rub cream into her dry little hands. She didn't need to come here for that.

Finally we are back in her room, and I breathe a sigh of relief. Dr. Brown and the nurses are leaving us alone, and I am glad, because right now I just want to reconnect with my little girl.

James stands in the doorway, watching me as I sit next to Emily and start to brush her hair, stroke by gentle stroke.

"This seems like a good place," he says, and I can't make myself reply. He knows how I feel. "I think Emily will like the music room." A pause that feels breakable. "Remember how she used to love to dance?"

For a second, I close my eyes, picture the scene: the kitchen of our old house in Newton, the one we were going to have at least two, maybe three kids in. I turn up some music on my phone, and Emily races from the family room as soon as she hears the beat. Her eyes are alight, the sunlight turning her baby curls to gold. She's not quite two.

"Dan!" she calls out as she starts to wiggle her hips and flail her arms, throwing herself into the movement. I know she means "dance". "*Dan*, Mama!"

And we dance, with me taking her hands and leading her in a little, laughing box-step, but after a few seconds, she wrenches herself away and starts twirling on her own, caught up in the sound, in the moment, everything about her so joyful that all I can do is look at her and laugh. She's beautiful. She's so, so beautiful.

I open my eyes and gaze down at the limp curl lying against her forehead. Her eyes move towards the door and back again, making my heart lurch, but Dr. Brown has told me—again and again—that it's just a reflex. *I know it looks promising, but I'm afraid it doesn't signify any awareness.* It would be a cruel thing to say, if his tone hadn't been so kind.

I take a deep breath. "Of course I remember. But please, James. Don't..." I lower my voice to a whisper. "Don't talk about her as if she's dead."

Another pause, as tense and fragile as the one before, starting to splinter. "I didn't mean to," he says quietly.

I start brushing her hair again, and then fasten a sparkly pink butterfly clip to keep it from sliding into her eyes. It's grown a bit. She'll need another trim, something that I am glad to have as my responsibility.

"I suppose I'll head back to work," James says after the silence stretches on, suffocating and heavy. "I'll come here tomorrow, as usual..."

"Okay." Generally, during James' visits, I try to stay for a few minutes, to pass on any relevant information, but I'm not sure I can do that anymore. Not if we're going to always have this between us, this heavy burden of disappointment and difference in the way we see not just Emily's care, but Emily herself.

After another moment he leaves, and I take out the bottle of nail polish—bright pink, Emily's favorite color. She used to insist everything was pink—her clothes, her cup, her bedspread. For her fourth birthday we gave her a pair of sparkly pink shoes she was barely able to wear, before she lost her mobility.

I wonder if she would still like pink now, if she could tell me so. I wonder if she would have moved on, found pink too babyish now that she's nearly six. Maybe she'd have become more of a tomboy, or maybe she would have gone through what seems like the inevitable princess phase, complete with tiaras and tutus.

We never found out, because when all the other four-year-old girls in her preschool were insisting on dressing as Elsa every day, Emily was forgetting how to talk. Having a seizure. Spending three weeks in hospital until we were released for another stint at home, until something else happened and we were back again, and then eventually we were there all the time.

In my alternate life, the one I can't bear to fantasize about but do anyway, Emily would be in kindergarten, learning her letters, getting ready to go into first grade in the fall. She'd be able to sound out words, and be learning to ride a bike, and maybe she'd even have a little brother or sister. We'd been starting to try again when we first noticed Emily's symptoms; we'd both wanted another child and I was thirty-eight already. We put it on hold, by mutual agreement, after Emily's first seizure, when we realized this was serious. Even then we had no idea how serious it would become. How we would end up here.

After I finish Emily's nails, I go to the kitchen area to make a cup of coffee. My body is aching with tiredness; I spent another sleepless night yesterday, anticipating today, spending too long online trying to find miracle cures when I know there aren't any. But I still try. I have to try, as long as Emily is breathing and being.

Now I switch on the electric kettle, my shoulders slumping as I stand there, my eyes roving blankly over the printed notices about keeping things in the fridge and wiping down the sink, along with the host of support numbers, including the suicide prevention lifeline.

As I'm waiting for the kettle to boil, a woman comes in, tired-eyed and slumped-shouldered like me. She shoots me an uncertain smile, which I make myself return as she goes to the fridge. There is an etiquette to hospital wards and sick children that I've learned over the last two years. You don't ask. Everyone tries to be supportive, and you might share some vague information— "Taylor has a scan today" or "We're discussing Brody's latest tests"—but you don't generally volunteer more information than that, and you definitely don't ask questions of other people. And so I don't now, as I step aside so the woman can access the fridge.

She takes out a carton of two percent milk and nods towards the kettle. "Do you want some?"

I am startled out of my thoughts, as if she's penetrated an invisible shield around me. It takes me a second to realise she means the kettle, my coffee. "Oh yes, thanks,' I half mumble, and we work in silence, spooning granules, sharing milk.

At the end of this awkward little ritual, I heft my cup in thanks, and then retreat back to Emily's room. I'm not strong enough for even those innocuous conversations. I don't have the emotional space to wonder about her life, her child, and yet my gaze tracks her as she walks down the hall, slipping into a room two doors down from Emily. Before the door closes, I glimpse a man sitting in a chair, his face set in haggard lines. I go into Emily's room.

Her eyes are closed now and I decide to put on some music—Baby Einstein's Lullaby Classics, which I played when I was pregnant and then, after she was born, when she was going to sleep.

Would she have outgrown these by now, along with the color pink? Of course, I don't know. Perhaps she can't stand Baby Einstein anymore, and she isn't able to tell me. The latest research suggests that patients in a state of unresponsive wakefulness may be more aware of their surroundings than we realize, a possibility which gives me terror and hope in equal, overwhelming measure.

I think once more of Martin Pistorius, the South African man who had been conscious but unable to communicate for years. They'd seated him in front of a TV playing endless episodes of *Barney* for hours at a time; he couldn't stand it, but he hadn't been able to say anything. What if Emily is the same—struggling to communicate, trapped inside her body, desperate to reach me?

As I sit and sip my coffee, I gaze at her face; her eyes are closed and her lips are slightly pursed, the way they used to be when she slept, as a baby. I can't see anything in her slack features that tells me she can hear the music, hear *me*, but I still hope she can. I hope she knows I am here, and she is comforted. I can't stand the thought that she might be afraid, that she might not understand what is going on, that she might feel lonely or frightened or hopeless.

I lean forward, needing to reach her, even if it's only in my own mind. "Baby girl, it's Mama. I love you. I'm here and I love you so, so much." My voice becomes huskier as I say each word, and I take a shuddering breath.

In the hallway, I hear someone crying quietly, like an apology.

I've got to get Emily out of here.

I've got to get Emily somewhere she can find hope.

Six hours later, as dusk starts to fall, I am out in the parking lot, fishing for my keys, ready to return home. Before Emily got sick, I was a high school English teacher. I'd returned to work when she was a year old and quit after Emily's first seizure, when it was clear she needed full-time care.

A few weeks ago, during one of our hospital hand-offs, James suggested I return to work, at least part-time. "I know this is hard to hear, but Emily doesn't need you the way she did before, Rachel." She'd been in a coma for less than six weeks, not even long enough to qualify as being vegetative. I wasn't remotely ready, and I couldn't believe he was. Still, I tried to stay reasonable.

"Even though Emily isn't awake the way she used to be, she still needs me," I said. Who else was going to brush her hair, play music, talk to her—do whatever it took to remind her brain it needed to wake up? "Besides, it's spring. Maybe I'll talk to the school about going back in the fall." Except I knew I wouldn't.

James nodded his acceptance, looking weary. I knew money was tight. He paid child support and alimony, and maintaining two separate households in an expensive city wasn't easy. When we'd sold our house, I'd moved to a duplex in Upper Falls, the cheaper end of Newton, while James had rented an apartment in one of Boston's most expensive neighborhoods. I couldn't help but wonder if he was reliving his bachelor days, but then he went and got married again.

Still, it felt as if he were constructing a new life for himself—the cool apartment, the beautiful wife—while I was treading water, just as Emily was. But I tried not to think that way. I didn't want a new life. I wanted my old one back, if not with James, then with my daughter.

On the way back home, I decide to stop by my mother's house in Brookline. Since Emily's illness started, she's been a rock for me—bringing meals, always listening, letting me cry. My friends may have fallen away after years of unrelenting illness, but my mother hasn't. She visits Emily once a week, always bringing her a little present, even though they just pile by her bed, unused, unseen.

As I pull into my childhood home, a brick split-level in a friendly neighborhood, the kind with sidewalks and big front yards, a wave of nostalgia breaks over me. When I was younger, Brookline was for families like my parents—college professors, doctors, teachers, the occasional plumber or carpenter—unpretentious and solidly middle class.

Now, however, the young families have been priced out; my mother's relatively modest four-bedroom is currently worth well over a million dollars. My mom doesn't want to sell; she still loves the neighborhood, or at least what it used to be, and she says there are too many memories of my father there that she doesn't want to lose, as if memories are keepsakes you can misplace. The thought is awful and terrifying. I can't lose my memories. One day they might be all I have.

Today she meets me at the front door, beckons me back to the kitchen, where the kettle is on, a batch of fresh gingerbread on the table. My mother retired from being a linguistics professor at Boston College last year, although she's still very active in her field—going to conferences, writing scholarly articles. But she's always had time for me, and I don't know what I would do without it, without her.

"How was it?" she asks gently, and I shrug.

"About what I expected."

"Emily settled in all right?"

"Yes, I think so. I did her nails and hair."

"Sweet." My mother smiles as she pours the tea. "Did you take a photo?"

"Yes." My mother always asks for photos. I swipe my phone to show her the picture of Emily with her nails and hair done, and my mother smiles at it, as if it is normal for a little girl to lie in bed like that, to stare at the ceiling, her jaw slack, her body unmoving, with pink nails and a sparkly butterfly clip.

At moments like this, I don't know whether to play along, as part of me desperately needs to, or scream. I end of up doing neither, putting my phone away and sitting down at the table.

"Anyway, it's done," I say, the words ones of acceptance even as I rail against them. I'd briefly considered filing a lawsuit, but I knew it wouldn't do any good. The money, and more importantly, the time, weren't there. I need another way to help Emily. "There's nothing I can do about it now," I tell my mom, "but I'm still going to fight. If I can convince Dr. Brown to try some of the experimental treatments that are out there…"

Every day I read something new on the internet, the research that is being done, the progress that's being made. The trouble is, we're still years away from being offered that treatment in a regular hospital, and Dr. Brown claims there aren't any clinical trials that Emily is eligible for. But in another hospital, another country…

My mother hasn't responded, and as she moves around the kitchen, I can tell she is a bit distracted. Her hair, usually styled in a sleek steel-gray bob, is ruffled at the back, a little bit of it sticking up in a tangle, and she keeps moving things around—a sugar bowl two inches to the left, the tea caddy an inch to the right. As if she needs to keep busy. As if she can't look at me.

"Mom? Is everything all right?"

She looks at me quickly—too quickly—and my heart contracts. I don't think I can take any more bad news.

"Yes, of course," she says. "Everything's fine. Have some gingerbread." She pushes the plate towards me and then sits down at the table, her hands laced together in her lap.

"It's just… you seem a little…" I'm not sure how to phrase it, or even if I can. Besides the bit of hair in the back, she looks normal. Tailored trousers, cashmere sweater, a smile. She's my mom, the person I've counted on the most, especially since my dad died of a heart attack when I was only seventeen. The two of us together, for so long. I'm being paranoid, I think, because of Emily. Because of everything. "I don't even know what," I finish with an uncertain laugh.

My mother runs a hand over her hair, her fingers snagging in the tangle in the back and smoothing it down. "I'm fine, Rachel. Please don't worry about me."

And even though she's smiling, I see the shadow of concern in her eyes, the truth that she'd hiding, and I know I'm not strong enough to force the issue. Not now, not with Emily. So I swallow down the questions, and the needling concern, and sip my tea, pretending that nothing is wrong, because so much is.

CHAPTER SIX

EVA

On Monday, when James comes back from work, having taken the morning off to settle Emily into the palliative unit, I ask him how it went. Of course I do, because that is the normal, expected thing for a wife to do, surely, and I do actually want to know. I want him to want to tell me.

Yet when I mention it, I get the response I expect—a shrug and a mumbled reply, before he turns away.

"She's settled?" I press, because part of me has to. "Transferring her wasn't... too difficult?" I feel as if I'm stumbling in the dark, because I don't even know if that would be an issue. I've read online a bit about Emily's condition, and what it means, but since I've never seen her and James never talks about her to me, it's so hard to know even what questions to ask.

"Yes, she's settled." James' tone is definitely final-sounding now. "I'm going to change."

He heads to the bedroom and I move around the kitchen, stirring the pasta sauce I've made—out of a jar with some portobello mushrooms added to make it seem a little more like homemade. Neither James or I are great cooks; we tend to rely on upscale ingredients to make up for the fact that everything is out of a box or a jar. I asked him once if he cooked when he'd been with Rachel, out of curiosity rather than spite or jealousy, but his expression closed right up and he looked away.

"Pancakes," he'd stated flatly. "My Saturday morning speciality, with Emily."

Immediately, I had an image of him and his little girl, measuring flour and sugar, cracking eggs, and my heart ached for them both. But when I tried to express that, he shrugged me off, just as he has now.

I'm not surprised. I understand why James doesn't want to talk about these things, because they hurt too much. Aren't I the same? Bury it down deep enough and maybe you can pretend it isn't there at all. At least James told me about Rachel and Emily, laid it all out, hiding nothing. The fact that he hasn't wanted to talk about it since doesn't change the fact he was honest.

But in moments like this, it leaves me feeling left out, cut off, and even more so when I see the teddy bear I'd bought Emily sticking out of his messenger bag. Why didn't he give it to her? I know it's a paltry gesture, but it felt wrong not to give her something for her new room, not to recognize she's part of my life, even if she really isn't. Even if I'm not sure I actually want her to be.

"You didn't give Emily the teddy bear," I remark when he comes back downstairs. I meant to sound curious, gently inquiring, but it comes out accusing. Normally I wouldn't have said anything at all. I don't know why I feel like stirring things up now; I should be trying to get things back to the way they normally are between us, easy and relaxed. Perhaps it's because this month's disappointment has hit me harder than usual, and James' silence feels thick and oppressive, like something is suffocating me, making me doubt how strong or good our marriage really is.

"There wasn't a good time," James says. "Sorry. I'll give it to her next time."

"Okay." I stir the sauce, willing myself to let it go. "Do you think Rachel would mind?"

He shrugs. "I don't know. It just felt a bit tense. She's not happy with Emily being there, so..." So she wouldn't want her daughter to have a teddy bear? This time I really do let it go. It's not about me. It was just a gesture anyway, a show of support, or maybe even some vaguely passive-aggressive way of letting Rachel know I'm involved. Even if I'm not.

"How is Rachel now?" I ask. "Has she… accepted it, do you think?"

"She has to. She knows a legal battle is way too expensive, and it wouldn't be good for Emily, anyway." He sighs. "She'll get there, eventually. It's a really nice place. There's a music room."

I nod, although if I were in Rachel's position, I think I'd feel the same way. I wouldn't care about a stupid music room; I'd wanted the best medical care for my child.

Really?

I silence that voice immediately by opening a bottle of wine. I hand James a glass, and he takes it with a murmured thanks. We've been off-kilter this last week, with all the stress and tension around Emily's move. I want to get back to normal. I want to think about us, to laugh and lie my legs in his lap and sip wine as we surf on our laptops or watch something mindless on TV. Or, even better, I want to go away for a Sunday—our only free day—maybe to a country inn in the Berkshires, or even up to Vermont. We could take the Monday off…

I wait until we've both had a glass of wine and we've eaten our pasta before bringing the whole pregnancy, or lack of it, up, although part of me is saying to leave it, that this surely isn't the right time. "You might have realized," I begin with what I hope is a somewhat wry look, "it didn't happen this month."

James looks back at me blankly. "What didn't happen?"

I tamp down the instinctive spike of irritation I feel. It's so uncharitable. His daughter is in palliative care; can I really be so insensitive as to talk about being pregnant—or not—now? To expect him to notice?

The answer is that yes, I can, because I've come to realize there won't ever be that mythical better time, not for us. There will always be Emily, in one way or another, and we still have to live our lives.

"I got my period."

James looks blank for another few seconds, and I do my best to keep my expression neutral. He *knows* we're meant to be trying. He's seen the ovulation kit in the bathroom. He bought that bottle of wine. He laced his fingers over mine and said *maybe this month*. Surely he realizes how important this is to me, five months in?

"Considering everything," he says slowly, "maybe that's for the best."

I let those words roll around in my mind like marbles. "Considering everything?"

"It's just... you know, Eva, with Emily..."

"But nothing has actually changed with Emily," I point out carefully, trying to keep my tone gentle. "In terms of her condition." I want to be sensitive and sympathetic, and I try so hard, I really do, but there comes a point. The research online has told me that Emily could live as she is now, with no change, for many years. Meanwhile, for me, each month matters. I feel guilty for thinking that way, but I have to.

"Eva." James blows out a breath as he leans back in his chair, cradling his glass of wine. "I know this is important to you, but... do we have to do this now?"

"We're not *doing* anything." My gentle tone has dropped. "I just told you I'm not pregnant."

"Okay, then."

We lapse into a silence, one tenser than any before. I realize how stupid it was to have brought it all up now, when James had just settled Emily *today* and was undoubtedly feeling raw. Why couldn't I have waited a few days, a few weeks, even? Or just kept silent? It wasn't as if I actually had any news; I didn't have to mention it at all.

I am kicking myself, wondering why I was so reckless, even as I know the answer. Because I wanted James to care. I wanted him to be as disappointed as I am, to hold my hand, to tell me we'll make a double effort next month, to promise me the trip I've dreamed about, a nice B&B with a king-sized bed and a bubble bath for two…

Foolishness, I know. He never would have done that. He's never been as on board with the baby idea as I am, even though he tries to be. His agreement was guarded, maybe even reluctant, and I pretended that it didn't matter. That he would change, once I was pregnant. And perhaps he still will.

"Maybe next month," I finally say, trying to turn it into a peace offering, but James frowns. He takes a sip of his wine as he looks away.

"Look, Eva, with everything that's going on…"

"What do you mean, everything? You mean Emily."

"And Rachel…"

I jerk back a little. "What does Rachel have to do with our family planning?"

"I don't mean like that, it's just…" He blows out a breath. "I'm not sure this is the best time to do this." He rakes a hand through his hair. "I mean, surely you can see that?"

"I know it's difficult." Words that are a massive understatement, but what else can I say? I know it's not *difficult*; it's torturous, agonising, but it's been that way for a long time, ever since I met him, and it's going to be that way for the foreseeable future. Somehow amidst all that, we have to find a way forward, for us. "James, I know now doesn't feel like a good time, but the reality is, Emily will always be…" I trail off, unsure what word to use. Around? Alive? Anything sounds horribly callous.

"No," James says quietly. "She won't."

I bite my lip, accepting that chastisement, even though none of us knows what the future holds for Emily—not James, not Rachel, not me. "But people in… her condition… they can live for years and years," I say, as reasonably, as kindly, as I can. Inside, I feel panicked. If James is saying we can't even think about trying until Emily is… I don't want to go there, not even in my own mind. I don't want to will Emily away at all, and yet I've read the statistics. Most children in Emily's state die within five years, but some live for much longer. Decades, and in any case, five years could be too late for me. "You agreed to start trying for a baby, James—"

"I know. I *know*." He raises his voice, so unlike him, and I sit back, silent, appalled. We don't do this. We don't argue. But right now I wonder if that is only because I've made sure that we don't. He sighs heavily. "I'm just not sure it was the right decision, considering everything. Emily, and also how quickly we… I love you, Eva, of course I do, but jumping into having a baby together when we've only known each other a year?"

"We jumped into getting married," I point out, trying not to let my voice wobble. "How is this any different?"

"I just think we need some time. I don't want to disappoint you, but…" He makes it sound like he's cancelling a dinner date.

My chest feels tight, and I have to concentrate on taking each breath, in, then out, slow and even. "What are you saying?" I finally make myself ask. "That you might never want a child?"

"I *have* a child." The words are sharp, and I close my eyes.

"I know that. I'm sorry. I didn't mean…" I shake my head, unable to continue, afraid I might cry. I never should have pushed the issue tonight. I never seem to learn not to want more than someone is able to give.

"Eva." James reaches over and touches my hand. I sniff, willing the tears back. "I'm sorry. I don't want to fight with you.

I'm feeling… all kinds of stuff right now." A big admission, for him. "I don't mean to take it out on you. It's just… seeing Emily in there, knowing… knowing she won't come out…" His voice cracks, and so does my heart. I haven't let myself think too deeply about what it actually means for Emily to be on the one-way road that is palliative care. I can't believe how insensitive I was, bringing up a baby now. When will I learn? "It affected me more than I expected it to," James continues in a ragged voice. "I tell myself—and you and everyone else—that I've come to terms with my grief, but there are moments…"

"Oh, James." I reach over and take his hand, blinking back tears that don't feel like my right to shed. "I'm so sorry. I shouldn't have mentioned this all now."

"Can we just… table this discussion for a bit? It's not an issue till next month anyway, right?" I nod. "So let's leave it for a few weeks." He squeezes my hand, giving me a rather watery smile. "I'm sorry you're disappointed, you know, that it didn't happen this month."

"Thanks," I murmur. I may feel guilty for bringing it all up, but it still stings that I can tell he's relieved. I know he's been reluctant, but I've been so sure he'll come around. Now I wonder if I've simply been wishing in a happily-ever-after that might never happen. *Again.*

I reach for the bottle and pour myself more wine, even though my head is already spinning a little. I need something to blunt this fear inside me, the terror opening up like a black hole, that I'm never going to get the chance to be a mother. That I'm never going to be able to make things right.

Two weeks later, James and I still haven't talked about babies or Emily or pretty much anything other than work, what's on TV, or whether we want to get takeout. On the surface, everything feels easy, the way it used to be—we meet friends for dinner downtown; we go biking along the river on a sunny Sunday afternoon. But underneath I sense something bubbling away, a corrosive acid attacking the foundation of our marriage. I tell myself I'm being fanciful, paranoid, but I know I'm not. There's so much we don't talk about it, and it's getting harder and harder to ignore all the no-go zones.

And meanwhile, according to the chart I've been keeping of my cycle, I'm three days away from ovulating. I know it seems far too scientific and entirely unromantic, doing things according to a rigid timetable, and once I would have rolled my eyes at it, but right now it is necessary… if I can work up the courage to mention it to James.

When I first started trying, five months ago, I attempted to make a game of it. One month, I taped the ovulation test to the front door and waited for him on the bed, in nothing but a scrap of silk underwear.

"Both clinical and romantic," he'd teased before he'd pulled off his tie and launched onto the bed, both of us laughing as our arms came around each other.

It had been fun then. It feels like a lifetime ago now, and it's only been a few months.

As the days pass, I try to focus on work, salvaging the ethical sourcing campaign that still hasn't picked up, despite my adjustment of the images and demographics. I talk to Mara about the launch of a new skincare line, offering a giveaway, free samples sent to our most consistent customers.

"I like your ideas, Eva," she says, and I sense a "but". I wait, a half-smile on my face, alert, professional as always. "But I have to say, you seem a bit distracted lately."

Mara sounds concerned, but I know I can't trust it. My working environment manages to be both caring and cut-throat—that's just the business world these days, for everybody.

Too many people needing jobs, too narrow a profit margin in every sector. I've heard Mara say, "self-care is so important" and then fire someone in her next meeting.

I lean back in my seat, giving her the full force of my confident, professional smile.

"I'm fine, Mara." I haven't told anyone at work about Rachel or Emily; it hasn't felt like my story to share, even though I sometimes feel guilty, as if I'm keeping them a secret. But considering I've never even met either of them, my actions feel reasonable.

"Are you sure?"

"Yes." I am firm now, brisk. I can't let my personal life interfere with my professional one. I'm so much stronger than that. "I'm disappointed in the results of the ethical campaign, but it's given us some helpful data that will prove useful to further campaigns." I sit forward, poised now for action. "So it's all good."

Mara gives me a considering look. "As long as you're sure."

"I am."

A beat passes, and then another, and neither of us breaks what is starting to feel like a game of blink. Then Mara gives me a brief nod of dismissal.

Back at my desk, my body sags. I'm not usually distracted at work, and I shouldn't be now. Yes, this whole thing with Emily has affected me more than I expected—the knowledge of her there in that unit, just waiting, and the unspoken tension between me and James. And yes, not being pregnant for the fifth time running might be one more disappointment than I am able to handle, but here I am, showing up for work, doing my job. Can't that be enough? Why am I always having to *try*?

I push the thoughts away as I focus on my work, and when I return home several hours later to an empty apartment, I can't believe I've forgotten that it's Tuesday and James is, as he always is on a Tuesday, at the hospital with Emily.

It's another beautiful evening, syrupy sunlight and bright green leaves, and I want nothing more than to curl up on the sofa, my head on James' shoulder, his arm around me, something brainless on Netflix. We've only been married a year, but I don't need romantic dinners or weekend getaways, as nice as they are. I just want to be able to laugh with James over an order of moo shoo pork and some spring rolls. I want to read bits of the *Boston Herald* out to him and have him snort in laughter or disbelief; I want to joke with him that there's only one real Red Sox fan in this family, since he was born in Connecticut. I want to be normal again, but lately everything has felt forced and off-kilter.

I flip off my heels and pour a glass of wine—I've been going down the liquid comfort route far too much recently, I know—and flop on the sofa. In an ideal scenario, James would be home, we'd have takeout, and then we'd get busy since it is peak ovulation time, maybe right here on the sofa. Maybe I'd dare him to leave the curtains open; that's about as risqué as either of us ever gets. He'd laugh and leave them open for about ten seconds, before he'd whip them shut and then reach for me…

As I sip my wine, I count back the days and realize we haven't had said sex since our two hurried and rather lacklustre attempts last month that didn't pan out. I know I need to stop thinking like this.

Another sip of wine, and then the doorbell rings, surprising me. No one comes to our door. Despite the bikes chained to railings, the vague talk whenever the weather is nice of a block party, it's not that kind of neighborhood. Maybe it's someone handing out flyers, asking for a few minutes of my time which I am really not in the mood to give.

Amazingly, absurdly, I don't recognise the woman standing there, her bag clutched to her chest, her expression determined but also a bit… frenzied. The look in her eyes alarms me. She's middling height, a little shorter than me, with dark hair pulled back into a messy ponytail, worry lines bracketing her eyes and mouth. She's wearing an oversized sweater in soft gray and a pair of skinny jeans, but the outfit looks haphazard, thrown together, as if she doesn't care much about clothes. The wrists poking out of the sleeves are too thin. I stare.

"Eva," she says, testing my name out, seeing if it works.

"Yes?" I have one hand on the doorknob, my body blocking the entrance, my eyebrows raised in a parody of politeness.

She looks at me levelly, her expression determined yet giving nothing away. "I'm Rachel."

CHAPTER SEVEN

RACHEL

Was it wrong to come here? Sneaky or manipulative or just inappropriate? James might think so, and Eva might well too, but it's too late to regret my choice. I've got to do something, and James and his refusal to discuss anything has driven me to this.

Admittedly, he has responded to my texts, but only to say he doesn't want to talk; he doesn't see the point. I sent him an email with links and copy-and-pasted paragraphs, pages and pages. Too much maybe, but this is our *daughter*. His only reply was to try to shut it all down.

I'd be angry, if I didn't feel so frustrated and frankly panicked. Time is running out. Every day in the palliative care unit is a day where no one is working on Emily's behalf, where she is just dwindling down and down. I can't stand to see it. I can't stand to sit there, next to Emily, listening to the murmurs and quiet weeping from other rooms, knowing everyone on the ward is just *waiting*.

Eva's lips part, her eyes widening as she looks at me. It stings me a little, that she didn't recognize me. Are there no photos of me at all in their apartment? Did she never even look me up on Facebook? I looked her up as soon as James told me about her, and she was exactly what I expected, strangely enough. The opposite of me, with her careful hair, her perfect makeup, her stylish power suit. *For heaven's sake, James,* I remember thinking. *It's a bit cliché, isn't it?*

Except I won't let myself think like that now, because I'm here to get Eva on my side, on Emily's side, as absurd as that may sound. It's the only card I have left to play, my last, desperate roll of the dice.

"May I come in?"

Eva looks like she doesn't want to move from the door, doesn't want to let me into her life. And I understand that, to some degree. We've been circling around each other's lives, important and yet unknown, for a year now. How exactly are we meant to relate?

"Um, yes. Of course." Her tone is stiff, her nod jerky.

She steps aside and I slip by her, into James' new home, where I've never been before.

I recognize some of the furniture. When we sold the house, we split everything—the furniture, the dishes, the wedding presents. It seemed only fair, and I didn't want to reconstruct our family home in a shabby duplex anyway, a second-rate version of what I once had. I let James have the good pieces, and I topped up with stuff from IKEA.

Now I feel a jolt as I see our leather sofa in the living room; James and I sat on that just about every evening. I can picture my feet in his lap, his palm spanning the curvature of my baby bump. I look away, and catch sight of the hall table we picked up at an antique store in the Catskills, after trying to haggle with the owner of the shop, a wiry, dapper gentleman with snow-white hair and a mischievous smile. Being here is going to be harder than I thought.

I walk towards the back of the apartment, noticing the new things too. Some nice lithographs of colonial Boston. Dining room chairs in white leather. How totally impractical, I think, but then, of course, they don't have children. Looking at Eva, one French-manicured hand resting on the living room doorway, her wasp-thin waist emphasized by the tailored skirt and tucked-in blouse, I wonder if they ever will. It's not a possibility I want to dwell on even for a moment.

"This is a surprise," Eva says eventually, when I haven't said anything. "Is everything okay?"

"Yes, I'm sorry to just come here like this." I don't want to be hostile, but it rises up in me anyway, a bubbling resentment I've kept at a sensible simmer for too long. I turn to face her. "I know I'm invading your privacy, your life, and I am sorry to do that…" My words trail away and she raises her eyebrows.

"But…?" she prompts coolly. She doesn't want me here. It's uncomfortably obvious, insulting, even though I understand it. I don't want to be here, either.

"James isn't answering my texts or emails anymore. He's refusing to engage with me about Emily's care, and so I decided I needed to find another way to discuss something with him."

"So you're involving *me*?" Her tone is not promising, as her eyebrows rise higher. She sounds incredulous and even horrified, as if she can't imagine why on earth I would do such a thing. I can't imagine it, either, and yet here I am. Desperation drives you to do the strangest things, and not even feel sorry or embarrassed.

"I just need him to listen, Eva. And he won't listen to me." I thought about cornering him in his office, trailing him out to the parking lot, but that felt too humiliating and I don't think it would work anyway. James needs to hear my viewpoint from someone else. Someone else who thinks like I do.

And that's Eva?

Who else could it be?

"Your relationship with James has nothing to do with me, Rachel," Eva says firmly. "Nothing at all."

"Doesn't it?" My words hover in the air and then fall softly to the ground. Eva gives a little shake of her head but says nothing. I decide to try another tack. "Look, this isn't ideal, is it? Divorce…

remarriage… we all know that this isn't the way it's meant to go, but life is messy and broken, and here we are."

"Thanks for that." There is acid in her voice now; I didn't mean it unkindly, but I see her bristle, and I curse myself for making this even harder than it needs to be.

"I'm sorry. I wasn't trying to…" I pause, helpless, wanting this so much to work and yet afraid it already hasn't. Afraid that it was a desperately absurd thing to do in the first place. "Eva, look, what I was trying to say, and making a mess of it obviously, is that I'm not… I'm not bitter. About… you know. You." There is a lie twisted up in all that truth, but I can't untangle it now. "I accept that it didn't work out between James and me, that he's happy with you now. I'm not here to rock that boat or cause any trouble between you." That much is absolutely true. "All that matters to me now is Emily," I say, and I hear the throb of sincerity, of feeling, in my voice, like a pulse. I see Eva's eyes widen and I know she hears it too. "And James is refusing even to talk to me about it. I need someone to speak sense to him, someone he'll actually listen to…"

"And you think I'm that person?" There is a disparaging note in her voice I'm not sure I understand.

"Who else is there?"

"What about his dad? He'd listen to him, maybe?"

I shake my head. James' mother died two and a half years after we were married, and his father remarried a woman from his gym six months later. James wasn't happy about it; the irony isn't wasted on me now. In any case, James' relationship with his father, a former bigwig in finance and undoubtedly once a workaholic, was always a bit distant, with that slap-on-the-back-instead-of-a-hug kind of affection.

"I don't think so," I tell Eva. "They've never had that kind of relationship." In fact, James became estranged from his father for a brief period after college, when he didn't go right into actuarial work, but spent a year traveling in the Far East, finding himself, something his father took a dim view of. But doesn't Eva know all that?

She moves from the doorway to the kitchen, picking up a half-full wine glass along the way, shaking her head all the while. "Whatever you want me to do, Rachel… I don't think I'm the right person to do it."

"I know it's not ideal, and it might feel a bit awkward." I follow her into the kitchen, which is a pristine hymn to granite and stainless steel, and looks untouched. "But you know Emily has gone into the palliative care unit…" I don't actually know what James has told her, how involved she's been; I've never liked thinking of the two of them discussing my daughter, or, for that matter, me. I haven't wanted to imagine James complaining about my attitude, not that I think he would. He's loyal, in his way. But it still feels deeply uncomfortable, to think of them talking about my life. My pain.

"I know, yes," Eva says briefly.

"And I suppose James has told you I'm not happy about it?"

"Yes." Eva sloshes more wine into her glass, filling it nearly to the brim. She turns to me, one eyebrow raised. "Want a glass?"

I do, I need something to steady my nerves, but it doesn't feel right, and besides, I'm driving. "No thanks."

"Suit yourself." She puts the wine bottle, only a mouthful left in it, back in the huge sub-zero fridge and then picks up her wine glass, closing her eyes briefly as she takes a sip.

Then she opens her eyes and stares at me hard, which is a little disconcerting. Is she looking at my gray roots that are at least an inch long, the lines carved into my face that weren't there three years ago?

I'm forty-two, and according to her Facebook profile, Eva is only thirty-six. She looks younger than me, by more than six years, with her smooth skin and clear eyes and styled hair. She is beautiful, but in a hard-edged way; I sense something brittle about her, ready to snap, and I wonder what attracted James to her. The fact that she is so unlike me? Or is it arrogant to think that way?

It doesn't matter, I tell myself. *He chose her. Here we are.*

She takes another sip of wine and then lets out a weary breath. "So what is it you want James to do?"

I pause, assessing the moment. Eva already looks resigned and we're both standing up in the kitchen. How much time will she give me? I need more than a few minutes' hasty, stammered recap standing by a counter.

"Can we sit down?" I ask, trying to sound humble. "I have to explain…"

A pause, and then she nods and walks into the living room, sinking into the sofa, with an air of something close to resignation to having me here, wrecking her evening. I tell myself not to mind. To focus on what's important. *Emily.*

"Thank you," I say, and I mean it.

I perch on the edge of a large, squashy armchair opposite her, my hands clasped between my knees.

"So you know Emily was moved into palliative care two weeks ago…" I resume and she nods. "And that was against my wishes. I'm not ready to give up on my daughter."

"And you think James is?" The words are without censure, more curious than anything else.

"Maybe," I allow, although it hurts. I'm not ready to write James off that much just yet; I know he is grieving too. "I think, perhaps, it's easier for him… with…" I trail off, not wanting to put it into words.

"With me?" she finishes, and takes another large mouthful of her wine.

"Yes, I suppose. With you. He has a new life…" Whereas I do not. It's so painfully obvious, and I don't even care, yet it hurts to admit it to this woman. My replacement.

I realize then, with a jolt of understanding, that as amicable as we've tried to make it, there is a deep, dark river of bitterness and hurt and even rage running beneath all of us, catching us up in its currents. Perhaps that's why we've never met. Why Eva has never seen Emily. It never even crossed my mind that she would, and James never once broached the idea of bringing Eva to see our daughter. Now I wonder if that is normal. Now I wonder if, beneath this surface of careful amicability, we actually hate each other.

Eva looks away from me, her lips pursed. "So what is it that you want him to do? You haven't said yet."

I take a deep breath. "I want to take Emily for some experimental treatment. I need James to agree. We have joint custody of Emily in regard to her medical care. We both need to agree to any treatment or change in her care plan."

She looks back at me, her gaze flickering over me, closed and opaque, revealing nothing. "And you don't?"

"James won't even engage with me about the possibility." I hear the despair making my voice waver. When, after hours of online research, I stumbled on the treatment a single clinic in Italy has been pioneering, I knew it wasn't a miracle. Of course I knew that. I'm not that much of a deluded dreamer, and yet it was the chink of light in the unending darkness that I needed. That Emily needed. It was a wonderful what-if that we could both hold onto. But when I forwarded the link to James, his reply was all too brief.

I can't do this, Rachel.

I fired an email back, too quickly, assuring him I wasn't asking him to do it. *I* would do it. All of it, everything—the money, the travel, the care. But as we both have equal control over Emily's medical decisions, I needed him to say yes, and so far he has refused even to have a discussion about it. It's like battering my head against a brick wall, and I'm bruised and bloody now, but still so determined.

"And you think I can convince him?" Eva arches one eyebrow, clearly skeptical.

Do I? I'm not even sure, but I don't have any other avenues. James won't talk to me, any mutual friends we had have dropped off, but he surely listens to his wife. "I don't know," I admit. "But I've run out of ideas, and I really need him to agree. Otherwise it means a court case…" Which I can't afford. Which will take too much time. Which will make everything worse.

She shakes her head slowly, and inside I am shrieking in protest. She can't say no, not yet, not when I haven't even told her the statistics, given her all the hope.

"Look," I say, cutting off whatever pitying refusal she is poised to make, "I know it's a long shot. I'm not naïve. This treatment is very new. Very untried. But Emily deserves every chance I can give her—just as any child does. And the research is compelling—this experimental treatment has been done on several patients in conditions similar to Emily's, and they have regained some con- sciousness, shown some awareness." Not huge gains, but *something*, and Emily's case could potentially be even more promising. She's been in a state of unresponsive wakefulness for less time than the patients who have already had the treatment, and she's young. I don't want to get my hopes up, but I am. Of course I am. They are flying sky-high, sailing along, euphorically buoyant.

"What is the experimental treatment?" Eva asks.

"It's a kind of nerve stimulation. The doctors would implant a sensor in Emily's chest that stimulates the vagus nerve, which connects to parts of the brain pertaining to alertness." I am reeling off what I now know by heart, having learned it from the internet. There's not that much out there about this treatment, because it's so new. It's been tried on a handful of patients in the last few years, that's all. Hardly conclusive. I can practically hear Dr. Brown, or even James, say the words as they shake their heads, murmuring about false hope, wild goose chases.

"The patients who have undergone the treatment have experienced some return of consciousness," I continue steadily. "Sometimes significantly. They're not jumping out of bed, it's true, but they can respond to stimuli, they sense a threat, they follow an object with their eyes, they *listen*. Some have even tried to communicate." My voice breaks and I draw a ragged breath, doing my best to hold it together. "I know that probably seems like very little to you, but the thought of Emily being able to recognize me again, of responding in any way to me..." I can't go on, not without starting to cry, and I really don't want to do that in front of Eva. "It would mean a lot to me," I manage to finish, my voice clogged with emotion.

Eva looks away again, and I have no idea what she is thinking. Did my little display of emotion move or harden her? Does she think I'm pathetic or admirable?

I wait, holding my breath, *hoping*. When I can't stand the silence any longer, I finally speak. "Please, Eva," I say quietly. I'm under control now, thankfully. "I know I'm asking a lot of you. I know this isn't your problem, that it's not your responsibility to care about me or Emily." Her lips twitch but she says nothing. "But you gave Emily a teddy bear, James showed it to me..." I stop, try again. "If you had a child, if you and James had a child..." It hurts to say those words, but I make myself. "Wouldn't you want to do whatever you could to try to help them? Help them to regain even a little bit of themselves, even if just for a little while? I couldn't live with myself, if I knew there was something I could have done for Emily, and I didn't do it."

Her face contorts briefly and she angles her head even farther away from me. Did I say the wrong thing? Have I lost her?

"You don't know what you're asking," she says, and I feel a sudden spike of irritation, almost rage. As far as I can tell, I'm asking for very little, no matter what I've just told her. *One* conversation. To advocate for a little girl who needs all the help and support she can get. It won't cost her too much, surely? James might be a bit annoyed with her for being overly involved, but surely he'll blame me for that, not her?

"I'm sorry," I say, doing my best to sound humble, even though for a second I feel like going over to her sprawled on the sofa with her big glass of wine and designer suit, the skirt hiked up mid-thigh, and giving her a good shake.

Do you even know what my life has been like?

Eva shakes her head. She's going to say no. I know it, I feel it, and part of me doesn't even blame her, because this isn't her life. Her child. It was a desperate long shot, to ask her to speak to James. If my husband would just man up and have a conversation with me… but so far he won't. And I was hoping that hearing it from someone else, someone like Eva, might give him a new perspective, change his mind.

But it's not her responsibility; it's mine. I accept that, even as I rail against the rejection I sense is coming.

Eva turns to face me, her expression set, her lips pursed. There is a distant look in her eyes, almost as if she isn't seeing me. She swings her legs off the sofa and deposits her empty wine glass on the coffee table with a clatter. I wait, holding my breath.

"I'll do my best," she says.

Dear Bean,

Let me tell you the story of your birth. It was the middle of the night, and I couldn't sleep. I kept tossing and turning, wedging pillows under my big, wonderful bump—that's you, Bean!—trying to get comfortable, but nothing worked. So I got up to make some tea, although I knew I'd be having to use the bathroom all night as a result. My bladder had become the size of a pea, Bean, but I didn't begrudge you any of it. I never would.

So there I was in the kitchen, waiting for the kettle to whistle, one hand resting on top of my bump, when I felt something pop. It was such a strange sensation, like a balloon popping inside me. And then there was a rush of water as if I was wetting my pants, but I wasn't. I stood there, feeling completely befuddled, and then your daddy stumbled into the kitchen and said, 'I think your waters just broke!' I should have realized that, right, Bean?

The next few minutes felt like a Keystone Cops routine as we ran in and out of rooms. We were chickens with our heads cut off, Bean, because of you. We were excited and scared and overwhelmed and excited. So excited, because you were finally coming. You were almost here.

Somehow we made it to the hospital and into the labor ward, all as if there wasn't a moment to spare, as if you were going to plop right onto the floor. Like most first-time parents, I guess, because let me tell you, the nurse wasn't particularly moved by our frantic urgency. 'First baby?' she said. 'Take a seat.'

When we finally got seen half an hour later, I found out I was only two centimeters dilated! Two, Bean! Just in case you don't realize, you have to get all the way to ten before you can push. We had a long way to go.

Dawn broke while I was walking back and forth in the room they'd given us, trying to get things moving along, but you weren't ready to come out. Was it just too comfy in there? I don't blame you for wanting to stay.

After several hours of nothing happening, and thinking nothing would, it suddenly all started to speed up. I was four centimeters, and then I was six, and then I was eight, and then you were almost here! I won't talk about the pain because it was worth it and I didn't care about how much it hurt. I refused an epidural because I wanted to feel everything; your daddy thought I was crazy.

And then it was time to push. The doctor said, 'You might feel a certain amount of pressure' and I remember bursting into laughter and answering, 'You think?!' He smiled at that, and I laughed again, because I was so very excited to meet you.

And then you were here. Your daddy let out a cry of joy as you slipped out without any fuss at all, and the doctor held you up, all red and screaming. You were angry, Bean. You were furious! But then he laid you on my chest and I put my arms around you and you tilted your head and blinked up at me and you stopped crying. We stared at each other and it felt as if there was nothing else in the world but us. I've never felt anything like it before or since. And I smiled, and I kissed your wrinkly little forehead, and I whispered, 'Welcome to the world, my little bean.'

Love, Mama

CHAPTER EIGHT

EVA

The wine bar where my friend Naomi asks me to meet is one of those understated places that is trying not to seem cool and so feels as if it is trying all the harder because of it. Scattered sofas, low lighting, mood music, and glasses the size of fishbowls. It's the last bit I like, although I told myself I wasn't going to drink anything tonight. I mean, what sort of woman trying for a baby has a glass or three of wine nearly every night?

Well, the answer to that one is easy. Me. Not that I'm actually trying to conceive, since my fertile period passed without so much as a goodnight kiss. I feel as if my marriage is ebbing away like the tide, and I'm not even sure how or why it's happening, or if it's all in my mind, because I'm so scared this isn't going to happen for me. That James and I are doomed to drift apart.

Rachel's visit a little over a week ago certainly didn't help. I haven't yet told James that she came to see me, never mind what she was asking me to do. When he returned home that night, I felt like some sort of adulteress; I'd actually sprayed air freshener in the living room, to hide the subtle, lemony scent of her perfume. I thought he might sense she'd been there, see one of her long, dark hairs on the back of a chair, but no. In the end, he barely saw me.

He said hello, got a drink from the fridge, and disappeared behind his laptop, citing work. Before all this—and I'm not even sure when *all thi*s began—I wouldn't have minded. We didn't live in each other's pockets, and I'd always liked my space, as did James. I might have sat opposite him with a drink of my own, and my laptop in front of me, making the occasional comment to one another, a sudden smile or met gaze. We used to have that, and I want it back.

Now I weave through the scattered sofas to Naomi, my friend from an earlier life, when we were both young, ambitious interns for a large consulting company in New York. She stayed in finance but moved to Boston a couple years ago, and I took a job at a consulting firm in Boston fresh off my internship, before moving to Maemae.

"Hey, girl." She grins up at me as she hoists her large glass. "I decided on a cocktail. Some kind of cosmopolitan."

I eye the maraschino cherry and spoonful of syrup hanging suspended in the alcohol like a drop of blood. "Looks fancy."

"You want one?"

"Maybe."

"What's wrong?" She raises her eyebrows. "Tough day at work?"

Naomi is probably my best friend, amidst a handful of work colleagues I could call friends, but even she doesn't know me that well. She doesn't know what I've been trying to bury all these years, and she doesn't know how I long for a baby now. She was surprised by my marriage, although she congratulated me when I informed her of our spontaneous destination wedding. I think that was somehow more acceptable than if I'd planned a big, blowsy occasion at a golf club on Cape Cod.

"Yeah, I guess." I don't have the energy to enliven the pretense, and Naomi frowns.

"Seriously, what?"

I shake my head. She doesn't even know about Emily, although I told her about Rachel. I never went into the details of it all, never wanted to. Easier all around if I didn't tell anyone; if I let my marriage be simple. Naomi has only met James a handful of times; his commitment to Emily has made socializing difficult.

Emily. She has dogged my thoughts since Rachel came into my home, reeking of desperation, oozing a mother's love, making me hate her and pity her in almost equal measure. Why did she have to get me involved, when I so very much haven't been? Why did she have to make me doubt, wonder, *care?*

"Eva." Naomi lays a hand on my arm. "Tell me what's going on, because something obviously is. And let me buy you a drink."

It doesn't take much to coax me into a cocktail, and it gives me a moment to compose myself and figure out what I'm going to say, if anything. When Naomi comes back with another cherry cosmopolitan, my stomach cramps with both anticipation and anxiety about it all.

"Here we are," Naomi says, handing me the huge glass. "Drink up."

I take a small sip; it's surprisingly strong as well as terribly sweet, like sugary cough syrup.

"Now tell me what's going on," Naomi instructs. "Is it work? Is it marriage?" She can't help but make a little face; she has never been big on commitment. We bonded over cocktails similar to this one back in New York, declaring we'd do everything for our careers and nothing for love. How things have changed... at least for me.

"I suppose it's marriage," I say after a moment, as the alcohol burns through me. "Sort of."

"Sort of?"

And so, haltingly, somewhat reluctantly, I tell her about Emily. And about what Rachel now wants me to do. Naomi's mouth drops open as soon as I let the first bombshell drop, and she doesn't close it until I trail away, the unfinished ending to this sad story. And then... *what?* What am I going to do?

"Seriously? She wants you to intervene, siding with her against your own husband? I mean, the *nerve*."

For some reason, I am annoyed that this is the first thing Naomi says. "She's desperate. She doesn't have any choice."

"This is not your problem, Eva." Naomi shakes her head as she sips her cocktail. "Not at all."

"James is my husband," I point out. "Emily is his daughter. They are my part of my life." Despite how separate they've been. How much of that was because of James, and how much was down to me? Because until Rachel showed up at my door, I didn't realize just how much I didn't want or need to meet my husband's first wife.

"And Rachel is his ex-wife. They can deal with their own problems. Dragging you right into the middle of it? I mean, what even *is* that?"

I can't get on board with Naomi's outrage, as much as part of me wants to. It would be so much easier, so wonderfully simple, to shrug this all off, to hold up my hands and say *nuh-uh. Not me*. "Don't you feel sorry for her?" I ask curiously.

Naomi stiffens, surprised, a little discomfited. "I mean, yes, of course I do," she says after a moment, looking annoyed and flustered. "Anyone would be. That's not the point. You can feel sorry for someone, Eva, and not have to swoop in and fix all their problems."

I think of Emily, lying so still in a hospital bed, not that I've actually seen her there, or anywhere else. I've only imagined it, too many times, like something out of a movie, some weepy drama. "I'd hardly be doing that."

Naomi regards me for a moment. "So, you're seriously thinking about this? I thought you were going to bitch to me about this Rachel, the nerve of her, but you're not, are you?" She shakes her head slowly. Wonderingly. "You're really thinking about doing something."

"I don't know if I am." I think of what I said to Rachel—that I'd do my best. What is my best? I don't even know, and yet she latched onto it as if it was some kind of lifeline, thanking me, even reaching for my hand, before she thought better of it. I felt like a traitor, because I wasn't one hundred percent sure I would actually dare to say anything. I certainly didn't want to, and yet…

If you and James had a child… wouldn't you want to do whatever you could to try to help them?

Could Rachel possibly know how much she hurt me with those words? How they would play over and over again in my mind, taunting me, tormenting me.

If. If. If.

If only…

"I don't get it," Naomi says, making me look up from my drink; I've only had the one sip. My stomach is churning. "This isn't like you."

"It isn't?" I don't know whether I should be offended. What *is* like me? Am I the tough businesswoman I try to be at work, briskly polished and coolly focused, or the easygoing, fun lover I want to be at home? Am I the dutiful daughter at my parents' interminable barbecues, or the quiet, seething rebel I feel on the inside? I don't know the answer to any of those questions, never mind Naomi.

"You're smarter than this," Naomi urges. "Savvier. Surely you realize what will happen if you do talk to James about it?"

I take another sip of my drink, wincing at the over-sweet taste that coats the inside of my mouth. "What will happen?" I'm curious to hear her opinion, considering she barely knows James and only heard about Emily a few minutes ago.

Naomi leans forward, her cocktail forgotten for a moment. "I'm certainly no expert on relationships, but even I can see this is a disaster waiting to happen."

"Oh?"

"Rachel and Emily—they're just not your business, Eva. If that sounds mean, sorry, but that's the way it is."

"Rachel has made them my business, at least for now."

"But she shouldn't have, and you shouldn't have agreed. Do you actually think James will listen to you about this?"

I recoil a bit at that. "Why shouldn't he?"

"Has he asked your opinion already?" Naomi counters. "Is this something you've already discussed? Does he value your input on how he conducts his relationship with his daughter and ex-wife?"

She speaks so knowingly, even though I haven't told her about the cone of silence around James and me when it comes to Emily. To Rachel. I feel exposed, even though I haven't said anything.

"No, he hasn't," I say with dignity, "but that doesn't mean it has to be that way."

Naomi shakes her head. "Put yourself in James' place. You have a kid with your ex, it's all kinds of difficult, and your new husband butts in and tells you how you should be handling that relationship, handling your own daughter, even though they've never even *met* your child."

My cheeks start to warm. She makes me sound like some kind of awful busybody. "I wouldn't be *butting in*."

"Yes, you would. Don't you think James has a good reason for not pursuing this experimental treatment, whatever it is? Don't you think he's thought it through?"

"Nerve stimulation. And I don't know if he has." I looked it up online. Besides a few articles in *Scientific American* and the like, there wasn't much information, but I ended up down a rabbit hole of internet clicks, leading me on to articles on brain function and current research and the fact that there is so very much we don't know. There was even an article about a guy in a coma who was actually conscious the whole time but couldn't communicate. It sounded utterly terrifying, and yet I can see from

Rachel's perspective how it might be the tiniest bit hopeful. A chink in the darkness. A chance.

"Well, assuming James isn't some kind of uncaring sociopath, which he didn't seem to be when we had dinner last month, I assume he wants the best for his daughter?" Naomi raises one eyebrow, all cool sarcasm.

"Of course he does." I do believe this, utterly. I can't imagine the devastation of not believing it. That, more than anything, would wreck my marriage.

"So he clearly has already decided what the best is," Naomi points out, oh so reasonably. "He's thought this through, Eva. Of course he has. Why would you want to weigh in with your two cents?"

"Because I'm his *wife*." I'm annoyed by how dismissive Naomi is of my opinion, my worth. Judging from her tone, she believes utterly that James would not value my opinion on this matter. And the worst thing is, I think she's probably right. But surely it isn't meant to be that way?

"And you spoke to Rachel, for what, five minutes?"

More like fifteen, but I shrug. "What's your point?"

"Don't you think James has researched this, probably a lot? Don't you think there are things you haven't considered, that you can't know, based on what little Rachel said?"

Of course there are, because I hardly know anything. "Rachel thinks it's worth pursuing, and I know she'll have done as much, if not way more, research than James. Emily is her whole life."

"Which suggests something kind of unhealthy, don't you think? I doubt she has proper perspective anymore."

I think of Rachel's frenetic energy, the intensity I saw in her eyes as she asked me to talk to James. Naomi is probably right, but I don't blame Rachel for how she is. Wouldn't any mother—any loving mother—be the same? "And you think James does have proper perspective?" I ask.

Naomi shrugs and sips her drink. "Maybe. The point is, Eva, you don't need to get tangled up in this. It's only going to end badly for you, with James feeling annoyed or resentful—or worse. I might not be married, but I've dated enough guys with exes to know they do not like you getting involved. Ever."

I roll the stem of my glass between my palms, sifting Naomi's words in my head, separating the wheat from the chaff. "But what if it's not about what's best for *me*?" I finally say. Naomi looks distinctly nonplussed. "What if it's about what's best for Emily?"

She lets out an exasperated sigh. "And you think you know what that is?"

"I think Rachel might." And I think James might not. The realization jolts through me. *Why do I think that? What does that even mean?*

Naomi throws her hands up in the air. "So be it. I don't know why you bothered to ask me, since it sounds like you've already made up your mind."

"I haven't." But it's not true. I just hadn't realized I'd made up my mind, not until now.

"I think you have." Naomi recrosses her legs. "And if that's the case, I won't bother trying to convince you otherwise. You have to do what you believe is right." She sighs heavily. "Even if it isn't. Another drink?"

"I can't. I'm driving." And I haven't finished my first one. "Sorry to lay this all on you."

Naomi waves my apology aside. "What are friends for, except to give you advice you don't want?"

I smile, and then I ask her about work, because that's only fair. It's her turn to talk, and she regales me with a story about some hapless intern, and I do my best to listen and laugh.

An hour later, I'm back home, and the house is still empty. It's Thursday, another Emily day. I've never resented them before, far from it, but I *feel* them more now for some reason.

I change from my work clothes and drift through the house, at a loss. I end up on the sofa, with James' and my wedding album on my lap. It's only a couple of pages, a complimentary book of artfully montaged snaps provided by the hotel that managed our wedding—the vows on the beach, the champagne in the honeymoon suite, the joint massages and scuba diving lessons. It was a wonderful, whirlwind of a week, and I smooth my fingers over the photos now—the two of us holding hands during the ceremony, the wind blowing my hair into an artful tangle. I'm wearing a maxi dress in cream linen that I bought off Nordstrom's rack—there was no time for a proper wedding dress. I didn't mind.

At least, I told myself I didn't mind. Our wedding—the whole idea of our wedding—happened so quickly, an idea that took hold of us and never let go. We'd been dating for just four months, a couple of dinners a week, the occasional Sunday afternoon brunch, inching towards something more serious, both of us cautious, because we knew it was serious.

Then, over a Chinese takeout in this very room, James looked up at me and said, "What if we got married?" There was a light in his eyes, a smile quirking of his lips, a recklessness in him that he so very rarely had. I smiled back, even as my breath hitched and my mind cartwheeled.

"What if we did?" I answered, teasingly, afraid to take him too seriously, to hope too much.

James grabbed hold of my hands. "I mean it. Let's get married. Life is short and when you find what you were looking for, you've got to hold onto it."

My heart lurched as the lightness dropped. "Am I what you were looking for?" I whispered.

"Yes, you absolutely are. I know it's soon, but I want to do this."

I knew I did, too. Forget being careful; we were both such careful people, plotting our courses, now determined to be

wonderfully reckless because we loved each other so much. "Yes,"
I heard myself say. "Let's do it."

James grabbed his laptop and we started looking at destination
weddings; it wasn't even a discussion, that was just where both
our minds leapfrogged to. We shared a sense of urgency, that we
had to do this *now*, before we turned sensible and cautious again.
We giggled incredulously as we booked it right then, a week in
St Lucia, a wedding on the beach. It was crazy and wonderful,
and as quickly as it all happened, it felt so right.

It still feels right. I'm not going to let this whole issue of Emily
derail us, turn us into strangers. I won't say anything. Naomi is
right. It's not my business. I don't want to make it my business.
I'll stop interfering, stop asking, even. If James doesn't want to tell
me about Emily, that's fine. I understand his reticence; if I were
in his position, I would share it. It hurts to talk about painful
pasts, to keep dredging up the details. It doesn't have to be this
big thing between us.

Yet as I make this resolve, remembering how we held hands
on the flight to St Lucia, sliding sideways, incredulous smiles at
each other, clinking champagne flutes, I already can feel it wither.

I can't let this go. Not for Rachel's sake, and not for mine. I
close the photo album slowly and put it away, in the cupboard
where it's lain unopened and unlooked at since we came back
from St Lucia, tanned and tired.

I think of pouring myself a glass of wine—there's an open
bottle of red on the kitchen counter—but I drank most of that
revolting cocktail and I've told myself I'm going to cut back.

But it leaves me restless, drifting around the apartment once
more, until I finally turn on the TV and stare unseeingly at some
mindless, obnoxious reality TV show—there's a lot of fake tan
and bleached-blond hair.

James comes in just as the credits start to roll. It's nearly nine,
later than he usually gets home.

"Hey." He sounds tired, and he gives me a weary smile.

"Hey." I reach for the remote and click mute. "How are you?"

"Okay." James sheds his jacket, loosens his tie, something I've always found sexy. He's such an understated man, some people might skip right over him, but he's always made my heart race, especially when I see those masculine fingers tugging at a knot, flicking open that top button…

I'm not going to say anything.

"What did you get up to tonight?" he asks.

"I had a drink with Naomi. I've just been watching TV since then."

He nods, only half listening, and sits on the sofa with a sigh of weary relief.

"How is Emily?" I can't *not* ask. It would be heartless.

"The same, really." He hasn't changed his position or his tone, but I *sense* his withdrawal. Or am I being paranoid? Fearful, because of Rachel's visit? Because of everything that's always been unsaid between us?

"The new place is working out okay?"

"It's fine."

I nod slowly, my mouth drying. I'm not going to leave it. Stupidly, I am not going to leave it. But why should this be such a big deal, anyway? It's just a conversation between a husband and wife, a loving, concerned conversation about the daughter he loves.

And yet I know it is a big deal. I know it will be.

James' gaze narrows as he stares at me; I must look nervous. "What is it?" he asks. "What's going on, Eva?"

I lick my lips. My heart is hammering. It's ridiculous and a little shaming that I'm so nervous. This is my *husband*, after all. We should be able to talk like this, battle it out even, if that's what it comes to, which it shouldn't.

We should be able to do that, but we don't. We never do. Our relationship, I am realizing more and more, is based on a mutually agreed foundation of certain silences and implicit agreements. And I am about to break them all.

James is still staring at me, and I know I have to speak. I remind myself that I am tough, that I've had to be. I straighten, gazing back at him directly.

"Something's happened," I say, and I know immediately that it sounds too melodramatic. "I need to talk to you about something," I try instead, and James leans back into the sofa and folds his arms, not exactly a position of openness.

"All right," he says. "So talk."

CHAPTER NINE

RACHEL

One Sunday morning, a few weeks after Emily has been moved, I wake up to beautiful spring sunshine spilling through the windows and a dream of my daughter lingering in my mind like silken threads of gossamer.

I don't often dream of Emily; the times when I do feel like a gift, but one that hurts. She lingers with me for a few moments after I wake up, so close I almost feel I can reach out and touch her, even as a leaden part of me knows I cannot.

Last night I dreamed of her as she used to be, although that's not always the case. Sometimes in my dreams she is a baby or a toddler; sometimes she is four or five or even ten or eleven, the image of her older self one I can never quite recall once I am awake. Sometimes she is Emily, but she looks entirely different, the way it is so often in dreams. *I was in my house, but it looked like a medieval castle.* It's Emily, but she has dark hair, or brown eyes, someone else's child, but I know, I *know* she is mine.

But today I dreamed of her when she was a toddler, before the symptoms came, one after another, like dark waves rolling towards the shore. In the dream, she was running through the backyard, the grass long like in a meadow, even though James always cut it regularly. I was sitting on the back steps, my face tilted to the sun, as she ran towards me, but then she never came. I looked back down at her, and she was still running, always running, and

I held my arms out, longing to swing her up onto my hip, to press my cheek against her soft, plump one—I could feel it in the dream, the smooth roundness of it—but still she kept running, arms stretched out, face full of joy.

If she can't come to me, I'll go to her, I thought, but when I rose from the steps, my limbs felt heavy and uncoordinated, and when I tried to move, it was as if my feet were stuck in concrete. I couldn't take so much as a step.

Call out to me, I willed to Emily—my conscious self, drifting somewhere in the dream, knowing that she wouldn't. *Say my name.*

But she didn't, of course, and I realized as I stood there, helpless and stuck, that she wasn't even aware of me; it was sun and trees and sky for her, not a mother waiting with open arms.

Awake, I lie flat on my back and try to hold onto the dream, because it feels like holding onto Emily. Of course, it doesn't take a would-be Freud to figure it all out. Me, helpless. Emily, unable to reach me. Yes, that about sums things up right now.

I swing my legs out of bed, feeling tired, even though I slept for ten hours last night—bed at nine, up at seven. I have a soul-deep exhaustion, a base layer of complete and utter spentness that I drag around with me like a fifty-pound weight.

Today is a Sunday full of possibility and promise—a bike ride? A trip to the park? Even a whiz around Trader Joe's with Emily in the shopping cart would be fun on a day like today, where the dew sparkles and the sun is trying to outdo itself. I picture us meandering through an aisle of organic snacks, Emily pointing to the ones she likes. *Rice cakes, Mama?*

Part of me is tempted to take the morning off. I could jog to the Charles River Reservoir, feel that satisfying burn in my legs and lungs; it would be glorious on a morning like this one, the cherry trees almost aggressive with their complete covering of pink puffball blossoms. Or I could tidy up a bit, do a proper grocery shop instead of eating takeout or just toast. Since Emily has been sick, meals have tended to be an afterthought.

My *life* has been an afterthought; in the two years since she first started being hospitalized, I've done little more than go from home to hospital and back again, with a swing-by the grocery store for anything essential, a stop at my mother's once or twice a week, a catchup on bills and laundry on Saturdays, when James is with Emily.

I've been living in this house for nearly eighteen months, but it looks like a low-end Airbnb; the only room that is properly decorated is Emily's, all in pink, with a gauzy canopy over her bed. She hasn't slept there in over six months, and even before that it was sporadic—a few days at home, a few more days in hospital. I wonder if she ever will sleep there again.

If this experimental treatment works… maybe she will. I could bring her home, if she didn't need so much constant monitoring; perhaps she'd even start communicating, *living* again, if only a little. I'm trying to keep my expectations low, but they try to rise, like a child with a balloon, desperate to hold onto it and yet at the same time wanting to see it soar up in the sky. They just can't resist seeing how high it will go.

I push aside any daydreams about a jog or a shop, knowing I won't risk being late to the unit, the still-there possibility of missing something, anything. Every day, without fail, except when James is there or the few times I've had an infectious cold and can't expose children to it, I have been with Emily from eight in the morning until seven at night.

I can't stop now.

I shower, dress, and force down a yogurt that is a day past its sell-by date, because I know I should eat something. I've lost my appetite for food; sometimes it feels as if I can't actually taste anything. The yogurt is slimy, but the strawberry flavor passes me by.

By half past seven, I have my car keys in hand, ready to make the twenty-minute drive to the hospital. There won't be traffic on a Sunday; I'll be at Emily's bedside by eight as usual. I imagine her turning to look at me, giving me a smile.

You made it, Mommy.

Of course I know that's not going to happen. I'm not deluded, not yet anyway. I'm not living in some sad fantasy world, thinking that one day Emily will wake up. It's just, sometimes it *helps*. To imagine she would, she *could*, that one day I'll get my little girl back.

When I get outside the house, though, I am surprised, because there is a big white van in front of the driveway, blocking my car in. I fight a burst of annoyance when I see there is no one in the driver's seat. Now I'm going to be late.

I turn around slowly, scanning up and down my street, but at before eight on a Sunday morning, it's completely empty. I don't know any of my neighbors, have barely seen them in my walk from door to car twice a day. I haven't seen my closest neighbor, the thirty-something woman in the other half of the duplex, in months.

I blow out a breath, repressing the urge to kick the stupid van. What am I supposed to do now?

Then a voice from behind has me stiffening. "Oh, sorry, are you blocked in? I didn't think anyone would be going anywhere this early."

I turn around slowly, trying to school my expression into something normal and neighborly. A man in his thirties with round cheeks and crinkly, hazel eyes smiles at me. I try to smile back.

"Would you like me to move the van?"

Um, yes? Obviously. I nod. "If you don't mind."

"Do you live here?" He gestures to the door of my half of the house.

I nod again.

"I'm your new neighbor, then." He sticks out a hand. "Andrew. And Jake. We're moving in today." He glances behind him and then calls, "Come on out, buddy."

While I shake his hand, a tow-headed boy of about five years old slips out from behind the screen door and then down the couple of concrete steps.

"My son," Andrew says proudly as Jake shimmies next to his father and presses his head against his side. Andrew rests his hand lightly on top of Jake's hair; the blond strands catch the sunlight, turn them to gold.

I haven't spoken, haven't been able to, although I know there are some niceties I should be spouting. I can't seem to manage them, not when the sight of this little boy, so close in age to Emily, feels like a fist to my gut.

It shouldn't. Usually it doesn't. I haven't been the type to avoid children in the supermarket, or to get grouchy or bitter when I see a healthy child skipping down the street. In fact, I've made an effort to say hello to children when they look at me, to send a card when a former co-worker has a baby. Proof so everyone can see that I'm well-adjusted and okay, despite everything.

But with the dream still hanging over me like a gentle cloud, and the van making me late, and the sheer unexpectedness of this moment, I can't quite kick my thoughts in gear.

Finally I manage something. "Nice to meet you. I'm Rachel."

"Hi, Rachel." Andrew gently nudges Jake between his chicken-wing shoulder blades. "Jake?"

"Nice to meet you," Jake mumbles, half hiding behind his dad.

He's polite as well as cute. I keep my smile in place as I explain, "I'm sorry, but I've got to run. Did you just arrive?"

"Yes, this morning. We got here early because we couldn't wait."

I wonder where the mother is, if she's in the picture. I sense something solitary from them both, a bit broken, but I'm not going to pry. The last two years have taught me not to ask personal questions.

"Sorry," Andrew says with a grin, "I'll move it now."

I wait with Jake, both of us unspeaking, as Andrew hops in the van and moves it forward a few feet. I wonder why he couldn't park in front of the house instead of the drive in the first place, but then I tell myself not to be so touchy.

"Thanks," I say as I head to my car. "Good luck with the move." There is a final-sounding note to my voice, as if I'm never expecting to see either of them again, and the truth is, I'm not, at least not more than in passing.

I force both Andrew and Jake out of my mind as I head to the hospital; it's already quarter to eight. I'm going to be late.

Not that she'll notice.

I force that voice to fall silent and I keep driving.

The unit is quiet as I am buzzed in, but then it is always quiet. Everyone here talks in murmurs and whispers, even the nurses. There is an almost sacred feel to the space that I want to ignore. As I head towards Emily's room, the nurse at the station gives me a kindly, sympathetic smile.

I'm so tired of sympathy. At first, I lapped it up, grateful that people cared enough to at least address what was going on in my life. Tragedy so often makes people ignore you; they act as if it's catching, or it's simply too awkward for them to bear, never mind you.

The acquaintances on the periphery of my life did just that. They gave me fleeting smiles at preschool and then dodged conversations, not that I would have started talking, because when I did, people listened but looked elsewhere, fixing their gaze above my head or slightly to my right.

When Emily left preschool because of her health, my circle of friends grew smaller. I still had some then—Denise, from work, who texted me regularly and would drop off meals, and Sara, a mom I met at a Mommy and Me class, before I went back to work, who would ask how I was, waiting for the real answer, which sometimes I gave.

But even Sara and Denise stopped making an effort a while ago now, and I don't blame them. I'm never around, and when I am, I don't want to talk. I resent them, even though I know I shouldn't. They don't understand why I am still going to the hospital every day, and when Denise hesitantly asked if I had to, a rift opened up in our friendship that I knew would not be healed.

"No, I don't *have* to," I'd answered with a distinct edge to my voice. "If you mean by that is there some rulebook, or someone putting a gun to my head, to make me spend time with my daughter?"

"I'm sorry," she'd stammered. "I only meant... it must be exhausting."

Except she didn't mean that at all. Now I think even the nurses are wondering why I keep coming. Most children in the palliative unit are here for a relatively short time; that's the nature of the place, after all. So parents camp out, friends and relatives come in and out, as everyone waits for the end, which is going to happen in a few days or weeks, or maybe just minutes.

But Emily isn't like that. She's here for the foreseeable future, however long that may turn out to be. I know there is one other child in a condition similar to Emily's in the unit, and his parents come in a couple times a week. I've seen the mother once, still in her work clothes. I tried not to look accusing.

Because if I did that, if I went back to my job, even part-time, or jogged in the morning or spent an afternoon having coffee with a friend... I will have given up.

And I am so far from giving up. The new research I've done into the nerve stimulation I mentioned to Eva buoys me, urging me forward. I Skyped the doctor a few days ago, a kindly-looking man named Marco Rossi, from the Centro di Neuroscienza in

Bologna, who is pioneering the research in Italy, after it was started in Lyon, France.

He made no promises, of course, but he sounded so *positive*. He thought it was worth trying. He warned me that results could be minimal, but they could be there.

As soon as we'd finished the call, I wrote down as much as I could remember. I printed out all the research I could, although there wasn't all that much of it because the treatment is so very new. I even drew up a preliminary budget, since our health insurance won't pay for experimental treatment in another country, and tried to think of all the hidden costs, all the things I might not be expecting.

Of course, James won't look at any of it, no matter how many emails I send. I am hoping that Eva can convince him to. It's been over a week since I spoke to her, and I haven't heard anything from James. I have no idea if Eva did what she said she would and my ex-husband didn't listen, or if she chickened out, or maybe didn't care in the first place?

If he doesn't get in touch by Tuesday, I tell myself, I'll call him again. I'll make him listen. Somehow.

Emily has a quiet day, sleeping for most of it, although she does wake up—if I can even call it that—for a few hours in the afternoon. I take off the polish on her nails and wash her hair, brushing it carefully. I talk to her the whole while, although the sound of my voice is starting to sadden me. How long can you talk to someone without ever hearing anything back?

As the sunlight fades from the sky, I gaze down at her slack face and unseeing gaze, and wonder, for the first time, if I should keep going down this lonely route. Or if I should, as James wants me to, let her go.

My heart feels as if it's been wrenched within me as I stroke her hair, and then reach for her hand. How can I be thinking like this? I never have before, not in all this time. I've held onto hope so hard.

And yet… outside, the last of the light is being leached from the sky. I missed the whole day; I've missed *every* day. My skin is dry and flaky from being inside all the time; I can count the people I talk to regularly on one hand, practically one finger. My life has been reduced to this room, this *silence…*

If I let her go, I could go back to work. Make my house a home, instead of just the place I sleep. Maybe even meet someone new. Rebuild my life from the rubble.

As soon as the thoughts flit through my mind, I am flapping them away, furious with myself. How could I betray Emily like that? How could I possibly live with myself if I just walked away from her, because I was tired of trying?

I lace my fingers with my daughter's and silently promise never to think like that again. I will her to squeeze my fingers, to *feel* me, will it with every desperate fiber of my being, but nothing happens. This time.

It doesn't matter, because I am determined. I won't let myself waver again.

It's dark by the time I pull up outside my house, and the van is gone. There are lights on in Andrew and Jake's side of the duplex, and as I get out of the car, I see their silhouettes moving in front of the window, hear music, some kind of jazz, drifting from the open window. The air smells of barbecue, mouthwatering and smoky.

I hadn't even realized my former neighbor had moved out, or that the place was for sale, which says something about how much I'm here, but now I witness these signs of life, of love and happiness, and something in me aches.

I am at my own door, reaching for my keys, when Andrew comes out onto his stoop.

"Hello again," he says, and I give him a tired smile. "You just got back?"

"Yes." It's after seven, and I am so tired. All I want to do is make myself eat something, take a shower to wash the hospital smell off me, and go to bed.

"You must be hungry." Andrew cocks his head. "Have you eaten?"

I can't fathom why he's asking as I answer. "No, not yet."

"Do you want to come over? It's just hamburgers on the grill, but…" He shrugs, smiling, making it sound so easy. "You're more than welcome."

I open my mouth to politely decline—what else can I do, after all—when I see Jake sidle up behind his father. He looks up at Andrew and then he smiles at me, and something in me breaks.

I'm so *lonely*. I haven't let myself feel it fully, haven't wanted to give over even a second of consideration for anything but Emily, but it hits me in the face now, a full body slam of breathlessness. In that moment, I could cry, not for Emily, but for myself.

"That's really kind of you," I begin hesitantly. What if he didn't mean it? Do I even know how to make small talk anymore?

"There's plenty," Andrew says. "Right, Jake?"

Jake nods, gives me another shy, smiling look. I throttle back the tears gathering in my throat and behind my eyes, swallow down the howl in my chest, and manage a smile.

"Thank you," I say. "That's really nice. I'd love to."

CHAPTER TEN

EVA

James is looking at me warily, waiting for me to speak. I feel frozen, poised on the precipice, except by speaking at all I've already leapt off. I'm in free fall and even though it's too late, I realize I don't want to do this.

"Well, Eva?" He sounds so tired, I almost drop it right then and there. Neither of us is ready for this conversation. "What's up?"

I draw a breath. "Rachel came to see me a few days ago."

"What?" James lurches upright, his elbows braced on his knees, his expression completely stunned. "What?" he says again, when I just stare at him, because even I didn't expect him to be that jolted.

"She came to talk to me," I repeat carefully. "About Emily." That, I suppose, is obvious.

James rakes a hand through his hair as he shakes his head slowly, clearly still reeling. "What... I mean why..."

"She wanted me to ask you to consider agreeing to the experimental treatment she's been researching." There. I've said it. I've done my duty. I don't have to say anything anymore. In fact, I could commiserate with James, give him a little of Naomi's attitude. *What a nerve, right?* We can both shake our heads at Rachel's chutzpah, leave it at that, and turn on the TV.

That's what I want to do. It would be so easy. I could assuage my unwieldy conscience, forget about Rachel, and just live my damn life, because, as Naomi said, as James believes, this doesn't actually concern me.

But even as I think that, yearn for it, I know I won't do it. In part because it would be unfair to Rachel, but mostly because it's not how I feel. I stay silent and wait to see how James will react.

"I just can't believe… why would she…" He blows out a breath. "I'm sorry she did that. She already knows how I feel about this. For her to draw you into it… I'll have to talk to her."

"How do you feel about it?" I ask.

He gives me a frowning look, clearly surprised by my question. "Eva…" He sighs wearily. "This doesn't have to concern you."

He's never said it so bluntly before, and a sudden fury rises up in me. "But it does," I say as reasonably as I can, but I still hear a throb of feeling in my voice, like a riptide. "I'm your wife, James, and Rachel and Emily are a huge part of your life. You can't cut me out of it. Of them."

"I'm not cutting you out—"

"That's what it feels like. I'm not allowed to ask about them. To know."

"You're being melodramatic—"

"Then surely you can tell me how you feel about the experimental treatment."

We stare at each other, a silent impasse. The very air between us feels as if it is pulsing. "Look, Eva," James says finally. "This is between Rachel and me. The decisions I make about *my* daughter…"

I fold my arms. "I'm not making any decisions. But the fact is, Rachel came to see me—"

"She shouldn't have."

"But she did. Why are you not even talking with her? She says you won't reply to any of her emails or texts…" I don't mean to sound accusing; I was going for confused, but I hear the sharp note and inwardly wince. James' lips compress.

"I did reply, at first, but I can't believe I'm having to justify myself to you. You sound as if you're on her side in this, and you don't know anything about it."

"Then *tell* me, James. I just want to understand." I fling an arm out, feel myself teeter onto that damnably thin ice. "Why is this such a no-go area for us? You never want to talk about Rachel or Emily with me. Never. And I'm your *wife*."

James is silent for a few seconds, his jaw so tense, I think I can hear the grit of his teeth. "Why would I?" he asks eventually, and his voice is low, agonised. "Why would I, Eva?"

"Because I *care*…" Yet I sound hesitant.

"I know. I'm sorry. It's just…" He releases a long, low breath. "This is hard for me, Eva," he says finally. "I don't like… It's too painful, to talk about Emily. Rachel. All of it. When I'm with you, I want to…" He doesn't finish the sentence.

"I understand that, but this is something else now." My voice is level; I feel calm all of a sudden, almost supernaturally composed, as if I'm a spectator to my own self. "Rachel came to me, James, because she said you refused to talk to her. To engage with her at all. She asked me to talk to you about this experimental treatment she wants Emily to have, to see if you'd just *consider*—"

"Do you even know what she's asking me to consider?"

"I know a bit." I pause. "What's going on?" I ask gently. "Why won't you even talk to her about it?"

"I did talk to her."

I wait. He sighs and shakes his head. Then he looks up, and the bleakness I see in his eyes softens the tough shell that's been forming around my heart. He looks so *sad*. Sometimes I forget. Sometimes I paint him in someone else's colors, because I've been here before, in a completely different way. But James is not, thank God, like Lucas. He's totally different.

"I replied to her text," he amends, and the shell hardens again.

"One text?"

"And an email. I wasn't trying to be heartless, Eva. But how much do you really know about any of this? What, exactly, did Rachel tell you?"

We're on thin ice again, tiptoeing across slick, treacherous surfaces. "She told me that she emailed you about the experimental treatment. It's some kind of nerve stimulation, and it's been successful in treating people in Emily's condition."

"Is that all?"

"I didn't ask for more detail, James. I just said I would talk to you." I fling my hands out, hating that we're fighting over this. Over Rachel and Emily. "Look, I'm not the enemy here. There isn't any enemy, unless it's Emily's condition. We don't have to fight about this. We can just talk."

James shrugs. "I'm not fighting."

But he is. I can feel that he is, everything in him tense and ready to spring.

I sigh and drop my hands. "So why won't you talk to her besides a text and an email?"

James leans back against the sofa and folds his arms. "Do you know," he asks in a level voice, "that the treatment is in Italy?" I don't reply, and he doesn't wait for me to. "Do you know that it is so experimental, only three people have had it, *total*, with varying results?" Another question he does not wait for me to answer, not that I would. "Do you know that the price tag of this treatment, of which not one cent will be covered by our insurance policy, is upward of fifty thousand dollars, and that's just for Emily to be there for one week? Rachel wants to take her for a month, minimum."

I open my mouth, but I can't think what to say, and James steamrollers on anyway. "Do you know that after I texted Rachel saying that I couldn't do this, after I responded to her first twenty-page email, telling her this was not feasible in any way, and that I do not believe it is in Emily's best interest, never mind hers or mine, she has continued to bombard me with texts, emails, and voicemails upwards of three times a day?"

No, I didn't know any of that, and James knows I didn't.

He leans forward, appealing now, his eyes bright with determination, or maybe even tears. He looks like *my* James, the one who laughs at my corny jokes, who stands behind me and wraps his arms around my waist, who puts my feet in his lap when we're watching a movie. "Look, Eva, if there was a treatment I thought would work, that was worth it, I would take Emily there in a heartbeat. A *heartbeat*. I love her as much as Rachel does, even if sometimes it feels as if nobody believes that, as if I'm some unfeeling…" He swallows, shaking his head.

"I don't think that," I whisper. "I don't think you're unfeeling."

"Then trust me when I say, this treatment—it's crazy. It's so experimental, it's not even in clinical trials yet. No one is considering it seriously—not Emily's medical team, whom I've *asked*, nor any other professional in this country that I've found online. It's not approved anywhere; *no one else* is doing this. Rachel's found one crackpot doctor in Italy who's willing to take her money and she wants to climb right on board, because she's so desperate for Emily to get better. I understand that, of course I do. I've understood it all along, and I used to feel it—when it seemed like Emily could still get better. When her symptoms weren't so severe." He swallows hard, his Adam's apple moving convulsively. "But, Eva, at some point you've got to say no, no matter how hard it is, no matter how much it hurts. This is not going to work. It's not worth the time, the money, or the emotional investment for everyone involved. And, most importantly, it's not worth it for Emily, for the health risks it poses, and the disruption to her life, such as it is, that it would cause." By the time he finishes, his chest is heaving, and my mind is spinning.

Part of me wants to agree with him. He makes so much sense, and yet… "How do you know?" I ask quietly.

James's breathing is ragged, as if he's run a race, climbed a mountain. He shakes his head as he looks at me. "How do I know what?"

"How do you know if it's worth it?"

He swears. I flinch. I meant the question honestly, from the depths of my being. *How do you know*? How can you balance those crucial scales—a life on one side, some numberless expenditure of energy, emotion, money, *whatever*, on the other? What tips them from one side to the other? Who gets to decide?

"You know what I mean," he snaps. "Don't make me sound as if I'm so heartless. I get enough of that from Rachel, trust me. What I mean is, is it worth all the money, the emotional energy of running on that hamster wheel of hope and then disappointment, the discomfort to Emily, the *risk* to Emily…?"

I can't help but cynically notice he mentioned money first. But then James is an insurance man. His job is to run risk assessments, to decide *exactly* how much a life is worth. Even, it seems, his own daughter's.

"But, James, how do you know it's *not* worth all those things?" I ask. I can't not ask, because the thought is blaring in my brain like a hand flattened on a car horn. "How on earth can you possibly know?"

I see James' expression close, like the snapping shut of a fan. He is done explaining himself, especially to me. "You haven't seen Emily," he says after yet another long, tense moment. I'm not sure I can take any more of them.

"You've never invited me to."

"I've wanted to keep the parts of my life separate, I admit it," James says. "It felt easier that way. Maybe it wasn't the right thing to do, but the truth is, you haven't seen her. You don't know what she's like now."

"No, but Rachel does."

"Yes," James answers evenly, "And as I told you, she's desperate. She's not thinking straight about this. She's lost all perspective. She'd take Emily to the moon if she thought it would help."

And you wouldn't? Why am I feeling so ungenerous to him? All his points were good ones; they appealed to my sympathy as well as my common sense. I still don't doubt he loves Emily. And yet…

There is, unfortunately, an *and yet*.

"I don't understand why you're taking her side," James says wearily. "I mean, I know Rachel talked to you. I understand she'd appeal to your sympathy. And maybe I've kept you more in the dark than I should have, because it's been easier not to talk about it. To have one part of my life that's free from thinking about it all, even if that sounds callous. It's just… I *need* that, Eva. I need us to be…" He shakes his head helplessly. "Separate."

"I understand that." I speak slowly, choosing my words with care, because I know how much they matter. "But, James, why do there have to be sides?"

"Because Rachel and I disagree on what is best for our daughter, and we happen to share responsibility equally for decisions about Emily's care." His voice has hardened again. "She can't take her to Italy unless I agree."

"And there's no way you ever would?" I have to ask, even though he's made it all too clear. I need to hear him say it.

"No." His voice is flat. "Not unless something huge changed—Emily's brain function improved, or the treatment became credited. But as things stand now? No. Definitely not. And that's for Emily's sake, as well as for Rachel's sake, if you can believe me. She has got to let go. It's not good for her, this holding on."

"And for your sake," I remark before I can think to stop myself. James looks as if I've slapped him, and I feel a rush of guilt. I'm being too aggressive. I know that.

"Yes, for my sake too," he says as he rises from the sofa. "Does that make me a monster, Eva? That I actually want this all to end? Yes, I've got to that point, and it's taken nearly three years. But do you think this has been easy? That I can just walk away without a backward glance?" His fists clench as his voice tears. "It's been fucking hard, okay? All the time. Every single second of my life. What we've had… finding you… feeling like there's something good in my life again…" He swallows. "Please don't take that from me."

He walks into the kitchen, where I hear him open the fridge, the door slamming against the wall. The next sound is the pop of the cork from a bottle of wine. I close my eyes, filled with a painful mix of regret and resolve.

Why did I keep pushing? Why did I have to make it such a *thing*? And yet I know I won't stop now. James asked me why I was taking Rachel's side, and no matter what I said, I know that I am.

I'm taking her side because I understand a mother's need to do whatever she can for her child. Even if it costs her. Especially if it costs her. And that need appeals to me so strongly, so intrinsically, that I can't separate myself from it, even as part of my brain is telling me to shut the hell up and let this go, in a way that Rachel can't.

I'm not Rachel. Emily is not my child. Just walk away, Eva!

But I don't. I walk to the kitchen, and I watch my husband drain his beer.

"I'm sorry, James," I say quietly, and everything about him softens, which makes what I say next all the harder. I want to put my arms around him, but I don't. Instead I speak. "But I really think you need to hear Rachel out properly, in person. You may have texted her back, but I don't think you've really listened to her." I pause, wanting to be fair to him. "At least, she doesn't feel listened to."

"She doesn't *feel*…? Eva, she'll never feel that way. If I listen to her, even a little bit, I'll just give her more hope, more reason to pursue this crazy path." He shakes his head. "You really don't get it, do you?"

"No, I don't." The words burst out of me, fueled by too much history, too much memory. "Emily is your daughter. Surely you should do—you should want to do—whatever you can for her? I get that it's hard. That it's been hard for three years. But as her father you shouldn't ever have to decide if it's *worth* it." The last two words come out in something like a snarl.

James stares at me for a long moment, his face slackening as he registers the full force of my feelings. "I don't want to fight about this," he finally says, sounding so tired and sad, I want to cry. "I don't want this to come between us." And yet I know, just as he does, that it already has. "But I'll say again that you haven't been where I am. Where Rachel is. You haven't seen Emily day in and day out, you haven't heard the doctors, run the statistics—"

"She's not a statistic."

"I know that. Don't you think I know that?" He glares at me, caught between exhausted frustration and a terrible hurt. "Of course I know that. But at some point—*at some point*—you have to make a decision. You *have* to. And I don't expect you to understand, because you've never been where I am." And there it is, the trump card people play when they have run out of arguments. *You have not had my experience. You are not allowed to speak into my situation.* No matter what. No matter why.

I take a deep breath. I almost say words I know I will regret. James' expression is implacable, his bottle of beer raised halfway to his lips. There is a look on his face, a slightly smug look, although perhaps that's unfair, as if he knows he's finally got the upper hand. I can't refute anything he's said, because I haven't walked that damned mile in his shoes.

Except I have, and he doesn't know it. No one knows it. I know what James is going through, at least in the broad strokes, if not the particulars. I know, because I've been where he's been.

The situation might have been very different, but the choice was the same.

But I've never told James any of that, and I know I can't tell him now, even though part of me is tempted.

I have been where you are, James, I want to say. *I understand perfectly, even if you don't think I do.*

But that's not even true, not really, and now is hardly the time to say it anyway. We're not playing some twisted game of one-upmanship here. So I will it all back, and I take a deep breath as I square my shoulders.

"Think about it, please," I say, and then I walk out of the kitchen and go into our bedroom, shutting the door softly behind me.

Alone in the room, I let out a shuddering sound that comes close to a sob. I pace the room as memories float like bubbles coming to the surface of my mind, fragile and translucent, ready to pop.

After a few moments of restless walking, I sit on the edge of our bed, trying to compose myself, trying not to let those bubbles pop, because what then? A few minutes pass, or maybe it's a few hours. Time feels like honey, slow-moving and viscous.

The apartment is quiet, the room so dark that I can only see the shapes of furniture—the chair in the corner, the bureau, the wardrobe. I listen, straining to hear, but all is silent. I wonder if James has left the apartment. Left me, even.

Then I rise from the bed, and, before I've even acknowledged to myself what I'm doing, I open the big oak wardrobe James and I share, and then go to the bottom of my side, rooting behind several shoeboxes and a clutch of discarded wire hangers I haven't yet thrown out.

It takes a few moments, but I finally find what I'm looking for, tucked deep in the dark recesses of the wardrobe, underneath the forgotten flotsam and jetsam of my old clothes and shoes. It is wrapped in a silk scarf I never wear; it's a little enamelled box, small enough to hold in the palm of my hand. There's very little in it—just two photos. I haven't opened this box in sixteen years, although it's come with me wherever I've gone. From college in Pomona to my first internship in New York, to the dark and cramped apartment I rented in West Roxbury, and then later to the first apartment I bought in Charlestown, and now here. This box is part of me.

I sit on the bed, the box in my hand, afraid to open it. Afraid to look. To remember.

But already I remember, already this whole issue with Rachel, with Emily, with *me*, is making me remember, and it's turning my insides into a froth of feeling, a churned-up mess of regret and fear and grief.

And even though James wants me to, even though I think I should, even though it might cost me my marriage… I know I'm not going to let this go.

Dear Bean,

You are six months old today. Half a year! It seems impossible to me. It's gone by so fast, and yet, I confess, Bean, some days are very slow. This motherhood thing can be tough. I wouldn't change it for anything, I promise you that, but some days feel as if they go on forever.

It always irritates me when people ask, 'Is she a good baby?' I want to ask them what they mean, and if anyone would ever answer no to that question. How can there be such a thing as a bad baby? Of course there can't, and you aren't.

Now, if the question was does she sleep ten hours a night without a peep? Well, Bean, the answer to that would be no. It took you four months before you slept more than two hours at a time, and two months on from that it's not much better. Sometimes you go four or five hours, and it feels like a miracle. One time—only once—you slept for seven hours and I woke up with a start, instantly alert and panicked that something must have happened to you.

I crept into your room and peeked into your crib and there you were, lying on your back in a pale pink sleepsuit, one hand flung palm up by your face. I looked down at you sleeping so peacefully, your little rosebud lips pursed, your cheeks so pink and round, and I almost wanted to wake you up for a cuddle, because you were just too delectable for words.

I didn't, of course, because no new mother wakes up a sleeping baby ever. But sometimes I look back on that moment, when the moonlight streamed through the window and you were an armful of joy, and I think, why didn't I wake you up? Why didn't I?

*   Love, Mama*

CHAPTER ELEVEN

RACHEL

Andrew's house is a mess of boxes and bubble wrap, toys scattered across the floor, unpacked books tottering in a tall, uneven stack.

As I step across the threshold, I am assaulted by this house's otherness—when have I paid a visit to someone else's home? The last time was when I spoke to Eva, but I don't want to think about that now.

"Sorry it's such a mess," Andrew says with a wry grin, scratching at his patchy beard. I can't tell if he's growing it out or cultivating the stubble, but it suits him. He has such a friendly look about him that just watching him makes me want to smile.

"You're doing well," I say as I step over a pile of mismatched Tupperware. "It looks like things are mainly unpacked." If not put away.

"Jake likes the unpacking part," Andrew says as he ruffles his son's hair. The unconscious gesture makes something ache inside of me, but I repress it. I don't want to feel sad right now. Jake is half hiding behind his dad, but he keeps peeping out to give me cautious, curious glances. "Not so much the putting away. But we'll get there."

"Where did you move from?" I figure if I ask Andrew questions, it might keep him from asking questions of me. And I remember, in an achey, atrophied sort of way, that asking questions is part of normal conversation. Getting to know people. Actually making friends.

"From about an hour away, near Worcester. This is a new start for us." There is a determinedly upbeat note to Andrew's voice that I recognize, and I must give an unconsciously questioning look, because he grimaces a little and glances towards Jake. The implication is obvious; he doesn't want to talk about it in front of his son.

I nod my understanding and turn to Jake. Looking at him feels a bit like looking at the sun—too much, too bright. I fight an urge to shield my eyes. His eyes are very blue, his hair a curly rumple, his skin smooth and soft.

"Are you in school, Jake?"

Jake nods, sliding behind Andrew's legs once more. "He's starting kindergarten in September," Andrew says. "At Angier. Do you know it?"

I shake my head. I looked at Angier Elementary School ever so briefly, when I still nursed hopes that, with the right specialist help, Emily might start there last September. I gave that up a while ago, when the seizures became worse and then Emily went into hospital for yet another infection and it became clear she would not be coming out anytime soon. But I don't want to explain any of that to Andrew.

Andrew rests one hand on Jake's shoulder and gently steers him to stand in front of him. Jake leans against his legs. "Jake is looking forward to school, aren't you, buddy?" He nods.

"That's great." It's clear Jake is shy, and I don't want to pressure him to make conversation with a stranger.

He gives Andrew a questioning look, and he nods back, the kind of easy, unspoken communication between parent and child I remember so well, and then Jake ducks his head and runs off, out to the backyard.

A surprisingly comfortable silence stretches between Andrew and me, expanding and elastic.

"He seems like a good kid," I finally say, because he does.

"He is," Andrew agrees. "I'm lucky."

Yes, I can't help but think. *And you don't even know how lucky you are.* But I don't want to go down that dark, twisting trail of conversation, so I smile as brightly as I can and ask, "Did you move to Boston for work?"

"Yes. I'm a graphic designer. I start work on Monday with Neo Designs. Have you heard of them?"

With an apologetic grimace, I shake my head. "I'm sorry. That's not an area of work I'm that familiar with."

"What do you do?"

I pause, as I often do at this stage in a conversation, not that I've had all that many, weighing up what I want to say, and how I want to say it. How much to reveal, knowing the shocked flood of sympathy it will cause, followed by the inevitable awkward silence, the change in conversation like the screech of tires.

I realize I don't want to go down that route today. I'm too tired, too weary and worn down. I want to be different, even if it's just pretend, just for a little while.

"I'm a teacher," I say when the pause has gone on a few seconds too long. "High school English."

"Oh, that's great. Here in Newton Upper Falls?"

Another pause, as I consider whom Andrew might meet, what he might discover about me. "No," I say, deciding to stick with as much truth as I can. "In Needham."

"That's not too far…?" His forehead crinkles. "I'm still getting used to the area. I'm from Rhode Island, originally."

"It's pretty close. Ten minutes, in the car."

"You must like it." He smiles at me, and I'm not sure how to respond. Yes, I did like it, but it feels like a lifetime ago. I can't imagine caring about George Orwell and Emily Bronte now, the five-paragraph essay, putting your hypothesis in the introduction… it all feels ridiculous. Unimportant, and yet I know it's not. Not for everyone else.

"Yes," I finally say with a smile and a shrug. "It has its moments, both good and bad."

"Have you lived here very long? I mean…" He nods towards the wall that separates his home from mine.

"About eighteen months." I pause and then because I can see the uncertain question in his eyes, I clarify, "I got divorced."

"I'm sorry." Another pause; there are so many, like molehills we have to move around. "I'm in the same boat, actually." He lowers his voice even though Jake is outside. "Jake's mother—my wife—left us four months ago."

I can't quite hide my surprise; his word choice is so stark, that I know there must be a story there. "I'm sorry," I say, because what else is there to say?

"Yeah, it hasn't been great." Andrew sighs and then shrugs. "Let me go check on the burgers before they're totally charred."

I follow him out to the small, scrubby backyard that is identical to mine in size and shape; the two lawns are bisected by a rather unsightly waist-high fence of chain link. Mine looks empty, deserted and forgotten, the grass patchy, the deck empty of anything but a trash can. In contrast, Andrew and Jake have already put a friendly mark on theirs. There is a barbecue on the postage stamp of decking, along with a table and a couple of chairs, and a battered, plastic jungle gym on the grass that Jake is scrambling on. A couple of bikes lean against the fence.

The sky is turning pink, and the air is still warm. The burgers smell delicious. Something inside me, amazingly, loosens. I'm not going to think about Emily right now. I'm not going to let myself feel what a betrayal that is. For once, for a few minutes, maybe an hour, I just want to *be*.

"I hope you're not a vegetarian," Andrew says with an uncertain laugh.

"Nope." I take another step out onto the deck. "They smell wonderful. Are you sure you have enough?"

"Yeah, I bought a package of four and decided to cook them all." He smiles at me. "But Jake will only eat one."

"Thank you. It's very kind to invite me over."

"You had a busy day?" There is a deliberately casual note to his voice that I recognize; he doesn't want to seem nosy, but he's wondering.

"Yes," I answer after another one of those pauses. "But not too bad." And I don't say anything else.

Andrew nods, letting it go. He's not going to be one of those people who press, thank goodness. He bends over the barbecue, intent on the burgers. "Can you give me any recommendations for the neighborhood?" he asks. "Good takeout places, playgrounds?"

"There's a good Chinese place on Oak Street, although I think technically it's Taiwanese."

"Okay." He smiles at me, but I can see he's waiting for more.

I take a quick, steadying breath. Why does this have to be so hard? "As for playgrounds, there's a small one on Chestnut Street. Emerson Park is probably the best one in the area." For a second, a memory pierces me—the winter before last, when Emily was having a good day. We'd moved to Upper Falls a few weeks before, and I'd walked to Emerson Park, Emily in a stroller, even though she was four and a half, old enough to walk. She'd been exhibiting symptoms for sixteen months by then, and her speech and mobility were starting to become limited. She hadn't been able to manage any of the climbing equipment, and I could see the other parents and carers giving us speculative looks, wondering about our story.

At one point, as Emily painstakingly moved across the tarmac, I heard a child say in a too-loud voice, '*What's wrong with that girl?*' and his mother shushed him.

I don't know, I wanted to cry. *No one knows, and it's killing me.* But worse, I was afraid it was killing Emily.

Now, as I stare unseeingly at Jake happily scrambling over his little jungle gym, I remember helping Emily into one of the accessible swings—the kind with a big bucket seat and straps with buckles to keep her in. The kind of swing you're supposed to steer your own children away from, so the ones who really need it can use it.

I remember how excited she was; she couldn't speak much, but she made little gurgling sounds that I recognized as joy. I remember her flying high in the air as I pushed her, her head tilted back, her mouth wide open. She was making a screeching sound that made the other people in the playground shoot us uncertain looks, but I knew she was happy. I *knew*.

And in that moment, I fought the sadness that she was like this—that she couldn't talk or walk properly any longer—and just let her be happy. But later, as I pushed her stroller back towards home, I had to fight off the black cloud of despair that threatened to descend on me and never lift. Why had this happened? Why Emily? Why me?

And yet, looking back, I'd take that moment in a second. I'd snatch it and hold onto it and live in it for the rest of my life, if I could. So Emily couldn't talk; she could still communicate. So she couldn't walk; she could still throw her arms around me. Joy still lit her eyes; her smile was the most beautiful thing I'd ever seen.

Oh God, I think now, *just give me that moment, or one like it again. That's all I want.*

"Emerson, huh," Andrew says, and I drag myself back to the present.

"Yes, I've heard it's a good one." That feels like a lie, but I'm not ready to go into the whole do-you-have-kids conversation.

"Come on, Jake," Andrew calls. "I think the burgers are ready."

The next few minutes are filled with busyness rather than conversation; I help set the table outside, and Jake climbs onto a seat. Andrew dishes out the burgers and asks if I want something to drink.

"I have a bottle of wine," he suggests hesitantly. "Or some beers…"

I'm tempted, but something in me resists. I'm not ready to let go that much. "A glass of water is fine, thanks."

"Okay."

Soon enough we're all seated around the little table, burgers with all the fixings in front of us. The sky is now the color of burnt orange, the air still warm but holding the faint promise of evening chill. It's the middle of May, everything is in Technicolor, and I am eating a burger with someone I could potentially call a friend.

I never expected to be here, in so many ways.

"Dig in," Andrew says cheerfully, and so we do.

The burger is juicy and delicious, and for a little while we just eat, happy to enjoy our meal. Jake is nibbling the edge of his bun, his eyes wide as he keeps darting me glances. I smile at him, trying to help him relax.

"So I guess your house is identical to mine," I say. I smile again at Jake. "Which bedroom is going to be yours?"

"The one at the back," Andrew answers. There are three bedrooms upstairs, two big and one small. "I'll use the little one for an office."

"Sounds like a good plan."

"And Jake's going to have dinosaurs on his wall, right?" Andrew smiles at his son. "We've got some stencils we're going to put on. Jake's going to help me paint."

I think of Emily's room, with its pink princesses on the walls, the canopied bed. Although she was only in it for a few months, Emily loved that room. "Sounds great," I tell Jake, and he gives me a slightly wider smile.

Andrew asks me about more local recommendations—the movie theater, the library—and for a little while our conversation is innocuous, easy, or almost. I tell him about the farmer's market in Wellesley, and the Hayfest at the Jackson Homestead and Museum. James and I took Emily there, when she'd just turned three. I remember sunshine and old-fashioned crafts and exhibits, sugary donuts and warm, spiced apple cider. A perfect family day.

I also remember noticing that she stumbled a bit, climbing over the bales of hay, but we didn't pay much attention to it then. She was only three, after all. We had no idea what was ahead of us. I feel a longing for that innocence, even as I curse it.

"There's a jazz festival in Newton, in September," I tell Andrew. "Although I've never been to it, I hear it's good. Really, there's enough in the Newton area, you never even have to go into Boston, if you don't want to."

"This is an amazing area," he agrees. "Worcester doesn't have half as much."

I smile politely, because I've never been there. I grew up in the Boston area, went to college here, made my life. I don't know anything else.

"So," Andrew asks when we are nearly done with our burgers, "when does school get out?"

I put the remains of my burger down and wipe my ketchupy fingers on the paper towel he provided. Now is the time when I have to start explaining, and I don't want to. "Actually," I say as lightly as I can, "I'm taking this semester off." He looks surprised, and a little guarded. "I have some… family issues I need to focus on." I give him a fixed smile, but my eyes are saying "no more questions", and thankfully Andrew understands that.

"It's great you can do that," he says after a moment. "Will you go back in the fall?"

I know James wants me to. "Maybe," I tell him. "I'm thinking about it."

He nods, and then Jake asks to be excused—so polite! —and runs off to the jungle gym again, even though it's getting dark, and the little yard is full of shadows.

By silent agreement, Andrew and I start clearing the table. Inside, the house is dim and he flicks on the lights.

"I hope we're going to be happy here," he says quietly as he starts to rinse the plate, his head lowered. "It seems like a good neighborhood."

I know next to nothing about the neighborhood. "I think it is," I venture.

"Jake hasn't had an easy time," Andrew continues, and I brace myself for some sharing. "I mentioned his mom left four months ago…"

"Yes…"

Andrew grimaces. "She just… went. We were having some problems beforehand—I was working too much, I know, trying to set up my own business, which failed. And Christina… she found motherhood hard, I guess." I wait, tense, not entirely wanting to hear these confidences. Not wanting to be responsible for them. "But I thought we'd make it, you know? It didn't seem like anything out of the ordinary, what we were going through." He glances at me, seeming to expect a response.

"Mm," I say, and nod. I am out of my depth.

"Anyway, she went to Bali on a yoga retreat. I thought she needed some downtime, and Christina had always enjoyed that sort of thing. It was only meant to be for a week." He sighs heavily. "But then she texted me to say she'd met someone, on the retreat. A guy named *Rain*." A slight sneer to the word, which I understand. "And she ran off to Seattle to be with him, without even coming back to say goodbye to Jake." He dumps some cutlery into the sink with a clatter. "That's the part I can't forgive."

I'm not sure how to respond. It all sounds awful, and I am sympathetic, of course I am, and yet… he still has Jake. I know it's not fair to think that. I know Andrew has had his own sorrows and trials. But I do think it. I can't help but have that thought beat through my brain. *You're still lucky. You don't know what real grief looks like.* Of course I would never say that. I feel guilty for thinking it. And so I stay silent, and Andrew gives me an abashed look.

"Sorry. TMI."

"No… no." I shake my head, feeling so miserably guilty. "I'm sorry. That all sounds hard. Really hard." My words are inadequate.

"Well, it sounds like you're going through some stuff, too?" The lilt to Andrew's voice is hopeful; it's my turn to share. This is how friendship works, an exchange of information, a sharing of stories that knit us together, bind us with mutual sympathy.

But I can't share mine. Even if I wanted to, I know it wouldn't be fair. Andrew would have to trip over himself to say how horrible it all is, and then he'd feel duty-bound to retract his own sad story, as if it doesn't count, which is invariably what happens in these kinds of conversations, few as they've been. *Sorry to have whined, what I'm going through doesn't even compare, I know that…*

No, it doesn't, but my story doesn't invalidate his. I recognize that, even if I don't always feel it. And in any case, I don't want to explain about Emily now.

"Yes," I say, giving him a smile that I hope is apologetic. "I am." And I leave it at that, and although he looks disappointed, Andrew leaves it, too. I feel as if I've just shut a door in his face. He won't open it again.

I'm battling a regret over closing down the conversation as I say my goodbye a little while later, even though I know I wouldn't have done anything differently. I doubt Andrew will ask me over again, and of course I won't reciprocate. This was nothing more than a pleasant little interlude, one that ends on a bit of a sour note.

"Good luck with the unpacking," I say as I head across to my door. It sounds so final. "Hope kindergarten goes well."

"Well, that's not till September," Andrew says with a laugh, and I smile, because I really don't think we'll have a proper conversation again before then, if ever.

Back in my empty house, I wish things were different. I wish *I* were different, that I could somehow find a way to live my life with Emily in the hospital. That I could be normal, or something close to it, instead of putting absolutely everything on hold. I think about texting Denise or Sarah, but I don't. I haven't contacted them in months, since before Emily went into the hospital for good.

Maybe I should have told Andrew about Emily. I feel the expected hot rush of shame that I didn't, that I betrayed her in that way, and yet it was so nice to pretend for a little while.

Pretend your daughter doesn't exist? The voice in my head is scathing, contemptuous.

No, I answer back sadly. *Pretend that my life is normal. That I'm happy, or almost.*

But pretending never lasts long.

CHAPTER TWELVE

EVA

For two weeks, I pretend things are fine. It's easy enough, because I think both James and I are relieved to fall into our usual rhythm—mornings moving around each other as we bolt coffee and get ready for work, and evenings chatting over our homemade versions of takeout and a bottle of wine. On Sunday, we even drive up to the Berkshires and browse antique shops.

We don't talk about Rachel or Emily; I don't even ask how his visits have gone, when he comes back from the hospital, looking tired and defeated. I tell myself it doesn't matter. I'm not willing to risk my marriage, my chance for a child, on somebody else's— someone I've never even met. Who would do that? Who should?

After our argument, when I sat on the edge of the bed and told myself I couldn't let it go, I made myself do just that. James came to bed in silence, his movements stiff and offended. When he climbed into bed next to me, I put my hand on his shoulder, felt him tense. The silence breathed on, and then he relaxed, and even though we didn't say anything, he turned to me and brushed a kiss against my forehead. I closed my eyes and breathed him in, willed us to be okay. It was as good as a conversation, and from that moment on I did not mention Rachel or Emily again. I didn't even want to.

And so I live my life, and I tell myself everything is fine—and it almost is.

On a balmy evening towards the end of May, James and I try the new tapas place downtown we've been meaning to for ages. We sip Rioja and nibble at huevos rotos and watch the world go by, and it's *fine*.

Later, as the sun streaks towards the horizon and everyone seems full of goodwill that nice weather always brings out, we hold hands as we stroll back to our apartment, sleepy and content with good food.

And even later, in bed, James reaches for me in a way he hasn't for a little while, fitting me close against his body, brushing my lips with a tenderness I've yearned for. I rest my palm against his chest and he fits his hand to the curve of my waist. We move sweetly, silently, finding an agreement, an understanding, in this, as we always have.

It's only after, when James has fallen asleep, that my mind drifts inevitably to the things that aren't so fine. The silences that still weigh between us, that I feel. The fact that I still think about Rachel and Emily—a lot. And, not least of all, the realization that, according to my ovulation predictor, tonight wasn't a peak time to try, so I can't even hope that anything happened there.

It's been three weeks since I spoke to Rachel, and I haven't contacted her; I don't think I even can. I don't know her number, and I'm not going to go hunting for it. No matter how resolved I once felt, with that precious box in my hand, I don't want to pursue this any longer. I am choosing not to, a choice I make deliberately, every day.

I roll over onto my side, tuck my knees up to my chest. Next to me, James snores gently. I think of Rachel, wondering what she's doing, how she is feeling, and then I make myself stop. I won't feel guilty. I *won't*.

Eventually, I fall into a light, uneasy sleep, to wake up the next morning and repeat the whole day again, and again. This is life, and it's good. It has to be good.

Things at work are fine, as well. The campaign for the new skincare line has taken off, and we're up for some minor award. Mara is happy, and I accept her approving smile as my due. Yet I realize I've lost the passion I once had for my work; I can't shake the niggling feeling that no matter how ethical our company is, no matter how responsibly resourced our makeup, it still feels so… *shallow*.

I've never thought of working for Maemae as unworthy before. I know it's not saving lives the way my brothers, the firefighter and the paramedic, do, but it's still something. Women wear makeup; we're giving them an ethical choice. And I was never going to become a nurse or a teacher as my parents expected—the only two careers they believe are truly open to women, although they'd never actually say so outright. So why can't I be happy and satisfied, doing something that is important and valuable in its own way?

I tell myself this restlessness will pass; it's to do with Rachel, and *all that*, and not how I actually view my career or my life. And yet the days slip past and I find myself starting to get touchy, a little short with my colleagues. I snap at a secretary, I make a mocking joke about the importance of mineral-based eyeshadow, and Mara gives me a questioning lift of a single eyebrow, a precursor to a more formal dressing-down. *Not good.*

I pretend I don't see it, and I try to rein in my temper. This too will pass. I can't risk my job, not yet, not until I'm pregnant, at least. *If* I can get pregnant.

But my peak ovulation time arrives and when I reach out to James, he rolls away, too tired. I don't feel brave enough to point out now is a good time for baby-making, and so I lie flat on my back, staring up at the ceiling, sleep eluding me yet again as I wait to start another day.

One Thursday in late May, when James is at the hospital with Emily, I end up swinging by my parents' house, even though I hardly ever surprise them with such a visit. I realize I am lonely; my nights feel empty, along with my days.

"Diva!" My father looks thrilled I've shown up.

I smile and hug him; I've never told him I disliked that nickname, because he's the one who gave it to me. And there is a kernel of truth in it; when I was little, I was the spoiled princess to his rough-and-tumble sons. I flaunted that fact to my brothers, because even though my dad cosseted me, I was never part of the impromptu football games in the backyard; I didn't go fishing upstate when they organized a trip one spring. That's just the way it was—unthinking, impossible to ignore or combat. That's the way it's always been.

"Is everything all right?" my mother asks anxiously as she presses her cheek to mine and then bustles me back to the kitchen, the women's domain. My father settles himself in the armchair, in front of the TV, having done his duty.

A gleam comes into my mother's eye as she looks up at me from the ground beef she is frying on the stove. "Or is there news…?"

"No. No news." I smile tiredly. *If only.*

My mother deflates. "Oh. I was hoping—"

"I know, Mom. So was I." My period is due in a couple of days, and I know there's no point in even using one of the pregnancy tests lined up in my underwear drawer, under a set of lacy thongs I never wear.

"You were?" My mother looks up, surprised, almost hopeful again. "Because you never *say*, Eva. To tell you the truth, I haven't even been sure if you've wanted children." Which is about the worst thing a woman could feel, according to my mother.

"I told you I do, Mom."

"I know, I know, but you're so *quiet*." She shakes her head, half in annoyance, half in affection. "You keep so much in. I have no idea what you're thinking most of the time."

I'm not sure what to say to that, because I know it's true. I shrug.

"Well, you're trying then?" Now she definitely sounds hopeful. "Because it can take some time, you know. With Steve, we had to—"

"Please, Mom. No details." I hold up a hand to forestall hearing about my brother's conception.

My mother gives a girlish little grin. "Well, you know, trying can be fun."

"*Please*."

Thankfully, my mother drops that line of conversation, although she's not done with talking about conception. Far from it. "James doesn't bicycle, does he? I've read that can limit sperm."

This is why I have avoided this conversation. This, and a lot of other, more complex and painful reasons. "He doesn't bike." Not that much, anyway.

"And I hope you're taking folic acid, because you know that's important? Right from the beginning. Otherwise, babies can get that horrible disease—the one where they have that awful bulge in the spine—"

"Spina bifida. And yes, I am taking folic acid." I have been for six months, so I'm definitely okay on the vitamin front.

"Well, it will happen then," my mother says as she pats my hand. "But, you know, you could always go to the gynecologist? Get things checked out? Make sure it's all working down there?" A faint blush touches her cheeks. My mother is the queen of euphemisms when it comes to a woman's body parts. She didn't seem to have the same kind of trouble discussing my husband's sperm.

I nod, reluctant but not wanting to admit it. "Yes, maybe I'll do that in another month or two." But I'm afraid to see my doctor, afraid of what she might say, the bad news that will be the end of my hopes.

"It can't hurt," my mom says, ever philosophical.

"No," I agree. "I don't suppose it could."

She smiles and pats my hand again. "Don't worry, Eva. Not every woman can pop out babies the way Tiffany can. It can still happen for you." I think that's meant to be reassurance, but it feels like a jab.

I nod and murmur something like agreement.

"And how is James?"

"He's all right. He's visiting Emily tonight." I don't normally mention Emily to my parents. It's easier not to, and it's not as if I ever have news to impart. I told them about her after James and I got married, because it felt necessary. They were sympathetic, anxious, a little bit horrified. And my mother continues to be all three as she shakes her head and gives me one of her looks.

"That poor, poor girl. You'd said she moved to palliative care… has there been any change?"

"I don't think so." I don't actually know. Emily has been in the palliative care unit for five weeks; James and I have been deliberately not talking about her for two.

My mother prods the browning beef. "It's just so sad, the way she's gone downhill so quickly. And no one can find out why?"

"No."

"Do you think…" My mother's voice drops to a hush. "Do you think she'll die?"

"One day," I say. "I mean we all will, Mom."

"Oh yes, Eva, but you know what I mean. Is she… is she *dying*?" She says this as if she's not meant to ask, and maybe she isn't.

"I don't know." My ignorance weighs on me heavily. I fight the guilt of disappointing Rachel. Is she waiting to hear from James? To hear from me?

"I mean, it's awful, it's tragic, but… it would be a mercy in a way, don't you think?" My mother shoots me an uncertain, apologetic look, as if she's not sure if she should say such a thing. My family is Catholic, and my mother believes firmly in the sanctity of life. Yet it's different when you're facing the issue head-on and not some abstract theory floating somewhere out in space, a *what-if* that is only meant to happen to someone else.

And yet... it would be a mercy. Wouldn't it? *A mercy for me.*

"I don't know, Mom. I don't know how... aware she is. Of everything." I usually picture Emily sleeping peacefully in a hospital bed, but I don't think she's like that all the time. When I researched her condition, the internet told me that she could be opening her eyes, exhibiting reflexes, jerking spasmodically, all of which seems a little bit... creepy.

"I thought you said she was in a coma," my mom says.

"A state of unresponsive wakefulness," I correct.

My mother frowns. "You mean, like a vegetable?"

I flinch a little. "You're not supposed to use that term anymore." Or so I read online, on one of the evenings I've spent alone, when James was with Emily, and I was searching the internet for more information about it all, about the research that might be a false promise, or might be her salvation. Who knows? *Who knows?*

"Oh, for heaven's sake." My mother prods the beef again, and the fat sizzles. "What's the point of getting upset over a few words?"

"They matter. They can hurt." I don't think Rachel wants her daughter being called a vegetable. I know I wouldn't.

"But that's what she is, isn't she?" My mother's voice has taken on a stubborn, pedantic tone that she often adopts when she suspects she's not in the right. "She's not talking or communicating or anything, is she?"

"I don't think so." I'm pretty sure about that, but I picture Emily with her eyes open, moving even a little, and I think how that could easily seem like communication, especially if you so desperately wanted it to be.

"Well, then." My mother gives a little nod, as if she's somehow proved her point, done her duty. "It would be a mercy, then."

I almost tell her about Rachel seeing me, about the new research and the experimental treatment, and how Emily might have a chance at a little more of life. But I don't, because I don't want to admit my part—or lack of it—in it all. I'm still pretending that it's over, that it's nothing to do with me, even as I acknowledge all along how I'm kidding myself. Really, I'm just biding time.

"So why did you come over?" my mother asks in her typically blunt way.

I shrug, blushing, embarrassed by my obvious need. "I just hadn't seen you in a while."

My mother softens. "Oh, Eva." She gives my shoulder a little squeeze. "It will happen. Don't worry."

I know she's talking about pregnancy, just as I know that isn't really why I came over. There is so much more I want to talk to her about—the tension with James, whether I should fight for this experimental treatment alongside Rachel—but my mother, loving as she can be, won't give me the kind of advice I need. If I told her James and I were having trouble, she'd advise me to cook him a steak and wear a negligee tonight. That's just her world. As for Rachel… I don't know what she'd say then. Stand by your man, maybe? It's heartbreaking, but you don't need to get involved?

Why don't I want to hear that?

I am surprised to find James at home when I get back. It's only seven o'clock, and he usually doesn't return till nine.

"Hey." I toss my keys on the hall table and come into the living room to see him sprawled on the sofa, his laptop on the coffee table in front of him, a carton of Chinese takeout in his hand "Is everything okay?" I ask cautiously. "With Emily?"

"Yeah." James shrugs as he digs for a piece of pork in his lo mein. "I was just tired, and there didn't seem much point to being there."

I stiffen at that, because he's never, as far as I can remember, left early. He's never *not seen the point*. I walk to the kitchen, telling myself not to ask. Not to stir that damned pot, because everything is *fine* and it can keep being fine.

Except, I realize as I reach for the wine bottle that is always in the fridge, it isn't really fine. On the surface, yes, but the truth is, I'm sinking a glass or three of wine every night, just to blunt the edges of everything. I'm starting to hate my job. And the list of things James and I don't talk about is becoming longer than the list of things we do.

I am not fine. *We* are not fine. I want more than this—for me, for my marriage, and yes, for Rachel.

Slowly, I pour myself a glass of wine and take that first, much-needed sip. From the living room, I hear James slurp a noodle. I walk back towards him, standing in the doorway, surveying the scene—the squashy leather sofa I love to curl up in, the carton of sesame chicken on the table that James knows is my favorite and has no doubt left for me. The warm light from the floor lamp we picked out at Room & Board pools on the floor in a golden circle; it cost more than we could afford for a single lamp, but we both loved it and we were so excited to make a home for ourselves.

It would be so easy, so wonderful, to curl up on the sofa next to James, idly ask what he's working on, nibble on a piece of sesame chicken. I want that so much, it is a physical sensation—a twisting of my gut, a pressure in my chest, a deep, deep ache to just *be*.

Why can't life be easy?

But it's not easy for Rachel, and it's not easy for me. And so, instead of doing all that, I sit in the armchair opposite, just as Rachel did three weeks ago, and I sip my wine. "Did you ever talk to Rachel?" I ask, trying to make it sound like a matter of general, casual interest. "About the experimental treatment?"

James looks up, his chopsticks—he never uses a fork—halfway to his mouth. His look is instantly guarded.

"I emailed her," he says after a moment. "To say the subject is closed, for all the reasons I told you before."

"And she let it go? She's okay with it?"

"As far as I know. She hasn't been in touch."

Fine. I should leave it there. It wasn't my job to convince James, just to talk to him. That was all Rachel asked of me, and I did it. Yet as James returns to his laptop, the discussion clearly over, I sip my wine and think of Rachel.

Five weeks Emily has been in palliative care. Five weeks of watching, wondering, *waiting*. Has she lost hope? Has she given up?

I realize I can't stand that thought. No parent should *ever* have to give up on their child, not when there still might be some hope left, no matter how small. No matter how slight.

But what can I do about it?

I tell myself nothing, even as the answer forms in my mind, taking shape with every passing second, gaining texture and weight. I know what I can do. I know what I'm good at, and how I can use it to help Rachel... if I dare. Do I?

I stay silent, sipping my wine, letting the moments slip by as James relaxes into the evening and my mind continues to spin.

CHAPTER THIRTEEN

RACHEL

"Hello?" I call out, my voice echoing through my mother's dark and empty house as I walk down the hallway towards the kitchen, where she is almost always bustling around, waiting for me. I decide she must be in the garden; she's always loved her flower beds, and the beautiful weather has held. It's almost June, and everything is burgeoning, the blossoms ridiculously blowsy.

I haven't seen my mom in over a week, mostly because there has been nothing to report. Emily's condition remains unchanged. My battle for experimental treatment has come to nothing, thanks to James' terse email informing me he'd read all the research and he still wouldn't discuss it because he doesn't believe it is "helpful for either Emily or you". As if he knows what's helpful for me.

I've thought about contacting Eva again, asking her if she ever talked to him, but I can't bring myself to do it. In the end, it doesn't matter anyway. James knows I won't start a big legal battle, although last week I did look into it. I spoke to a lawyer whose name I got off the internet, a sharp-voiced woman who promised no fees unless we won, but I didn't like her manner. She sounded ruthless, and the way she talked about Emily, so coldly yet with a syrupy overlayer of false sympathy, had me silently clenching my fists.

So I decided to speak to someone else, someone recommended to me from a Facebook group for parents of disabled kids whose posts I can only bear to read every few weeks, because they're all so desperately upbeat, trying to act as if everything is okay, as if our children aren't in agonizing circumstances.

Another mother gave me the name of someone really good, or so she said, and yet I found this lawyer even harder to talk to, because she was so terribly kind.

"I feel for your situation," she told me. "I really do. And normally I would advocate exploring absolutely every avenue for treatment and diagnosis of a seriously ill child. But with what you've told me about Emily's condition, as well as the rate of deterioration she's experienced so far, I think a legal battle, in this instance, is most likely unwise. It will end up costing you a lot of money, and there are no guarantees that you'd win. The treatment is just too new, too experimental, without enough data to show its value. If you wanted to try another kind of therapy, something that's been more tested, is already in clinical trials…"

"Like what?" I asked, trying not to sound either angry or hopeless, and the woman's apologetic silence was answer enough. I hung up the phone, not caring that I was being rude. Why was I always running up to a dead end, a determined no from every quarter?

Except for Eva. She'd said she'd do something, but if she has, it hasn't worked. And so I've let the weeks slide by, and I've sat by Emily's bed, and I've felt my hope start to drain away, which is the worst feeling in the world. *Almost.* I know there is a worse feeling, but I'm not thinking about that yet.

"Mom?" I call again as I open the back door that leads to the yard, a strip of lawn bordered by flower beds that are bursting with colorful blooms. I can tell from the stillness, however, that she's not out there, and I start to feel a little bit uneasy.

I texted her this afternoon to say I'd stop by after James came to the hospital, and it's after six now, a time when she should almost certainly be up and about. Her car is in the driveway.

"Mom?" I call again, and then I hear a creak on the stairs.

"Sorry, Rachel," she calls as she comes down the stairs and then into the kitchen. "I didn't hear you come in. I was just upstairs."

She smiles at me, but she seems distracted; her hair is rumpled and her cardigan is buttoned wrong. I watch her move to the kettle, the slump of her shoulders seeming more pronounced than I've ever noticed before.

"Is everything all right, Mom?"

A long, telling pause and suddenly I feel as if I could stagger. She hasn't said anything, but I know from that pause that there is something she has to tell me, just as I know I don't want to hear it. I've known it for weeks, sensed it since the last time I saw her, like something dark lurking in a corner.

"Tea?" she asks finally, her back to me as she rummages in the kitchen cupboards. "I've got chamomile or wild berry?"

"Wild berry, please."

I feel weirdly numb as I take a seat at the kitchen table. Everything about this room is familiar—the dark wood cupboards that were popular in the 1980s but not so much now; the linoleum floor that is peeling up at the corners; the table I am sitting at, of solid oak, with its scarred surface and the pottery bowl of fruit in the middle, although right now there is only a single, browning banana resting there, forgotten.

My heart lurches, like a drunk stumbling across the floor. I'm not ready for this. Whatever it is, I'm not ready. And yet even so, I tell myself it may be nothing. That I'm overreacting, as I always do, because of Emily.

That mole? Must be cancerous. That cough? It's pneumonia. That unmarked letter in the mail? It must be bad news. I can't help it; it's become my default, even as I struggle not to be so discouraged, such a downer. Who wants to be around someone like that? Not that anyone actually is.

"I was just having a nap," my mother says as she gets out two mugs—a Boston College one, and another with Shakespeare quotations all over it in curly script.

"Are you feeling under the weather?" I ask. My mother doesn't normally have naps. She's always been go, go, go—a novel on the counter as she stirs the soup, an essay she's writing on her laptop while browsing the newspaper. She is the queen of multitasking; I remember my dad saying he'd never met someone who could do not just two things at once, but six.

"Oh, I'm fine." My mother's smile seems a little vague. The kettle whistles shrilly, and she makes the tea. How many times have we sat here together, sipping tea, sharing confidences? It became a ritual for us, especially after my dad died in my junior year of high school. I'd come home from school, and we'd download our days over mugs of chamomile or peppermint or lemon. Always herbal, accompanied by something my mother had baked. I wonder now how she found the time, with her busy life, her career at the college, but she did. She always did.

Even when I was attending Boston University, I'd come home a couple of times a week to check in, to chat. I've never left the Boston area, and a big part of that is because of my mom. Because of how important she has always been to me. Now, as she comes to the table and hands me my tea, she gives me a tired smile. I don't like it.

"Mom…" I trail off, letting that be enough. I place my palms around my cup, savoring the warmth, waiting for whatever it is she has to say.

She sits opposite me, her hands around her own mug. The silence expands between us, like something breathing. "This is hard," she finally says, quietly, and I think, *no*. No, no, *no*, damn it. I don't want to hear this. Whatever it is, I know I can't take it.

"Mom," I say again, and my voice wobbles.

"Oh, Rachel." She reaches over and squeezes my hand, her smile full of sympathy. "I haven't wanted to say anything because you have so much on your plate already."

No.

"But it's not fair to either of us, to keep it from you." She sighs, and it feels as if she's not going to say anything more.

"Keep what?" I finally manage, the words squeezed out of my too-tight throat, because I still don't want to know.

My mother sighs again, and the sound makes me think of someone laying a burden down. "I've been having some symptoms," she begins and already there is part of me that is jerking back, the chair screeching across the floor as I stand up and walk out of the room. I don't move, but that is what I want to do, what I am doing in my head. I can't take any more *symptoms.* "I went to the doctor," my mother continues steadily. "I had some tests done."

I know this story. I've been living and breathing this story for years. And I hate it. "And?" I manage, and to my surprise my voice sounds calm. Level.

"And I've been diagnosed with Parkinson's. They think I've had it for some time."

Neither of us speaks, and in the distance I hear the steady dripping of the kitchen faucet. A robin flits across the window, a flash of red and brown.

The silence continues on, like a thread being pulled. My mind is blank; it's as if what my mother said has just bounced off its hard walls. I can't take it in. Some part of my psyche won't let me.

"I'm so sorry, Rachel."

"You don't need to be sorry." The words come automatically.

"This is the last thing you need—"

"This is the last thing *you* need." I can't bear it, that my mother is thinking of me at a time like this, when her life has just been unbearably limited. "Parkinson's," I say, trying to remember what

I know about it. "But you don't have tremors…?" I look at her hand as if I expect it to shake.

"I do sometimes, and that's only one symptom. The others…" She sighs and shrugs. "Lack of balance, slowed movement. I didn't even realize it at first. I just wondered why everything was taking such a long time." She gives me a wry smile. "But then my writing was affected, and my speech."

"Your *speech*…" Why have I not noticed?

"It takes more concentration," my mother says. "I've been trying to hide it from you, Rachel, so don't beat yourself up for not seeing the signs."

"How long have you known?"

"I started having tests back in April. The diagnosis came a few weeks ago."

I scan her face, flinching inwardly at the sorrow in her eyes. Is it my imagination, or does she look older now than she did even a few minutes ago? Her hair seems whiter, the wrinkles on her face carved deeper. I can't bear it. I can't bear any of it.

"What does it mean?" I ask, even though I don't want to. "People can… they can live with Parkinson's for a long time."

"Yes, they can. With the right medication, symptoms can be lessened or delayed. People have lived with Parkinson's for decades." Something in me relaxes a little at that, even though I still feel scared. It's not going to be like it has been with Emily. "But it is a degenerative condition," my mother informs me gently. "It only gets worse." Which is like Emily. I can't stand the thought of the two most important people in my life both inexorably declining.

"Still," I say. "You could be okay for years."

"Yes." There is a note in my mom's voice that I recognise; she is shielding me. She's done it often, especially since Emily got sick.

"What is it?" I ask. "What are you not telling me, Mom?"

She shakes her head as she takes a sip of tea. "It's just, already I don't feel like myself. I've lost something. That's why I went to the doctor in the first place."

"But…" How could I have missed this? How could I have been so *blind*? "You've seemed like yourself to me." And yet, even as I say the words, I think… *has she*? The ruffled hair a few weeks ago… it seemed like nothing at the time, yet other memories float through my mind, snatches of conversations, moments in time. When I stopped by and my mother had forgotten that I was coming. The shopping list she'd left on the counter, with the writing looking more like a child's than my mother's usual copperplate script. The teapot she'd asked me to carry, when she was the one who always brought it to the table.

And I'd dismissed it all, I hadn't even let it register, because I was hiding too. I was protecting myself, knowing I couldn't cope with the information, the possibility that something else was wrong. Yet here we are, and there is no going back. There never is.

"So what happens now?" I make myself ask. "You go on medication that helps…"

"Yes, there are some things," my mother agrees. "Still no cure, though."

No. No cure. I am silent, as realization filters through me. My mother is going to go through the same experience Emily already has, albeit in a different way. She is going to lose her faculties. Maybe not for years, decades even, but eventually she is going to become entirely dependent on other people, on me. She is going to decline and die.

"I've been prescribed something," my mother says after a moment. "Levodopa. It helps with some of the physical symptoms—the tremors, the slowness, at least at the beginning."

"So you're still in the early stages." That, at least, is some tiny glimmer of hope in all this suffocating darkness.

"Possibly. It's hard for them to know."

"But you're…" I gesture to her, her hands resting on the tabletop, without a tremor. "You're *fine*.…"

"It isn't like that, Rachel." My mother's voice is quiet, a gentle reprimand. I need to stop denying what she's told me, finding ways out when there aren't anyway.

A sudden rage swells in me, like a tsunami building force and power. This is so *unfair*. First Emily, now my mother. I don't *have* anyone else to lose. Not anymore. But I can't say any of that to my mom; I can't make this about me.

"I know," I tell her heavily. "I know."

She reaches over and places her hand on mine, and that's when I feel a tremor, as faint as one of Emily's squeezes. "Rachel," she says, almost sounding severe, "I don't want you to worry."

"Of course I'm going to worry—"

"No." She speaks firmly. "I won't let you take on my care as well as Emily's." Something I hadn't even thought about yet; I haven't even begun to think about what this all means, how the landscape of my life, along with my mother's, has changed irrevocably, become even more cratered and desolate. "Look, this might not happen for years and years, and I hope that is the case, but I've arranged to go into a nursing home when… when it's time."

I blanch. "Let's not think about that yet, please, Mom…"

"We don't need to think about it, because it's sorted," my mother says briskly. "I'd rather have it all arranged, so you're not burdened."

"I don't mind—"

"You have enough to do." And even though I know she's only being kind and considerate, it hurts a little. It feels as if she is blocking me out from an important and intimate part of her life. "Also, Rachel." Her voice gentles, and I tense. *What now?* "I want you… if you can… I want you to try living life again."

What? "What is that supposed to mean, Mom?" The words come out in a rasp of angry hurt.

"For the last two years you've lived and breathed the hospital. There's been no time or space for anything else, and I understand that, Rachel. I've supported you in it, because it felt necessary and right. But Emily isn't… she isn't getting better, and you need to…" She pauses, biting her lip, her forehead creased with concern. "Not move on exactly, but—"

"I'm not *moving on*." I can't believe she is saying this. Thinking it, even. She never has before.

"I know you're not. I don't mean that. I'm just asking you to get a little bit of your life back. Maybe spend only *half* the day at the hospital. Reconnect with friends. Exercise. Eat healthily, instead of whatever you can grab on the go. Work part-time… see a counselor, perhaps, to help you process everything that has happened."

It's nothing I haven't thought of myself, in a vague way, when I'm feeling weak, but I resent it coming from my mother, who has been my biggest supporter, who has absolutely understood why I've spent every day at the hospital, with Emily. "I don't want to do that," I say flatly. *Any* of that.

My mother leans forward, urgent now. "Rachel, I don't want to leave you without any support, any friends, any *life*. Please, for me, do this. Do something. It doesn't have to be big. Just… something."

For a second, I see the bleak picture she is painting—the barren landscape of my life, without my mother in it to offer a bit of comfort and companionship. With nothing but days at the hospital, nights alone, on and on and on. Is that all that's left—for me, for Emily? *And for how long?*

"You know I'm looking into some experimental treatment," I say, and my mother nods slowly.

"Yes, but you said James won't agree."

"I haven't given up," I say stubbornly. "I'm going to talk to James again." I think of Eva.

My mother frowns. "But taking Emily to Italy for this treatment… it would have its own difficulties."

"Yes, but I can handle them." Although I haven't even thought about them properly yet—the travel, staying in Italy, arranging everything. I haven't got that far, because there hasn't seemed to be much point, with James in the way. But now, more than ever, I need to find a way forward for Emily. For me. Because one day Emily might be all that I have left.

I am still thinking about how to talk to James again when I drive home through the dark and park in front of my house. As always, I check Andrew and Jake's side, to see if they're home, even though I've only seen them in hurried passing since I had dinner there a couple of weeks ago.

The lights in the living room are on, the curtains drawn, making it look cozy. I get out of my car and walk into my own empty house.

I am just heating up some pot noodles when, to my surprise, I hear a determined rapping on the door; three short, sharp knocks, made by a person with intent.

The microwave pings and I take out the plastic cup with its lurid yellow liquid and stringy noodles, leaving it on the counter before I hurry to the door. Maybe it's Andrew, and he saw me coming home. I don't know whether I want it to be him or not. I have a horrible feeling I might start to cry if anyone asks how I am.

But when I see the figure behind the frosted glass, I can tell it's not him, it's a woman, and I try not to feel disappointed.

Then I open the door, and my mouth drops open, because it's Eva.

CHAPTER FOURTEEN

EVA

I shouldn't be here. Even now my heart is racing and my palms are damp, and I feel as shocked as Rachel looks, even though I'm the one who drove here, who knocked.

"Eva…" she says faintly.

I swallow. "May I come in?"

For a second she looks reluctant, and then silently she steps aside.

It was easy to find her address; James has a little leather book of all his work and social addresses, kept by the kitchen phone. It was no more than a fifteen-minute drive from home to here, yet it feels like so much more. By coming here, I am stepping across a chasm I created, one that will only grow wider by my actions now.

"I hope I'm not interrupting anything," I say, pointlessly, because it's obvious that I'm not.

"No. I was just grabbing something to eat." Self-conscious now, she moves into the little kitchen in the back of the house and grabs a cup of noodles.

I look around the place, trying not to let it show in my face how depressing it all is. Bland, beige furniture that looks unloved and unlived in—a futon-like sofa, a medium-sized TV, a coffee table of fake wood. The living room doesn't hold a single other thing—no books, no photos, no vases of flowers or little knick-knacks that show a life that has been enjoyed rather than endured.

The kitchen is the same—white units, fake granite worktop, soulless. The only thing in it is a stack of unopened mail, mostly leaflets and junk.

"Did you want something?" Rachel asks, politely, and I realize she has no idea why I'm here. How could she? When we last spoke, I was reluctant at best.

"Yes, in a manner of speaking," I say. I sound nervous, because I am, and I'm not even sure why. Am I afraid Rachel will scoff at me—or that she'll agree? "I spoke to James."

She pauses mid-noodle, giving me a searching look. "When?"

"A few weeks ago."

A resigned shrug. "So it didn't make a difference."

"No. I'm sorry. He feels… quite strongly about it. Emily's treatment, I mean."

Her face twists and then she irons out her expression, like a hand smoothing out a crumpled piece of paper; the lines are still there. "So do I."

"To be fair to James," I say, my voice wavering a little, "he isn't trying to be callous or unkind. He believes not allowing Emily to have this treatment is the best thing for her. I know he does."

"And you came here to tell me that?" There is an edge to her voice, which I understand.

"No, no, I wouldn't… That's not why I'm here." I can't believe how nervous I am. I feel like pacing, but I stand still, smoothing my hands down the sides of my skirt. I'm still in my business clothes, and I wish I'd changed into something more comfortable. I already feel constricted enough.

"Why are you here then, Eva?" Rachel asks, her tone bordering on unfriendly.

"I… I want to help you."

"*Help* me?"

"I can't stop thinking about Emily," I blurt. "About this treatment. I've been wondering if there is something I could do…"

Rachel stares at me. "You've done enough. Thank you for trying. I really do appreciate that." She sounds less hostile now, and more resigned.

"But it doesn't have to end here, Rachel."

She sighs heavily as she half collapses into the sofa, still holding her wretched little cup of fluorescent noodles as she tucks her legs up and twirls her fork. "Look, I know you mean well, so thank you for that. Really. But if I can't get James to agree, there's not much more I can do. I wish there was. I've thought about it so much. I've wanted..." She lets out a long, low breath. "I even spoke to a lawyer and I don't think I can go down that route. All the money, publicity, the acrimony... none of it would benefit Emily, and I'd be spending all my energy and emotion and time on something other than her, and that's not a sacrifice I'm prepared to make." She gives me a smile that is fragile and brave and just about breaks my heart. "I've been reading a lot about music therapy with patients like Emily. How familiar music can access a certain part of their brain... I just hope Emily still likes Baby Einstein." Her smile wobbles and slides off her face.

"But what if she could still have the treatment?" I ask. The words feel loaded, a grenade I am casually tossing in my hand like a tennis ball. "What if it could still happen?"

Rachel stares at me, baffled, wary. "What do you mean?"

"Will you tell me about the treatment? I mean, what it entails exactly?"

She still looks confused, and as if she wants to refuse, because really, what am I doing here? Rachel doesn't know. I'm not sure I do. *This isn't my business.* How many times have I felt that? Been told it?

And yet somehow it still is.

"I told you about it," she says finally. "It's stimulation of the vagus nerve, with electrodes. Ideally, Emily would have the stimulation for thirty days, while the doctor—Dr. Rossi—closely monitored the results."

"And this… James said it was in Italy?"

Rachel gives me a defiant look. "Yes. But Dr. Rossi is willing to waive his usual consultancy fee… there would be no cost for the treatment."

"James said it would cost fifty thousand dollars for Emily to be there for one week."

She frowns, resentment flashing in her eyes. "That is one estimate, and I think it's a bit high. But yes, it would be expensive. The specialist travel is a big part of it, as well as the ongoing care Emily would need while in Italy… it would be a lot. I'm not pretending it wouldn't."

"So how were you thinking to pay for it?" I try to speak reasonably and not as if I am trying to catch her out, because I'm not. I just need to know.

Rachel slowly stirs her noodles, although she's barely eaten any since I came into her house. "I have some savings. Some inheritance from my mother. I'm not saying it would be easy, but…" She trails off, before she shakes her head, impatient now. "What exactly is the point of all this, Eva?"

"I want to help you." I blurt the words, and Rachel cocks an eyebrow, clearly and utterly skeptical. As I would be, if I were in her situation.

If someone had offered to help me…

"Please," I finish.

"*Please?*" Her voice rises incredulously. "Please, what? Please make you feel better, so you can be happy about your good deed for the day? You think you're losing sleep over this? You think it matters to you?" Her words ring out, each one an accusation. "What even *is* this?"

Disgusted, shaking her head, she rises from the sofa and goes into the kitchen, hurling the pot of noodles into the trash can. Then she turns to me, hands on her hips, her eyes narrowed.

"I don't know why you're here, and I'm trying to see the positive side, knowing you mean well, but…" She shakes her head again, slowly this time, back and forth, back and forth. "I really don't understand why you're here."

"There are other options. Options I can help you with."

Rachel stares at me, nonplussed. "I don't know what you mean."

I keep her gaze, everything in me straining, racing. "Ways to get James on board. To raise the money."

"What are you talking about?"

I take a deep breath. *Why am I doing this?*

Because I have to.

"Have you heard of crowdfunding?"

"You mean asking for money online?" Her tone is slightly derisive.

"Sharing your story, Emily's story, to people who are interested and want to support you," I correct swiftly. I'm not in marketing for nothing. "People who can help, who want to help, if they just knew how."

Rachel looks as skeptical as she ever did; I haven't changed her mind at all. "So that's your plan? I put up one of those websites telling random strangers about Emily, giving them my sob story, and then ask them to pay for me to take her to Italy?"

"You raise awareness," I say. "Not only would it help Emily, but it would benefit the research on her condition, as well as any potential treatment. You wouldn't be doing it just for Emily; you'd be doing it for any child who suffers the way she has. For the doctors who can't get funding for their research, because it's too new or too weird or people think they don't care about kids in states of unresponsive wakefulness. You can *make* them care. You put a face to a condition and it changes everything. It humanizes it. It makes people want to help." Although raising awareness didn't always help when it came to buying makeup. Still, this is different. This actually matters.

Rachel walks back to the sofa and slowly lowers herself onto it. There is a deep crinkle in the middle of her forehead, a hard set to her lips. I wait.

"I don't know," she says slowly, after a long, tense beat of silence. "I've never thought of doing something like that before. Perhaps I should have, but…" She shakes her head. "I just didn't."

"This is what I do for a living, Rachel. I can help with this."

"You crowdfund for a living?" She looks bemused.

"I'm in marketing, digital marketing in particular. I try to get things to go viral. I use the algorithms, the keywords, the trends, to raise awareness, to garner interest. It's amazing what you can do online."

"I don't want Emily to become some sort of poster child." Rachel shakes her head again, harder this time. "I've seen those articles in the paper or the tabloid stories online. Desperate people with their ill child, asking for money, sharing their sob story… it's awful. They open themselves up to all kinds of criticism and even hate. The comments… I couldn't do that. I couldn't put myself through that, or James." She shoots me a searching, almost accusing look. "What about James, anyway? He would never agree to this, you know. You *must* know."

"He doesn't have to agree." I can hardly believe I'm saying the words.

"He would hate it, Eva." Another look. "And if he found out you were behind it too? How do you think he would take that?"

"He'd feel betrayed," I say quietly. "He… he doesn't like me asking about you or Emily. He's compartmentalized his life. Us."

She stares at me for a moment. "Yes," she says finally. "I can see that. James has always seen things in black and white." She shakes her head slowly. "And yet, knowing that, you're still here."

"Yes. This… this is important to me, Rachel." The words feel jagged in my throat. "But, trust me, I don't want to hurt James."

"So how would you propose not to? Because, contrary to what you might think, I don't want him to be hurt, either. I know he believes what he says. I know he loves Emily." Her voice thickens. "We just have different ideas of what that looks like."

I nod, remembering. "He said virtually the same thing to me."

"So." She draws a clogged breath. "How on earth could this work?"

"James wouldn't have to be referenced in whatever you decide to put online," I say carefully. I've thought about this, but it still feels loaded. Dangerous. "Even if he did agree, you'd still probably need to raise some amount of money, wouldn't you?"

"Yes, I suppose… but do you really think having Emily's story splashed about on the internet will make James change his mind?" She releases a breath. "It might just make him dig in all the more."

"Attention might exert some… pressure," I say.

"That sounds manipulative."

"All marketing is manipulative, to a degree. We're appealing to people's emotions, to their better selves. But, in essence, we're playing them." It sounds stark, but it's the reality, at its base. "But you don't have to think of this about just you getting what you want. It's about helping others—helping people who want to help, as well as helping people like the doctor in Italy who wants to make a difference."

Her mouth twitches and I realize she is smiling; it's the first time I've seen her do it, and even that little quirk of her lips transforms and lightens her face. It makes me realize how she might have been, before Emily got sick. I wonder if, in another reality, we might have been friends. "You really can spin things, can't you?" she says.

I smile back, the stretching of my lips like exercising an old muscle. "It's my job."

"You're good at it."

"Thank you."

A long silence follows, one that expands and fills the room. Are we actually getting along? It's so unexpected, but it feels good. I realize I don't just feel sorry for Rachel; I *like* her. At least, I think I could.

"I just don't know," she says finally. "I just don't know. I hate the thought of Emily being out there, for public consumption. You read comments online… they can be so awful. I really don't think I could handle that, and I know James would hate it. He would never forgive me, for going public with our lives. With Emily." She gives me a piercing look. "He might never forgive you."

My stomach churns and I taste acid in my mouth. *Why am I here? What am I doing?*

"It could all be very sensitively done," I say after a moment. The words taste metallic in my mouth. "And nothing would be posted that you didn't sign off on, a hundred percent. Plus, it can all be taken down in the blink of an eye if you change your mind."

"But you must know that's not true, if you're in marketing. If it's posted on the internet, it's on there forever. Screenshots, forwarded emails… you can't get rid of it."

I incline my head. "That's true."

"And people can be so cruel…" Rachel takes a shaky breath. "I really don't know. And I don't understand why you're doing this. Why do you care so much, Eva? I mean, I know the whole thing is sad to the average bystander, but… Emily isn't your child." She doesn't say this nastily, just a gentle statement of fact. "Why do you care?"

The question hangs in the air, suspended, weightless. I think of how I could answer, the story I could tell, my own little tale of sorrow and grief, but I don't, because this is Rachel's story, and in any case, I don't want to reveal mine. "I can't stop thinking about Emily," I say, which is true. "And I want to help her. At least, I want to try. If you want me to." Rachel still doesn't look convinced, and how can I blame her? I don't believe myself. "This means a lot to me, Rachel. I don't expect you to understand that, but it does. It really does." And that is all I can say about that.

I glance at my watch; it's after eight and James will be coming home soon. I should be there. I certainly shouldn't be here. Yet I don't want to leave it like this.

"I'll think about it," Rachel says at last. "Although I'm not sure how—even if we can raise the money and awareness—doing this would get James to agree."

"He'll see how strongly you feel about it. How other people care. He'll be given another perspective." Although, like Rachel said, all that might just make him dig in deeper. Still, it's a risk I think is worth taking.

"All right." She nods slowly. "I'll think about it. Why don't you give me your phone number so we can be in touch?"

"Okay." We spend a few minutes inputting each other's details into our phones, it feels odd, like we're planning for a date. When we're finished, I rise to go. "Thanks for listening to me, anyway," I say as I head for the door.

"No, I should be the one thanking you, Eva." Rachel smiles tiredly. "I'm sorry if I seemed… suspicious. Hostile. I don't… it's just that I didn't expect this."

"I understand." I didn't expect this, either, even though I was the one who planned it. Who has been thinking about it pretty much nonstop for the last few weeks, even though I haven't wanted to. It still feels like a surprise, to both of us.

"And I'm sorry if I seem… like I don't care enough." Rachel's eyes fill with tears and she swallows hard. "As if I wouldn't do everything I could for Emily, even this. I would, I always would, but…" She makes a gulping sort of sound. "Today's been a hard day. My mother… she's not well." She sniffs. "Not that that… I just… please don't think I'm… I'm a bad mother."

I stare at her, appalled. "Rachel, I couldn't think anything *less*." She gives a watery smile and sniffs. "I think you're amazing," I tell her sincerely. "I've never doubted that for a single second."

"Really?" She looks at me almost hungrily, and I wonder if there is anyone left in her life who can tell her these things.

"Of course I do. You've given your life over to take care of Emily. You've never stopped fighting for her. I admire that. It's part of the reason why I want to help."

Rachel brushes at her eyes. "Thank you," she whispers, and suddenly I feel guilty. Who am I, to push her into anything?

"Look," I say in a rush, "please don't feel any pressure to take me up on this. This is your call, completely. Your decision, not mine. Not mine at all. And it sounds like you have a lot going on with your mother anyway…"

"She has Parkinson's." Rachel gulps. "I just found out."

"I'm so sorry." I wish I had more words. "I really am. But in terms of this… Emily… I just… I just wanted to offer. I just wanted you to know this is an option."

She sniffs again and nods. "Thank you."

There doesn't seem to be anything more to say, and so I murmur goodbye and then I leave.

Outside, the night is soft and dark. It's almost June, the start of summer, the air full of the incessant whine and chirp of cicadas. An easy time of year, when you slip from work early, kick off your shoes, and relax. Bare feet in soft grass, fruity cocktails on a deck, burgers smoking on a grill. That's what this time of year should be about, what it has been before.

I slide into my car and rest my hands on the wheel, my heart flip-flopping in my chest, something treacherous and fearful snaking along my skin.

I try to untangle my feelings—do I want Rachel to agree? Or would I rather she refused? I really don't know. Surely now I can say I've done my duty. I can walk away with a clear conscience, secure in the knowledge that I've done everything I possibly can, and it really, *really* does not concern me any longer. I can finally be free.

Except I know that's not how it's going to work. And as I drive back to the apartment in Beacon Hill and James waiting for me, I know I will have to lie to him about where I've been. And what should be, in an uncomplicated world, a way of working together for an innocent child, is starting to feel difficult and dangerous and even wrong.

Yet I know I'm not going to back out now.

I don't back out, and I don't tell James what I'm doing, as I kiss him hello and say I was with Naomi. I don't tell him as we watch Netflix curled up together on the sofa, joking about the corny thriller we've chosen to watch, or when we've gone to bed, snuggled together, his arm wrapped around my waist.

I say nothing of it the next day, as he pours me coffee in the kitchen, or when I kiss him goodbye before going to work. And I say nothing of the text that makes my phone buzz that evening, as we stand in the kitchen, waiting for the microwave to ding with our warmed-up curry.

James raises his eyebrows in silent query as I glance at my phone and then put it back face down on the counter, giving him a smiling shrug. I'm not lying. Not precisely.

Because the text was from Rachel, and it contained only three words.

I'll do it.

CHAPTER FIFTEEN

RACHEL

That night, after Eva leaves, I don't sleep. When the door first closed behind her, I simply sat and stared. My mind was spinning, spinning, a thousand thoughts dancing through it, yet I couldn't hold on to a single one.

Could this really… Should I even… Why had she?

I paced the downstairs for a while—to the back door, turn around, past the sofa, to the front window, and again. It felt like a march, as if I were going somewhere with purpose, and yet still I couldn't think.

At one point, I heard a creak from behind the adjoining wall—Andrew in his kitchen, moving around like me. Could he hear my methodical treads? What did he think I was doing?

What *was* I doing?

Eventually I got on my laptop and found my way to a crowdfunding site, this one particular to ill children. I've stayed away from these over the last few years; they're far too sad. Now I steel myself as I read page after page of sad stories—Kaycee's Story, Jackson's Story, Chloe's Story. All children with terrible diseases, usually cancer. Often they were thin and bald, smiling bravely, breaking my heart, with medical bracelets encircling birdlike wrists, tubes snaking away in the background, scrawny collarbones protruding from those awful, shapeless hospital gowns.

Kaycee has been so brave... Jackson has touched the lives of everyone he has met... Chloe has smiled through all the treatment—all the needles, all the noise, everything! We're so proud.

At some point, I pushed my laptop away. I felt a flash of envy, which was ridiculous yet real. These children were total troopers, little sick superstars. And while I wanted to believe Emily was too, she wasn't like this. She wasn't being brave, at least not so anyone, even I, could see. And it felt unfair, that those parents of cancer kids still had their children, in a way that I did not. They could talk to them, and hug them, and their children would hug them back, wrapping their arms around their necks, cheeks pressed to cheeks, telling them they loved them...

How wrong was it? To find myself *wishing* Emily had cancer? Anything but this. *Anything.*

And yet what if Dr. Rossi's treatment gave me a little bit of that? *Emily's been so brave...*

I could see myself saying it. Typing it. Experiencing it—seeing Emily's eyes open, her lips curving in a precious, lopsided smile. Just that would be enough. Yet I still wasn't sure I was ready to do this.

At some point, I took myself off to bed, staring gritty-eyed at the ceiling as the hours marched past and I waited till morning. I thought about all the what-if possibilities of the future, the wonderful along with the horrendous. And then, as my mind grew fuzzy yet my eyes still couldn't close, I let myself drift back, to the past.

Emily's first birthday. Her sixth was next week, a day that would be painful yet necessary to celebrate. Back when she turned one, my mom had come over, and James' parents; his mother had been ill but smiling, his father jovial yet also a bit distant. A few friends had come along too—Denise and Sarah, as well as Bryce, a friend of James' from college.

I'd chosen a duck theme, because Emily had always loved feeding the ducks at Bulloughs Pond, and so there was a duck topper on the duck-shaped cake, hook-a-duck in a paddling pool on the deck, duck party favors, and a big yellow helium duck balloon.

In retrospect, it was all a bit much, but I'd been so excited to celebrate Emily's birthday. To celebrate Emily. And she'd loved it all, even if she couldn't yet speak—she'd reached for the duck balloon, arms outstretched, a huge grin splitting her face. She'd played hook-a-duck, as we'd gently and lovingly guided her—so obvious the parents of only one child, the absolute center of our existence—and she'd tossed the pole aside and reached into the water with both hands, crowing triumphantly when she'd managed to grab hold onto one of the rubber ducks. Everyone had laughed, and James and I had exchanged smiling looks—*Isn't she funny? Isn't she amazing?*

Of course, I'm not so forgetful or deluded to think every memory is rose-tinted. There were some shadows to that day— James' mother coughing, her thin frame wracked to pieces, a cancer diagnosis just weeks away, and then his father taking a call in another room and disappearing for an hour. Later, we found out he'd been having an affair; he ended up marrying the woman on the phone, at least we assumed that's who it was—Laura Lee, a frosted blond with steely eyes and a Southern accent like syrup.

Still, overall, it was a good day. A happy day. At the end of it, I held Emily heavy and sleepy in my arms, her thumb tucked in her mouth, her head on my shoulder, and felt that rush of gratitude no one feels often enough. *I really am so blessed.*

I want that again, in some small way. *But is this the way to get it?*

I fall asleep sometime after six in the morning, and waken groggy and heavy-eyed at quarter past eight. I'm already late for Emily.

I scramble out of bed, clumsy with fatigue, and shower and dress in a matter of minutes. I forgo food and grab my bag, heading outside by half past, breathless with exertion.

Andrew is coming out of his door at the same time, and he smiles at me. "Hey, long time, no see."

"Yes." I give him a harried, fleeting smile as I fumble with my keys at the door.

"How have you been?"

"Oh." I wave a hand. "Fine." I feel guilty, although I'm not sure why. I haven't been avoiding him, at least not exactly. But I haven't been seeking him out, either. "What about you? Are you settled in?"

"Getting there."

I've locked my door, and I turn to him with what I hope is an it's-been-nice-to-see-you kind of smile. In other words, goodbye.

Then Andrew surprises me by saying, "Are you in a rush? Would you like to get a coffee?"

I blink at him, too startled by the invitation to speak. Doesn't he see—can't he tell—that I'm in a rush? Everything about me says *must be going now*, surely.

And yet… why am I rushing?

Emily will still be there in an hour. Emily will be there forever. *Unless…*

I jangle my keys uncertainly. "I'm not in a rush," I say after a moment. "Not exactly. But don't you have to get to work?"

He shakes his head. "I'm working from home today. Jake's at playgroup till one, and I was just about to head to Stacks to set up a mobile office."

"I love Stacks," I say before I can think better of it. "Much better than Starbucks." Stacks is an artisan espresso bar and community space in Newton Highlands with a welcoming atmosphere and great coffee. I haven't been there in ages.

"Join me?" Andrew asks, lifting one eyebrow, a hint of uncertainty in his voice, as if he suspects I'll say no. "I'll need to start work, so it won't take up your whole morning."

"All right." I am surprised by the words, by myself. When do I do this? *What about Emily?*

And yet the thought of doing something different, even just the once, of sipping excellent coffee and feeling the sunshine on my face, is too much to resist. Plus I need the caffeine.

I'll be at the hospital by nine-thirty, I tell myself. At the latest.

Andrew and I drive separately to Stacks, finding parking spaces on the street and then meeting inside the little café, where the smell of roasting beans provides a welcoming aroma. I order a tear drop, vanilla and half and half, mixed together and layered with espresso, and Andrew has a latte.

Within a few minutes, we're sitting at a table in the window on a beautiful summer's day, and I am feeling the awkwardness. I'm not sure what to say to him, so I take a sip of my drink.

"I'm sorry if I'm being too nosy," Andrew says after a moment, "but what have you been up to? I see you leave every day pretty early in the morning, and you don't come home until after seven. And you told me you were taking time off work…" His forehead crinkles as he shakes his head. "Sorry, I am being nosy. I just wondered."

Of course he did. "I go to the hospital." I practically blurt the words, and Andrew looks half taken aback, half horrified, clearly thinking he's been socially clumsy.

"Oh, I'm sorry, you don't have to say…"

"I'm visiting my daughter." It is a relief to say it. As much as I dread having to go through the halting, painful explanation of the where and why of my life, it never sat comfortably with me, not to tell Andrew about Emily. To pretend she doesn't exist, even for a few moments.

"Your daughter? Oh, I thought…"

"I have a daughter." I speak firmly now. "Her name is Emily. She's six next week. She's in the… the palliative care unit at Boston Children's Hospital."

Andrew's face crumples, his shoulders slumping, the universal gesture of compassion. "Oh, Rachel…"

"But she's not dying," I say.

Andrew looks understandably confused, and so I explain about her symptoms, her lack of diagnosis, her current condition. I've done this so much that it sounds like a soulless sales patter, and yet every detail rips through me, every time. It never stops hurting.

"Rachel, I… I don't know what to say. I'm so sorry…" He's looking like a landed fish, mouth open and closing, and I'm used to it. I'm so used to it.

"Thank you," I say. "It's been hard."

"I can't even imagine…"

"No, you can't," I agree frankly. Andrew looks a little surprised by my bluntness, although, of course, he doesn't disagree. "But I couldn't either, before this all happened. And I wouldn't have wanted to."

"No." His voice is quiet. "I don't suppose anyone would."

I take a sip of my coffee, savoring the vanilla-flavored sweetness, letting him absorb everything I've said. I know it takes a while. And I hope this won't make things stilted and awkward between us, as it has for so many other people, even those I called my friends, Emily being laboriously acknowledged in every single conversation. *I know I shouldn't complain… you've got so much more to deal with…* on and on and on. It annoyed me when they said it, when they so clearly felt they had to, and yet it would have been worse if they hadn't.

"Actually," I say after the silence has lengthened, "I'm looking into an experimental treatment for her."

"You are?"

"Yes…" And so I talk some more, about the nerve stimulation, and then about Eva's idea for crowdfunding. "We're not friends or anything, and I don't know why she's putting herself out there, considering my ex-husband's position, but she is, and I'm seriously thinking about taking her up on her offer."

"Yes, I can see that," Andrew says. "I mean, why wouldn't you?"

For some reason, his words strike me; they clang through me like a bell, the reverberations rippling. *Why wouldn't you?* It sounds so obvious, so elemental.

Why wouldn't I?

"I'm worried about the publicity," I say slowly. "You know how things can go crazy so quickly online… I'd hate to be caught up in that, and I know my ex-husband would, too."

"Yes," Andrew agreed, "but very few things go viral, in the grand scheme of the internet. I mean, think about how many things are posted or tweeted or whatever every day. Thousands. Millions."

"Yes…"

"And why should it go viral? I mean, it's not particularly controversial, is it?" He gives me a sad smile with a touch of whimsy. "An ill little girl seeking treatment?"

"It's not that." I realize I haven't explained everything. "My ex-husband won't agree to the treatment."

Andrew is silent for a moment. "Would he stand in your way?" he asks finally. "If it got to a point where it was truly feasible financially?"

My heart tumbles in my chest. I feel as if I'm on my tiptoes, arms outstretched. Ready to fly… or fall. "I don't know," I admit. "I really don't know how he'd take any of it. He won't talk to me about it at all. I know he finds it painful, but… I want to have a conversation."

Andrew takes a sip of his latte. "Putting up a page on a crowdfunding site doesn't have to be this enormous deal. In most cases, it wouldn't be. But it could be a start, an experiment, to see how it goes. See how you feel about it." He pauses. "If you like, I could design a logo for you, for the page." His eyebrows lift. "Only if you wanted, of course. Free of charge."

"Thank you." I am touched by his offer, but I am also overwhelmed. This is suddenly starting to feel real, as if it might actually happen, and I don't know how I feel about that.

Andrew must see something of that in my face, for he reaches over and touches my hand lightly. "I don't mean to pressure you into anything. This has got to be your decision entirely, Rachel. I could understand why you would decide either way."

I nod. Gulp a little. "If it was Jake," I ask, feeling as if we've waded into deep, deep waters over a single coffee, "would you do it? Not just the crowdfunding thing… but the treatment?"

Andrew's forehead crinkles as he gives my question his full consideration. "Yes, I would," he says finally. "I think I'd do anything for Jake. Anything at all." I nod, and he gives me an apologetic grimace. "Sorry. I didn't mean that to sound…"

"It's okay."

"I'm not in your situation, Rachel. It's easy to make decisions from the outside. Much, much harder from where you are, actually experiencing it."

"Yes." I nod again, but I am becoming more resolved by the second. *Why wouldn't you? Anything at all.* "Thank you, Andrew," I say, and I smile, and when he smiles back, I feel like we've navigated that awful, awkward abyss that so often opens up when I've told people about Emily, and maybe, just maybe, we've made it to the other side. Maybe I can call Andrew my friend, something I haven't really felt I've had in a long while. "You've been really kind. So often people don't know what to say to me when I tell them about Emily, and so I end up saying nothing at all."

He gives a grimacing nod. "I'm not trying to compare my situation to yours, not remotely, but I think I understand a little. When Christina left… no one knew what to say. I mean, it was so sudden, and it was so obviously not your usual trying-to-be-amicable split…" He shrugs. "People started avoiding me rather than speak to me. They didn't mean to, I know that. They weren't trying to be cruel. It was just… easier."

"Yes." I am nodding, gratified that he gets it, in his own way. "Yes, that's exactly how it is."

"That was the big reason we left Worcester. A clean slate, you know? A place where no one knew our story." He let out a gentle huff of laughter. "And then I go and tell you, anyway, so…"

"It's hard not to tell, though, isn't it? It's so much a part of who you are. You feel as if you're lying if you don't say anything."

"Yes." He nods, as I am nodding, our gazes locked, some deeper level of understanding connecting us now, binding us together. "Yes, exactly."

It is so strange, this feeling of being understood and accepted, that it makes me nervous. I glance at my watch, and then Andrew makes a big show of checking his phone, going through his messages.

"I should let you get to work," I say, the obvious get-out.

"Yeah, I really should get some stuff done." He smiles at me, standing as I do. "Thanks for coming out for a coffee. And thank you… for telling me about Emily."

Suddenly my throat is tight, even though I've been feeling, if not happy, then something like it. "You're welcome," I manage.

"Let me know what you decide to do. I mean it, about the logo."

Twenty minutes later, I am hurrying down the corridor of the palliative care unit; it is almost eleven. Sheila, one of the nurses I have to come to know, raises her eyebrows as I make for Emily's room, walking quickly.

"Busy morning?" she asks, and I try not to feel guilty. I've been here every single day, save for the Saturdays when James comes, and even then I usually manage a few hours either before or after.

"Yes, a bit," I say, and I duck into Emily's room, smiling at the sight of my girl, even though seeing her like this still breaks my heart. Her eyes are open, and hope and longing blaze through me as her gaze tracks me to the door.

"Hello, darling girl," I whisper. "It's Mommy."

One hand twitches against the bed sheet, and I come closer, sitting next to her bed.

"Emily? Em? It's Mommy." I'm not sure what I'm expecting; I've been here before, so many times. Still I take her other hand, the one that's not moving, and I thread my fingers through her smaller ones. "Have you been waiting for me, sweetie?" I ask, trying to keep my tone light even as my throat thickens. "Have you been wondering where I am?"

I feel the slightest of pressures on my fingers; was that Emily, or just my yearning imagination?

"Have you missed me, Emily?"

Her gaze, which has been staring straight ahead, moves slowly towards me. For a second, I feel pinned in place, terrified and hopeful in equal measure. *My daughter is looking at me.*

"Emily…" I breathe, but before I can say anything more, the moment passes, her gaze moves on, her fingers slacken in mine.

I lean back in my chair, longing for Emily to look at me again, to feel that faintest of connections, but nothing happens, and that's when I decide. The resolve that has been building ever since Eva knocked on my door explodes like a firework inside of me, and I know what I need to do.

CHAPTER SIXTEEN

EVA

The Saturday after Rachel texts me, I am on the doorstep of her house, my laptop under my arm, my heart beating hard. James left for the hospital half an hour ago. I feel, bizarrely, as if I am cheating on him.

"Thank you for coming." Rachel sounds oddly formal as she invites me in.

It's as bland and charmless as before, a place to sleep rather than a home. I wonder if that's intentional; if she doesn't want to make it a home as long as Emily isn't there. Sometimes it's easier to care less.

"Tea? Coffee?" Rachel asks as she rubs her hands down the front of her shorts. Her dark hair is pulled up into a haphazard topknot, and she's wearing a faded T-shirt and cut-offs, making her look younger than her forty-something years, despite the crow's feet I see by her eyes, the lines of worry rather than laughter that bracket her nose and mouth.

"Umm… coffee would be great. But only if you're making it."

"Sure, I'll have some, as well."

She goes to the kitchen, and after putting my laptop on the coffee table, I follow her. This is so very *odd*. Rachel has been part of my life for the last year, and yet I don't know her at all. And she doesn't know me. I don't know if we should try to get to know one another now, or just conduct the business we're both here for. I don't know what Rachel wants.

"I'm glad you decided to go ahead with this," I offer hesitantly and she shoots me an uncertain look from under dark brows.

"I still don't know why you're doing all this."

"I know."

She turns to me, leaning back against the counter, her arms folded, as we wait for the coffee to drip through. "So there *is* a reason. Something you haven't said."

"I told you, I can't stop thinking about Emily…"

She shakes her head. "A personal reason."

I am shaken and trying not to show it. "Can't someone do something good without having a personal reason?" I try to sound curious rather than defensive, and she shrugs.

"It's just a feeling I have. But if you don't want to tell me, you don't have to. God knows I don't like being asked questions; I'm not going to press you for information you don't want to give."

"Thank you," I say humbly, and she nods.

We lapse into silence, the only sound the drip and hiss of the coffee machine. Outside, the sunshine is burning off the morning clouds, although it has forecast rain this evening, perhaps one of those spectacular summer thunderstorms that lights up the night sky. I picture curling up with James later to watch the lightning fork the sky, his arm around my shoulders. I want that moment; I just need to get through today and I'll have it. I'm not going to think about what being here might mean to James, or for him and me. I can't go there in my mind, not yet.

Finally the coffee machine beeps, and Rachel pours us both large mugs. We take them into the living room and sit on the sofa side by side, because there is nowhere else to sit. This is starting to feel really weird now, and yet also surprisingly comfortable at the same time.

"So, how do we start?" Rachel asks. "I looked at some of the kind of pages you were talking about the other night, and some of them seem a bit… saccharine." She makes a face, half grimace, half apology. "Which sounds a bit mean, I know, considering, but…"

"I understand," I say as I put my coffee down and reach for my laptop. "We don't want to go for something schmaltzy and sentimental."

"Absolutely not." She shudders, or pretends to. "I'm not referring to her as my little angel, even if she is. That's just not me."

I smile, and Rachel's lips tremble as she smiles back. "Noted."

"Good."

After Rachel gives me the password for her Wi-Fi and I am on one of those pages, I see what she means. Some of them look a bit sentimental, as heart-rending as they are. The language is too flowery; the emotions too gushing, although it feels mean to think it. These are expressions of people's pain, personal and important. And Emily's page needs to reflect her, as well as Rachel.

As I click through the pages, I start to feel more in control, more prepared to handle this situation, with my computer open and my fingers on the keyboard, my mind starting to leapfrog through ideas. This is my world. "In any case," I say, "you can decide how to design the page, Rachel. You don't have to put in anything you don't want to. It can be as simple or as flowery as you want."

She sighs and takes a sip of her coffee. "I don't even know where to begin, which is a bit ridiculous, considering I am—at least, I used to be—an English teacher." I realize I didn't know that. "But this feels too personal. Too close. I don't have any perspective. I can't even think about what details to include. And I'm not sure I can write it, even if I did. I think that would just about…" Her lips tremble a little until she presses them into a line. "It wouldn't be good."

"I understand." I'd feel the same if I were in her position. Detailing all the milestones of grief and loss for any stranger to read? It would be like prodding exposed nerves, pain radiating out with every word you typed. "Would you like me to try to write something?" I ask, flinching inwardly at the presumption of the question. "And then you can edit it?"

Rachel doesn't answer for a moment, and I see the conflict of her emotions on her face. Neither of us can quite forget that I am her husband's second wife. That he left her and found me. That her child is gravely ill, not mine. I've never even *met* Emily. I barely know Rachel. And yet I'm going to try to tell her story?

"All right," she says finally, sounding a little reluctant. "We can give it a try."

I pause, my fingers poised as the enormity of what I am doing hits me all over again. How can I presume to tell Rachel's story? How can I dare? I shouldn't even be here.

It's been thirty-six hours since I started lying to James, deception by silence, and every one of those hours has eaten me up with guilt. I need to tell him what I'm doing. I need to explain why I'm doing it. I know that. I just haven't yet.

Cautiously I begin to type.

Emily Harris is almost six years old. Nearly three years ago, she began to develop symptoms no one—not her family and not even her doctors—could understand. Nothing helped, and her symptoms became worse and worse. Today she is in a state of unresponsive wakefulness—a step down from a coma—and we—her family—would do anything to help her, even just a little. Just to see her smile again, or open her eyes, would be the most amazing thing for us, as well for her.

There is a very new experimental treatment available in Italy. We are hoping to take her there, even though we know it is risky and it makes no promises. We believe it's still Emily's best chance at a little more of life, and we want—we need—to take it. For her sake, and for ours, because every child should be championed and fought for.

I pause, letting out a shaky breath, feeling emotional about what I've written, and yet without any real right to.

"What do you think…" I begin, turning to Rachel, only to see tears streaming down her cheeks. I am jolted, horrified that I've hurt her with some insensitivity I didn't even realize I had, and so I simply stare as she shakes her head, wiping her damp cheeks with her palms.

"Sorry… sorry," she mutters.

"No, I'm the one who is sorry. I didn't mean…"

She rises from the sofa, hurrying to the kitchen, where she rips off a sheet from a roll of paper towel and blows her nose. "Sorry, I really didn't expect to do that," she says when she has composed herself a bit. Her voice is still clogged, her eyes reddened. "I don't usually cry anymore, at least not in front of other people."

That simply spoken statement has tears rising to my eyes. How does she endure it, day after day? How does she go *on*? "I'm so sorry, Rachel. I didn't mean to upset you."

"You didn't." She lets out a ragged laugh. "It's just… what you wrote… it's the first time someone has expressed what I'm feeling, exactly. It's the first time someone has really *gotten* it. How did you do that? How do you know?"

I am humbled; I am also exposed. I don't know what to say, so I just look away.

"Sorry," Rachel says after a moment. She sounds more subdued. "That was actually meant to be a rhetorical question. You don't have to say anything."

"Sorry," I say, although I'm not sure what I'm apologizing for. Not telling her? Making her cry?

She lets out another raggedy laugh. "I didn't mean to fall to pieces on you. I know that's awkward."

"No, no." I turn back, ashamed that she might think that, when I'm the one who doesn't know how to respond, how to be. "It's fine. I mean… I understand why… I would if…" I can't seem to finish any of those sentences. "Do you want to edit it?"

"Maybe a little." She blows her nose again and then comes and rejoins me on the sofa.

With a questioning lift of her eyebrow, she reaches for my laptop, and I nod. She places it on her lap and I watch as she rereads what I've written and then makes a few small changes.

"Do you think it should really be 'we'? Isn't that implying James is on board?"

"Well, 'we' could be lots of people. Your parents, for example…" I trail off uncertainly.

"Yes, my mom." She nods, and then shoots me another searching look. "My dad died a long time ago."

"I'm sorry." What else can I say?

She chews her lip, scanning the page, and then she starts typing.

An hour later, we have a few paragraphs about Emily and the proposed treatment, as well as a template for the page that isn't, according to Rachel, "too corny". It's pale yellow, with a light blue ribbon framing it. Rachel tells me that her neighbor is going to make a logo to go with the page, and I assure her I can add it on at any time.

"So is that it?" she asks. "Do we publish it now?"

"It would be good to add a photo of Emily, if you didn't mind," I say. "But if you think it's too invasive…"

"No." She hesitates though, thinking it over. "That makes sense. Nothing recent, though. Not when she's been…"

"An older one would be fine, I'm sure."

Rachel nods and gets her laptop out. Soon she is flicking through a folder of photos; I don't know whether I should look or not. It feels too personal, too private, to look over her shoulder. Then she angles the laptop so I can have a better view of the screen, and I turn my attention to the photos flickering past.

Here is Emily. I've only seen the one photo of her on James' dresser, in black and white and artfully blurry, but now I see her in full color, at every age. As a baby, cradled in Rachel's proud arms, or draped over her shoulder, mouth open, a milk bubble frothing at her lips, fast asleep. A chubby six-month-old or so, giving the camera a gummy grin. Around a year, taking her first faltering steps. A lifetime, captured in moments that make me ache.

She's adorable, with her strawberry blond curls—a couple of shades lighter than James' hair—and her round cheeks and button nose. Her eyes are bright blue, brighter than James' gray-blue eyes and a far cry from Rachel's hazel ones. I can't believe she's lying in a hospital bed, unresponsive, barely breathing. I *can't*.

"Which one?" Rachel asks, and her voice is a bit unsteady. I wonder if she doesn't usually look at these photos. I know if I were her, I wouldn't. It would hurt too much.

"Maybe something more recent…? Around her third or fourth birthday?" I know from James that she started showing symptoms at three, but it didn't get truly serious until she was four.

"All right." Rachel nods. "Her birthday is actually next week, you know." Her lips tremble and she turns back to the laptop, frowning with concentration.

We flick through more images—Emily splashing in muddy puddles, going down a slide, opening a Christmas present, holding an Easter basket, licking batter off a spoon in the kitchen—and then finally come to one from her fourth birthday, just two years ago and yet a world away.

She is on the beach, the wind blowing her curls into a golden halo, her rosy cheeks speckled with sand. She is staring straight at the camera, her unabashed grin triumphant and full of joy. She is reveling in the moment, in life itself.

Neither of us speak and then finally Rachel says, "That was our last vacation together, the three of us. She loved the beach. She would have made sandcastles for twelve hours a day if we'd let her."

And now, quite suddenly, I am the one overcome with tears, my eyes filling, my throat closing. I force it all back, because this is not my pain. It feels wrong to take it on as my own, even in part, to presume. Really, I have no idea of the depth of what Rachel feels.

"She's so beautiful," I say, and Rachel nods, almost fiercely.

"Yes," she answers. "She is."

We look at a few more photos, and soon enough I can see the signs that something is going wrong. Emily with new pink glasses; Emily using a tiny, improbably-sized walker. Still smiling, still Emily, but the losses are encroaching, a tide moving inexorably towards the shore.

After a few minutes, Rachel stops clicking the mouse for the next photo. "Let's use the beach one," she says, a bit abruptly, and we do.

The page is pretty much set up; all we have to do is click to publish. I tell Rachel about some easy tricks I'll use to promote the page—the usual social media outlets, like for likes, parenting forums I'll post on. She nods, looking a bit overwhelmed by it all.

"How do you think James will feel about you doing this?" she asks when we've both fallen into silence, and I shift my position on the sofa, unable to meet her gaze.

"I don't know."

"When are you going to tell him?"

"I should…" I sound so halfhearted, and Rachel shakes her head.

"Eva, you really should tell him as soon as possible. If this all happens without him knowing—"

"Yes." I know that. Of course I do. "I will."

"Why haven't you yet?" She shakes her head. "I know you mentioned how you've never really talked about… about Emily, and James can be a bit one-sided about this, but… you're his wife. He loves you." Her voice wobbles a little at that, but her gaze is direct. "Surely he'd understand why you've gotten involved? Or, at least, I don't know, accept it?"

"I'm not sure if he would or not." I blow out a breath. "When I said we never talk about you or Emily, I meant we *really* don't."

"Yes…" Rachel frowns. "But I guess that's understandable…?"

"I mean, we *never* do," I emphasize. "Never, ever. James told me about you and Emily on our second date and then it was as if he never wanted to talk about you again. At least to me."

Rachel blinks, looking diffident, as if she doesn't know how to process that information, or what it means. I'm not sure what it means, either. Is it because our marriage isn't strong enough? James wants to keep our relationship separate from his earlier one? Emily is too sacred a subject for me? I really don't know.

"Really, never?" she finally asks.

"Pretty much never. He told me everything in one shot—"

"Everything?" She sounds skeptical, and for one heart-stopping moment I wonder if there is something I don't know. Something James *didn't* tell me, when he was being so honest. Something that would change things.

"As far as I know," I amend, and Rachel does not reply. "Why… why did you divorce? In your opinion? I mean, James said you'd grown apart…" I trail off, realizing what an invasive question I am asking my husband's ex-wife, and yet I want to know. I want to hear Rachel's side of the story.

Rachel lets out a long, weary sigh. Her gaze is distant, hooded, her chin tucked low. "I think," she finally says, "not many marriages could withstand what happened to us, with Emily. I don't know who would be able to keep going, faced with all that."

Which I understand and should accept, yet for some contrary reason, I press. "But shouldn't you, at least in theory, want to support each other through it? Lean on each other in a time of crisis? I mean, isn't that the *idea* of marriage?"

"Yes," Rachel says, a wry twist to her lips, her gaze still settled on something other than me. "In theory, it is. But when you're both hurting so much..." She sighs. "It felt like we were both on life support. We couldn't be each other's oxygen."

Which sounds so bleak, and yet I understand it. "Sorry. I don't know why I'm asking these questions."

"I suppose I'd be curious, if I were you. I'd want to know what went wrong besides the usual."

I'm not sure what to say to that. "So what did go wrong?" I ask. "In your opinion?"

She throws me a look—a bit wry, a bit scornful even, but without hostility. "The easy answer—the one he gave you—is we did grow apart."

"And the real answer?" I dare to ask, although I'm not sure if I should, or even if I want to.

"Who knows what the real answer is? It felt like one day we were happy, the three of us, a family. We were even trying for another baby." I try to school my expression into neutrality. James never mentioned that. "And then the next, our daughter was sick, so sick, and we were barely speaking. We had nothing to say to each other that wasn't about Emily." She shakes her head. "But, you know, I've had enough time to think about it now, and I know it wasn't like that. It wasn't so quick." She lapses into silence and I wait for more. "I think we were drifting apart even before Emily got sick," she says quietly, a confession. "I don't like to think that, but I think it's true."

"Why?" I can't not ask.

"I don't even know. Maybe there wasn't enough to keep us together in the first place. I mean, we loved each other," she clarifies quickly. "I know we did. But sometimes it felt like we got together mostly because it was easy, and neither of us was getting any younger." She makes a face. "That sounds terrible."

"No..."

"But I think he fell properly in love with you," Rachel says without rancor.

"I don't know." I look back on those first heady days, that moment when I saw James waiting for me at the entrance to the bar, and I knew he was going to ask for my number. It had felt like a shot of adrenaline, right into my bloodstream. And that first date, when I'd spilled all the wine and we'd both laughed... I remember thinking, *Yes. This is what I've been looking for. This is who I've been waiting for.*

Why, just a year later, do I feel as if I am doubting that?

"Eva," Rachel says, and she sounds serious. "I know I'm hardly the right person to be saying this, but don't jeopardize your marriage for Emily's sake. I did that, and I don't want you to do it, too. It's not fair to you, and it's not fair to James."

"Wow." I try to smile. "I really didn't expect you to say something like that."

"Yeah, well, I'm not a saint. I wouldn't have been able to say it a year or even six months ago." She unfolds herself from the sofa and takes our coffee cups into the sink, a sure sign that she doesn't want to say anymore about that. Neither do I, particularly. "So what now?" she asks as she stands in the archway between the kitchen and the living room, her hands on her hips.

"As soon as you want to, we press publish. I'll try to direct some traffic towards the page through various means, and then we see what happens."

"And... the money?"

"The crowdfunding platform takes five percent for hosting, and another three percent for donation by credit card. Everything else goes to you, and they'll pay it out on a monthly schedule."

Rachel shakes her head slowly. "It feels wrong, somehow, to just... get money like that."

"People don't have to give, if they don't want to. You're creating an opportunity, Rachel, that's all."

She nods. "And what about James?"

I tense but try to sound normal. "What about him?"

"I suppose I need to tell him about this, even if you don't. Before it's live and starts getting attention."

"Yes, I think that's a good idea." I try to picture James' reaction and can't. Or at least, I'm not sure I want to.

"Should I mention your involvement?" Rachel asks, a sceptical look on her face.

I swallow. "I'd rather you didn't. That should come from me."

Rachel's eyes narrow as she gives me a look that is hard and yet with sympathy. "You need to tell him, Eva. Soon. It's not fair to him if you don't."

"I know."

"James won't like feeling as if he's been tricked or ganged up on."

"It's not like that—"

"I know it's not, but he might not see it that way, especially since we're working together." She shakes her head as she gives me a small smile. "Who would have thought?"

"I know." I smile back, enjoying this bizarre camaraderie, even though I still feel tense about everything. "I will tell him." As soon as I work up the courage and find the right moment. "So, should we hit publish?"

Rachel hesitates, and then nods. "All right. Yes. Let's do this." She glances towards my laptop as if it is a live grenade. "I'll tell James tonight. It will take a little while to publish, won't it?"

"Not really, but it will take a day or two to start getting some views. And you can edit the page or take it down at any time," I remind her. She has all the login information.

"I know." She lets out a little laugh and shakes her head. "I don't know why it feels scary. There are so many pages out there... this one probably won't even get any views."

"It will get some." I'll make sure of it.

"Okay." She sits back on the sofa, and so do I. The laptop is in front of us, the screen bright and glowing, *Emily's Story* on the top of the page, along with her photo. I look at her smile, those beautiful little baby teeth, her bright eyes, her joy. This child deserves a chance. Every child does.

I glance at Rachel. "Do you want to do the honors?"

"All right." She gives me a shaky smile, lets out another uncertain laugh, and then navigates the trackpad so the arrow is on the publish button. Click.

A few seconds later, after the colorful circle has spun around, we are taken to a new page. *Congratulations, Emily's Story is live!*

Rachel clicks on the mouse to reload the page, and there it is, *Emily's Story*, for everyone to read and see. I picture it being retweeted, shared on Facebook, Instagram, Snapchat. I imagine a newspaper picking it up, splashed on a million users' homepages, with the thousands and thousands of comments that can result, in just a matter of minutes.

I know it probably won't get that far, and that will probably be a good thing. A media deluge is in no one's best interest. And yet… *someone* will see it. It's out there, available for public perusal, consumption, judgment.

This is really happening, and I am part of it. For better or worse, this is about me now too.

CHAPTER SEVENTEEN

RACHEL

After Emily's page goes live, I am buzzing inside, filled with excitement, anticipation, and more than a little fear. I know I should tell James what I did, I was planning to that evening, but I didn't, and somehow the moment never comes and, in any case, so few people are reading the page that I tell myself it doesn't matter yet. Three days after I hit publish, there are only forty-four views. I'll talk to James when it starts to matter, when I actually have something to discuss and share. That's what I tell myself, anyway.

"It will gain momentum," Eva assures me, when I work up the courage to phone and ask her about it. "Don't worry."

I'm not worried, at least not in that way. Actually, the thought of just forty-four people reading about Emily, knowing her story, makes me feel a bit anxious. What are they thinking? What do they feel, when they look at her photo? I'm not sure I want to gain any more momentum, even as I am desperate for it to, for this to *work*.

Just a few hours after we put up the page, Andrew comes over with Jake and asks if he can brainstorm with me about potential logos. I'm already feeling kind of raw, having gone through everything with Eva, seen all the photos of Emily, and it hurts to see Jake in my house, asking me why I don't have any toys. I force myself to get a few books and blocks from Emily's room, even though it rips me apart inside.

When Andrew asks if Emily had a favorite teddy bear or book he might incorporate into the design, I feel even more fragile. I'm not used to accessing all these memories, offering them up to others, and yet talking about her feels good. Painful, but good.

"She loved ducks," I tell him as I show him the photos from her first birthday—the yellow cake, the hook-a-duck on the deck. He smiles at each one. "And she had a toy elephant... it's at the hospital." My throat closes on the words. Emily's ragged toy elephant, Blue, is lying next to her on her bed, forgotten and untouched for months now, but still there.

"Is there any particular image you'd prefer?" Andrew asks, his voice gentle.

I force down the lump of emotion that has lodged in my throat. I don't want him to see me cry.

"No... I mean, I don't know. Just something simple, I think. Not too sentimental or corny or anything like that."

"Okay."

He smiles again, and then reaches over and touches my hand, a butterfly brush of his fingers against mine. I do my best to smile back and then I look away. It seems so strange that I have people in my life again, people I might even call friends, although I'm not sure I'm ready to think of Eva like that. Still, she helped me, and so has Andrew. It feels like a lot; it feels, miraculously, like enough, at least for now.

"Are you doing anything today?" Andrew asks, and I blink, startled. It's early afternoon, but this day already feels momentous.

"No, not really." Saturday is usually my day for sleep, or shopping, housework and maybe visiting my mom. "I'm seeing my mom for dinner." I don't know why he's asking.

"It's just... Jake and I thought we'd try Wellington Park. We haven't been there before." I stare, saying nothing, still unsure what he wants from me. "I wondered if you wanted to go with us," Andrew explains gently. "We might take a picnic, although we've had lunch. Some snacks, at least."

"Oh…" Emotions tumble through me, too many to name. Does Andrew feel sorry for me? Do I want to go to a park with him and Jake? Can I handle that?

"You don't have to if you don't want to," he says quickly. "I'm sorry if asking is…" He pauses. "Insensitive."

"No, it's not." Of course it's not. I can go to a *park*. I can go to a park with a child almost the same age as Emily.

Can't I?

Andrew gives a little shrug. "I just thought… it's so nice out, although it's meant to rain later. Make hay while the sun shines, and all that." He gives me a lopsided smile, and I smile back.

"Yes. Right." I take a breath to steady myself. "Thanks. I'd… I'd like to go." I almost said I'd love to, but I couldn't quite make myself, because the truth is, I don't know how I feel about going, but some part of me realizes that I need to. Like my mother said, I need to do something. Take some small steps towards living again, even if everything in me resists.

We take Andrew's car, since Jake's booster seat is already installed in the back, and just the sight of that innocuous object causes me to catch my breath. I took Emily's car seat out a few months ago, when it was clear she wasn't coming back home, at least not for a long while. I only did it to stop any questions, but it felt like a surrender.

Jake is excited as we head off, a few gray clouds lurking on the horizon, reminding us of the rainstorms predicted for tonight. Still, it's sunny now, the sky a fragile blue, the air balmy. Jake bounces in his seat, kicking his legs against the back of Andrew's, and laughingly he tells his son to settle down. There's so much love in his voice, so much easy affection, that it makes my eyes sting. This afternoon is going to be harder than I thought.

I've never been to Wellington Park, even though I grew up a town away, and my spirits lift a little as we park on the road and head towards the playground in an oasis of green planted in a residential neighborhood.

"Apparently a group of volunteers tend the garden," Andrew tells me, with a nod towards the neatly tended herbaceous borders.

Jake starts running towards the swings, clambering on one with adorable effort.

"He's only just moved into the big boy swings," Andrew says. "I'm teaching him how to pump his legs."

"Always a tricky one." I'd only just been teaching Emily to pump when she fell sick. She never really learned how. But I don't want to think about Emily now, at least not in that way. She'll always be in my thoughts; she's practically here with me, and yet I don't want to keep thinking *I never got to do that. Emily missed this.* Instead, I want to think about what she *could* do, what she might be able to do if I take her to Italy, if the nerve stimulation works. Maybe she won't be able to pump her legs, but she might be able to sit in a swing again. She might tilt her head back and laugh for joy, like Jake is doing now, as Andrew sends him flying high, running underneath the swing as it soars up, making his son squeal with delight.

I amble over to a bench to watch them, and curious to see what has happened, I load Emily's page on my phone. A ripple of shock goes through me when I see there have already been eleven page views, and it's only been an hour or two.

I slip my phone in my pocket and tilt my face to the sun, determined to enjoy the day.

Jake scrambles off the swing a little while later and makes his way to the sandbox, which is thoughtfully scattered with communal toys—a plastic truck, a battered bucket and spade. Andrew joins me on the bench.

"This should tire him out," he says with satisfaction.

"And he'll sleep well tonight."

"Was Emily a good sleeper?" Andrew asks. "I mean, as a baby?" I must look startled, because he adds, "Sorry, I don't know if you want to talk about her or not. Tell me to shut up if you need to. It's just… I know what it's like when people tiptoe around a subject, and you just want them to ask about it."

"Not really," I say after a moment, when I've absorbed everything he's said. "She wasn't a particularly good sleeper. She was colicky when she was a newborn, and then she used to sleep very lightly. We used to not even flush the upstairs toilet after she'd gone to bed." I give a little laugh at the memory, one I'd forgotten.

"Jake was like that too. You'd tiptoe out of his room, holding your breath, praying he was asleep for good this time, and then the floor would creak or something and his head would pop right up. I remember once I had just laid him down in the crib when my phone went off with a text. Ping! It took another hour to settle him."

"Rookie mistake," I tell him with a smile. Surprisingly, this doesn't hurt as much as I thought it might. "Bringing your phone in while you were rocking him. Classic newbie error."

"I know, I know." Andrew shakes his head, smiling. "What was I thinking?"

I glance back at Jake, who is industriously filling a bucket with sand. "What about you, Andrew? What is it you want people to ask you about?"

"Oh, um…" He lets out an uncertain laugh as he scratches his chin. "Christina, I suppose. No one wants to talk about her. They act as if she's dead, but she isn't."

"Does she see Jake at all?"

"She keeps saying she will, but I'm not so sure. She hasn't yet, and it's been six months." He sighs. "I always knew she was a free spirit. That was one of the things I loved about her. She was so full of joy—dancing in the kitchen, deciding we should wake Jake up and get ice cream at nine o'clock at night, because it was so beautiful out." He slides me an apologetic look. "I know that could sound like bad parenting, but—"

I shake my head. "I'm no judge."

"Well, she was a lot of fun, and Jake and I both adored her. But when he was three or so, she started to get restless. I pretended to ignore it for a while. And then when I couldn't ignore it anymore, when she was leaving Jake with babysitters every day and coming back later and later, I encouraged her to get a job. Retrain, if she wanted. She'd worked as a physical therapist, but she said she didn't want to go back to that. That's when I suggested the yoga retreat." He sighs heavily as he leans back against the bench, his features drooping with the memory of it.

I touch his hand lightly, just as he touched mine earlier. His skin is warm, and his hand moves under mine, a little twitch. The contact feels strange, and far more important than it should. I realize, besides my mother's hugs, I haven't been touched by another human being in a very long time.

"I'm sorry," I say quietly. "It all sounds incredibly difficult."

"Yes." He shoots me a look of grateful understanding. "It is, mainly for Jake, because, of course, he doesn't understand. Not that I do, really, but for him… he kept asking when she'd come back, and that broke my heart. And then he stopped asking, and that broke my heart even more."

"Yes." I can understand that. I remember two years ago, when we thought Emily might have epilepsy, how terrified I was, breaking down in tears, not wanting it to be real, praying for it to be something else. And then, later, thinking almost savagely, *why couldn't it have been epilepsy?*

"Maybe Christina will come home one day," Andrew says on a sigh. "It's only been a little over six months."

"Yet I bet it feels like forever." Emily has been in a state of unresponsive wakefulness for nearly that long, and yes, it feels like an age. And yet at the same it feels like no time at all.

We lapse into silence, and like a nervous reflex, I check my phone. Sixteen views. Andrew glances over and I show him.

"Who do you think is looking at the page?" I ask.

"Could be anyone. Maybe some people who have pages themselves. Do you belong to any support groups?"

"Yes, on Facebook, but I'm not very involved. It just feels a bit overwhelming sometimes." But it occurs to me, as I sit there in the sunshine, that perhaps I've chosen to isolate myself all this time. I was the one who stopped returning calls, not my friends. I chose not to go back to work, even though about a year ago they offered me flexible, part-time hours. I go to the hospital every day and choose not to make more than chitchat with the other devastated parents in that unit, even though I see their pale faces and haunted eyes, just like mine.

Why have I cut myself off so much? Was it because it was easier; I knew I couldn't handle anything more than Emily? Or was it because, as James said, I was making it into some sort of competition? Whose cross is bigger to bear? Who is suffering the most? *Me. It has to be me.*

I don't like the thought. It makes me sound so petty, so, well, *unhealthy*. Unhinged, even. Surely I don't really think like that? It's not about me; it never has been. Now, more than ever, I want to think of Emily, and I want to think of her with something other than fear or sorrow. But I can't ignore the fact that I've cut myself off deliberately, for whatever reason. I was the one who did it.

"Penny for your thoughts?" Andrew asks lightly and I let out a little laugh.

"Oh, nothing. Just random stuff." I hardly want to blurt out all the things I've been thinking. "This is nice," I tell him. "I know I don't get out enough."

"You've been busy."

"Yes." At least Andrew understands that. I know most people would wonder why I go to the hospital, day after day after endless day, when Emily doesn't even seem to recognize me. But I do, and I will keep doing it, because stopping feels far worse, and now, for once, I have something to look forward to, to aim for. I wonder if James could at least understand *that*.

The clouds that were skirting on the edge of the horizon an hour ago are now rising up in a dark, menacing bank. The air feels humid, with the promise of rain. Jake has left the sandbox and is trying to climb a slide. Andrew goes to help him, and I watch as he patiently guides him up the rungs, and then waits at the bottom, arms outstretched, to catch him as he comes down. I watch, smiling a little, as Jake does it again and again. Emily was scared of the slide. She was definitely more of a swing girl—*is* more of a swing girl. Could be again.

By the fifth time Jake heads down the slide, it is starting to rain—at first just a spattering of drops, but as we gather our things and head for the car, it becomes a downpour, the rain coming so hard and fast, we are soaked in seconds.

We clamber into the car, dripping and laughing, and lightning forks the sky as we head back home. For a second, it almost feels like this could be my family—it could be James in the driver's seat, raking his wet hair back from his face, and if I twist around, I'll see Emily in her car seat, her thumb in her mouth as she kicks her legs happily.

All right there, Em?

I blink and it all disappears; Andrew is frowning as he navigates the unfamiliar road in the driving rain, and Jake is asking if he can have his iPad. I turn to look out the window, at the rain streaking steadily down it like tears.

That evening, after saying goodbye to both Andrew and Jake, and spending the rest of the afternoon doing housework and checking my phone—nineteen views!—I head over to my mother's.

I haven't seen her since she told me about her diagnosis, and as I pull into the driveway, I realize that is at least somewhat intentional. Yes, I've been distracted, but more so, I've been lost. I'm not ready to think about letting go of my mom, not even in part. I'm not ready to start living with the knowledge of what she has, what is going to kill her eventually, and yet I know, as I step out of the car, that I am already seeing the signs everywhere. They are there in the weeds in the flower beds lining the front walk, that I know my mom wouldn't normally countenance. I see them in the dirty dishes piled in the sink, and the notice scribbled on the calendar for a Memory Clinic on Monday, the handwriting far more of a scrawl than I recall it being.

"Mom?" I call out, a note of trepidation striking my soul. Is she sleeping again? Or what if she's fallen and hurt herself, and can't get up? Surely we're not at that stage yet.

"Up here," my mom calls, sounding cheerful, and with relief I head upstairs. No, of course we're not there yet.

I walk down the upstairs hallway, following the sound of her voice, to the fourth bedroom, which has been the junk room of the house for as long as I can remember, filled with crates of clothes and boxes of photos, stacks of books and papers no one has bothered to file.

My mother is on her knees, riffling through a box of sweaters. I stop in the doorway, staring.

"What are you doing?"

"I thought I'd have a bit of a clear-out."

"Is this to do with…?" I can't not ask. Neither can I finish the sentence.

My mother sits back, her hands on her thighs. Her hair is a bit ruffled, the sleeves of her pinstriped button-down shirt rolled up to the elbows. "Well, yes," she says. "Everything is to do with that, Rachel, unfortunately." She gives me a brisk smile. "I'm trying to be practical, not maudlin. And I don't want you to have to do it. Nearly fifty years of stuff in here... you can't be bothered with all that."

The remnants of the afternoon in the sunshine, the hope I was starting to feel, fall about me in tatters. "I want to do it, Mom."

After James and I divorced, and we had to sell our house, my mother asked if I wanted to move in with her. I thought about it seriously, because she certainly had the space and I knew I could use the company. Yet I didn't, in part because my mother was working full-time and I didn't want to burden her with worry over and care of me, and also because my life already felt as if it were falling apart; moving in with my mother at almost forty years old felt like a step too far.

Now I wonder if I should, even as I recognize my mother will resist. She'll think I'm doing it to keep an eye on her, and maybe I will be. Besides, I realize with a jolt, I don't want to leave my little house, sad as it is. I don't want to leave Andrew and Jake, and the friendship we're only just beginning to form.

"There will be enough for you to do, Rachel," my mom says. "Trust me on that. I'm just going through some boxes of old clothes." She reaches for a sweater. "Would you like a cashmere cardigan, circa 1985?"

I eye the bright pink cardigan with the sewn-in shoulder pads, not my sort of thing at all. "Maybe."

My mom laughs and tosses it in a garbage bag that's clearly meant for donations. "I can't see you wearing that."

"Do you really have to do this now?" I ask.

My mother glances up at me with a sympathetic smile. "I'll stop, if you want. I know this is hard."

Which makes me feel selfish. "Harder for you."

"No, it feels good. I've held onto this house for so long, and everything in it. All the memories of Dad..." Her smile wobbles a bit. "It feels good to let go. Freeing. It's certainly been long enough."

"How did you go on, Mom?" I ask suddenly. "When Dad died? I don't even remember you crying."

"I cried." She smiles sadly.

"I just remember you being there for me. Every day after school. Baking cookies even when you had a full-time job, papers to mark…"

"I knew it was important."

"It was. I just…" I shake my head slowly. "I don't know how anyone faces it. Losing someone."

"You've lost someone, Rachel," she reminds me gently. "You know what it feels like. You lost your dad when you were only seventeen."

"I know." Have I forgotten how wild the grief was, how consuming? Maybe I have. Maybe that's the only way you can go forward, by forgetting. "It just feels different now. Thinking about Emily." A lump forms in my throat and I will it to dissolve.

"I know it does. Losing a child… it's unnatural. It feels wrong."

"Have I already lost her?" The hope I felt, looking at those paltry page views, vanishes in an instant. "Should I not be doing this, Mom? Seeking this treatment?" I look at her anxiously, waiting for an answer, and she pulls me into a hug. Her body trembles against mine as I rest my head on her frail shoulder.

"You're doing this out of love for your daughter, Rachel. It's not wrong. It might not have the outcome I know you're longing for, but it's not wrong."

I close my eyes as I breathe in her familiar scent—Tide detergent and lavender perfume. "Thank you. Thank you for saying that."

"I believe it," my mother says staunchly. "I will always believe it."

Later, as I'm unlocking my car to head home, I check my phone. Thirty-one views. A ripple of something—I don't know what—goes through me. Who is looking at the page? Who is reading Emily's story?

Over the next week, I kept checking Emily's page on my phone. Andrew designed a logo that Eva uploaded, and it was perfect—a little, smiling rubber duck with a pink bow in her quiff. Eva even designed a sticker of it that people can put on their social media, when they've donated.

We do all this, and still neither of us tell James what's going on. There's opportunity, of course. He comes to the hospital on Emily's birthday, and we sit together as we watch our daughter silently and try not to think of the birthday that could have been—the cake, the candles, the party, the presents. Our little girl, gap-toothed and grinning, twirling around the house in her excitement. I can picture it so perfectly, so easily, I can't believe it hasn't happened… and that it never will.

We sing happy birthday to her, softly, so the words feel like an apology. Her eyes flicker back and forth, making me catch my breath, but then she sinks back into herself, as she always does. I touch her hand, wishing there could be more to this moment, even as it slips away.

James hands me a card, and I see it is from both him and Eva, in her handwriting. This is the perfect opportunity to tell him about the page, but I don't. I can't. The words crowd in my throat and press against my tongue and it feels as if I physically can't get them out of my mouth. I don't know why; I'm not scared of James' reaction. I just don't want this ephemeral feeling of optimism to pop, and I know it will once James finds out, and he is either furious or hurt, and definitely disapproving.

So I convince myself it doesn't matter, because so few people have seen the page. But over the course of the week, the number of views has kept creeping up, slowly, slowly. Forty, then sixty, then one hundred. A week after Eva and I put the page up, it's at two hundred and forty-one, hardly life-changing. A veritable drop in an endless ocean of need and desperation.

And yet. Two hundred and forty-one people know my story. Emily's story. And, I see, when I check the donations page, almost six hundred dollars has been donated for the cost of her treatment.

Those figures both hearten and discourage me. At least someone cares, enough to read the page, give some money, although, of course, it's not nearly enough. The cost of Emily's treatment will be in the many thousands, most likely in the hundreds of thousands. Who am I kidding? Who is Eva? *How is this going to help?*

The realization of how little it is, even though it feels like so much, throbs through me. Hope that was starting to unfurl inside me like the tenderest green shoot begins to wither, and it's only been a week. It feels worse to have hoped and then lost than to have never hoped at all. I go to bed on Sunday night sick at heart, tomorrow stretching ahead of me bleakly.

Then, on Monday morning, as I bolt a cup of coffee, I check my phone again, because there is still some small hope pushing up through the dry, desert soil of my heart, and I nearly drop it in shock. There are *four thousand* views. I check the donation page, letting out a little gasp at the number there. Three thousand dollars. *What…? How…?*

I am still reeling from those numbers as I shower and dress and head to the hospital. I check it again before I go inside—seven thousand five hundred views, nearly double what it was a mere hour or two ago. I am thrilled and terrified in equal measure. *What is happening?*

All through the morning, I check it—refresh, refresh, refresh. Eight thousand. Ten thousand. Twenty-five thousand. The numbers continue to soar, and I have no idea why. People have donated *twenty-eight thousand dollars*.

Then, when I am standing in line at the hospital cafeteria, my phone rings. It's a blocked number, and I answer it as I always do, because there is the chance it could be about Emily, an emergency that I must know about.

"Is this Rachel Lerner?"

My heart lurches up towards my throat at the officious tone. A nurse? A doctor? "Yes…"

"I'm calling about the webpage regarding your daughter, Emily Harris, and how your former husband James Harris doesn't seem to know anything about it?"

CHAPTER EIGHTEEN

EVA

Things got out of control very quickly. That's my only excuse, and I know it's not much of one. I was *going* to tell James. Every day, I was going to tell him. The words formed a pressure in my chest, bottled in my throat... and then stayed there.

I told myself that, despite my efforts, not many people were actually looking at Emily's page, so it didn't really matter. Another excuse. I knew that, but I let myself believe it anyway. And despite the dark cloud looming over me, James and I had a nice week.

We went to see a new indie film at an arthouse cinema, and met up with some of James' work friends for drinks. It was full summer, the most social season of the year, when everyone wanted to be outside, when the days were long and balmy instead of short and dark and encased in ice.

A weight seemed to have slid off James' shoulders, while another one rested squarely on mine. He was more relaxed, coming home an hour early from his evening visits with Emily, spending only half the day on Saturday. I noticed, but didn't say anything. I wondered if Rachel knew, and suspected she didn't, and that if she did, she wouldn't like it, but I didn't say anything to anyone.

It wasn't my problem, or so I told myself, even as I continued to furtively and obsessively check the views on Emily's page. Even as I continued to tweak the keywords and settings of the page, and post on Facebook groups and Twitter.

A week after we put the page up, I set up an Instagram account with Emily's duck logo as the profile photo and posted every day—facts about experimental treatment, neurological conditions, anything to raise both awareness and interest. It was all part of what I'd promised I'd do, and I found it both interesting and heartbreaking, so it wasn't any trouble. For some reason I didn't choose to articulate even to myself, I didn't tell Rachel about any of it.

Even as I sipped sangria with James' friends; even as we discussed the moody, black and white film we'd thought was too self-conscious over Thai food; even as we made love slowly and languorously, as the last of the summer sun spilled over the bed, I thought about that stupid page and I never told James.

It was as if I had been fractured into two selves—the wife I was to James, and the woman I was inside. I'd become obsessed; even in the midst of it all, I could see that. I started checking the page at work, sometimes every hour or more, and then, in a reckless moment of determination, I used my work contacts—lifestyle and beauty bloggers who were meant to *care* about things—to promote the page. It was just a few emails asking for favors—a mention, a post—but I knew, on some level at least, that what I was doing was risky, if not actually wrong. The lines had blurred so much, my whole life felt like a canvas of gray, and yet it felt right. Whether it was or not, I couldn't say.

And then Mara discovered what I had done. Stupidly, while at my desk, I was checking Emily's page and updating the Instagram account I'd created for her when I heard someone clearing her throat behind me, and I turned to see Mara standing there, dark brows drawn together in a damning, straight line.

"Excuse me, Eva, but are you working on something personal during work hours?" Her voice rang out through the open space, and everyone glanced up from their laptop before ducking their heads down again quickly, ears perked up for the drama.

I hesitated, and then decided to play it light. "Sorry, Mara, I'm on a break and it's a favor for a friend." I wasn't about to mention the complicated relationships involved—me and Rachel, me and James, me and Emily for that matter, even though we'd never met. I swiveled around in my chair and gave her a quick smile without any apology in it. "Her little girl is really sick—terminally, with a very rare condition—and she wanted me to manage the social media to raise awareness. Actually, I thought Maemae might like to be involved, but we can talk about that later."

"I see." Mara's gaze was penetrating as she stared at me for a long moment. I held her gaze and my smile, and then finally she turned around and walked back to her office, her heels clicking ominously across the floor. I let out a shaky breath. I wouldn't make that mistake again.

But I still checked and posted on my lunch break, at home, before bed. As James came into the bedroom, toothbrush in hand, I slid my phone in the drawer of my bedside table, instead of keeping it on top as usual. He noticed, his gaze moving from the drawer to my face before he turned back to the bathroom. He didn't say anything, and I didn't know what that meant. Everything in my life felt tenuous, and yet just a few minutes later, when we were both in bed, James rolled over to me and kissed me gently on the lips. I kissed him back, and as his arms came around me, I made myself forget everything else.

And then, on Sunday night, after a weekend where I'd hardly thought about Emily or checked her page at all, everything changed. With only half-hearted interest, assuming things wouldn't be much different, I checked the page's stats before going to bed. They were at four hundred. My tweaks and posts were helping, but not nearly enough, and I felt both relieved and frustrated. I didn't know what to do with either emotion, and I told myself, yet again, that I wouldn't check the page tomorrow. I'd managed all weekend, more or less. It was time to let this go.

And tomorrow I would tell James. I'd explain it all to him matter-of-factly, apologize for my deception but help him to understand why I'd done it. In my head, it all sounded so simple. So easy. And yet somehow I never managed to start that conversation.

As morning breaks and James heads to the bathroom for the first shower, I keep to my promise. I don't check it all morning, as I shower, dress and sip coffee in the kitchen while James scans the news on his phone, kissing my cheek before he leaves and suggesting we go somewhere downtown for dinner. I murmur my agreement and wave him off with a smile.

I'm not going to check it.

I walk to work and my phone stays firmly in my pocket. I work all morning on a new campaign, and I don't do anything but what I am supposed to do. Just after my lunch break, a salad eaten at my desk, Rachel texts me. I don't read her message. She's texted me a few times, asking me about any updates on the page, as if she can't see them for herself. It's never anything urgent, and I decide to look at it later. I want to stay focused on my job, my life.

And that's what I'm doing—working hard, staying focused—when everything begins to fall apart.

"Eva?" Mara's voice, calling from the doorway of her office, is noticeably tense. I turn around in my chair. "A moment, if you please?" Her formality is ominous.

I ignore everyone's furtive stares as I walk towards her glassed-in box of an office, trying not to feel nervous. *I haven't done anything wrong...*

Except I have.

I stand completely still, my face starting to burn, as Mara goes through the list of my offences—from being distracted, to using company time for personal matters, to accessing work contacts and pressuring—her word—them to feature my friend. Apparently some of the bloggers were unenthused about my suggestion and let Mara know. Somehow I'm not even surprised about any of it.

"I'm really shocked by all of this, Eva," Mara says as she shakes her head. "Shocked and saddened." She pulls a face, and I know exactly how this is going to go. Mara, my boss, is going to be disappointed in me. She's going to lament about how much potential I've had, how thrilled she's been to see me develop the digital marketing strategies for seven *years*, and then she's going to sigh and shake her head and say how sorry she is to have to let me go.

And that's exactly what happens. I'm fired, effective immediately.

Twenty minutes later, I am clearing out my desk—not that there's much for me to take. My laptop belongs to Maemae, and since we change desk spaces every few days, all I have is a photo from my wedding day and a potted cactus Naomi gave me for good luck when I started. It's survived longer than I have.

I am numb, my mind seeming as if it is full of buzzing bees. I can feel people's glances, burning and inquisitive, and a few colleagues I've called friends hug me and say we must get together for drinks. I wonder if we will, or if I've become that person no one talks about, a work pariah because I've been fired.

Fired. I can't believe it, and for a few seconds I consider my options. I could file a complaint of unfair dismissal, register something formally with HR, consult a lawyer. I know I won't do any of it though. Even if I hadn't been fired, my time at Maemae had been coming to an end. I'd been getting bored with makeup, ethical as it was. I'd lost my passion and my drive, and I don't blame Mara for firing me. Using work contacts, updating Emily's page on company time… all of that was just an excuse to get rid of dead weight. Me.

I feel leaden inside as I say goodbye to everyone, a flurry of air kisses and pressed hands. I've worked here for seven years, and

I've made some friends, albeit not very close ones. Occasional drinks, idle chitchat as we get coffee, the odd bridal shower or bachelorette party. It never went much more beyond that, and I didn't mind, because I was focused on success, and then I was focused on James, and then I was focused on getting pregnant.

And here I am, one already lost, one starting to slip away, one I might never have. A tremor of terror ripples through me as I realize I have to tell James about everything. If Mara can find out, if I've lost my job over this… I have to tell him. There are no more excuses.

As I leave the office, I reach for my phone. I see another two texts from Rachel, and my trepidation intensifies. Something must be going on. When I swipe to see what she's written, I swear under my breath.

A local TV station just called me about Emily's page—and how James doesn't know?! What should I do??

I duck into a café, order an espresso and then load Emily's page as I wait for the barista to make it. Twelve thousand views. Over a thousand in the last twenty minutes.

Shit.

I realize, in this moment, that I didn't want this. That my ambivalence about it all was actually a dread, a fear that I would start something that would snowball and snowball and never stop. And it might cost me everything.

I check the Instagram account Rachel doesn't even know about, and scroll through the comments on the last post, which was a more personal one about Emily. I'd written it recklessly on Friday night, after I'd promised myself not to check the page all weekend. There are now over six hundred comments. *How did this happen?*

And yet I know how it happened. This is what I do, what I'm good at, despite having just been fired. My gaze flicks over the comments—*Poor Emily, God bless. People need to know about these conditions. What a sweetheart. Am donating now.*

I let out a shuddery breath and the barista hands me my espresso. Then I call Rachel.

"Eva?" She sounds panicked.

"It's all right," I soothe, even though I am feeling as on edge as she is, if not more. "This is a good thing. The publicity—"

"The publicity sucks," Rachel cuts across me. "Some *viper* from a local news channel called me and wanted to know why my ex-husband didn't know about any of this, and what did I think about the fact that he's actually opposed to the treatment. *That's* the angle she's going for—"

"How did she know he didn't know?"

"Because she called him. He's *spoken* to her, Eva. She saw something on Instagram… I didn't even know we *had* anything on Instagram… and from that she ferreted out his details. Eva, what am I supposed to do? I want to take it all down."

"Don't do that." Even now, when everything in my life is at risk, I don't want her to stop it all, not that it even could be. These things become juggernauts. "I know this feels overwhelming, Rachel, but this is good. The comments are all positive." Except for a few horrible ones that I deleted so Rachel can't see them. Hopefully she hasn't already looked. "If one desperate journalist wants to make some story about James not knowing, that's a small price to pay." For her, not for me. It might be a much bigger price for me… although surely I can explain. Surely I can make James understand. "I'll talk to him today. Make sure we're all on the same page. Then there's no story there, and she'll drop it."

"But what if we aren't, Eva? What if he doesn't agree to any of this?" Her voice is high and thin. "I should have told him. I'm so *stupid*…"

"I'll tell him now." I know I have to.

"I'm the one who needs to talk to him, Eva," Rachel says, her voice hard all of a sudden. "You might have had the idea, but Emily is James' and my child. This is about us, not you." I am silent, winded, absorbing the hostility of that statement along with its truth. "I'm sorry," Rachel says more quietly. "I'm not trying to hurt you. But you must know I'm right." And then she hangs up.

I spend the afternoon being a domestic goddess, as if that is going to make any difference. I clean the kitchen, even though it's already pretty clean, since we hardly ever use it. I scrub the bathrooms, I pick up the dry-cleaning and sort the laundry, I blitz the living room with air freshener and dust and vacuum everything. It helps to keep busy, but I am still filled with dread, checking my phone constantly for updates from Rachel or something from James, but there is nothing.

And then he comes home, his shoulders stooped, weary lines of resignation etched on his face. I stand in the kitchen, holding a dish towel, filled with fear. Should I confess right away, or let him speak first? What is the right thing to do, never mind what feels easier? Safer?

"Sorry," he says, apropos of nothing, as he puts his messenger bag on the floor. "It's been a crap day."

I hesitate, then ask in a voice that wobbles a little, "What happened?"

"Rachel…" He blows out a breath. "She's gone and done something without telling me, and now it's blown up." He shakes his head. "I just wish she'd *told* me."

I bite my lip. I have to say something, I have to confess, and yet somehow I can't. "What has she done?"

James shrugs off his jacket. "Created this whole page online about Emily, asking for donations for her treatment. The treatment I have not agreed to," he emphasizes, his voice rising. "I mean, what is she really trying to do?" Then he deflates again. "I know she's desperate, and she really wants this treatment to happen, but…" Another weary shake of the head. "This morning I was contacted by some news reporter who wants to make it a thing, that I didn't know. Because I *didn't* know. I get this call out of the blue… well, you can imagine."

Yes, I can. I open my mouth to say I don't even know what, but then James smiles at me, and kisses my cheek.

"I'm going to go change. You still want to head downtown for dinner? There's a new Lebanese place I wanted to try."

I see in his smile that I'm his oasis, his shelter from the storm with Rachel, and I can't bear the thought of taking that from him. Do I have to tell him? If Rachel says she did it on her own…

My heart thuds as I murmur some agreement while James goes to change. I've got to tell him about my involvement, I know I do. I also need to tell him that I've been fired. Our world is about to be upended and it's all my fault. I close my eyes.

"I know it will blow over," he says as he comes back into the kitchen. "These things usually do. It's just… well, it's something neither Rachel nor I need right now. I don't think she anticipated this, to be honest."

"Have you spoken to her?" My voice sounds strange and mechanical.

"Only briefly. We're going to meet up tomorrow. She apologized, said she didn't realize this would happen. I think she's a bit freaked out by it all, actually."

"Mm." I pointlessly wipe the kitchen counter as I don't meet his eyes.

"Eva?" The sudden, serious tone in his voice makes me still. "Is something wrong?"

I force myself to meet his gaze. "What… what do you mean?"

James frowns and puts his hands flat on the kitchen island. "I don't know. You just seem a bit… off. Is everything okay?"

The concern in his voice is the end of me. I can't lie to him. And even though he's given me the perfect opening to tell him about being fired, to make it only about that, I say something else instead. "James, I already know about Emily's page. The internet stuff." He stares at me, still frowning, not understanding. "I helped Rachel to make the page. It was actually all my idea, to set it up, to try and make it go viral."

"What…" The word comes out of him like a breath and he shakes his head slowly, still not understanding. Not wanting to.

"I created the Instagram account," I continue relentlessly, needing to say it all, a confessional. "And I posted on Facebook, and a bunch of other sites, and basically did it all to drum up interest."

"Why…" He looks winded, shell-shocked.

"I… I wanted to help. I thought Emily deserved that chance. I still do."

"*Emily?*" The disbelief in his voice hurts me, somehow, as if he doesn't think she matters to me.

"Yes, Emily. I care about her—"

"You've never even met her."

"And why is that?" I counter. "Besides, she's just a child. She's your *daughter*. If there is treatment that can help—"

"I told you about the treatment, Eva!" James rakes a hand through his hair, looking too stunned to be angry. Yet. "How experimental, how expensive, how *hopeless* it is—"

"I know what you said, but—"

"This wasn't your decision to make." The words are quiet and certain; he sounds hurt rather than angry, and that makes everything so much worse. I watch as he collapses onto the sofa, his head in his hands.

"James…" I let his name trail off into nothing. He doesn't answer. Then, with a rush of horror and guilt, I realize he is taking deep breaths, trying not to cry. Because of me, and what I did. "*James…*"

He shakes his head, still cradled in his hands, and then he gets up from the sofa and reaches for his jacket.

"Please, let's talk…" I say, my voice cracking, but he just shakes his head again, his eyes bloodshot, his lips set.

"No." He shrugs his jacket on and grabs his keys. "I can't. Not right now."

"James—"

"I *can't*."

The words are a broken cry, and then he is gone.

CHAPTER NINETEEN

RACHEL

The doorbell rings and my heart turns over before I take a deep breath and go to open it, telling myself this meeting is going to be okay, that we'll handle this like the two mature and responsible adults that we are.

"Hello, James."

He nods his greeting and I step aside as he comes in. He looks defeated rather than angry, which surprises and saddens me. I was pitching for some sort of battle, but I feel as if it is already over, or as if it never happened at all.

Since Emily's page exploded all over the internet—admittedly in a fairly minor way, at least in internet terms—my emotions have been all over the place—regret, fear, excitement, *hope*. The last one I hold onto, cling to it with my fingertips, because it's been so long since I've felt it properly, and it's so, so fragile. In the end, I know it's the only one that matters.

"I'm sorry about all this," I say as James sinks into my sofa and gazes around my bland, beige living room without interest. He's never actually been here before.

"Are you?" He sounds tired. It's Tuesday evening; he's come from being with Emily. I don't know what he wants to say to me, although I can guess. *How could you. How dare you. This is not what we agreed on, Rachel.*

"Yes, I am, James." I try to keep my voice from turning strident. "I never meant… well, I never wanted you to come out the bad guy in this. That was absolutely never my intention." In the thirty-six hours since the news reporter contacted me, the story has broken online on a local news page that James is opposed to the treatment, and there has been a slew of horrible, hateful comments under it, as well as on the Instagram post I didn't even know about. *How could a father deny his daughter treatment? I feel sad for the mom, but she needs to know when it's over. What a bastard. What a saddo. These people are desperate. Why don't they pay for it themselves? Poor kid, but it's not my problem.*

Each comment felt like a slap or a punch; I made myself read them all, and by the end, I felt bludgeoned, bruised and bloody. I can't even delete them, because I don't have the password to the account. Yet as much as I try to feel angry with Eva for creating the account without telling me, I recognize that I basically gave her permission to do anything online, wanting her to boost the visibility of Emily's page. Never truly thinking through what could happen, despite my vague apprehensions about a scenario, it turns out, exactly like this. Something going viral. Hatred being spewed. James alienated and even more intransigent, turned into the bad guy by a bunch of faceless consumers, because it's a better story.

James doesn't reply to my stammering apologies, and I sit on the opposite end of the sofa, my hands clasped between my knees, unsure what to do, how to handle this. He asked to meet me, and I was expecting blustering demands to take down the page, to stop it all, to just *go away*, Rachel. Isn't that what he's wanted from me all along, even if he's never said? That's what it's felt like.

But I'm not going away. When I last looked, Emily's crowdfunding account had eleven thousand dollars in it. The page has over thirty thousand views. Despite the admitted backlash, I don't want to take it down.

"What were you thinking, Rachel?" he finally asks. He sounds so tired, so resigned and so *sad*, that everything in me cringes with guilty remorse. I realize I'd far prefer him to be angry than hurt. I know I didn't handle this the way I should have, but his record isn't unblemished, either. If he'd just *talked* to me… "I mean, I understand the need to do something," he continues. "I can see why you'd start the page, even though you knew I don't agree with the treatment." He draws a shaky breath. "But to not even *tell* me about it… to have me find out from a news reporter, who actually came to my office…"

"I didn't mean for that to happen."

"I know you didn't, but the fact is, it did. And you made the page over a week ago, so…" He rubs a hand over his face. "Surely there was time to tell me? Mention the page, the funding, all for a treatment I've already said no to?"

"Which is why I didn't tell you." My voice wobbles, and then rises. "You would have just told me not to do it—"

"Yes, I would have, because I don't think this is the right course for Emily, or for that matter, for you."

"For *me*?" I swell with indignation, feel myself getting bigger. "How can you presume to know what's best for me, James? You don't know anything about me anymore. You have no right to pretend you do. You *left* me." The words are ripped out of me and hurled at him, words I've never actually said, because I've been determined to be so reasonable, so understanding, about everything, for Emily's sake. Right now I don't feel any of that.

He shakes his head, lips compressing. "I may have been the one to end the marriage, but that's because I was the one brave enough to call time. You know we were basically strangers for months before that, Rachel. We barely spoke, never mind touched or acted like a husband and wife. I've been willing to be the bad guy if you need me to, but let's be honest about that for once."

I can't argue with the truth of his words. "I wouldn't have left you," I state. Of that I am sure.

"No, you would have just endured. Sorry, I'm not the same kind of martyr." He shakes his head. "In any case, this isn't about us, Rachel. I'm sorry, I have always been sorry, for any hurt I've caused you, but right now this is about Emily."

"Yes, and that's where we differ. I think the experimental treatment is best for Emily, and you don't." I speak flatly. "And if we're going to talk about not telling each other things, James, how about the fact that you refused even to have a discussion with me about this? All I've got from you are one-liners by text and email, and then a complete shutdown."

"I didn't think either of us had the emotional energy for a big drama over such a remote possibility—"

"I've got the emotional energy." I lean forward, my fists curling. Maybe there will be a battle, after all. I'm ready for it. I almost want it. I've suppressed so much over the last three years, because I didn't want anything to take away from my focus on Emily. From doing whatever I could to help her… including this. "I've got the time and the space to get Emily this treatment," I tell him. "All I need you to do is agree, James. You won't have to do anything—"

"Do you honestly think this is about me feeling put out or something?" There is a spark in his eyes I haven't seen before, or at least not in a long time. "Do you honestly think this is about me not wanting to be *hassled*?"

"I don't know what to think. You won't even talk about it—"

"Because there's no *point*!" His voice rises to something like a roar, and suddenly I am shouting too.

"*You* don't think there's a point. Just you. Not me. And I have as much of a right, if not more of one, to decide on Emily's care—"

"More of one?" he repeats, nodding as if he knew I'd say that. "That's how it has always been with you, Rachel. You have to win, and it is *not* meant to be a contest."

"No one is winning here," I say in a voice that throbs with both anger and emotion. "*No one.*"

"Yet it's still some sort of sick competition with you. *You* have more right to decide. *You* feel the grief more—"

"We're not grieving," I shout, even though I know that's not really what he meant. "Not yet, even if you almost seem as if you want to—"

"*Don't.*" The single word is savage, and I know I've gone too far. But I'm so angry, my body practically vibrating with it, with the unjust intractability of my ex-husband's position. He just won't budge.

James takes a deep breath and lets it out slowly. I wait, my hands bunched. We've never fought like this. That taut conversation in Starbucks is the closest we've ever come, but even that was nothing like this. I want to scream. I want to slap James' face. I want to cry and cry and have him hold me, but I know he never will, and that makes me even angrier.

"This isn't about me not caring, Rachel." James speaks slowly, enunciating each word as if he has to take time and care to form them. "This isn't about me not having time or patience or energy for Emily. It isn't about me jaunting off into the sunset with Eva, and forgetting that I had a family, that I *have* a daughter."

My nails dig into my palms. "Are you sure about that?" I squeeze out of my too-tight throat.

"Yes, I am absolutely sure. I love Emily, Rachel. I have always loved Emily. It destroyed me as much as you when she started to get sick—"

"It can't have." The words burst out of me before I've thought them through. "It can't have, because you've moved on, James.

You might not think you're *jaunting into the sunset* or whatever, but you have definitely moved on."

He looks at me levelly. "Perhaps you should, too."

"And yet you tell me this isn't about you not forgetting you have a family?" I choke. *How dare he?* How dare he pretend he is still in torment over Emily, when he so obviously isn't? "That this isn't about you not wanting to be hassled?"

"Of course it isn't—"

"The nurse yesterday told me you left on Saturday at lunchtime." I didn't believe her at first. I was so sure James would never do that. "And that you have been leaving early since she's been in the palliative unit." I can barely get the words out. "And I thought it was Dr. Brown who would be forgetting about Emily."

The look that flashes across James' face is impossible to discern—a potent mixture of fury, hurt, and guilt. I take a shuddering breath, trying to rein the emotions back in, when in truth I feel like sobbing and sobbing and never stopping.

How did we get here? The summer before last, we rented a cottage on Cape Cod and sat on the beach with our legs entwined while the sun set and Emily made sandcastles, patting the damp sand so industriously, flipping the bucket over with endearing expertise. It was past her bedtime, but she was having so much fun—it was her first time at the beach when she wanted to do something other than eat the sand—that we couldn't bear to bring her in. The sunlight had looked as if it were melting over the surface of the ocean, and the only sound was the shoosh of the waves and our daughter's laughter.

How did we get here?

And how do we get back—if not there, because I know that can't happen, then to somewhere else, somewhere survivable, at the least?

James hasn't spoken for a few minutes and neither have I. Have we reached an impasse built of anger and resentment? Neither of us knows how to cross it.

"If this isn't about you forgetting you have a family," I finally ask, my jaw aching with how hard I am clenching it, "then what is it about? Why won't you even talk about this treatment? Why are you so quick, so determined, to believe there's no point? Why can't you crack your mind open just a little?"

James doesn't answer for a long moment. Outside, I hear Andrew call to Jake, and then the sound of him opening his front door, followed by Jake's piping voice, all of it a stark contrast to the palpably taut silence in this frozen room.

"Emily is not going to get better," James finally says, choosing each word with care, making me think of someone stepping from stone to stone over a rushing river, carefully placing his foot on each slick spot. "Everything—*everything*—we have experienced since she first became sick, has pointed to that. Dr. Brown believes that. His entire medical team believes that. *I* believe that."

I take each word like a blow, absorbing their impact. It is at least a minute before I manage to speak, my tone, I hope, reasonable, or almost. "None of you have considered this treatment."

James leans forward, his elbows braced on his knees, his expression caught between pity and exasperation. "Rachel, I *have* considered this treatment. Do you think I didn't do the research you did? Do you think I didn't read the articles in *Scientific American*? Do you think I didn't see the report about the man in a vegetative—"

"*Don't* use that word."

James rolls his eyes, he actually *rolls his eyes*, and then continues. "In a state of unresponsive wakefulness. Fine. I saw it, okay? I saw how little was achieved. He was barely better than before—"

"Little to you, maybe. You've already consigned Emily to the *grave*—"

"Stop it." The words are low but fierce. "Stop making this a damn competition."

"It's not a competition, James. I'm not trying to win here. God knows, I wish you felt as I did. I wish that more than anything."

My throat is closing up and I blink furiously. I will *not* cry. Not in front of my ex-husband, who is treating this so unemotionally. He might say he cares, but his words, his actions, say differently right now. And that hurts as much as anything else—when did my ex-husband stop caring about our daughter? The two evenings and Saturdays every week are just a chore to him now, I realize. A burden he has to bear. He wants it all to be over.

James leans back, rubbing his hand over his face. "Rachel, I don't think this treatment is a good idea for you, either."

"What is that supposed to mean?" Not that I want to know. In fact, just about the last thing I want is James giving some kind of half-baked pseudo-therapist assessment about my emotional state.

"It means I think it is time for you to let go, as hard as that is. Look at you." I recoil as he nods towards me, as if I'm exhibit A of what? A wrecked woman? A nutcase? I'm a little thin, admittedly, and my hair and skin aren't the best, but *still*. "Look at this place." Now he nods towards my living room, which admittedly is uninspired, but who is he to judge? Should I be getting a swanky place in Beacon Hill like he did, filling it with impractical white leather? Marrying up? "Do you do anything other than go to the hospital? Do you see your friends?"

"I see my mother." I haven't told James about my mom having Parkinson's yet. He always got along with her, and I know he'd be saddened, but I feel right now he'd just use it against me. *You can't deal with both your mom and Emily.* It might be a fair point, but it's not one I'm willing to give him.

"Besides your mother, I mean. And what about work? You loved being a teacher, Rachel. You were good at it—"

Yes, in another life, a life that didn't include watching my daughter diminish day by day, hour by hour. Now the thought of spending my days telling fifteen-year-olds about *The Great Gatsby* instead of with Emily feels pointless and offensive.

"I've made my choices and I'll stick by them, James. Emily is the most important thing in my life. Not my job. Not my friends. That's a choice I made, and I am one hundred percent glad I made it. No regrets whatsoever." I gaze at him levelly, a hint of challenge in my voice, my eyes. Can he say the same about his choices?

James stares at me for a long moment, and then he looks away. From next door, I hear footsteps, and then Jake laughing. Life being lived.

"What exactly are you proposing to do?" he asks finally, and it's the first time he's entertained the prospect, even in theory, that I could take Emily to Italy.

And so I outline the plans I've only been able to dream about so far—a month in Bologna, the treatment at the Centro di Neuroscienza that Dr. Rossi has agreed to provide for free; the guesthouse that has offered me a discounted rate for thirty days; the room at the Centro that could be made ready for Emily at a few days' notice, the repatriation agency that will offer a door-to-door air ambulance service.

"And the money?" James asks heavily. "I know you don't think that's important, but neither of us have one hundred and fifty thousand dollars or more lying around, Rachel."

"With Dr. Rossi offering his services for free, it might not be that much."

"It could be more. Transporting Emily? That alone will cost fifty thousand dollars, I should think."

"It depends whether she has to travel by air ambulance," I counter. I've done my research. "She might be eligible to travel accompanied on a commercial flight."

James shrugs, conceding the point. "Even so, there is the around-the-clock care she'll need, in a foreign country for a month?" He shakes his head. "None of that will come cheap." He holds up his hand to forestall my reply, although I haven't even opened my mouth. "I know it's not about the money. If I thought this treatment had any chance of working, I'd do all that I could to get my hands on that kind of cash, whatever it took. I *would*." He pauses, gazing at me steadily, willing me to believe him. I don't reply. "But I don't believe it will, and I'm not willing to pour my life savings into this... this wild goose chase."

"I'm not asking you to," I retort. *Wild goose chase*? "I'll use however much I get from the crowdfunding, and the rest from my inheritance."

James frowns. "Your inheritance?"

"From my mother." I know my mother has put aside money for me. When she dies, the house will be mine, as well. It doesn't sit exactly right banking on that money before she's gone, but I know she'd want me to use it for Emily. She'd offered me money before.

"You've discussed this with your mother?"

I lift my chin. "I will."

James sighs again. "You're really willing to gamble your entire inheritance, as well as a lot of other people's money, on this?"

"On *Emily*." Why can't he see that? Why can't he feel as I do, that nothing is more important than doing all I can for her? Why can't he realize that *any* improvement will be a total triumph for me, an absolute joy? It's not about *quality of life*, as if we're testing mattresses and deciding which are worth being rated a ten out of ten. It's about a living, breathing person we both love having the best chance at life that we can give her.

But James doesn't see that. He only sees the expense and the waste and the ongoing dilemma. He can't see the possibility, the need, the *hope*.

Which is why his next words shock me.

"If you're really sure you want to do this," he says slowly, heavily, "and you really believe it's worthwhile, then I won't stand in your way any longer."

I open my mouth to say something—thank you? —but James just shakes his head. He looks defeated, and terribly sad, which makes it hard for me to feel as jubilant as I want to.

"But please take down that Instagram account. The crowd-funding page—fine. I'll accept that. But let's not turn our lives, or our daughter's life, into some kind of social media circus."

"Yes, fine," I say, my voice a whisper. "I'll do that." I feel a sudden need to apologize, but I don't.

James nods and then rises from the sofa, looking older and more careworn than when he'd come in. It occurs to me then, no matter what insults and accusations I hurled at him earlier, that he really believes this treatment is not in Emily's best interest, or mine. He's acting on his genuine convictions, not just because he's tired or hassled. And that leaves me silent, fighting uncertainty, as he walks to the front door and out of my house.

CHAPTER TWENTY

EVA

Somehow, in the midst of everything, I didn't manage to tell James I was fired. And so when Friday morning rolls around, and for the first time I stay in bed, unable to continue the pretense that I have a job to go to, James looks at me blankly and says in a voice devoid of emotion or interest, "Aren't you getting up?"

My limbs feel leaden as I struggle to sit up. I've slept badly the last three nights, caught between a terrible, corroding guilt and a furious self-righteousness. Since walking out of the house after I told him about my part in the whole crowdfunding scheme, James has not spoken to me. I realize I am getting a taste of what Rachel experienced when she broached the idea of experimental treatment—his complete emotional shutdown. The only words he has said to me—more than once—are "I can't."

I accepted that at first; I was humbled, penitent when he came home at ten o'clock at night, having been out for hours, and still didn't want to talk. The next morning, I got up, even though I had nowhere to go, and made the coffee.

"James," I said as I poured him a cup, "Please, can we talk about this? I'm sorry—"

"I can't." The words were so flat and final it felt like he'd put a hand over my mouth. He left for work—twenty minutes earlier than usual—as soon as he'd put down his cup.

I mooched around the house all day, feeling restless, knowing I should do something with my resumé, figure out my life, but I felt so adrift that I ended up watching several hours of trashy TV and forgetting to have a shower.

James was back late, and when I asked him where he'd been, he just said briefly, "To see Rachel."

"Can we talk—"

"I can't."

Not again. "You can't talk?" I repeated, a scathing note entering my voice that I knew didn't help matters. "What are you, *mute*?"

"Yes, when it comes to this. To you. I just don't even…" He shook his head, and then he went into the bedroom and shut the door. He didn't seem angry, which was frightening. He was something worse, something deeper, as if I'd mortally wounded him.

I veered from guilt to self-righteousness then; it wasn't as if I'd cheated on him. I'd tried to help his daughter, for crying out loud. I'd been doing his family a *favor*.

Except I knew James didn't see it that way, and in truth I didn't either. He felt I'd betrayed him, and no matter what my motives, I knew that I had.

I pounded on the door, stupidly, because it wasn't even locked. "Are you going to hide away forever?" I shouted, tears of anger and worse, despair, springing to my eyes. "Are you never going to talk to me again?"

No reply. James didn't come out; I didn't go in. Eventually I curled up on the sofa and fell asleep until sometime past midnight; when I crept into bed, James was already asleep, his back like a brick wall to me.

And now, Friday morning, here I am, blinking sleep out of my eyes, having to tell him another unfortunate truth.

"I'm not getting up," I say. "I was fired."

James pauses in the act of knotting his tie. "Seriously?"

"Do you think I'd make that up?"

"What for?"

Some contrary streak in me makes me lift my chin. "For using company contacts to boost Emily's Instagram account." Even if it wasn't really just that. It's almost as if I want him to hate me, or maybe I just want to come completely clean.

James presses his lips together and turns away. He leaves the room, and by the time I motivate myself to get up ten minutes later, he's already gone.

Is this the end of my marriage? I consider the question like a dusty artefact, examining it from all angles, feeing weirdly distant from it, from James, from my own self. *Is this all it took—one step out of line, one little push, and it's over?*

It's not even that I blame James; I knew all along what I was risking. I knew what we had was precarious, even if we pretended it wasn't. We've only known each other a little more than a year. How could such a new relationship be strong enough to withstand this kind of stress and pressure? In any case, deep down I knew not to trust it, just as I've never trusted anyone, or any relationship, since I was twenty years old and my world fell in fragments all around me, because Lucas, another man I loved, told me he was there for me when he actually wasn't.

Now it all weighs on me, the past along with the present, a burden too heavy for me to bear, and so I don't. I don't think about it. I act as if I don't care. I've done this before; this feels familiar. Act the part and you will become it. To one degree or another, I've been doing this all my life for whomever I need to—my dad, my high-school boyfriend, Lucas, James. All men I ached to trust, tried to impress, in one way or another. I tried to be what I thought they wanted me to be.

And so, while James is at work, I clean the apartment, I grocery shop, I tinker with my resumé and then send it out to several marketing firms. I text Naomi to go out for cocktails this weekend. And I check Emily's page—one hundred thousand views, thirty-six thousand dollars. I don't know how to feel about any of it; looking at those figures makes me numb. So I put my phone away and open some jars of expensive pasta sauce for dinner and pretend everything is going to be fine.

When James returns home, he looks around at the clean apartment, the sauce bubbling on the stove, the expression on my face that I think is a combination of eager and desperate. His shoulders slump a little.

"I don't know if you've spoken to Rachel, but she's decided to go ahead with the treatment. I gave my agreement."

"You… did?" I haven't spoken to Rachel since this all broke, even though I've wanted to. It felt easier, not to.

"Yes. I can't fight you both. I don't want to fight either of you."

"James, I never meant—"

"I know you didn't. Rachel didn't, either. None of us did." He puts his messenger bag down on the table and I stand there, a sauce-splattered spoon in my hand, unsure what to say or do. Where we go from here. It feels as if we've climbed a mountain, but there is still a whole range in front of us.

"When is Rachel… When will the treatment start?"

"I don't know. I haven't spoken to her about the details."

But Emily is your daughter. I swallow down the words, the useless protest. "Will she go to Italy on her own? Just her and Emily?"

James shoots me a look; these aren't the questions I should be asking. He was, I realize, giving me an opening to move on. To paper over the cracks. "I have no idea, Eva. I imagine she will." He shrugs. "Perhaps her mother will go with her."

"But her mother has Parkinson's," I say before I think better of it.

James turns to me, his mouth dropping open in surprise. "What?"

"She found out a few weeks ago. When… when we were talking about setting up the page." I look away, feeling guilty for all sorts of reasons. It wasn't my place to tell James about Rachel's mother. She obviously chose not to.

He shakes his head. "Then I guess maybe she'll go alone. I didn't realize…" He shakes his head again.

I know he doesn't mean to sound indifferent. I know this has been too much for him, one hard thing after another; this morning I checked the comments on Emily's page and saw how many of them were about James. Horrible, spiteful, deliberately cruel comments, and I know he must have seen them too. Still I speak.

"That will be so tough on her, to go it alone." I picture Rachel alone in a foreign country, navigating everything on her own: the foreign language, the unfamiliarity, the emotional highs and lows of the experimental treatment… "Will you… visit?"

James presses his forefinger to the bridge of his nose as he closes his eyes briefly. "No, I don't think so. No."

Somehow, even now, I am taken aback. "But it's a whole month…"

"I'm well aware of that, Eva." James turns away, his shoulders hunching. "It was hard enough for me to agree to the treatment in the first place. Do you really think I want to see it—Emily being zapped by some medical version of a stun gun? Do you think it's going to be *pleasant*?"

"But Rachel—"

"Rachel is up for this. I am not. Besides, if I went, I would just make things more difficult for her. Trust me on that one."

"I do," I whisper. I feel badly for pressing the point, and yet my heart still aches for Rachel, coping on her own. "I do trust you, but—"

James throws his hands up in the air. "There is *always* a but."

"I just think you'd want to be there, at least for some of it. I mean, what if the treatment works and Emily is…" I'm not sure what she'd be. "What if it doesn't work?" I continue. "Either way…"

James turns slowly to face me full on. "Do you think I haven't thought of that? Do you think that isn't one of the *precise* reasons why I haven't wanted to go down this route?"

I am silent, shamed by the raw pain I hear in his voice.

"I'll say my goodbyes here in Boston," he says bleakly, and then he walks out of the room.

Another night passes where we don't talk. Now neither of us can.

Despite everything, I continue to think about Rachel, and her plans to go to Italy, even as my own life continues to implode. I don't get called to interview for any of the jobs I applied for. James maintains a stiff formality, a chilly politeness that is worse than his silence. I ask him when he is going to thaw and he gives me a bleak look.

"I'm not trying to be difficult," he says. "Despite what you may think. I just… I don't know how to be with you anymore, Eva."

And the truth is, I don't know how to be with him either. Has this been too much for our marriage, or has it just revealed what we never had in the first place? Part of me wishes I'd never spoken to Rachel about making a damned page. Another part—a larger part—is still glad that I did.

After another few days of mooching around the house, I end up calling Rachel. I need to know how she is doing. What her plans are. I feel far too invested, more than she wants me to be, but I am.

Her phone switches to voicemail, and I realize she must be at the hospital, with Emily. It is two o'clock on a Wednesday afternoon; where else would she be? And I know where that is—the palliative care unit of Boston Children's Hospital. It's not even that far, a few miles. I could bike it, since James has the car.

An hour later, I am being buzzed into the unit. I explained I was a friend of Rachel's—which felt like a lie—and she had to approve my entry. She is waiting for me as I come through the heavy doors, blinking in the dim lighting. Everything is both cheerful—primary colors, murals of animals—and yet terribly, terribly sad, a hush hanging over the hallway like a thick blanket.

"Eva." For the nurse's benefit, she offers me a tense smile. "I wasn't expecting you."

"I know. I'm sorry."

The nurse has gone back to the station. Rachel lowers her voice. "What are you doing here?"

"I wanted to see how you were doing. James told me he agreed to go ahead with the treatment."

"Yes." She pauses. "Thank you, for your part in it. It wouldn't have happened without you." The words feel more dutiful than heartfelt, and I wonder if she can possibly realize what this has cost me. I decide that she probably can't.

"I'm so glad it's working out." I glance at a couple who are emerging from one of the patients' rooms, their heads bowed. "I… Can we talk?"

Rachel looks a little hesitant, but then she nods. "All right. I suppose…" She hesitates. "That is… Would you like to meet Emily?"

Even though I knew I was coming here, I hadn't considered that I would actually see Emily. Meet her. I feel emotional suddenly, like a hand grabbing my throat. "Yes, I would," I say. "Thank you."

A minute later, Rachel is ushering me into a quiet room, sunlight streaming through the windows, a little girl lying in a bed. I recognize her from the photos, and yet I don't. Her eyes are open, which is jarring, even though I knew to expect it, her face slack, her body still. I swallow hard, knowing I need to get this right and yet feeling entirely out of my depth.

What would I want Rachel to do, if this was my child?

And then, bizarrely, it suddenly feels natural. *My child.*

I walk towards Emily, a smile spreading easily across my face, like butter on toast. "Hello, Emily." I sit next to her and touch her hand; her nails are painted pink. "What a beautiful day it is. And look at this!" I touch the teddy bear I bought her, propped by her head, which makes me smile wider. "He looks familiar."

There's no response, of course, and I wasn't expecting one, yet the ensuing silence feels like the saddest thing I've ever had to endure.

"I wonder what his name is. I think he looks like an Elmer to me. Although Elmer is an elephant, isn't he?" I glance at the other stuffed animal on her bed—a faded blue elephant, clearly well-loved, once upon a time. "You've already got an elephant, I see. What's his name?"

"Blue," Rachel says softly.

I glance back at her, and she gives me a tremulous smile, fighting back tears.

"Thank you for that."

"You don't have to thank me."

"You understand more than… well, you understand. I don't know how or why, but you do."

She sits in the only other chair in the room, on the opposite side of the bed, and the three of us stay like that, breathing in the silence.

"I'm planning to go to Italy in two weeks," Rachel says eventually. "That's when the ambulance agency can fit the travel in. She has to go by private plane… it's not easy. Or cheap." She lets out a shaky laugh. "But I've got the money together, from the crowdfunding, and also from my mom. She was happy to give me as much as I wanted. This is really happening."

My heart swells; it's as if I can feel it getting bigger in my chest. "I'm so glad, Rachel."

"I know you are. I don't totally understand it, or you, but I know you are."

I glance down at Emily; her eyes are moving, back and forth, back and forth, which jolts me. I must make some sound of surprise, because Rachel explains, "The doctors say it's just a reflex, but it doesn't feel that way to me." Her voice hitches and then evens out. "It feels like more."

I can understand that. If my daughter's eyes were open, moving around, *looking* at things, I would think it was more too. I would have to. "Have you told them you're taking her to Italy?" I ask quietly.

"Yes. Dr. Brown, the head of her team, wasn't too pleased. He thinks the travel will put her at risk of infection, and the treatment is so new as to be completely unverifiable. I *know* that." She sets her jaw. "But there's nothing he can do about it, thankfully. I still have control of the medical decisions for my daughter, along with James, no matter what the experts advise."

"So it's really happening."

She folds her arms, nods. "Yes."

I touch Emily's hand; her skin is soft and cool, and very slightly damp. I can hear her breathe. "It's going to be hard, doing this all alone."

"I know." Rachel takes a deep breath. "My mom wanted to come, but the way she is... you know she has Parkinson's..."

"Yes. You told me."

"She's started some treatment, and the travel will be difficult for her." She pauses, then admits, "And the truth is, I don't think I can manage her and Emily. I'm not sure I'll even manage Emily."

It's the perfect opening for the thought that's been forming in my mind, my heart, all along. The idea that is ridiculous, absurd, that I'm pretty sure has crossed no one's mind but my own.

"I could come with you." I speak softly, my eyes on Emily, but I know Rachel hears me. I hear it in her soft gasp, and I look up to see her eyes wide, her lips parted.

"What..." she begins, shaking her head slowly.

"I could come with you to Italy. To help. You'll need another pair of hands. And emotionally... I know we're not exactly friends, but this isn't something you should have to do alone."

"But how could you..."

"I've been fired from my job. For using some company contacts for Emily's account, among other things."

"Oh, Eva..."

"It doesn't matter. I don't mind. I didn't like working there anymore, anyway. And James isn't speaking to me, not really. I don't know if he'll ever forgive me, for betraying him this way. Because that *is* how he sees it." My lips tremble and my eyes fill with tears. I didn't mean to fall apart; I don't want this to feel like some sort of emotional blackmail, and yet... "Let me come with you, Rachel. Let me do this." I draw a shaky breath, and Rachel's glance falls to my hand. Unknowingly, I've laced my fingers through Emily's.

She stares at our joined hands and then slowly she nods.

Dear Bean,

Today was a hard day. You were grizzly, getting teeth, and I was feeling bored and lonely and so very tired. We got on each other's nerves, Bean, but I should have risen above it.

I tried everything to help you settle. I put on our favorite Rod Stewart song—you have a fondness for "You're in My Heart"—and danced around the kitchen with you, doing our little two-step. You'd get into it for a second—I could see you thinking about smiling, but then you'd wrench away from me, practically trying to launch yourself out of my arms, and you'd start your grizzling noise that makes me think of a grumpy bear.

I can handle those noises. They can even make me smile, because they almost feel like you're putting it on. But then you started to cry, and I mean howl, and you didn't want to be held by me, but when I put you down, that made you sadder, and I just didn't know what to do! Five straight hours of this—up, down, dance around, deep knee bends because sometimes they help, but nothing did. Nothing! And then you got really fed up, and you started screaming. The whole works, Bean—tears, snot, your face as red as a tomato. And you wouldn't let me comfort you, you just wouldn't.

In the end, I put you down in your bouncy seat and walked out of the room. I just walked away, Bean. I went into the bedroom where I couldn't hear you and I put my hands over my ears and breathed in and out, trying to calm myself, because the truth is, I felt angry. Not just normal irritated-angry, either. I felt rage, and I didn't know what to do about it, and I was scared—of myself.

I stayed in that room for six minutes, which seems like far too long. Six minutes before I felt ready to go back and face you. And when I did… oh, Bean! You'd stopped crying. You'd tired yourself out, and you had your fist in your mouth, and your face was covered in tears and snot, and you were making these shuddering sounds that just about broke me.

I picked you up and you snuffled against my neck as if you were trying to fuse into me and I held you and held you, kissing your head, rocking you and singing you songs, and feeling so guilty, so sorry for having let you down.

And even though part of me knew what happened was normal for any mother, another part of me couldn't forgive myself for failing you… even as I recognized that I would again, and again, because I'm human, and you are too. But I'll do my best not to, Bean. I will do my very best always.

Love, Mama

CHAPTER TWENTY-ONE

RACHEL

I open the latticed shutters with a dusty creak, summer sunshine spilling through the windows and bathing my face with its warmth. Below me, the narrow, cobbled streets of Bologna bustle with activity—a shopkeeper sweeping his front steps, a boy on a bicycle, two women with clacking heels, heads together, as they walk to work.

I am in Italy. Emily is in Italy. *Eva* is in Italy.

I draw a breath of warm, sun-scented air, feeling almost as if I'm on vacation. Bologna is impossibly quaint, or at least what I saw of it sitting in the front of the ambulance from the airport, with narrow streets, terracotta-colored buildings, sidewalk cafés and sprawling plazas.

Eva and I flew here on a commercial flight with Emily; when I made the arrangements with the air ambulance service, they told me she was in fact eligible to travel by regular flight, on a stretcher and accompanied by medical personnel, rather than on a privately hired air ambulance. It meant I saved thousands of dollars, but I was conscious of the speculative and sometimes appalled looks of the other passengers, followed by naked relief that this wasn't them or their child, as Emily was brought past them, a nurse walking alongside, with her canisters of oxygen and fistfuls of tubes and wires. Her stretcher was placed in the back of the plane, where some seats had been removed.

When we arrived in Bologna, I went with her in an ambulance straight to the hospital, while Eva took a cab here, to the guesthouse.

I was able to see Emily settled into her room at the Centro di Neuroscienza that Dr. Rossi had arranged, before coming here, to this shabby, friendly little place on a tiny side street run by a smiling, round-faced woman who kissed both my cheeks when I told her who I was.

Everything feels good. Hope is overflowing, like a fountain of milk and honey, scoopfuls of it for the taking. Emily managed the trip fine. *Fine.* Despite Dr. Brown's grim warnings, and James' insistence that flying wouldn't be good for her, she didn't have any trouble on the flight and Dr. Rossi ran all her checks when we arrived and there have been no problems—no spike in temperature, no drop in heart rate. Her treatment will start the day after tomorrow, when they've monitored her long enough to ensure she is truly stable.

Now Eva and I have come here to unpack and get some rest. The last few days have been utterly exhausting, running around, making all the arrangements, making sure all the forms were signed, the provisions made, the money there. The crowdfunding donations topped out at fifty-three thousand dollars. My mother gave me the rest, without any strings, protestations, or modicum of concern about handing over such a huge amount.

"All you had to do was ask. Anytime, any amount," she said, and I tried not to feel guilty that this was her money, not mine, or that she'd let slip, without meaning to, that she wasn't on a certain prescription drug for Parkinson's because it was too expensive. "Eleven thousand dollars for six weeks' worth of some inhibitor or other," she'd scoffed. "I'm not willing to pay that."

Yet she was willing to give me ten times that amount for Emily.

But I don't want to feel guilty about that now, not when I'm finally here, and with her blessing. With everyone's blessing, even James', more or less. He texted me this morning, wishing both me and Emily a safe journey and asking me to keep him informed. We've reached a truce, an understanding, even if it's not one borne of agreement.

Andrew and Jake invited me over for dinner last night; they'd bought a cake all covered in pink that almost made me cry. *Good luck Emily.* They'd blown up balloons, and after dinner we played an epic game of Candyland; it felt like a celebration of what was to come, rather than what had happened. Afterwards, as I was leaving, Jake tackled me around my knees and I bent down, my arms closing around him in surprise; he'd never hugged me before. I was still recovering from that emotional shot to the heart when Andrew gave me a hug and a kiss on the cheek.

"Let us know how it all goes," he said quietly, looking into my eyes, meaning it. "And if there's anything I can do. Anything at all…"

"Thank you. For everything." I meant it, too.

I said goodbye to my mother, as well, as if I were going on a long journey, as if I were some sort of old-world adventurer, an explorer off to unknown lands, the Arctic or the Amazon. That's how I felt, and as I looked into my mother's worn face and saw her smile try to hide the worry, her hands trembling against my back as she hugged me, I wondered if she would be much changed upon my return. If I would. And most of all, if Emily would.

"Tell me everything," she insisted. "I so wish I could be there, Rachel. Skype me whenever you want, as often as you can."

"Of course I will."

And I said goodbye to James. He'd texted and called me several times over the last few weeks, asking about the preparations for the trip, meeting me at the hospital to sign medical forms. We didn't talk much beyond the logistics of getting Emily to Italy; everything emotional had already been said and lay between us like a frozen river, but one at least we could now cross.

The last time I saw him, two days before now, at the hospital, he hugged me. We hadn't hugged or even touched in what felt like years, and the feel of him—the smell of him—was like falling back through time. It was a quick but tight hug, and then he stepped back.

"Keep me informed about everything," he said almost brusquely.

"I will."

He turned to Emily, his throat working. I watched, my eyes filming with tears, as he bent over and pressed a kiss to her forehead. "Bye bye, sweetheart," he whispered. "Have a good trip. You're going to Italy, and I've never even been there."

I swiped at my eyes; I couldn't recall the last time James had spoken to our daughter in my presence.

He stepped away from Emily, his face back to its usual mask as he looked at me. "I hope… I hope you find what you're looking for, in Italy."

"Thank you." I tried not to let that rub me a little bit raw; he made it sound almost as if I were going on some indulgent, self-help trip, like Andrew's wife Christina jaunting off to a yoga retreat. But I knew he meant well, that he was trying, and I swallowed down the reply that had sprung to my lips, that the only thing I was *looking for* was for Emily to get better.

Now I lean my arms on the windowsill and stretch my head to glimpse more of the narrow street below. Window boxes spilling over with bougainvillea decorate every house, and in the distance I hear the melodious peal of church bells. I can't believe I'm actually here.

From behind me, I hear a knock on the door of my bedroom, and I go to answer it. Eva stands there, looking fresh and pretty, her hair still damp from a shower. She is wearing a pink sundress and she looks softer than I've seen her before, as if her hard edges have been rounded off.

"I thought you were back from the hospital," she says. "Emily settled in okay?"

"Yes, fine."

Eva has been remarkably unfazed by Emily's needs. Most people I know would school their face into what they think is a bland expression when they see Emily, but the horror is visible in the widening of their eyes, the higher pitch of their voices. They can't quite make any of it seem normal, and I don't blame them. How can I? It *isn't* normal.

But Eva, to my surprise, didn't exhibit any of those signs. From the moment she met Emily, she treated her like a person, not a patient, or worse, a thing. She talked to her as if she wanted to, as if she knew Emily was listening, and she *touched* her—her hand, her cheek—something most people never do. I wasn't expecting it; Eva has always seemed so polished and professional, almost cold, that this sudden warmth emanating from her towards my daughter took me completely by surprise and moved me almost unbearably. I needed another person in my life who saw Emily the way I did. It was what made me agree to let her come, and I've been glad of her presence since. Already she's made herself indispensable in a dozen small ways, from bringing me coffee while I waited with Emily at the airport, to taking my mind off everything as we chatted about the best series on Netflix on the plane.

"How's the jet lag?" she asks, and I shrug.

"I slept for an hour or so when I got back. You?"

"The same. I'm not sure my body knows what time it is." She makes a face. "Anyway… are you hungry?" Her eyebrows rise. "We could go out to eat? There's a cute little place I spotted on the corner—actually, there's a dozen cute little places. Take your pick."

I hesitate, because my imagination had not stretched past a hurried meal somewhere charmless—food has been a matter of expediency rather than enjoyment for a long time. Yet right now, with the sun still shining, and the jabber of joyful conversation audible from the street—everything in Italian sounds emotional—I think, why not? Why not enjoy myself here, if just a little?

"I suppose we could," I say, still cautious, and Eva gives an expansive shrug.

"We should. I've never been to Italy before, and Bologna looks beautiful."

I haven't either, and yes, it does. I realize I don't feel guilty for wanting to enjoy myself, because I know—I *know*—Emily is in the best place she could possibly be right now. "Sounds like a good idea," I tell Eva. "I don't mind where we eat."

"Why don't we walk around and see what we like?" Eva suggests. "It's so beautiful out."

I thought it would feel stranger to be here with Eva, and yet somehow, so far, it hasn't been. As we head out into the balmy evening, I am amazed at how companionable we can be. I've never disliked my ex-husband's second wife, but I have, at times, resented her existence. Yet now I am thankful for it, for her, and that she chose to come to Italy with me.

Music spills out from the open shutters of a bar as we stroll down the street, people jostling for space, yet everyone seeming to smile, and we soak up the atmosphere. Everything feels different, more vibrant and alive, the street full of people and noise, everyone living life to its overflowing brim—the wine, the music, the laughter, the smells of delicious food and moped fumes, and the bougainvillea in the window boxes combining to form a heady scent. *We are alive.*

The thought of eating a nice meal in a restaurant in a beautiful city fills me with a happiness and even an excitement that I haven't felt in a long time.

Soon enough, we find ourselves in the back courtyard of a little trattoria, sitting at a rickety table with a bottle of Chianti with a candle stuck in it between us.

"This would seem cliché, except it's real," Eva says with a laugh, and I have to agree. I feel almost as if I'm in a movie, the imagined version of Italy rather than the real thing, and yet it all feels wonderful—the food, the wine Eva insists we order and which I am more than happy to drink, the violinist who serenades us as we eat our antipasti, insisting that we are "*Bella, bella, molto bella!*"

"Can we make a deal?" Eva asks as a white-aproned waiter clears our plates, ready for our main course—parmesan and truffle risotto for me, tortellini in cream for Eva.

"A deal?" The wine has made me relaxed, but I am still the tiniest bit wary.

"Yes, just for tonight. That we won't talk about… any of it." She bites her lip, her gaze searching my face. "Not the social media stuff, not the treatment, not Emily or James or anyone. Let's just… let's just have a regular conversation. Talk about anything else. Just to relax. To be." She continues to scan my face, looking anxious. "Is that okay?" I can tell she is afraid she's offended me, but she hasn't.

"That sounds like a pretty good deal to me," I say, and Eva smiles in relief.

And so we don't mention any of it, and it feels like such a *relief.* We end up sharing our life stories, in dribs and drabs. I tell her about being a bookish nerd in high school, working on the school newspaper and avoiding all sports, with academics for parents, and how I tried to become cool in college and failed, but that was fine, because I realized I didn't actually want to be cool. I wanted to be me.

Eva tells me she was a cheerleader for all four years of high school—I snort my wine as I burst into laughter, saying I am not surprised—and she laughs, too.

"I know. I annoy myself, thinking about it. I had it all—the pom-poms, the high ponytail, the short skirt. I thought I was amazing."

I bet she did. There is a whimsical cast to her face now, something almost a little sad, and so I ask, "What happened?"

She smiles and shrugs. "I went to a college that didn't have a cheerleading squad. A college where even admitting you were a cheerleader was embarrassing. So I didn't."

"So if you weren't a cheerleader, what were you?"

"Something almost worse." She laughs. "A pretentious college student. I even bored myself back then. And after that, I was a career woman in the making, city-smart and focused, living in New York, trying to get to the top." She shakes her head ruefully. "It's always something, isn't it? You always have to be something."

"Yes, you do." It surprises me, to realize how similar we have been, reinventing ourselves to suit the circumstances, to fit other people's expectations. Eva became the straight-A student; I became the best hospital mom. Do all women do it? I wonder. Do we all bend ourselves into whatever shape we think others want to see, so somehow we fit, even if it hurts?

Our main courses come, and we exchange conversation for food, both of us savoring the rich sauces. I've drunk too much wine, and my head is starting to spin, but I don't care. I want this evening to go on forever, almost as much as I want tomorrow to come. For Emily to start her treatment, and begin to get better. For everything, finally, to change.

Yet right now, with the food and wine, the music and laughter, with *Eva*, I don't think about Emily. I don't think about anything, except the pure enjoyment of the evening, the setting sun sending vivid orange streaks across the sky, and my friend sitting across from me, sipping her wine and smiling.

CHAPTER TWENTY-TWO

EVA

I sneak a glance at Rachel as we sit on hard plastic chairs in the waiting area of the Centro di Neuroscienza, where we've spent most of the last week. Her face is pale and wan, her gaze abstracted as she nibbles on her lip. We haven't spoken in over an hour as we wait for Emily to finish today's treatment—something we are not meant to see. Rachel balked at that at first, but Dr. Rossi gently insisted.

"Sometimes the stimulation can cause effects that seem troubling," he said, and Rachel's face leached of color.

"It doesn't hurt her—"

"Not in the way that we experience pain. But it is stimulation. And, to tell you the truth, Signora Lerner, we do not want to be distracted. This is treatment for your daughter, but it is also research, in controlled conditions."

Rachel nodded, accepting, even if she looked frightened. "I can see her afterwards, though?"

"Yes, of course."

As a result, the last seven days have been mostly about waiting, with less time with Emily than either Rachel or I expected. With the treatment, the recovery period, and Dr. Rossi's assessments afterwards, we are only allowed to see her for a couple of hours each morning, and then for a little bit in the evening. I try to give Rachel some alone time with her daughter in the mornings, and so I end up wandering around the outskirts of Bologna, trying not to sweat into a puddle in the relentless heat, or wonder what I am doing here.

I was amazed that Rachel actually agreed for me to come, just as I was amazed that I even asked. We're not friends—at least, we weren't when I asked to come. Maybe we are now. But still, I'd met Emily once before Rachel said yes. I don't regret coming, not at all, but I still wonder.

I still remember, and I keep thinking what if.

What if I'd…

But I can't bear to finish that question, much less answer it.

I've texted James every day that I've been here, just as I know Rachel has. It feels important to keep him involved, even as I wonder what the state of our marriage is. When I told him I was going with Rachel, he didn't even look surprised. It was as if I'd already shown him my where my loyalty lay and this was just another piece of proof.

"I'm glad she'll have someone with her," he said, which would have been kind, except it sounded so defeated. He wasn't angry anymore, or icily silent, just broken. And I continued to veer wildly between a terrible, penetrating guilt and an exasperated self-righteousness. *All I did was try to help.* But, of course, we all know where the best intentions lie.

I turn my gaze from Rachel to the view of the outside—a world full of summer seen behind a plate-glass window. The sky is an achingly bright blue, so it almost hurts to look at it, and the heat radiates up from the pavement in visible waves. I feel trapped in here, but I don't want to leave Rachel alone while she waits to hear how Emily responded. She always insists on sitting vigil through her treatment, even though it doesn't do any good and I think it might irritate Dr. Rossi. He's here to do an experiment as much as he is to make someone better, something neither Rachel nor I fully realized until we'd met with him on the first day, and he'd explained in full how this was all going to go.

"Rachel." My voice sounds loud in the stale stillness of the room. She startles and then turns to look at me. "Why don't we go out for a bit? Get some fresh air? This can't be good for you."

"But Emily…"

"You're not going to be able to see Emily for hours," I remind her as gently as I can. "And meanwhile you need to take care of yourself, for her sake. Recharge. Relax, if just a little."

Her teeth sink deeper into her lower lip as she starts to shake her head. I struggle against a well-meaning exasperation, because I understand why Rachel feels she needs to be here. The possibility of missing something, anything, is too terrible to contemplate. But she looks both washed out and highly strung, and she needs a break. So do I. I wait, and after another endless moment, she nods.

"All right… for a little while."

I suggest we visit MAMbo, the Museo d'Arte Moderna di Bologna, a clean, open space dedicated to "visual culture and experimentation", and, I hope, a place that will take us out of the realm of hospital and hope, illness and uncertainty.

But as we are crossing Piazza Maggiore, a huge esplanade, the central square dazzling under the bright summer sun, Rachel pauses, her gaze fixed on a sign, and then she heads down a narrow street towards a large church on the Via Clavature—the Chiesa di Santa Maria della Vita.

"I love old churches," she explains, and she heads inside. I follow her a little reluctantly, because I don't love old churches. I spent enough time in them growing up—church every Sunday, first communion classes, the whole good Catholic upbringing. I stopped going in college, although I don't think I ever stopped feeling guilty.

I stand in the nave of the church, next to Rachel; it is a beautiful, Baroque building, all marble friezes and soaring space. As we start to walk through it, we don't speak; this church, like every other I've seen, is a sacred space, an expectant hush falling over it, and us, like a gentle blanket. Words would feel profane.

Rachel pauses in front of a Renaissance-style oil painting of the Madonna and child. She is beatific, with her blue veil and distant gaze, a slight Mona Lisa-like smile curving her lips. The child is a rotund baby with a serious expression and dimpled rolls of fat, a rumpled loin cloth his only clothing.

Rachel stares at that painting with a fixed expression that is starting to make me nervous. She almost looks angry, or at least determined. I wonder what she is thinking while looking at that mother and child, and then I wonder what I think.

Why was she so lucky?

But then I remember what Mary must have endured—the death of her son, painfully and publicly at that. *But at least she got thirty-three years with him.* Is it wrong to think like that? Blasphemous, even?

Finally, after what feels like a very uncomfortable age, Rachel moves on. I want to get out of the church, back into the bright sunlight and the sultry air, away from the echoes of footsteps and hushed whispers. Away from mothers and babies, whoever they are.

But we're not done yet, for Rachel pauses in front of an enclosed space that advertises something called the Lamentation of the Dead Christ. I don't know what that is, but we have to pay four euros to see it, and Rachel hands them over without a word. Feeling anxious for a reason I don't fully understand, I do the same.

The Lamentation of the Dead Christ proves to be—what a surprise—exactly that. Instead of a painting, however, it is a set of life-size terracotta sculptures—Christ lying on the ground and six figures surrounding him, each with an expression of grief or pain on their face as they behold him.

The realism of the figures is strangely shocking, far more visceral than a painting—Mary's fists are clenched, and another woman—Mary Magdalene, perhaps—has an expression of pain, almost agony, on her face, her clothes blown by an invisible wind. One of the disciples is silently weeping, his chin under his hand.

We gaze at the figures in silence; they transfix me, but they also make me want to run away. How can a six-hundred-year-old statue speak so rawly into our own experience? Because I know that is what is happening here—these statues are an echo of the grief that is surely waiting for Rachel, if not now, then one day.

After several tense seconds, she turns and walks quickly away from them, and I nearly trip in my haste to follow her. Rachel strides right out of the church and into the street; the sunlight is dazzling, blinding, and the hot air has a baked feel to it that makes it hard to breathe.

"Rachel…" I begin, and then don't finish, because I don't know how she's feeling or how to respond to it.

She shakes her head and draws a quick breath as we stand there in the street. "I shouldn't have gone in there." I try to think of something to say, but no words come. In any case, it doesn't matter, because Rachel keeps talking. "Eva, I'm scared."

I can deal with that, or so I think. "Dr. Rossi said it would take several weeks before he could tell if the treatment was working—"

"Not about that." She shakes her head. "I'm scared I've done the wrong thing." She turns to look at me, her eyes dark and full of fear. "I'm scared I shouldn't have brought Emily here."

I stare at her helplessly. "But why…?"

A man shouts at us to move out of the way—at least that's what I'm assuming he's saying, based on his hand gestures—and I take Rachel's elbow and steer her towards the side of the street.

"Let's find somewhere quiet and get a coffee," I tell her. "And then we'll talk about this properly."

She lets me lead her by the arm to a café on a quiet side street. Once inside, I order us both macchiatos and steer Rachel to a table in the back. The noise from the street is muted, the only sound the murmur of a few other customers and the clinking of cups.

Rachel cradles her coffee as if she craves the warmth, even though it is boiling outside and only a tiny bit cooler in here.

"Why are you saying that?" I ask quietly. "Why do you think you might have done the wrong thing?"

"It just…" She bites her lip. "It doesn't feel the way I expected it to. When the money started coming in… when James agreed… when we got here… I felt so hopeful. I really did. Everything was finally happening." Her eyes fill with tears as she looks at me and I have to force mine back. "It felt like a beginning, at *last*. And that's what I so wanted it to be…"

"It still could be, Rachel. It's only been a week. You need to give it time."

"I know, but it's just not… Dr. Rossi…" She sighs and shakes her head. "I'm afraid Emily is just a statistic to him, something to add to his precious data."

"He's nice," I protest, even though I know what she means. Dr. Rossi is more of a clinician than a consultant; his manner is gentle, but even I've noticed the way he refers to Emily like exhibit A. Still, if he gets the results…

"I wonder if I've been selfish," Rachel says quietly. "If I came here for me instead of Emily."

"What do you mean?"

"Because I needed to feel hope. I needed to feel like I was doing everything I could for her, not for her, but for me."

I ponder her words for a few moments, thinking of how similarly I have felt. "That's not a bad thing."

"Isn't it? All along, James has been insisting he was saying no to the treatment because it was best for Emily. What if he was right?"

"And what if he wasn't? The jury is still out on this one, Rachel. Give it some time."

"Yesterday Dr. Rossi told me that this kind of nerve stimulation appears to be more effective on patients who are unresponsive because of traumatic brain injuries rather than neurological disorders. Something he didn't mention before, although I suppose I could have guessed it. I just didn't want to."

"He doesn't know for sure, though," I say quickly. "He hasn't done enough research…"

"Which might be why he is researching Emily." She sighs again, shaking her head. "I don't blame him. He's doing good, important work. I'm just mad at myself for secretly hoping for some sort of miracle, even as I told myself there wouldn't be one."

"There's no shame in that, Rachel. We're all hoping for miracles."

She gives me a frank look. "Are you?"

I shrug. I haven't told Rachel that James and I are trying for a baby, not that we actually have been for the last two months, but informing Rachel of my desire for her ex-husband's baby seems weird, not to mention the height of insensitivity. "Rachel, the point is, you weren't wrong in coming here. Even if… even if the treatment has no discernible results. You came because you wanted to give Emily every chance you could. There is absolutely nothing wrong in that."

"But if it doesn't work at all? The money alone—"

"Who cares about the money? I mean," I clarify quickly, "yes, it was a lot of your money—"

"My mother's money, and I know she gave it willingly, but all those other people…"

"They gave it willingly too. They weren't investing in a stock, Rachel. They're not looking for that kind of return."

She manages a wobbly smile. "That's a relief."

I reach over to put my hand on top of hers. "Don't feel guilty. You are a mother who loves her child, and you'd do anything for her." A lump is forming in my throat as I speak. "You'd sacrifice your own happiness and well-being for her… I've seen that time and again with you, and I admire it." I force myself to swallow past that wretched lump. "More than you could possibly know."

Rachel sniffs and dashes a tear from her cheek as she looks down at our joined hands. "Sorry," she says with a shaky laugh. "I don't know why I'm feeling so wobbly now. It must be PMS."

I smile my sympathy even as a sudden realization blazes through me. *PMS*. I haven't had my period in…

I sit back, trying to remember when it was; I'm always regular, and I track my cycle with an app on my phone. But as I sit there, I realize I haven't had my period in over two months, since right after Emily first went into palliative care. Two months. How could I have missed it? After all my ovulation monitoring and test taking, how could this have slipped my mind?

Hope unfurls inside me, along with panic. James and I are barely speaking. I'm in Italy with Rachel. And anyway, I've probably missed my periods because of stress. Surely I can't be pregnant now?

"Eva?" Rachel leans forward to look at me in concern. "Are you okay?"

"Yes, yes. Sorry. I was just…" I push the thoughts away. I can't tell Rachel about that; I can barely think about it. "Why don't we go to the modern art museum?"

Rachel shakes her head. "No, I should really get back. But you go ahead, if you want to."

Is that her subtle way of telling me she wants to be alone with Emily? I decide to take it as such, not because I want to see the modern art, but because I want to take a pregnancy test.

I part ways with Rachel at the Piazza Maggiore, and then spend fifteen frantic minutes looking for a *farmacia*. I finally find one on a side street so narrow it's more like an alley; the shop has old-fashioned bow windows and a cheery, balding man at the till who doesn't speak a word of English.

"*Avete…*" I manage, thanks to an hour on Duolingo on the plane. *Do you have.* But when it comes to *pregnancy test*, my knowledge fails me. "*Un testo di…*"

He stares at me blankly. My phone only works with Wi-Fi while abroad, so I can't even search for the right words now.

"*Un testo,*" I say again, and he shakes his head, seeming sorrowful.

Desperate now, I gesture to my front, rounding my hand as if I have a lovely big bump.

The man stares at me as if I'm crazy and then his expression brightens. "Ah! Ah! *Test di gravidanza!*"

I nod, even though I don't know if that's right or not, and he bustles behind the counter, appearing seconds later with a slim white box. The words might be in Italian, but oh, how I recognize its shape.

"*Si,*" I say excitedly. "*Si, si!*"

He grins, all benevolent bonhomie, and I hand over my euros. "*Buona fortuna, signora!*" he says with a vigorous nod. "*Buona fortuna!*"

I am still smiling as I take the box in its white paper bag back to the guesthouse. I am already imagining how I might tell this story to my son or daughter one day, about how I found out I was pregnant. How I found out about them. Just the thought makes me press one hand to my middle, as if I can feel a tiny little baby fluttering in there.

I may not even be pregnant, I remind myself. Stress can be a huge contributing factor to infertility, and I have definitely been stressed. Really, it would be no surprise at all that I've missed a couple of periods due to all the worry and uncertainty I've felt.

And yet just as Rachel has been hoping for a miracle while telling herself she isn't, so am I.

There's no point reading the directions, because they're in Italian, and anyway I've been here so many times before. Pee on a stick, wait, one minutes or three, the more lines, the better.

I sit on the edge of the tub in the tiny square of a bathroom, the test turned over so I can't watch the dye flow through the window. I've made that mistake before, incredulous hope withering away as the promising lines fade and blank.

Three minutes has never seemed so long, every tick of the clock in beat with my heart. Dare I hope…? *What if I am?*

Finally, with fingers that feel numb, I turn the test over. It takes me a second to focus on that precious little window and what it is telling me.

Two lines. *Two lines.*

I let out a sound, I'm not sure what, something between a sob and a laugh, with a huff of disbelief in there, as well.

I'm pregnant. *I'm pregnant.*

I think of all the wine I've drunk over the last few months, and then I think of James being so cold to me, and then of Emily lying so still in a bed. The look on Rachel's face, the look on the statue of Mary's face. Mothers longing for, and grieving, their children.

I'm pregnant. I'm pregnant again, finally. It's wonderful and incredible and so very terrifying.

With the stick still in my hand, I feel the warm, salty tears trickle down my face.

CHAPTER TWENTY-THREE

RACHEL

The hot, summer sunshine of the first week in Bologna has given way to a damp and oppressive heat, with an oily fog rolling in and blanketing the city in gray. Apparently this is fairly normal, as Bologna rests in the Po Valley and the fog is trapped in it like water in a basin; it will only lift when the winds blow and the weather finally changes.

The dank skies don't help my mood, which has been plummeting steadily since we arrived. I've tried to keep my spirits up, hoisting them again and again like a tattered sail, but it has been getting harder with every passing day. No matter what Eva said about coming here being the right thing to do, I'm more and more afraid that it isn't.

And I'm even more afraid that it isn't working.

Since that first buoyant evening, when everything seemed possible, nothing has felt the way I thought it would. The hospital feels sterile; Dr. Rossi is kind but clinical; and worst of all, Emily feels like an experiment. Here, more than anywhere else, she is a statistic. *Data*. And I find myself missing the massage therapy and music room I once scoffed at. I miss the familiarity of the doctors and nurses back at the children's hospital in Boston, the routines, the colorful murals on the walls, the smiles of the staff, the *language*. I miss my mom, and Andrew and Jake, and I even miss James.

I've texted and spoken to them all over the last two weeks, and although they've tried to be positive in their own ways, they haven't helped.

On the phone, my mother's voice sounds suddenly old—wavery and thin, as if she's already fading away, but I tell myself she can't be. She's only just been diagnosed. Yet when I asked, she admitted the tremors have become a little worse.

"It's all expected, Rachel," she said, as if somehow this made it better. "This is exactly the progression they told me to expect. It's not a surprise, even if it feels like one."

"Right." I didn't know what else to say. An awkward silence ensued, like something we had to stumble over. Then my mother asked another question about the treatment, and I answered it, and I thought we'd found our way back to a stable place, only for her to pause for a few terrible seconds a little while later, as she tried to sound out words that once came so naturally to her, taking her time with the syllables. Her speech, like her movement, was affected, and it would only become more so.

"I'm sorry, honey," my mom said, apologizing, even though she didn't need to. Of course she didn't. "I know it seems... well, I don't know how it seems. I'm slowing down. My hands tremble. And sometimes my head feels blank, as if there's nothing in there. Literally nothing." She let out a choked sound that I thought was meant to pass for a laugh. "Some days I don't feel it at all. Other times... it feels like a mental free fall, like I don't know who I am anymore. But I'm sorry. I know this, on top of everything with Emily, must be distressing to you, and I hate that."

"You don't need to be sorry, Mom." It saddened me unbearably that this was happening to her, and even more so that I was missing it. When I returned from Italy, would she seem like a different person? Was she already becoming one? Another cost to this trip that I hadn't envisaged.

"Still." She sighed. "I know it's the last thing you need."

"It's the last thing *you* need," I said automatically, but she was right. Worrying about my mother on top of worrying about Emily felt like a weight I wasn't strong enough to bear, and so I ended up trying not to worry or think of her at all, which felt awful in a different way, yet I knew there was only so much my soul could take at one time.

Outside, the clouds swell and darken with rain, turning violent shades of purple that would be beautiful if they didn't look so ominous. Eva told me a thunderstorm is predicted for tonight, and I think the rain might be a relief. I'm so tired of waiting.

Last night, I spoke to James to give him an update, even though there wasn't much to say. Every day Emily gets the nerve stimulation, which I'm recommended not to see, and then a brain scan, which I also don't see. After a period of recovery, I can finally sit with her, but she's covered in electrodes monitoring everything all the time, and it all feels far more invasive than I expected, the hospital more sterile and clinical, the future more unknown. Part of me just wants to go home, even as I desperately hope and wait for not a cure, no, I know better than that, but something. Anything.

The despondency that I can't quite hide has turned James, improbably, into my comforter. "They said it would take some time before there are any potential results," he reminded me when I admitted just a fraction of my doubts on the phone last night. "You need to be patient, Rachel. I know it's hard."

"I know. I just…" I couldn't admit to him that I'm afraid I was wrong, that I really have been holding out for a miracle like he accused me of, that this whole thing can sometimes feel like the wild goose chase he said it was. "I know," I said again. "I just didn't expect it to feel this way. Maybe I should have, but…"

"I know." He sounded sad, and I was grateful that he didn't remind me that he'd been predicting something like this all along.

I haven't asked James about Eva, although she has said she's spoken to him. It's not my place to ask about their marriage, even though I've been put smack in the middle of it. It feels strange, that I actually want them to work out. I don't want this to come between them, even though it already has. Yet maybe, just maybe, this can be something that makes them stronger, helps them to grow. A trial doesn't have to mean the end for a couple. And, I realize, I *like* Eva. I can see how her boldness and focus could be good for James. As bizarre as it feels, I am happy for them in a way I never was before.

A few raindrops spatter against the windowpane and then subside; they feel like a warning. I rise from my chair and walk around the room, rolling my shoulders and flexing my feet. Sitting still, strangely, can be exhausting.

During these long hours of waiting, I've found myself turning back time inside my head, something I don't normally do because it's too painful. Yet here, in this strange place, with so many strange voices and people around me, I need it, to anchor me to the present, to the reason I'm here at all.

And so I return to the plastic chair next to Emily's bed and remember. I remember when I found out I was pregnant; we'd only just started trying and I was so surprised, so disbelieving, that I took three tests and lined them all up on top of the toilet. I tried to think of clever and funny ways to tell James, but both of us were too down-to-earth for that. In the end, as he came through the door one evening, I just blurted it out. The look on his face, his total shock, was comical and endearing. I wish I'd taken a photo.

I remember Emily as a newborn, sleeping on my chest, a solid and pleasing weight, a milk bubble frothing at her lips. I remember her at four months old, staring up at her activity gym in wide-eyed wonder, as if a plush green frog dangling from a yellow string was the most incredible thing she'd ever seen.

Of course, not all of it was wonderful. I remember feeling as if I were going out of my mind when she was teething at six months old, and cried for six hours straight. I remember picking her up from her bouncy chair a little too firmly, my hands squeezing her middle, and hearing her shrill cry pierce the air. I was sorry immediately, and I hugged and kissed and quieted her, but four years later that memory still skewers me. How could I have lost my temper, even for a second? *If only I'd known…*

But, of course, you never know. And when I stomped into her bedroom in the middle of the night, wretched with lack of sleep, or secretly wished that she would just *shut up*, or when, as a toddler, she insisted on fastening the lid onto her sippy cup and juice spilled everywhere and I shouted at her… all those moments when I gritted my teeth or snapped at her or rolled my eyes or wished that moment away… Well, now I know you don't always get them back.

But thankfully there are far many more good memories than hard ones. Snuggles in bed in the morning, when she'd clamber up and wriggle under the duvet. *Snuggle, Mama*, she'd say as she fit her chubby little body next to mine. Except she couldn't say snuggle at first; it came out as wuggle instead. Eventually James and I started calling it that, too. *Do you want a wuggle, Emily?* Her answering grin would light up her face. Even when she was old enough to say snuggle properly, she still said wuggle. We all did. I picture the three of us in bed on a Saturday morning, arms around each other, sunshine spilling through the windows, wuggling.

Oh God, it hurts so much to bring back these memories, to remember those happy mornings. It leaves me breathless and reeling, gasping for air, one hand clutched to my chest as if I'm having a heart attack.

Wuggle, Mama. Wuggle.

My breathing is a loud, hatcheted sound in the silent room as I try to rein my emotions back in. I blink away the film of tears gathering in my eyes and focus on Emily, my beautiful girl, with her eyes closed, her face slack, her body still.

Dan, Mama! Dan!

I picture her dancing, whirling around. I take her chubby hands in mine. I laugh; she sings for joy. Her head is tilted back, her smile wide. My beautiful, beautiful girl. I wipe my eyes and draw a steadying breath.

Then, in the terrible silence of this fractured moment, Emily opens her eyes. Dr. Brown has told me again and again this most likely means nothing, there is no real awareness, yet right now it feels different. Slowly her gaze moves from left to right, searching the room. Finding me.

I lean forward, almost forgetting to breathe. I reach my hand out to hold hers. Her gaze fastens on me and she doesn't look away, she doesn't keep scanning vacantly, unable to truly see anything. She looks at me. My daughter *sees* me.

"Emily…" My voice is a hushed whisper, a sacred sound. "*Emily.*" Gently, so gently, her fingers squeeze mine. "Yes, Emily, yes, it's Mama. I'm here, baby girl. I'm here." I'm laughing and sobbing at the same time as I try to get the words out. "Can you hear me, darling? Can you hear me?" She is still looking at me, her gaze seeming so focused, so aware. Yes, aware.

I defy Dr. Brown or any of the other so-called experts to tell me this means nothing. I can feel her fingers squeezing mine again, and I know, I *know* she is in there, and she is trying to communicate. She's *trying*.

"We're getting you better, sweetheart. I know it's been hard, but I'm here and I love you. Daddy too…" I wish, with a fierce desperation, that James was here. That he could see this. "It's all going to be okay. You don't need to be afraid. I'm here. I'll always be here."

Emily's fingers start to loosen on mine, and in panic I feel her ebb away. I want to hold onto her, but I know I can't. Still, as her eyes flutter closed and her hand rests so still and slack in mine, I am buoyant. That was real. She was there, I know she was. I need to tell Dr. Rossi what happened.

But when I do, a little while later, practically gibbering in my excitement, he just smiles and nods. He doesn't seem particularly pleased or impressed; in fact, I wonder if he is skeptical that it happened at all.

"She was really looking at me," I insist, a strident note entering my voice. "I felt it. Like that man, the first one who had this treatment… they said he *looked* at people. He was trying to communicate."

Dr. Rossi nods and says nothing. He's holding a clipboard and he glances down at it.

"Don't you think so, Dr. Rossi?" I ask, my voice a little too loud. I need him to agree with me, to tell me it really did happen, because suddenly I am doubting, as surely as he is. "Don't you think she was trying to reach me?"

"It is very easy, in these situations," he says in his careful, halting English, "to see what you wish to see."

"You think I'm imagining it." My voice is flat, my euphoria draining away.

"No, not quite that. I believe she looked at you. But… we must have more… proof. Reliable data. The scans of the brain do not show that level of awareness."

"Then maybe your scans are wrong." I'm so sick of scans, and percentages of brain function, as if a human soul can be measured and ranked. *Your daughter is in the fortieth percentile of being.* That's basically what they're saying, and I despise it. My daughter is my daughter, and today she tried to reach me. I know she did.

I turn away from him, furious and unable to hide it, and Dr. Rossi puts one hand on my arm.

"This is difficult, I know. I am sorry."

Usually I'd murmur some kind of thanks for this useless platitude, but today I can't. This isn't *difficult*. It's impossible, unbearable, and I don't feel as if I can stand a second more of it without screaming. He has absolutely no idea how that feels. *None.*

He has never had a child lying in a bed like Emily; he has never seen her open her eyes and look at him. He's viewing all of this from behind a computer screen or a clipboard, charting progress on a graph, discussing it—her—with his colleagues.

"Never mind," I choke out, and I walk back to Emily's room. She is lying in bed—she's *always* lying in bed—and for a second I want to grab her by the shoulders and startle her awake. *Wake up, Emily! I know you can do it. I know you're there. You've got to be there. Just wake up, damn it!*

My fists ball at my sides and for one horrifying second I almost do it. I almost grab my daughter by her shoulders and shake her. I can see myself walking over to the bed; I can see myself grabbing her. I can even see her body flailing uselessly in my grasp, her head lolling back, and I let out a stifled cry of despair before I fling myself into the chair by her bed and drop my head into my hands.

Moments ago I was jubilant, and now I feel as low as I've ever been. For the first time, I realize that I may not be able to take anymore, that I can't *do* this, and that thought is terrifying.

"Rachel?" I look up at the sound of Eva's tentative voice. She's standing in the doorway, looking pale and a bit washed out, a little nervous. I could use some of her brisk good humor, her cheerful determination, but she doesn't seem to have brought it along today. "Are you okay?"

I shrug, unable to find the words, much less say them.

"I saw Dr. Rossi walking down the hall. Has anything happened?"

I glance at Emily's slack face, her closed eyes, and I wonder if I'd actually imagined it all. I've been so tired, so lost in memories… what if none of that happened? What if she didn't open her eyes, didn't squeeze my hand? What if I just wished she did, so much so that I imagined it happened? With a ripple of horror, I realize it is perfectly possible.

"I don't know," I whisper. I feel as if a tsunami is building inside me, a tidal wave of despair I've kept back for almost three years. I can't let it out now. "I don't know," I say again, and I drop my head into my hands once more as a breath shudders through me. I can't take anymore. I really can't.

"Oh, Rachel." Eva comes over and rubs my back, as if I'm a child who has had a bad dream. How I wish this were nothing but a bad dream. I'd wake up, I'd blink the sleep out of my eyes as the vestiges of the nightmare clung to me, and then Emily would run up to me and scramble into my lap, snuggling against me. *Wake, Mama? You awake?*

Yes. I'm awake. I'm wide awake. Because it's not a dream. It has never, ever been a dream.

"Today's a hard day," Eva says, and I let out a sound that is meant to be a laugh but isn't anything—just a ragged huff of breath.

"Every day is a hard day, Eva."

"I know. I'm sorry. I didn't mean…"

"I know you didn't. Never mind." I'm so *tired*. I feel, suddenly, as if I could curl up right on this cold tile floor and go to sleep. I'd sleep and sleep and maybe, if I'm lucky, I'll never wake up.

Somehow, with a strength I thought had gone, I pull myself together. I rub my face with my hands and stand up and smile, or sort of. My lips move, at least.

"I think I need a coffee. Can I get you one? Espresso, right?"

Eva looks discomfited, and some instinctive, internal radar makes me frown.

"What is it?"

"Nothing…" But she looks a little shifty, her gaze darting away, and I feel as if we are in a kaleidoscope and someone has just given it a twirl.

"It's something." I don't how things shifted so quickly, only that they did. "Do you not want a coffee?" If she doesn't, why on earth would it be a big deal?

"No, no," Eva says quickly. Too quickly. "I mean, yes. I'll have a coffee. Let me get them." She fumbles for her purse, not meeting my gaze, and I am trying to think why she wouldn't want a coffee, why she'd insist on getting it, and most of all, why she would look so guilty about it.

"I'll get them," I say. "I need to get out for a bit. Your usual?" Which is a double espresso.

Eva hesitates, biting her lip. *What is going on?*

"Actually," she says. "I think I've been having too many espressos lately. I'm starting to feel jumpy. I'll have a latte instead. Decaf." It all sounds so innocuous, and yet it isn't, because she is explaining too much and her tone is false. Falsely casual, the same as her smile, with an almost manic look in her eyes.

I stare. She looks back at me, the smile trembling at the corners of her mouth. And then I realize, the knowledge falling on me as if from a great height, landing with a thud, flattening me. "Hold on," I say slowly. "Hold on. You're… you're pregnant, aren't you?"

And even though she doesn't answer, I see it in her face—the rush of guilt, along with the fierce joy she can't hide.

CHAPTER TWENTY-FOUR

EVA

Rachel stares at me, a dazed, blank look on her face as I try not to feel wretchedly guilty. I didn't want to tell her. I knew it could only hurt her, that I'm expecting her husband's child, this new life that is full of hope and promise, unlike that of the little girl lying in the bed right next to us. Of course I didn't want to tell her, and certainly not now. Not here.

"You're pregnant," she says again, and she slowly lowers herself into the chair next to Emily, as if she is an old woman.

"I'm sorry." I blurt the words.

"How long have you known?"

"I took the test a few days ago." I realize that I will answer any question she asks me; I will be completely honest. It feels only right.

Rachel shakes her head, a slow back and forth. "Well," she finally says. "Well. Congratulations." And then her face crumples, and somehow I am kneeling in front of her, my arms around her as she draws shuddering breath after breath, trying to hold onto her composure.

"I'm sorry," I say again. It feels like the only thing I can say. "I'm so sorry."

"Don't be sorry," she manages after a moment as she pulls away from me, wiping her face. "For heaven's sake. What kind of absolute ogre would I be, to be angry that you're having a baby?"

She looks up at me, her face smeared with tears, a smile trembling on her mouth like a butterfly about to take a wing. "I mean, that is, you're happy about it, I assume? You were… trying?"

"Yes, and yes." But I sound hesitant, uncertain, and now it's my face that is threatening to crumple, my lips that can't quite quirk into a smile. I look away quickly, wanting to hide my emotion, knowing this isn't the place or time for it, but Rachel's not having any of it.

"Eva." She puts a hand on my arm. "What's going on? You are happy about it, aren't you?"

And that's when I realize I'm going to tell her. I'm going to tell her something I've never told anyone else—not James, not my family, not a single friend, not a counselor or doctor. No one. But Rachel, of all people, deserves to know. And, I realize, she'll understand.

Either that or she'll judge me, just as I've judged myself.

I take a quick breath, willing the tears back, the emotion that threatens to consume me now more than ever. "It's complicated."

"Okay." Rachel gestures to the room, the bed. To Emily. "I understand complicated."

"But it's always been so simple for you," I say with a sniff. Rachel looks as if she's going to object and I hasten to clarify. "With Emily. What I mean is, you've always been so sure about what you're willing—what you need—to do for her."

"That's not true." Rachel's face takes on a pinched look. "I've second-guessed myself a thousand times. Even today…" She gives a kind of gulp as she shakes her head. "But we're not talking about me right now. God knows I've talked and thought about myself way too much recently. What's going on with you? Why aren't you happy about this pregnancy?"

"I am happy," I insist. "So happy. More than anyone could possibly know."

"Okay." Rachel waits for more, because of course there's more.

"It's just…" Where to begin? How to explain? I stay silent, trying to order my thoughts, control my feelings. It's so hard.

"Eva, whatever it is," Rachel says, "I can hear it. I can listen."

"I've been pregnant before," I finally say. "A long time ago."

Her face has that carefully bland look people get when they don't know what you're going to say, only that they have to brace themselves for it.

"Okay," she says again.

"It was during my junior year of college. I was so in love. With a guy called Lucas." My mouth twists with the old hurt, the angry cynicism that covers it like armor. Sixteen years ago and I still feel it all, as fresh as ever. Will it ever fade?

"So what happened?" Rachel asks quietly.

"We were going to get married. I had it all figured out. He was a teaching assistant, doing his graduate work at one of the Claremont Colleges. I was at Pomona. Far from home for the first time, so full of myself. I hadn't meant to get pregnant, of course, and I knew it wasn't ideal. My family would be horrified, I knew—they're pretty strict Catholics, and I was always my dad's little princess." I sigh as the memories and regrets rush through me in a weary river. "Lucas wasn't thrilled at first, but he wasn't… you know, actively opposed." Or so I'd thought. "We had it worked out. I would take a year off while he finished his graduate work and I stayed home with the baby. Then I'd finish my degree—I was studying joint business and English—and we'd both find jobs, back in Boston, maybe. My mom would love to help with the childcare, once she got over the shock." She grimaces. "And yet I was too nervous to tell her I was pregnant, that I'd gotten pregnant in college, without being married. That wasn't… that wasn't how it was done in my family."

Rachel frowns. "But surely she would have understood…"

"Yes, I think she would have, in time." I have to admit that, even though it hurts. "The truth is, Lucas wasn't on board enough to make me trust what we had. Part of me was just waiting for it all to go wrong." And then, of course, it did.

Yet even so I remember dreaming about how it was all going to work out, so confident that I could have everything—the man, the baby, the job, the *life*. All mine for the taking, simply because I wanted them. I tried to make myself believe it, and yet I never quite could.

"So what happened?" Rachel asks when it seems as if I'm not going to say anything more, and the truth is, I don't want to.

"I had an ultrasound at twenty weeks. You know the one—where they count the fingers and toes, tell you if you're having a boy or girl?"

"Yes." Rachel's face has that pinched look again, and I know it is hard for her to hear this. What if she hates me, for what I did? After everything we've shared and been through together, it would hurt. However complicated our relationship, I would call her my friend.

"They flagged up a concern at that ultrasound. They didn't tell me what it was right away." My throat grows tight as the memory flashes through my mind like a video replay. I can see myself, my shirt pulled up, my precious bump so neat and round. The technician is poking and prodding me with the metal wand, and the black and white image on the screen dances and blurs. *A baby.*

Even though I'd started to feel fluttery kicks, even though my clothes were getting tight and I'd thrown up for six weeks, it amazed me, that image on the screen. I had a baby inside of me.

Lucas didn't come to the ultrasound. He was teaching, and I couldn't reschedule it. Maybe that should have been a warning sign; couldn't he have missed one class? But I was lost up in the clouds back then, determined to believe in my happily-ever-after. Even though I hid my pregnancy from my family, since I wasn't married, and even from my friends, who I knew would be shocked and disapproving. Baggy sweatshirts and saying I had the flu helped, and I didn't see my family on the east coast until it was all over, buried deep down inside.

"I had more tests," I tell Rachel. A blur of needles, scans, the frown of the ultrasound technician as she stared at the screen. Her murmured "excuse me" as she left the room without an explanation. The panic creeping over me with icy fingers, the sudden sensation of how cold and exposed I was, with my top up, my belly on show, my baby kicking. "And my baby—my daughter—was diagnosed with a fatal heart condition."

Rachel's eyes widen. "Oh, Eva…"

But I have to explain, because it's not that simple. "One side of her heart hadn't developed properly, and most likely never would. The doctor told me she'd need open heart surgery as soon as she was born, and it was extremely high-risk. Based on the severity of the defect, she was likely to have a shortened life span." I recite the facts as I remember them, each one emblazoned on my brain, my heart. I can see the cardiologist's compassionate look, hear his careful recitation. "Most children with the defect, the doctor told me, only lived a year at most, sometimes only a few months. Even if they'd had the surgery." But some lived longer. A precious few lived compromised lives, lives with lots of medical intervention and surgeries, but they made it to adolescence or even beyond. But he'd told me the percentages, and they hadn't been good. They'd been overwhelming.

"I'm so sorry." Rachel's face is creased with pity, and I wonder if it actually helps her, to focus on someone else's pain. Not everyone is living a charmed life, even if it may sometimes seem that way, especially to her.

"I told Lucas about the defect." He hadn't come to any appointments, saying he had class, and I hadn't let myself care. I can't really remember those weeks of waiting, of endless doctor appointments, my mind a blur as I pushed myself through the days. And then the verdict, given with such devastating kindness, followed by a question I hadn't even realised could be asked: *What do you want to do?*

"And?" Rachel asks. "What did he say?"

"He wanted out," I say bluntly. "He could just about handle a baby, but one with defects? One that would require so much care, that would mean an entire life change? He wasn't on board at all. He said I should end the pregnancy. We broke up over it." Which, funnily enough, had felt like a relief, rather than another heartbreak.

"Bastard." Rachel is silent for a moment, thinking. "Why do women so often carry it all?" she asks, almost to herself. "Why are we the ones who have to bear the load?"

Does she feel James didn't? The thought gives me a lurch of alarm, because one of the reasons I fell in love with James was because I thought he did. Because he'd had a child—still has—who was desperately ill and he hadn't walked away. Tears prick my eyes as I realize what a mess I'm still in, just like before.

Rachel turns back to me, her gaze narrowed. "So what did you do?" Am I imagining that note of judgment in her voice? I'm afraid I'm not. That she knows the end of the story, and she condemns me for it.

"I thought about going it alone," I say slowly, wanting to delay the moment when I have to tell her everything. "I wanted to." I lapse into silence, and Rachel's gaze nails me to where I stand.

"But?" she says, and of course she already knows.

"But I didn't," I say quietly. "I wasn't strong enough. I was scared and alone and I hadn't told my family or friends or anyone. I didn't have the money or the resources… I didn't think I could do it. And so I didn't." I blink back tears I still don't feel I have the right to shed. "I had an abortion at twenty-four weeks." It had taken that long, from scan to termination, to get the tests, to make a decision—the longest and shortest four weeks of my life.

I've read the articles since then, each one torturous to me, that have shown that a baby born at twenty-four weeks is viable. They can live outside the womb on their own. I've seen the photos of the tiny scraps of humanity born at that gestation or sometimes even earlier—the mother's tremulous smile, the effusive praise for the medical team, the joy in the miracle.

Of course, it didn't happen that way for me.

"It was the hardest thing I've ever done," I tell Rachel. "The worst thing." My throat is getting tighter and tighter and I can't look at her face. Memories bombard me—cold stirrups, sinking down into sedation, the fear paralyzing me, and then the sad, empty sack of my stomach afterwards. It had only taken half an hour, and yet my entire world had shifted, shattered. I've spent the rest of my life trying to hold it together even as everything always threatens to fall to fragments in my hands.

Rachel doesn't speak and I still can't look at her.

"I think of her all the time," I say quietly. "I wonder so many things. How long she would have lived. What would she have been like. I never got to see her." Obviously. I wouldn't have wanted to, and when I really want to torture myself, I think about how she was wrenched out of me and just... *discarded*.

I found out later that I could have requested the fetal remains to be buried respectfully; I could have had a funeral, given her the ending she deserved, but at the time I didn't know. I just walked away from it all and tried to forget, all the while knowing I never would.

I take another breath and dare to look at Rachel. Her expression is distant, her face slightly averted. I have no idea what she is thinking. She doesn't speak, and so I do, still trying to explain myself all these years later, to make her understand the depth of my sorrow.

"I wonder if she might have had a good life. I mean, I know it would have been incredibly compromised. Even if the open heart surgery had been successful, the doctors told me she would have had serious ongoing conditions. Problems." Still nothing, and so I persevere. "And in all likelihood, she wouldn't have lived past her first birthday. The percentages for five-year survival were so low… less than ten percent. And the truth is, I didn't think I couldn't handle any of that—her health, her death, how consuming it all would be… I was only twenty, and entirely on my own. I really didn't think I could do it." I sound as if I am begging now, pleading with her to understand, to forgive me.

"It must have been very hard," Rachel says quietly, after another endless moment. I can't tell anything from her tone.

"That's why—one of the reasons why—I admire you so much. You've *done* the hardest thing. You've lived the life I was too afraid to."

She lets out a huff of sound, caught between laughter and a despair. "Is that what I've done?"

"Part of the reason I wanted to come here, to help you, is because… because I didn't make that choice before, and so many times I've wished I had." A tear trickles down my cheek and I dash it away. "I wonder how it would have been, if I hadn't… if I'd…" I can't finish those sentences. "How she might have made me a better, stronger person," I continue haltingly. "What joy she might have given me, if I'd let her."

"And what heartache," Rachel says, her voice so low I strain to hear it.

"Yes, but isn't it worth it, in the end?" I ask, my voice rising on a desperate note. "Although maybe that's the wrong question. Maybe I shouldn't be asking whether it is *worth* it at all." Because, just as I asked James, who gets to decide whether another's life is worth living or not? Who gets to make that call? It's a question I've been asking myself for sixteen years, ever since I decided that I did.

"I don't think you can say whether something is worth it or not," Rachel says slowly. "We don't have a crystal ball to know where life is going to lead us, and that's a good thing." She turns to face me. "I can see that you've been tormenting yourself over this, Eva, and it must have been something so incredibly difficult to decide. To bear, for all these years." I sniff and nod, grateful for that much understanding. "But maybe that's the trouble with science today, with technology, with everything. We know too much. We have too much choice. If I'd been told what was going to happen to Emily…? That I was going to end up here, with her like this?" She nods towards the bed. "God knows what I would have done. God *knows*."

"But do you regret it?" I ask, the words bursting out of me, revealing how desperately I need to know.

She turns to look at me, an odd look on her face. "Are you asking me if I regret my daughter's life?"

I cringe in shame. "No…" But I was. We both know it; it's there between us, dark and heavy. And I know, before she says a word, what her answer is. Of course she doesn't regret it. No matter what decision she may or may not have made nearly seven years ago, she would never wish Emily away now.

Just as I wouldn't have wished my daughter's life away, had I let her live. The realization thuds through me, a truth I've been trying not to face for half my life. But I can't any longer; I have to face it now. Because of Rachel. Because of Emily. Because of the love and care Rachel has always shown for her daughter, no matter what.

Of course she doesn't regret having Emily. Being her mother. And I wouldn't have regretted it, either. It would have been hard, agonising even. It would have completely changed my life, and not always for the better. But I wouldn't have regretted it.

"I'm sorry," I gasp out when Rachel still hasn't said anything more. "I didn't mean that. Of course you don't regret it. Her." I shake my head, wiping my eyes. "Of course you don't. You never would."

"I'm not saying it's been easy," Rachel says quietly. "Or that I haven't had thoughts sometimes…" She looks towards Emily. "But the first three years of Emily's life were the best of mine, and even now…" She brushes her fingers against Emily's still hand. "Even now, I don't want to let her go, to move on, whatever you want to call it. I want to be right here with her, all the time."

Which makes me wonder what I've missed out on. What I've denied myself, as well as my daughter. What joy might I have known, what memories could I now treasure, if I'd decided differently, if I was strong enough? It hurts too much to think about, and yet it's the only thing I can think about. The thing I've been thinking about for sixteen years, all the while trying so desperately not to.

"Eva." Rachel puts a hand on my shoulder. When I look at her, she smiles sadly. "You seem as if you've been letting yourself be eaten up with guilt and remorse over your decision, and that's no way to live a life."

"I can't help it," I mumble. Tears threaten yet again.

"I know. And considering how reluctant I've been myself to do it, I can't believe I'm saying it to you, but I am. You've got to let go. Move on. For your sake, and James' sake, and… and this baby's sake." She nods towards my middle. "What happened, happened, for good or ill. Whether you regret it or not…" She draws a hitching breath. "All I know is, at some point, you have to put it aside. Forgive yourself, and move on." Her gaze moves inexorably to Emily and rests there.

I am silent, accepting what she said, and yet wishing she had said more. Wishing she had said *I understand, Eva, completely. You did what you thought was best at the time—for you and your baby. It's okay.*

But, of course, she couldn't say that. She wasn't even the right person to say that. And I realize I can't keep looking for someone to say that to me, or for me to say it to myself. Sometimes it's *not* okay, and you have to make peace with that and move on.

Like Rachel said, I have to let go. I have to accept that I will always wonder, I will always have some regret, but I don't have to let it control or define me. It doesn't have to make a shipwreck of my future with my husband and my child.

And yet… that's only the beginning of my complicated life. Because I haven't told Rachel that I don't even know if James wants this baby, or if our marriage is stable enough to have it. I haven't told her how terrified I am of being pregnant at all. What if the heart defect wasn't a fluke, as the doctors assured me it was? What if it's genetic, and it happens again?

But I can't say any of that now, not when I'm feeling so raw, and not with Emily right here in the room with us. I've made this about me too much already.

But then Rachel lets out a soft sound of surprise, and I stiffen. I look at Emily first, but there's no change. Rachel's gaze is fixed on the door. And so I turn, and my mouth falls open and my heart lurches, for standing there, looking haggard and tired, is James.

CHAPTER TWENTY-FIVE

RACHEL

For a second I think I'm dreaming. Hallucinating maybe, because, God knows, I'm exhausted enough, emotional enough, to conjure up the image of my ex-husband, or my mother, or even my elementary school teacher, Mrs. Ryan, who was so nice to me. Who even knows what's going on in my subconscious, and who I will make appear in the doorway?

But, no, James really is here, and he's smiling, although he looks too sad to call it that. He looks at Emily, and then Eva, and then he looks at me.

"Hello, Rachel," he says.

Eva's face looks stricken, and she throws me a panicked look, as if she's afraid I will blurt all her secrets—secrets I suspect James doesn't know—to him right here and now. As if I would. As if I would want to tell him something so personal, so tragic, so overwhelming.

"James," I say faintly. I can't say anything more. I don't know what to say, or even how to feel. Everything is a jumble in my head, in my heart—Emily lying in bed, Eva's pregnancy, all that she said, what I saw before. Did Emily really open her eyes and look at me? Did she squeeze my fingers as if she was trying to say something? Did I imagine all of it, because I've wanted it so much?

Eva glances between James and me. "I should go," she murmurs. "You'll want to talk…"

Will we? Or has James come to see Eva? I realize I have no idea why he's here, and so I ask him.

"Why am I here?" he repeats, looking startled, and also a little abashed. "To see Emily." He makes it sound obvious, but I'm not sure it is.

We both glance to the bed. No one says anything for a moment. Then Eva edges to the door. "I'll be back at the guesthouse," she says, either to me or James, I'm not sure which. She closes the door softly behind her, and then it's just me, my daughter, and my ex-husband. The air feels thick with expectation, with memories.

"I talked to you only last night," I remark after a long stretch of silence. "You didn't mention anything about coming here."

"I decided after we spoke."

"Why?"

He hunches one shoulder, hands deep in the pockets of his wrinkled khakis. "It felt like the right thing to do. Maybe I should have been here all along." His confession, the wavering note of uncertainty in his voice, surprises me. James has never seemed anything but a thousand percent certain that this experimental treatment is a complete mistake.

"Really?" I try not to sound skeptical, knowing it won't help. "You've seemed so sure, James, that she shouldn't be here. That the treatment won't work." It hurts to say that, even though I've known it, been living it, for months now.

"I'm not so sure," James says quietly. "About anything." He sinks in the chair on the other side of Emily's bed and glances down at our daughter's face. "How is she?"

"I don't know anymore. A couple of hours ago, she opened her eyes. It seemed as if she was really looking at me, trying to communicate."

"Really?" James' expression brightens so much, hope so clear in his eyes, that I feel ashamed. Did I really think he didn't care? That he didn't want Emily to get better, if she could?

"Now I'm not sure if I imagined it," I say with a shake of my head. "I don't think I did, but Dr. Rossi says her brain function hasn't improved enough for that, and I'm so tired…"

"He says that, from what he's seen on a scan?" James almost sounds scoffing. "That's not proof."

"Isn't it?" I feel almost dizzy now, by his seeming about-face. "You've always thought it was before." I don't mean to sound accusing; I'm more confused than anything else. Why is James changing his tune now? Why is he sounding more like me, after all this time?

"Maybe I was wrong." He speaks quietly, his head lowered, his gaze still on Emily.

"I don't understand you, James. Where is this all coming from?"

James doesn't speak for a long moment. As I wait for him to explain, I am conscious of many things—the rain that has begun to fall gently outside, streaking down the window. Emily's hand giving one little twitch against the sheet. The silence, the emptiness, the *waiting*… it has gone on for so long. I've spent over two years in rooms like this one, always waiting for something that hasn't yet happened, and now I am starting to believe never will. And maybe, just maybe, that *isn't* giving up. It's a new thought, one that feels like both a relief and a fear, but not quite as terrifying as it once might have been. I can actually start to envisage it, something I was never ready to do before.

"I feel…" James begins, and then stops again. He won't look at me, only our daughter, his fingers laced together in front of him. "I feel I haven't handled any of this as I should have," he says finally.

"What do you mean?"

"When Emily started to get sick… I wasn't prepared for it. I know you weren't either, no one was, no one could be. It was so sudden. It felt surreal. I kept just waiting for it to stop. I told myself it was some weird virus, it was going to clear up. Anything…"

"I know," I say softly. My throat is starting to ache. I'd done the same thing. Panicked, even as I told myself there was nothing to panic about, that whole first year as we ignored symptoms and then went to the doctor, at war with ourselves and our unspoken fears.

"You read stories online about stuff like that," James continues in a low voice. "People who fall mysteriously ill, who die for seemingly no reason, and every time, you think, 'that's horrible, that's sad, but that would never happen to *me*.'"

"Until it does."

He looks up at me then, the expression on his face so bleak that it makes me want to reach over and hug him, or at least touch his hand. But I don't, because we haven't had that kind of relationship for a long time, and I don't know whether we can start now. "Yes," he agrees. "Until it does."

He lapses into silence again, and I realize I still don't know why he's here. Did he come because he felt guilty? Or because he wanted to see Emily, or support me? And what about Eva? I feel too tired, too sad, to ask him. To hash it all out. Maybe it's too late, anyway. I glance again at Emily.

"I've been thinking a lot," James says, "about everything. Since you've come to Italy." I wait. "And how I handled it all." He glances up at me again. "Not very well, I mean."

"It was a hard situation. The hardest." If we're going to do confessions, then I'll give him mine. I don't have any pride left to hold onto; the self-righteous fury that buoyed me for so long has trickled away. "I didn't either, James. I can admit now that you were right, I did make it a competition. I didn't mean to, but I can see that's how it felt. I think it was a way to feel in control, when, of course, I wasn't. I couldn't be."

"Still… I just shut down. That had to have been hard for you to deal with. I suppose that was my way of being in control, but it didn't work."

"Nothing did."

"I really did believe we would be happier apart." He sounds as if he is asking my forgiveness.

"I know you did. And I came to see that, too." Although I still wonder if we'd both been different, stronger, maybe our marriage could have made it, even if our daughter didn't.

But just like I told Eva, I know there is no point in raking over the past, languishing in regret. What happened, happened. James has a wife now, a wife he loves, who is having his baby. We can't wonder what if.

"When you set up that page…" James begins in a low voice, and I tense. Now come the recriminations? "I felt so guilty."

I start at that. "*You* did?"

"It was like looking at some sort of alternate reality, seeing how our lives could have been. I thought, why didn't I do that? Why didn't I think of that? Why did I…" His voice wavers and then breaks. "Why did I just *give up*?"

"You didn't give up, James."

"Can you really say that—"

"Yes, I can." I realize it's true, no matter what I've accused him of. "You've always been there, always been supportive. And you advocated for the decision you believed was in Emily's best interest."

"I don't know if that's true." His voice is so low, I can barely hear it. "Maybe it was just easier for me." Which are the same words I once flung at him, but I'm not sure I ever meant him to take them to heart. "I've wanted this to be over, Rachel," he confesses. "Because it hurts so much."

"I know it does."

He clears his throat, straightens. "Anyway, I came here to see Emily, but I also came to see you." His gaze lifts to mine, resolute and still so bleak. "I'm sorry, Rachel. I'm sorry I wasn't a better husband. A better father."

"Oh, James…" My throat is too thick and aching to get any more words out. I shake my head and manage, "Don't."

"I have to say it. I've been thinking it for a long time. I told myself if I was upfront with you about everything, if I showed up for Emily, then I was doing a good job. I was doing more than most men would, even. But all along I felt I was failing, and that just made me dig in even more, and act as if I was right. As if I was some martyr." The sneer in his voice is unmistakable.

"I think I was the one acting like a martyr." I shake my head again, forcing the ache in my throat to ease. "We both made mistakes, James. We both tried our best. What more can we say than that? What more can we do?"

"Do you forgive me?" His look is so pleading that I feel ashamed. Did I make him feel this guilty? Did I bully him into this corner, with my wild accusations, my fierce sense of self-righteousness?

"There's nothing to forgive, but if you need it, then yes, I forgive you. And I'm glad you're here."

Silently, he reaches for my hand, and I take it. We lace our fingers together over Emily's bed, and both of us gaze at our daughter.

The next day Dr. Rossi sits down with both of us, a look of sorrow on his face that I realize I've been expecting. It's been several weeks since Emily started the treatment and there has been no change in her status, no improvement in the scans of her brain.

"In fact," Dr. Rossi says, looking at us both, "her brain function has decreased since she's been here. Only slightly, but I see a definite downward progression. I'm sorry."

"So the treatment isn't working?" James sounds incredulous, even though this is exactly what he predicted would happen. There are no surprises.

"The nerve stimulation techniques we have been researching appear to be more effective with traumatic brain injuries," Dr.

Rossi says in his careful, hesitant English. "And not as much with degenerative neurological conditions, where the decline is less reversible."

Even undiagnosed conditions, where the ignorance can feel like hope, if you let it. Or it can be defeat. "So what are you saying?" I ask. My voice feels as if it is coming outside of myself. "Are you saying we should stop?"

"I am recommending an end to the treatment, yes."

There is surprisingly little to say after that. Dr. Rossi talks about travel arrangements, and I say something about contacting the air ambulance service. I feel numb, as if I'm hovering somewhere above the room, watching this play out.

At some point, James takes my hand and we walk back to Emily's room. We stand at the foot of her bed and gaze down at our beautiful daughter, her blond curls spread across the pillow, her lashes fanning her cheeks. She's so little, so precious, so *still*.

This isn't the end of her life, not yet, but it is the end of my hopes. Emily will be transferred back to the palliative care unit, and that's what it will truly be. Palliative care, a wait till the end, whenever it comes.

"Do you remember how she liked to turn on the light switch in the mornings?" James asks softly.

I can picture it—Emily safe in his arms, reaching out one hand to flick on the switch in the morning, bathing our kitchen in a warm, electric glow. "She was so proud she could do it."

"And she'd always say the same thing—"

"Dark in here," we say together, in the sing-song voice Emily used to have. "*Light.*"

We both smile and laugh softly, and then the tears come, spilling down James' cheeks, a sob ripping out of me. He puts his arms around me, and I rest my head on his shoulder. Neither of us speak; we just let each other cry.

We spend the afternoon with Emily, sitting by her bed as the world rushes around us. James handles the phone calls to the air ambulance and the children's hospital back in Boston, and I am glad for him to do it. I can't be the strong one anymore.

My thoughts drift and ebb, memories pulling at me and then letting me go, until I am just sitting in the sunshine that has come after last night's wild thunderstorm, watching my daughter's face.

Eva has made herself scarce since James' arrival, and so, in the early evening, I tell James to go be with her, back at the guesthouse. "She needs you," I say, and he looks discomfited.

"We haven't been…"

"She needs you."

He goes. Alone in Emily's room, I watch the shadows lengthen and the hospital begin to quiet around me. Whatever visitors have come are leaving now, nurses and doctors clocking off. I've been here so many times before; I know the rhythms of the day and night in a hospital, the way I know how to breathe.

And it is strange to think that one day, perhaps one day soon, this won't be my life anymore. I won't be sitting by Emily's bed, talking to her, being with her, dreaming of when she's better. I won't wake up in the morning to rush to the hospital, and I won't come home at night, simply to fall into bed.

Thinking about that doesn't hurt as much as it used to, and I wonder if that's because I came to Italy. No matter the treatment's result, or lack of it, this trip hasn't been a waste. It's brought me acceptance and a form of peace that I can see on the horizon, even if I can't quite feel it yet. It's brought me closer to James, as well as closer to Eva. It's brought me a strange, new sort of hope. And it's brought me to this moment, where I can brush Emily's hair from her eyes and kiss her cheek.

"Baby girl," I say, with all the love in my voice. "It's time to go home."

Dear Bean,

Today is your third birthday! Three years old and full of spit and fire! I love your spirit, Bean. I love the person you are becoming.

So let me see, what are some things you like at just turned three? Well, you love princess pink, of course. That practically goes without saying. You love graham crackers and Play-Doh and dancing to Rod Stewart—still a favorite!

You're just starting to talk in complete sentences, and you screw your forehead up when you do it, as if it takes an immense amount of concentration, and then this look of incredulous delight passes over your face when you manage it, like you've just discovered quantum physics or rocket science. You're brilliant, Bean.

You have a little lisp that I love. I don't ever want it to go away. Yet I know it will, and you'll start speaking properly, and putting more and more words together, and even though I'm so excited for all that, I almost can't bear it. I want you to stay exactly as you are, Bean, because you're perfect.

Love, Mama

CHAPTER TWENTY-SIX

EVA

It is raining when we land in Boston, a misty drizzle that reminds me of walking through a sprinkler. It has been the strangest and saddest forty-eight hours, and I don't know how to feel about anything.

James and I haven't talked, not properly. I knew it wasn't the time or place, and so I kept myself in the background while he spent time with Emily and Rachel.

When he came back to the guesthouse the day after he arrived, looking so weary and forlorn, he told me that Dr. Rossi had said the treatment wasn't working and Rachel had agreed it was time to go home.

"Oh, James." I couldn't say anything else and I didn't need to.

James reached out and hugged me, and I realized I couldn't remember the last time we'd actually touched. It felt so good, being back in his arms.

"I'm sorry," I said, hoping he knew I meant for more than the news he'd just given, and James just nodded, his arms still around me. There would be time to talk later. Too much time, perhaps.

Rachel has been quiet and distant since we started the journey back to Boston, lost in her own world, and I've let her be, sensing she needs her space. This time, she barely seems aware of the stares in the airport, the whispers in the plane as Emily, buckled onto a stretcher, is boarded into the cleared section in the back.

We were lucky to get a passage so quickly; sometimes the wait for commercial travel with a stretcher can be as long as two weeks. It makes me wonder who else needed these cleared seats, the space for a stretcher. Who else was gambling everything on hope, desperate to get somewhere?

Back in Boston, Rachel travels in the ambulance with Emily, to see her settled back at the palliative care unit. James takes a cab to help on the other end, and I take our car home. Everything feels as if it is ending, and yet this life is in me, demanding to be acknowledged and known.

I've started to show, just the tiniest bit, the smallest, slightest of bumps, bigger than I was at this stage last time.

Last time. I know I need to tell James about that. I need to tell him so much, and I hope, I pray, we'll be stronger for it. But even if we aren't, I know I need to speak the truth.

I need to speak the truth to myself, the truth I've been hiding from for so long. Since finding out I am pregnant, since telling Rachel about everything, I've realized what I've been doing all these years. How I've been tricking myself into believing that if I get pregnant, if I carry a baby to term, I'll somehow make up for my lost daughter. I'll have balanced some invisible set of scales that I didn't even realize existed in my own mind.

But, of course, that's not going to happen, just as Rachel having another child would never make up for losing Emily. It's so obvious, such basic psychology 101—if someone had told me that's what I was doing, I would have laughed at them. Sneered, even.

Of course I know you can't replace a child. Everybody knows that.

But you can know something in your head and still believe it in your heart so deeply and secretly that you don't even acknowledge it to yourself.

And in the days after I found out I was pregnant, as we travel back to Boston, I realize that's exactly what I've been doing all along.

Alone in our apartment, I wander through the empty rooms, feeling as if I have been away far longer than a couple of weeks. The air smells slightly stale, and there is nothing in the fridge but some limp lettuce and moldy cheese. I wonder what James has been eating, what has been going through his mind and heart during this last month, and I realize I have no idea. I have become so distant from my husband over the last three months that I don't know if we'll ever be able to close that gap, even with the best will in the world. But I know I am going to try.

I close the door of the fridge and make my way to the bedroom; the duvet is rumpled, and the sheets look as if they haven't been washed in a while. I strip the bed and bundle everything into the washer, but I know I am just stalling for time. I know, already, what I am going to do.

And ten minutes later, with an online grocery order made and the washer running, I do it. I dig behind the hangers I still haven't thrown out and unwrap the patterned scarf to reveal the little enamel box I've never opened.

Sixteen years ago, I put the two printouts of my baby's ultrasound into this box, closed the lid, and never opened it again. I held it many times, and I thought about opening it more than once, but I could never bring myself to do it.

Now I do. The lid sticks and I have to ease it off gently, my heart beating so hard, you'd think I was defusing a bomb. I set the lid aside and take out the two photos—slips of silky paper, the image faded with time, the edges curling, but I can still see her.

She is curled up like a promise, her thumb in her mouth. I remember the technician telling me that, before she looked at her heart, before the bad news came. *Look, she's sucking her thumb.* I'd laughed, marveling, even though I couldn't really see it.

Now I can. Now I can see her perfectly—the tiny toes, the little hand, the thumb in her mouth. In this image you can't tell that her heart is shrunken, malformed. It's just a black blob in her chest, the way it's supposed to be. She doesn't look anything but perfect. I remember the flutter of her kicks and I close my eyes.

I've been sad for sixteen years, and yet I've never let myself grieve. How can that be possible?

"Eva?"

My eyes open in shock as I see James standing in the doorway of our bedroom, looking rumpled and tired. The photo of the scan is still in my hand.

"What are you doing?" he asks, nodding at the photo. "What is that?"

I hesitate, because I never wanted to tell him like this, when I'm feeling so raw and I'm not prepared, and he's just come from Emily.

"It's a picture." I put it back in the box, but when I try to put the lid on it sticks again. I leave it. "How is Emily?"

"The same." He pauses. "Worse, really."

My heart lurches, a seismic shift inside me. "Worse?"

"Dr. Rossi was right. Her brain function is decreasing. She's... she's less there, if that makes any sense. Even Rachel sees it. Feels it. Something more is missing."

"So what does that mean for... for her future?"

"Dr. Brown is going to run some tests over the next few days. After that, we'll... we'll have to make a decision."

"You mean...?" I can't say it.

He nods. "Yes."

"Oh, James." I rise from the bed, leaving the photos behind, and go to him. He wraps his arms around me and I press my head against his shoulder.

"Eva..."

"I'm so sorry," I whisper. "For everything."

"So am I." His arms tighten around me. "So am I."

And I wonder—I hope—*Is that it? Are we good now? We can move on?* It would be so easy...

Except it wouldn't be. Because I've lived with enough lies, enough silences. I didn't choose the easy path before when I decided to help Rachel, and I won't choose it now.

Gently, I disentangle myself from James' embrace and take a step back. He looks down at me, a wrinkle creasing his forehead, fear in his eyes.

"Eva…?"

"James, I'm pregnant."

Something flashes across his face; I can't tell if it's mere surprise, relief, or something else, something I don't want to name.

"When did you find out?" he asks after a pause.

"A few days ago. But I think I'm at least eight weeks along." He doesn't say anything, and I force myself to ask, "How do you feel about it?"

He rakes a hand through his hair, making it messier. "Honestly? I don't know."

"Okay." That's better than some of the things he could have said, things I've been half expecting him to say.

"It's just… with Emily…" He looks at me, anguished now. "I know I've been saying that all along, and it probably sounds like an excuse, but we're… we're close to the end now. And it doesn't feel the way I thought it would."

"How did you think it would feel?" I ask quietly.

"I thought I would be relieved." His voice breaks on the damning word. "I know how terrible that sounds, but it's been so long, and she's only gotten worse and worse. I wanted it to be over." He draws a breath, which shudders through me. "I tried to pretend that wasn't what I wanted, but Rachel saw through me. You did too, I think. And I feel so guilty…"

"Oh, James." I shake my head, my arms wrapped around myself. "I think we've all felt guilty."

"It's been so hard to know what the right thing to do is. And then to separate what you want from what you hope and what you fear… what is selfish and what is altruistic, what's best for you, what's best for Emily. I've been in knots."

He's never said so much before, and it fills my heart. "I know you have."

"And now that the end is actually here, on the horizon… I feel like I've wasted so many opportunities. How many times have I sat by her bed and just been on my phone? Or the evenings I let Rachel handle everything, when I could have been with my daughter? I should have taken time off work, a leave of absence…" A sob escapes him then, and when I see the tears rolling down his face, I put my arms around him and draw his head to my breast as if he were a child.

"James," I say. "James."

We make our stumbling way to the edge of the bed, and he weeps into my shoulder for a few tender minutes while I stroke his hair. Then he eases back, wiping his face, and his gaze falls on the little box, the lid next to it, the photos visible inside.

"What is that?"

I take a deep breath. Surely now is not the time, yet what other time is there? "That's an ultrasound photo," I say quietly.

James looks at me in confusion. "But you said you're only eight weeks…"

"They're not from this pregnancy." James stares at me. "I had a daughter," I say softly. His eyes widen. "She… she died when I was twenty-four weeks along."

"*Eva…*"

Of course I can't leave it there. And so I explain, as I did to Rachel, haltingly, hesitantly, afraid of his shock and judgment, but neither come.

"Oh, Eva," he says, shaking his head, looking so very sad. "Oh, Eva."

We embrace again, without words, without tears, simply leaning on each other as the sky darkens to twilight and the shadows lengthen in the room. For once, nothing more needs to be said.

The next few weeks pass as if in a hazy dream. Normal life, yet nothing feels normal. James spends a lot of time at the hospital, nearly every evening, and I spend time there too, with Rachel.

Rachel and I really have become friends, even though it's so unexpected. Even if it doesn't entirely make sense.

The tests and scans Dr. Brown did confirmed what was becoming plain to everyone, even me: Emily was fading before our very eyes. Considering her condition before, it seemed strange that she could be even less there now, but that's exactly how it felt. She wasn't gone, not yet, but she was going.

"I feel as if I'm living someone else's life," Rachel said as she held Emily's hand and I refreshed the water on some flowers James' father had sent. "I feel so distant from this, from her. Maybe it's just a coping mechanism. The numbness."

"I think it is." I remember I felt numb after the abortion. I acted as if it hadn't happened. Nobody knew, Lucas had gone, and that made it all easier—and harder, because no one knew my pain. Not even me. But maybe, like Rachel now, that was the only way I could get through the days, and then the weeks, and then the years.

"I've started therapy," I blurted to Rachel, and she raised her eyebrows. "Because of… you know."

She nodded slowly. "That's probably a good idea. God knows I'll need some therapy." Her gaze moved to Emily, who was utterly still, her breaths barely visible. Her face crumpled for a second and then smoothed out. "Why is life so hard?" she asked, and I didn't give an answer, because of course there isn't one.

Life *is* hard, and painful and messy and disappointing, but amidst all that there's hope, fluttering and ragged, the last thing left in the box. I feel it when I go for my first appointment with the obstetrician and I have to fill out my medical form.

Before she examines me, she asks me about my previous pregnancy, and I explain it all to her, and for once my voice doesn't waver.

Dr. Stein reaches over and puts her hand over mine briefly.

"I'm so sorry," she says. "That must have been incredibly difficult for you."

"It was." I pause. "It still is." And, somehow, saying that helps.

I find hope when I visit my parents and tell them about my pregnancy, and my mother tears up while my father beams. I could have left it at that, again it would be so easy, but I don't.

"Mom," I say. "Dad." They falter at my serious tone, my grave expression. "This isn't my first pregnancy."

And so I tell them, just as I told Rachel, and James, and Dr. Stein, and my mother weeps and my father looks diminished, shrinking into himself, shocked by my admission, by the fact I kept it a secret for so long. I always expected them to be shocked, disappointed, even condemning. But I didn't expect them to feel *hurt*.

"Oh, Eva," my mother says as she hugs me. "I wish you'd told us. I wish we could have been there for you, back then."

I put my arms around her, feeling her frailness. "I didn't want to disappoint you…"

"Eva." My father's voice is a growl to hide his own emotion. "You could never disappoint us."

"If you'd kept her," my mother says tremulously. "We would have helped. You know that, don't you?"

"Yes." I can barely get the word out as I acknowledge the regret and longing in their voices. "I know."

"But it would have been so hard," she continues. "Too hard, maybe…" The questioning lilt at the end of her voice tells me she doesn't really believe that. She is trying to find me a way out, because that's what mothers do.

I won't let her give it to me. "I don't know, Mom, if it would have been or not. But it was the choice I made." And that is the trouble; that has always been the trouble. I am tormented by the not knowing, by the what if. But, like Rachel said, no matter what or how much I regret, I have to let it go. And telling my parents is part of that.

We hug and cry some more, even my dad, and it isn't easy, because I know there is now a rift between us, a rift made of love rather than hurt, but a rift all the same. It will heal, like all things heal, but it will leave a scar, as all deep wounds do. And that, amazingly, is okay, because scars do not have to be marks of shame. They are signs of survival.

In early September, when I am about to start my second trimester, I start to do some freelance work, helping people with their digital marketing and social media. I know I want to be home with my child, but we need the money and I want to keep an outside interest.

James agrees, and he helps me set up a website, making suggestions, more interested in my fledgling career than he ever has been before. We're finding our old rhythms, as well as making new ones. He calls my bump Frodo, and jokes about the absurd names he's thinking of—Thor, Optimus Prime.

We start looking for a new house, because this apartment isn't big enough for a baby. We're thinking somewhere a little bit different, maybe on the North Shore, Marblehead or Rockport. It would be a longer commute for James, but there would be beaches and playgrounds and fresh, clean air. It's exciting to think about, for both of us.

One weekend in August we went house-hunting and spent the night at a romantic bed and breakfast right on the beach, making love with the sound of the waves in the background. Later, we walked along the moonlit beach and James told me about how Emily loved making sandcastles, how the last time he'd remembered her being well was when they were on vacation in Cape Cod.

I held his hand as he spoke and I let the words come, knowing he was telling me not because he needed to, but because he wanted to. He wanted to include me in his grief, and that was a good thing.

It is a beautiful day in the middle of September, the leaves touched with crimson and gold, the sky the bright, aching blue of fall, when Rachel calls me. I haven't spoken to her in a few weeks; after the initial crisis of our return from Italy, and my visits to the hospital, things dropped off a bit between us, which felt okay. James still continued to spend most evenings at the hospital, and he kept me informed; Emily was, more or less, the same.

"Eva? It's Rachel." Her voice is quiet and composed, and for some reason that alarms me. "It's Emily," she says in that same calm voice.

"Emily…"

"It's time."

CHAPTER TWENTY-SEVEN

RACHEL

It is strange to me, how ready I am for this. After years of refusing even to think about it, of fighting it with every breath in my body, now that the time has come, I feel strangely settled inside, in a way I never, ever would have expected.

The last few months, ever since we came back from Italy, have been hard. They have felt endless, and yet far too short, because they have been leading, always leading, to an end, and there is part of me that needs and craves it to come, and part of me that can't stand the thought.

Emily has continued to steadily decline, her brain function growing less and less. I see it, I feel it, and for once I don't fight it. Whatever condition—whether it was a virus, a blip in her DNA, a mystery—it is taking her life. I accept that now, in a way I was never willing to before.

When I first returned from Italy, it was with a sense of finality. I'd done all I could. My sense of striving was gone, replaced by a numbness that I was afraid to test. What deep emotion was lurking underneath it? Did I want to know?

"You'll find out eventually," Andrew told me with a wry, sad smile as we shared a takeout pizza. It was August, and the weather was oppressively muggy, the kind of day where you broke a sweat before you'd gotten out of bed. "Emotions don't hide away forever. They bubble up, like lava."

"I know." You couldn't hide from grief. Delaying tactics were just that. "I only hope I'll be ready for it, when it comes."

I put my half-eaten slice of pizza down, my gaze on Jake scrambling over the little plastic jungle gym despite the heat. He was full of joy; he had blossomed since coming to Boston, leaving the past and all its hurts behind.

"I'm scared to get my life back," I confessed to Andrew in a low voice. "Even beyond what that means for Emily. I'm scared of what it will mean for me." I looked at him bleakly, trying not to feel guilty for having these thoughts, for being scared for myself, instead of focused on my daughter. "I'm not sure I even know how to be anymore or whether, outside the hospital, I even exist."

Andrew reached over and held my hand, and I let him. I'd been trying to allow more people into my life—James and Eva, and now Andrew. Even my old friends Sarah and Denise; I'd texted them both recently, and they'd responded right away, seemingly eager to be back in touch. But it all felt hard, like exercising muscles you'd forgotten you had. The stretching was good, but the pain made you question whether it was worth the effort.

"You'll learn how to be again," Andrew said. "It may not be easy, or quick, but it will happen. And I'll help you. If you want me to."

I nodded, not trusting myself to say anything more, or even knowing if I had the words.

I visited my mother, soon after coming back from Italy, and realized she had declined even more in my absence, which gave me another load of guilt to wrestle with—should I have stayed, seen her through this? Was it worth it—the time and money and energy and hassle—to take Emily to a place where she didn't get better?

"Of course you needed to go," my mother told me, even though I hadn't actually voiced my fear. She knew me too well. "A mother needs to do everything she can for her child, no matter what." Her face softened, and I realized she was not just talking about Emily and me. She was talking about herself. "No matter what," she said again. Had my mother sacrificed her own health and the expensive prescription she'd been recommended to enable me to go to Italy? She insisted she didn't, but I wondered. And I knew she would do it again, if she could.

Just as I would.

I continued to spend all my days at the hospital, but less from a sense of frantic duty, and more from a place of peace. I was enjoying the time with my daughter, as simple as that. One afternoon, I came across the woman I'd seen months ago, in the little kitchenette, making tea. She gave me the same uncertain smile; she looked exhausted.

"Hi," I said. "Tough day?"

She grimaced. "Every day is tough, but yes. This one was bad." Her lips trembled for a second before she pressed them together. "It's all going to happen a lot faster than we thought, it seems. Than we hoped."

"I'm sorry." I put my hand on her shoulder, fleetingly, just to let her know I understood, because, God knows, I do. She smiled at me and nodded, blinking back tears, and we made our tea in silence. It's more than I did before; it's enough.

Now it is September, a beautiful time in Boston, the leaves just starting to turn, everything bright and fresh and filled with promise. Children going back to school, yellow buses trundling along, people walking with a spring in their step. September has always seemed a much better time to me for new year's resolutions than icy, dark January.

And it is on a beautiful, bright day when Dr. Brown tells me Emily is dying. She's been dying for a while, but now it is really, finally happening, the absolute end. It is no longer a distant day, something ambiguous to skirt around, to wonder when or if. Her body is beginning to shut down—her heart pumping slower, her breathing labored, her kidneys starting to fail. Everything closing up shop and creeping away.

He tells me quietly, kindly, his eyes full of sadness, and I am not surprised by what he says. I am glad, in fact, that I have never had to make the agonising decision to withdraw life support, to actively end Emily's life, a severing rather than a seeping away. That decision was made for me, and it is happening now.

"How… how long will it be?" I ask him. I am in his office, as I've been so many times before, with James next to me, his face stony, his eyes agonized. Dr. Brown asked to talk to us both this morning, and from his tone I knew what was coming. James did too, but even in the absolute expectedness of it, there is an element of disbelief.

"At this stage?" Dr. Brown steeples his fingers together, his smile full of sympathy I can finally accept. He didn't abandon us, after all. "I'd say no more than twenty-four hours, perhaps forty-eight."

As quickly as that. Despite all the preparation I've had for this moment, that named figure shocks me. In forty-eight hours, maybe much less, my daughter will be dead. The concept feels too big for me, like quantum physics or calculus. I simply cannot get my head around it, even though I am not surprised.

"How… how does it happen?" James asks. "I mean… you know, the… the actual logistics." His voice is scratchy and hoarse, his fingers plucking at his sleeve. Neither of us know how to be. What are the logistics of death? It feels so strange to need a schedule, to be told what to do, to have some rules to follow.

Dr. Brown takes us through it all, how they'll turn off Emily's monitors, to give us both privacy and peace. All the staff will be alerted to our situation. This is the palliative care unit, after all. They have a protocol, and they enact it seamlessly, because that is their job and they are very good at it.

I've seen it from a distance, when people go in and out of a dimly lit room, closing the door so quietly, and nurses tiptoe past, a look of compassionate concern on their faces. You just know. Even if no one tells you, it's obvious. And now it is our turn.

And so we head back to Emily's room, everything feeling stilted, as if things don't fit. I feel clumsy as I walk, even though I know I must look normal from the outside. Or maybe I don't. Actually, I realize, I have no idea what I look like, what I feel like, anything. I am existing somewhere outside my body, even as I feel entirely present in the moment, aware of every breath I draw, the coolness on my skin, the creak of a nurse's chair across the hall.

"We should call people," James says after a moment. We are both standing in the middle of Emily's room as if we don't know where we are. "Your mom… my dad…"

"Now?" I resist the notion of expending my emotional energy on relatives, explanations. It would be so much easier to call after. At least, I think it would. The truth is, I don't know how anything will feel.

James turns to look at me. "We don't have to wait for my father," he says slowly. His dad has come to see Emily only three times since she's been sick, and he's been increasingly uncomfortable each time, not even wanting to look at her, much less touch her or talk to her. "But your mom… wouldn't she want to say goodbye?"

"Yes, she would." My throat thickens and I force it back. Right now, I need to be numb. It's the only way I'll get through this, the only way I know how.

"Anyone else?" James asks vaguely, looking around the room as if someone will pop out from behind a chair, and I stare at him, because of course there is someone else.

"Eva," I say, my voice firm. "She needs to be here."

I call Eva, because it feels right, and then James call everyone else as I sit by Emily's bed. I hold her hand and I stroke her hair, part of me incredulous that this might be the last time I do it. I think of how, when she first went into a coma, I used to torment myself with all the last times. When was the last time I'd kissed her goodnight in her own bed? When was the last time she'd smiled at me properly? What was the last word she'd ever said?

I don't know the answers to any of those questions, because I didn't realize they were the last times.

But this time I know.

My mother comes an hour later, looking teary-eyed and determined. Her hair isn't brushed in the back and her cardigan is buttoned wrong. She came by bus because she's become too nervous to drive, with the tremors and clumsy movement. "Oh, Rachel," she says, hugging me. "Oh, James." She hugs him, as well. And then she turns to Emily, and bends over her and kisses her cheek. "My darling girl," she whispers.

Seeing them together is jarring—youth and age, beginning and end, and yet it is Emily we are saying goodbye to. I still resist the idea. *Twenty-four to forty-eight hours.* How on earth can that be possible? She's barely moving, she's been in this state for months, and yet I still can't believe it.

Eva comes a little bit later, standing uncertainly in the doorway. I usher her in; she belongs here.

"Rachel…" she says, and that is enough.

I nod a greeting, an acceptance of the rightness of her being here, and she sits on a chair one of the nurses has brought in. It almost feels like a party, in a weird, awful way, except no one makes chitchat. No one speaks at all. All we are doing, I realize, is waiting.

And I don't want to just wait. I don't want these last minutes and hours—that's all we have now—to be an empty space of time I won't be able to remember. And yet I don't know what else to do, how to be. How can anyone? There are no handbooks, no etiquette guides, no rules. That's the thing about death. It surprises everyone.

An hour passes, some moments too quickly, others too slow. I feel as if time is moving up and slowing down, coming in fits and starts, like Emily's breaths. A long silence, a sudden gasp. I can tell everyone finds it jarring, although no one says so.

I can see my mother is tiring, and James offers to accompany her outside to get a taxi, although I know he doesn't want to miss a moment with Emily. She kisses Emily's cheek, strokes her hair, tells her she loves her. I gaze on, still strangely numb, while Eva tries not to cry. I want to tell her it's all right to cry, that this, surely, is a time for crying, and yet I feel so frozen inside I can't get any words out.

When they leave, for a few minutes, it is just Eva and me... and Emily. She lies between us, like a photograph fading, every moment more diminished. The unit is quiet; no one else seems to be having a day like ours. There are only a few noises—light footsteps, hushed murmurs. Outside, the sky is a dazzling blue and the sun is turning a birch's yellow leaves to incandescent flame.

I have no idea what time it is; it feels like the middle of the night, but obviously it isn't. I am gazing into space, feeling so shut off from everything, when Eva's voice breaks the stillness.

"Do you want to... touch her?" she asks softly. I blink her into focus, trying to make meaning of the words. "Talk to her, if you want? I can leave, if you want some privacy..."

"You don't have to leave." My voice sounds as strange as I feel, almost guttural, as if I am learning how to speak.

I look at Emily, and I realize again that I don't just want to wait this out. I will miss these last moments with Emily, however many they are, so much. I will wonder, as I have about so many things, why I didn't savor them more. And so I scoot my chair closer to the bed, and I look down into my daughter's face.

"Hello, darling girl," I whisper. Now, more than ever, I doubt that she can hear me, but somehow that doesn't even matter anymore. "I love you so much, Emily. Mama's right here. You don't need to be scared." I take her head, threading her little fingers through mine, savoring the warmth her body still possesses. "I'm with you." I squeeze her hand, but this time she doesn't squeeze back, and I know she never will again, and somehow that is the thing that nearly breaks me.

I've grieved so many losses over the last few years, but this one small thing? The simple squeeze of her fingers that doctors told me was just a reflex anyway? It seems I must grieve that too.

I bow my head, fighting back tears, not wanting to cry now. I want this to be, if not a happy moment, then a good one. I hear Eva move and then I feel her hand on my shoulder, a solid, comforting weight. Squeezing.

I have no more words but weeping, and I don't want to do that. So I stop speaking, and instead I hum, a lullaby song James made up for Emily when she was just a baby. We sung it to her every night, and if we forgot, she always asked for it. Sleep song, she called it. *Sleep song, Mama.*

I hum the tune, and then I make myself sing the words. "Go to sleep. Go to sleep. Go to sleep, my dear." I repeat it, and then the second line: "I'm right here. I'm right here."

I squeeze her hand again. I wait. Eva's hand remains on my shoulder and, outside, the sun starts to set.

I don't know how much time passes then. It has slowed right down, each moment suspended before it passes onto the next.

James returns, taking his place quietly next to me, finding the rhythm of the moment, even in its silence. I start to sing the lullaby again, and he joins me. On the second time through, Eva, haltingly, sings it with us.

Go to sleep. Go to sleep. Go to sleep, my dear. I'm right here. I'm right here.

The shadows lengthen. The hospital parking lot is a front-row seat to a Technicolor sunset of spectacular crimsons and golds, the world, for a breathless moment, lit up, on fire.

And then it goes very quiet, and I know she's gone. I'm the first to realize. James and Eva are still sitting quietly, and I look down at my daughter's face and I feel, to my own surprise, nothing but relief.

I know the grief will come later. It will come and come and come, doubling back on itself, crashing over me, hissing and spitting like a wild thing, an enemy I will have to learn to live with and maybe to tame and befriend, but right now I feel relief, that the struggle is over, that my daughter is at peace, and so am I.

I rise from my chair and go to the window, laying my palm flat against the cool glass. The sky is full of violets and mauves.

James starts, and then he lets out a muffled cry as he realizes what has happened. Eva gives a soft gasp.

From the window, I watch a couple walk from the hospital to a car. The woman is shuffling slowly and the man is holding a car seat. I can't see inside, but I know what is there—a newborn baby, born today, or maybe yesterday. Brand new and beginning. And in that moment, I don't begrudge them their baby. I don't begrudge them a thing. They are beginning, and here we are, ending. And everyone must experience both.

"I'll tell the doctor," James says in a ragged voice.

"I can do it," Eva says. "If you want to stay…"

"No, I'll do it." James sounds firm; this duty, it seems, falls to the father. "If that's okay? Rachel…?"

I nod, my gaze still on the couple outside. "Yes. That's okay."

The next few moments are taken up with mundane details, which feels strange after the profound transcendence of death, the ending of life that feels both beautiful and wrong. We must sign forms, and discuss practicalities, sort out next steps. The doctors are quiet and brisk; they have done this many times before, and it shows, but not in a bad way. They make me feel reassured, even though the bottom of my world has dropped out. I just haven't dared to look down.

Then, even more strangely, after we've signed a few forms, we have to go. We have to leave Emily here, leave the nurses and orderlies to take her away. I cannot bear to think about it, where she will go, wheeled away on some metal gurney, *gone*.

And it feels wrong, to just walk away like that. To leave it all to someone else. At the doorway to her room, I stumble, and then whirl around as I realize I'll never actually *see* her again. I glimpse a nurse pulling a sheet over her head and I let out an animal sound of protest.

She looks up, startled, and James puts his arm around me to hold me up. On my other side, Eva touches my arm lightly.

'I'm sorry,' the nurse murmurs, but she doesn't pull the sheet back down. Emily is already gone.

I walk on wooden legs out of the room, out of the palliative care unit, all the way to the parking lot. The sky has darkened to indigo and the wind holds an autumnal chill. I stand by the doors to the hospital, clutching my bag to my chest, feeling as if I don't know where to go.

"Rachel, do you want to come back to our place?" James asks, his arm around Eva. "I don't like the thought of you being alone."

I don't either, but I'm not sure I want to go back with them. My ex-husband is holding Eva close, her bump visible beneath her loose top, and somehow all of that is okay. That is right, but I don't want to be a part of it right now.

I shake my head slowly. "I'll be okay. I'll talk to you soon. About… the funeral."

He nods, and then he comes over to me and gives me a quick, tight hug.

"You were the best mom," he whispers. "The absolute best."

I close my eyes. *Were.* Past tense.

I walk away from James and Eva, into the darkness of the parking lot. Slowly I unlock my car and slide into the driver's seat. It's as if I have to remind myself to do everything. *Lungs, breathe. Heart, beat.*

I think of Emily with the sheet over her head, and then I close my mind to the image, the thought. She is gone. She is free. That is what I need to remember, not what she looked like after. That wasn't her, anyway. She'd already gone by then.

As I drive home, I feel as if I am coming back into myself from a long way away. I notice everything—the brightness of the traffic lights, the beauty of the turning leaves on the trees, the streets of my city so familiar. I feel the smoothness of the steering wheel under my hands. The tick-tick-tick of the indicator sounds abnormally loud. I am fully present in a way I haven't been in a long, long time, and it is both painful and good. I am *here*.

I pull up in front of my house on my quiet street. Outside, the air smells of freshness and wood smoke. The sky holds a thousand stars and, with one hand on my car to balance myself, I tilt my head back as far as I can, to take it all in, earth and sky.

The moon is large and luminous, ridiculously pearlescent as it rises in the dark night sky. The stars are twinkling like glimmers of promise.

Dan, Mama!

I picture Emily doing a determined jig, her face flushed with joy, her body vibrating with energy, with life. *Dan!* I can almost hear her voice ringing out. I smile.

Slowly, I lower my head and blink the darkened world back into focus. My side of the duplex is dark, the living-room curtains drawn tight. I haven't spent more than a couple of hours there at a time in weeks; there is nothing in the fridge and most of my clothes are in a dirty heap in front of the washer. I know the place will smell stale and empty, unlived in and unloved, a house, not a home.

The other side of the duplex is warm with light and life. I see Andrew's silhouette against the drawn curtains. He is carrying dishes back to the kitchen. I see Jake's shape as he follows him, bouncing a little.

Slowly I walk to the stoop of my darkened house and reach for my keys. They are cold and sharp in my hand, and after a second, I put them back in my bag.

I cross the scrappy yard in front of the house to the other side of the duplex, feeling as if these ten steps are imbued with meaning, with choice, each one more than a mile.

From inside, I hear Jake laugh, a pure, crystalline sound. I take a deep breath and then I knock on the door.

A LETTER FROM KATE

Dear Reader,

Thank you so much for reading *A Hope for Emily* and for sharing in Rachel and Eva's story. I hope you enjoyed it! If you are interested in learning about my upcoming releases, you can sign up for my newsletter here. Your email address will never be shared and you can unsubscribe at any time.

www.bookouture.com/kate-hewitt

The idea behind this story was one that I believe is a parent's worst fear—the inability to help your ill child. When I was writing the letters from Rachel to Emily, I had in mind they were letters from every mother to every child; this is Rachel's story, but also every mother's, every parent who wants what is best for their child. They simply have to figure out what that is.

As I was researching the medical background to this novel, I found myself incredibly conflicted about the choices my characters were making. With each point of view I wrote, I ended up agreeing with that person! With all the information I learned about fatal conditions and end-of-life care, I realized there are no right answers in these heartbreaking situations. At the end of it all, there is only hope—and I truly believe that can be found in the strangest and darkest of places, in suffering as well as in joy.

If you enjoyed this story, please do leave a review or get in touch. I love to hear from readers, and I have a Facebook group,

Kate's Reads, where we discuss all kinds of books. It would be lovely to have you there! You can also sign up for my newsletter if you'd like to get updates about new releases, usually no more than three or four times a year. Thanks for reading!

Kate

🐦 @katehewitt1

📘 @katehewittauthor

🖥 www.kate-hewitt.com

ACKNOWLEDGMENTS

So many people are involved in creating a story, from my writing friends who cheer me on when I'm struggling in the saggy middle of the story, to my non-writing friends who always ask what I'm working on and then listen to my convoluted answers, to my fantastic editorial and marketing teams at Bookouture.

Many thanks go to all the amazing people at Bookouture, especially my brilliant editor Isobel, who always helps to make my stories better. I am also very grateful for all the marketing and publicity the team does, and I must give thanks to Kim and Noelle in particular, along with all the others on staff. You're all amazing, and I am very fortunate to be working with you.

Thanks also to my friends Ian and Deborah, who won't even know how their own amazing attitudes have shaped so much of this story. When I was in my twenties, they lost their third child as an infant to a genetic condition, and their love and grace throughout the experience affected me deeply, to this day. Thank you for your inspirational example!

Thank you also to my own family, who have always been supportive of my stories and accepting of me so often having my head in the clouds. A special shout-out to Teddy, who I think is starting to believe I do actually work during the day, and to Anna and Charlotte, who like to ask about my stories as I'm writing them, and are hoping for me to name a character after them. And also to Caroline and Ellen, for offering suggestions when I ask and reading my books. Last, but most definitely not least, many thanks to my wonderful husband, Cliff, for being such a staunch and loving supporter all along. I love you all!